HOT ICE

Praise for Aurora Rey

Recipe for Love

"[A] few things that always get me excited when Aurora Rey publishes a new book…Firstly, I am guaranteed a hot butch with a sensitive side, this alone is a massive tick. Secondly, I am guaranteed to throw any diet out the window because the books always have the most delectable descriptions of food that I immediately go on the hunt for—this time it was a BLT with a difference. And lastly, hot sex scenes that personally have added to my fantasy list throughout the years! This book did not disappoint in any of those areas."—*Les Rêveur*

Lambda Literary Awards Finalist *Crescent City Confidential*

"This book will make you want to visit New Orleans…Rey does a really wonderful job of creating the setting. You actually feel like you know the place."—*Amanda's Reviews*

"*Crescent City Confidential* pulled me into the wonderful sights, sounds, and smells of New Orleans…It was slow burning but romantic and sexy too. A mystery thrown into the mix really piqued my interest."—*Kitty Kat's Book Review Blog*

Summer's Cove

"As expected in a small-town romance, *Summer's Cove* evokes a sunny, light-hearted atmosphere that matches its beach setting… Emerson's shy pursuit of Darcy is sure to endear readers to her, though some may be put off during the moments Darcy winds tightly to the point of rigidity. Darcy desires romance yet is unwilling to disrupt her son's life to have it, and you feel for Emerson when she endeavors to show how there's room in her heart for a family." —*RT Book Reviews*

Winter's Harbor

"This is the story of Lia and Alex and the beautifully romantic and sexy tale of a winter in Provincetown, a seaside holiday haven. A collection of interesting characters, well-fleshed out, as well as a gorgeous setting make for a great read."—*Inked Rainbow Reads*

Praise for Erin Zak

Beautiful Accidents

"This book kept me engaged from beginning to end. I enjoyed the chemistry between Stevie and Bernadette."—*Maggie Shullick, Librarian, Lorain and Cuyahoga County (Ohio)*

Create a Life to Love

"Erin Zak does unexpected attraction and sexual awakening late in life really, really well."—*Reviewer@large*

"*Create a Life to Love* is a soulful story of how love can conquer all. I laughed, cried (sobbed) and got butterflies more than once, and did you see the cover art? Fantastic."—*Les Rêveur*

Breaking Down Her Walls

"I loved the attraction between the two main characters and the opposites attract part of the story. The setting was amazing…I look forward to reading more from this author."—*Kat Adams, Bookseller (QBD Books, Australia)*

"If you like contemporary romances, ice queens, ranchers, or age gap pairings, you'll want to pick up *Breaking Down Her Walls.*" —*The Lesbian Review*

"[A] charming contemporary romance set on a cattle ranch near the Colorado Mountains…This is a slow burn romance, but the chemistry is obvious and strong almost from the beginning. *Breaking Down Her Walls* made me feel good…"—*Rainbow Reflections*

Falling Into Her

Falling Into Her "is an age gap, toaster oven romance that I really enjoyed. The romance has a nice burn that's slow without being too slow. And while I'm glad that lesfic isn't all coming out stories anymore, I enjoyed this particular one because it shows how it can happen in a person's 40s."—*The Lesbian Review*

"[A] great debut novel from Erin Zak and looking forward to seeing what's to come.""—*Les Rêveur*

Praise for Elle Spencer

The Road to Madison

"The story had me hooked from its powerful opening scene, only got better and better...For anyone who has read my rev it's no secret that I love romances that include lots of angst, and *Road to Madison* hit the bull's-eye."—*The Lesbian Review*

"Elle Spencer weaves a tale full of sadness, remorse but one fi, with those little moments that make you have the flutters... T book grabbed my attention and had me turning the pages throu the night. A delightful story that I thoroughly enjoyed. I cann wait for the next adventure Elle Spencer takes me on."—*Romant, Reader Blog*

Unforgettable

"If you like angsty romances, this is the book for you! Both stories pack a punch, with so much 'will they or won't they' that I kind of wondered how they'd turn out (yes, even though it's marketed as romance!)"—*The Lesbian Review*

"I was stunned at how Elle Spencer manages to make the reader feel so much and we end up really caring for the women in her novels...This book is perfect for those times you want to wallow in romance, intense feelings, and love. Elle Spencer does it so well."
—*Kitty Kat's Book Review Blog*

Casting Lacey

"The story is full of humour, wit, and saucy dialogue but also has angst and drama...an entertaining and enjoyable read."——*Lez Review Books*

"This is the romance I've been recommending to everyone and he mother since I read it, because it's basically everything I've bee dying to find in an f/f romance—funny voices I click with, off-th charts chemistry, a later-in-life coming out, and a host of fun trop from fake dating to costars."—*Frolic*

By the Authors

Aurora Rey

Cape End Romances

Winter's Harbor

Summer's Cove

Spring's Wake

Autumn's Light

Built to Last

Crescent City Confidential

Lead Counsel
(Novella in *The Boss of Her*)

Recipe for Love

The Inn at Netherfield Green

Elle Spencer

Casting Lacey

Unforgettable: Novella Collection

The Road to Madison

30 Dates in 30 Days

Erin Zak

Falling into Her

Breaking Down Her Walls

Create a Life to Love

Beautiful Accidents

HOT ICE

by

Aurora Rey
Elle Spencer
Erin Zak

2019

HOT ICE

ISBN 13: 978-1-63555-513-4

This Trade Paperback Original Is Published By
Bold Strokes Books, Inc.
P.O. Box 249
Valley Falls, NY 12185

First Edition: December 2019

Credits
Editor: Barbara Ann Wright
Production Design: Stacia Seaman
Cover Design by Tammy Seidick

CONTENTS

ICE ON WHEELS

Aurora Rey

CHAPTER ONE

Brooke called off the jam, and Tracy signaled from the sideline for a time-out. Brooke skated toward her coach and grabbed a bottle of water. A glance at the scoreboard told her what she already knew. The lead they'd given up at the start of the second half was within reach. With twenty seconds on the clock, the next jam would be the last of the bout. And it would determine who walked away with the Louisiana Women's Roller Derby championship trophy and who went home runner-up.

After a quick discussion about strategy and a rally cry, the Big Easy Bruisers lined up with the Cajun Queens one final time. Brooke had managed to secure the inside position and found herself staring down a wall of rival blockers. The whistle blew, and she launched herself into the fray.

She pushed through the pack and saw her ref's arm go up. She'd claimed the lead jammer spot. That meant the title was in reach.

Not quite yet. She tamped down her excitement and made a loop, looking for her next opening. She pushed her way past a pair of blockers that lagged back to slow her down.

And then she saw it. Like the heavens parting in some mythical moment of clarity, the route around the outside of the track cleared. She angled herself to take it, hugging the outside line. A quick glance back told her the Queens jammer was gaining on her. This was her chance.

She rounded the curve, the taste of victory already in her mouth. They were going to win. Even better, she was going to score the game-deciding points.

By the time she saw the blocker out of the corner of her eye, it was too late. Not that she could have done much to stop her. She cut across the inside of the track at full speed. Just like a car accident, the split second before impact felt like slow motion. Just long enough for her to tense, even though she knew that would only make it worse. The blocker plowed into her shoulder-first. The momentum lifted her off the ground; the pain in her ribs paired with the feeling of her skates losing contact with the track.

As her entire body hit the concrete, her brain went fuzzy, then black.

She opened her eyes. A sharp pain radiated from her right hip. Not the, oh God, I broke something sort of pain, but the kind that screamed for ice and would leave a massive bruise for the next couple of weeks. Wuthering Hits and Crashin' Cali hovered over her, looks of concern on their faces.

"Are you okay?" Cali asked.

She blinked a few times, remembered how she got where she was, and groaned. "We lost, didn't we?"

Hits offered her a wry smile. "If you're asking, I'm taking it you're okay."

She was so not okay. She'd been a hundred feet from taking her team to the state championship, and she'd blown it. "I didn't black out, did I?"

Cali shook her head. "No, it's only been a few seconds. Do you remember getting hit?"

Oh, she remembered. But she didn't know who'd been the one to do it. "Who took me out?"

"Does it really matter at this point?"

"Yes." She hauled herself to a seated position and realized that every pair of eyes in the place was trained on her. Members of the opposing team had taken a knee. Fuck. "But not now. Help me up, will you?"

Understanding the urgency behind her request, they each grabbed a hand and pulled her to her feet. Despite the flush of embarrassment in her cheeks, she lifted a hand to signal she was unhurt. The requisite applause was quickly drowned out by the roar of cheering.

Right. The Queens had held off on their celebrations until it was clear she'd not been seriously injured. While such sportsmanship was usually one of her favorite things about derby, today it just made everything worse.

She made it to the bench and collapsed in a chair. Her teammates crowded around her, a mixture of concern and well-meaning support on their faces. She'd have been no different had the tables been turned. Even at its most competitive, the camaraderie mattered above all else.

But not today. Today, she'd failed, and all she wanted to do was crawl in a hole and die.

"Are you sure you're okay?" Cali asked.

"I am." She forced herself to look at the faces of her teammates. "And I'm sorry."

Her apology seemed to unlock a floodgate. Everyone started talking at once. Brooke made out "she came out of nowhere" and "still the most amazing season ever." The rest was a jumble that made her head spin.

"Who? Who was it that took me out?" She looked at Hits, who winced.

"Moby Dyke."

Brooke closed her eyes. Of course it was. She'd never talked to her before, but the blocker had definitely caught her eye. Her skating skills for sure, but it was more than that. Moby Dyke was tall and built and butch and gorgeous. And now Brooke was obliged to hate her.

After a rowdy victory toast, Riley's teammates dispersed to chat with their friends and wives and husbands and such. She scanned the crowd for the Bruisers jammer. Maybe with a drink or two in her, she'd give Riley the chance to congratulate her on putting up a hell of a fight. Championship bout or not, derby was about kicking ass on the rink and being a good sport off.

Riley spied her surrounded by a group of people, laughing. That was a good sign. She took a long swig from a bottle of Abita, and Riley wondered if she'd taste the Purple Haze on her lips if they kissed.

Whoa. Where did that come from?

Riley shook her head. She shouldn't be surprised, really. Femme Fatal was just that: deliciously femme with just a hint of fatale simmering under the surface. Sure, her type was more easygoing girl next door, but even she couldn't deny the appeal.

She took a sip of her own beer and crossed the room. She nodded hellos and exchanged pleasantries with a few members of the opposing team, working her way closer and closer to the jammer she'd taken out, quite literally, an hour ago. She chatted with a Bruisers blocker, complimenting her on her technique and stamina in the second half. All the while, she half eavesdropped on Femme Fatal's conversation. Her voice was low and sultry; her laugh made Riley think about doing a lot more than kissing her.

It wouldn't be the first time she'd gone home with a member of the opposing team. Not that she did derby to pick up women, but she wasn't opposed when the opportunity presented itself.

She was imagining the juxtaposition of hard lines and soft curves when she found herself face-to-face with the most gorgeous chocolate-brown eyes she'd ever seen. Riley had to swallow the wave of desire that swept through her. This was not the moment to get ahead of herself.

"Hi."

Despite offering her friendliest smile, Riley watched those amazing eyes flash with recognition, then cool. Actually, cool would be a massive understatement. Her eyes went from warm and inviting to subzero in about two seconds flat. They went from Riley's face to her outstretched hand and back to her face. And then, without a word, she turned on her heel and walked away.

"Don't mind Femme. She's taking the loss a little hard."

Riley turned in the direction of the voice. It belonged to Sister Mary Mayhem, one of the backup jammers for the Bruisers. "A little?"

Mary shrugged. "A loss is one thing. What you did was more of a personal affront."

Riley lifted both hands. "Hey, there was nothing personal about it."

"I know, but she thinks you should have been called for an illegal block."

"That's bullshit." The denial was out of her mouth before she could stop herself. Not that she would take it back, but there was no point in antagonizing the opposing team. Especially after snatching a win from them in the final seconds.

"I agree, but it could have gone either way, and Femme doesn't like that it was the move that cost us the bout."

"Is she always a sore loser?" Again, maybe not the most tactful approach, but she liked to know what she was dealing with. And sore losers were second only to cheaters in her book of people she considered a waste of time.

Mary smiled. "Not usually. I think this one hurt her ego as much as anything else."

"Ah." She could understand that. Sort of. "Well, I wanted to congratulate her on a great bout."

Wuthering Hits smiled as well. "We'll pass it along. And congratulations to you and the Queens. Pretty epic win."

It really was. Derby bouts were rarely close when it came to the final score. The fact that this one came down to the final seconds made it unique and made the win all the sweeter. "Thanks."

"Y'all heading back to Lafayette tonight?" Mary asked.

"A few people are, but most of us are staying over and doing the Quarter tomorrow. My sister lives here, so I'm crashing with her."

"Is that who was at the bout with the kids? The ones so excited to see you?"

"Yeah." She loved that even opposing teams would notice that sort of thing. Annie and the kids hadn't stayed for the after-party, but they'd made it through the whole bout. Given that Lucas was just three and a half, she'd been impressed. And of course, Annie had managed both Grace and Lucas with no help from her husband, who couldn't even be bothered to come along.

"They were really cute."

Riley shook off the flash of anger that came every time she thought of Jason. "Thanks. They're good kids."

A couple members of her team waved at her. She had a feeling they weren't waiting until tomorrow to hit Bourbon Street. She excused herself and went over to wish them a good night. Aunty Maim tried to cajole her into joining them, but she resisted. Not that she had a problem with a night of rowdy drinking, but she was starting to feel as if she'd outgrown it, a fact that managed to be both comforting and alarming.

The crowd started to disperse. Riley couldn't help but scan the bar once more for the antisocial Femme Fatal, but she was nowhere to be seen. Riley shrugged. It wasn't like she'd ever see her again.

CHAPTER TWO

Four months later

Brooke finished lacing her skates and pushed herself off the bench. She'd only been completely off the rink for a few weeks, but it felt like a lot longer. She missed it. The slick slide of concrete underfoot, the way her limbs settled into the stride of skating. She did a few laps before returning to the bench to chat with her teammates.

She'd stayed in touch with most of them during the brief off-season, working out together when they could, grabbing drinks or the occasional dinner as schedules allowed. But there was no substitute for the camaraderie of practicing together. It had taken her a long time to get comfortable, but her teammates were like family, and this was their living room.

"You been keeping in shape?" Hits asked as she pulled on her own skates.

The jab was part of their usual banter. Hits was a gym rat and teased Brooke pretty hard about hating, and therefore refusing to set foot in, any gym.

"Do I need to out-plank you again to prove that I have?"

Hits lifted both hands in a show of concession. She'd challenged Brooke last season and had been bested. "No, no. I learned my lesson."

Brooke smirked. "Good, because I'd hate to embarrass you. Again."

Hits chuckled. "Glad to see you're in top form, Femme."

She couldn't tell whether Hits was talking about her physical shape or the caliber of her comebacks. Not that it mattered. She prided herself on both.

"How's everybody doing?" Tracy yelled the greeting, signaling the official start of practice.

Brooke snagged her usual spot, sitting on the ground at the front of the group so she could stretch during the announcements and pep talk. Tracy welcomed everyone back and did a quick recap of the last season. The sting of defeat had mostly faded, and everyone had settled into the accomplishment of finishing second in the state. She felt good about that, too, even if the final moments of that bout remained etched in her brain and could rile her up on a second's notice if she let it.

Tracy moved on to introducing new members of the team. Brooke had missed tryouts to do an open house for a client, so she was looking forward to seeing the fresh meat in action. Chances were, none of them would make the varsity squad this season, but it was still nice to see who'd be working their way up the ranks. It made her nostalgic for her early days. She'd been awkward and completely lacking in grace at first, not to mention way too timid. But she'd learned quick and taken the spirit of derby to heart, becoming more assertive in her personal life as much as on skates. It had been hard work, but she wouldn't trade it for anything.

"And last but not least, we have a transfer joining us from the reigning state champion Cajun Queens. Please give a Big Easy Bruiser welcome to Riley Fauchet, or as you may know her, Moby Dyke."

Brooke froze. It couldn't possibly be. But as she followed the gazes of her teammates to the back row, she already knew it most certainly could.

Riley raised a hand in greeting. She'd been a little nervous about joining the ranks of the Big Easy Bruisers after the way last season ended, but she didn't have a lot of choice. Moving to New Orleans to help her newly divorced sister meant joining a new team or giving up derby. And she wasn't about to give up derby.

Tracy continued, "Moby has four years of skating with the Queens, three of it on their A squad. And anyone who was at last year's championship bout knows her blocking skills are second to none."

There were a couple of groans and a few laughs, followed by applause. Exactly what she'd hoped for. Yes, she'd played a role in defeating this team, but now she was on their side. It was a relief that most of them got that and seemed glad to have her.

She braved a look at Femme Fatal, the jammer who'd completely dismissed her when she'd tried to make nice. If she'd been frosty then, today it looked like she might spontaneously combust. Her cheeks were flushed, and the expression on her face was pure rage. Great. Before she could really analyze it or contemplate what to do about it, Tracy put them on warm-up laps. That was followed by sprints and some basic drills. Not unlike practices back home. Despite the newness of the space and all the people in it, the routine proved comforting and made her feel welcome.

When they shifted to the heart of practice—mock jams and specific blocking strategies—she followed along and tried to learn the ins and outs of working in a new pack. She had some ideas already but knew better than to stir things up at her first practice. She might have a solid reputation, but she still needed to prove herself as a skater and also as a member of this team.

She held back some, as she would in any practice. No point risking injury to herself or anyone else before the first bout. She took her spot in a wall, managed a few good hip checks. She even let Femme through a couple of times as sort of a goodwill offering. Femme still wouldn't make eye contact with her, but she didn't storm off in a huff. That, she supposed, counted as progress.

When practice ended, several of her new teammates surrounded her. They offered words of welcome and encouragement. There was a bit of ribbing about enemy infiltration, but it was all good-natured. She offered assurances of her loyalty and promised to share whatever secrets she had. She even scored an invitation to drinks.

She pulled off her skates and stowed her gear, looking for Femme. They should talk, try to clear the air. Otherwise, it was going to make for a tense season. And while she couldn't speak for anyone but herself, the whole point of derby was working off tension, not the other way around.

Riley spied her off to the side in what appeared to be a heated conversation with Tracy, the coach. They could have been talking about anything, but she got the immediate impression they were arguing about her. Ugh. Maybe it was going to be a tense season after all.

❖

"You don't think maybe you should have told me?"

Tracy had the good sense to look sheepish. "I never run transfers by the team. It's standard practice to let established players switch teams if they relocate."

"But there's a history." One that still haunted her.

"Brooke, try to look at it objectively. If it hadn't been you she took out, you'd be thrilled to have a blocker from a championship team join the squad."

But it had been her. And it felt really fucking personal. And even if part of her rational brain might see how it could be otherwise, her gut didn't. Her ego sure as hell didn't. "You should have told me. I was completely blindsided."

Tracy winced. "Okay. You're right. I'm sorry about that."

"Thank you." She might still be mad, but she wasn't in the business of making enemies.

"No hard feelings?"

She wasn't ready to go that far. "I'm working on it."

"Let me buy you a beer. That makes everything better."

Drinks after the first practice of the season was a tradition. As much as she didn't want to be in the same room as Riley, she refused to let her presence drive her away. Or create a rift between her and her other teammates. It might not be a popularity contest, but there was no way she was giving up ground to Riley. "I think you probably owe me two."

Tracy smiled, relief evident on her face. "Deal."

She packed up her gear and tried to find some calm headspace. She and Tracy were the last to leave, so they locked everything up and headed to their respective cars.

At the bar, the dozen or so members of the team who could make it broke into smaller groups. One of her favorite things about her team was that it wasn't cliquey at all. A few people had close friendships, but everyone talked to everyone else, and you never knew what would unfold or with whom. Riley's presence threw all of that into disarray. Brooke found herself actively avoiding any conversations she was part of, a strategy that proved tricky since she seemed to work the crowd like a politician.

It was annoying. It was ingratiating. It was—

"Hey."

Brooke spun around and found herself face-to-face with the woman she'd spent her whole evening trying to avoid. "Hey."

"We never got the chance to officially meet. I'm Riley." Riley stuck out her hand.

"Brooke." She reluctantly shook it. "But we mostly go by our derby names."

Riley offered a smile that was way more charming than it had any right to be. "Of course. I just like knowing everyone's real names. Feels friendlier that way, more personal."

"Sure." Even though the last thing she wanted to do was get friendly, or personal, with Moby Dyke.

Riley angled her head. "You seemed surprised to see me tonight. Did you not know I was joining the Bruisers?"

She didn't want to throw Tracy under the bus, even if she was still a tiny bit mad at her. "I missed tryouts, so I must have missed the announcement then."

Riley nodded slowly. "Ah. I hope the dust has settled enough on last season that there aren't any hard feelings."

Oh, there were hard feelings all right. Lots of them. "Of course not."

Her face must not have matched her words because Riley looked far from convinced. But after a moment she offered a smile and clinked her beer bottle to Brooke's. "Excellent."

Brooke bit her tongue to keep herself from saying what she really wanted, which contained probably a few too many expletives and a detailed description of how much she loathed everything about this arrangement.

"I feel really lucky to be able to transfer to such a good team. I don't think I could ask for better."

Brooke smiled. Did she have to be a suck-up on top of everything else? She glanced around, desperate for an escape.

"So, what do you do?"

Seriously? Was this woman seriously going to stand there, looking both ridiculously hot and completely relaxed, making small talk? "I'm a real estate agent."

Riley narrowed her eyes like Brooke had just announced she was a pet psychic. "Really?"

She took a deep breath and tried not to roll her eyes. "Why do you seem so surprised?"

Riley looked at Brooke and tried to decide how to answer. If it was anyone else, she might make a joke. Hell, if it was anyone else who was half as good-looking as Brooke, she'd find a way to make it flirtatious. But she got the feeling either approach would fall flat, if not earn her a black eye. She decided to keep it simple. "I am, too."

It was Brooke's turn to look surprised. "You are?"

Riley chuckled. At this point, how could she not? "Yeah. What are the chances?"

"What are you two laughing about?" Hits offered Riley a nod of greeting, then looked at Brooke.

Brooke glowered. Riley couldn't decide if it made her feel better or worse that Brooke seemed to be a little nasty to everyone. Since Brooke showed no sign of answering, she decided she might as well. "We just discovered we're in the same line of work."

Hits raised a brow and looked at Brooke as though seeking confirmation. Brooke shrugged. "So it would seem."

"That's awesome." She elbowed Brooke. "You can help Moby learn the area."

"Oh, I'm sure she'll get everything she needs from her office. Now, if you'll excuse me, I need to chat with Tracy about the schedule."

Brooke walked away and made a beeline to where Tracy stood chatting with a couple of the new recruits. At least Riley thought they were new recruits. She was good with names, but it would take her a couple of practices to learn everyone's, especially if she went for real names as well as derby ones. She turned her attention to Hits. "She really doesn't like me, does she?"

Hits shrugged. "Well, she takes a little while to warm up."

Forget warming up. She'd take anything even remotely resembling a thaw. "You're just saying that to be nice, aren't you?"

Hits smirked and clinked her beer bottle to Riley's. "You're going to do all right, Moby."

She had no idea whether the comment referred to her place on the team or her attempt to make friends with Brooke. At this point, she'd just as soon not have either of those things ruled out. She lifted her bottle in response. "I'll drink to that."

CHAPTER THREE

B rooke slept like the dead—she always did after practice—but still woke up in a foul mood. The iced coffee from PJ's helped some, as did the prospect of meeting with three potential clients over the course of the day. She got to the office early and managed to snag twenty minutes with Cassie before any of the other agents pounced. They'd just put the final details on the open house she'd scheduled for Saturday when Pam emerged from her office.

"Everyone, I have an announcement."

She glanced at Cassie, rolling her eyes but smiling. As managing broker, Pam liked making big announcements even though there were rarely more than four or five agents in the office at any one time. Cassie and Brooke stood and moved to the doorway of Brooke's office. Indulging Pam kept her happy, and a happy Pam meant a happy office.

"We have a new member of our team joining us from the Acadiana branch. She's just relocated to be closer to family." She took a step to the side, revealing the person who'd emerged from the office with her. Brooke blinked, disbelief quickly giving way to dread.

"You've got to be fucking kidding me." It couldn't be, but it was. Just like at practice. Brooke closed her eyes for a second and shook her head.

"What? What's wrong?" Cassie asked.

Brooke opened one eye, then the other. Unfortunately, it wasn't a figment of her imagination. Or a case of mistaken identity. Or any other thing she could think of that would make the person standing across the office anyone but Riley Fauchet. "Nothing."

She looked away to avoid any chance of eye contact and found

Cassie studying her with a look of exasperation. "Well, clearly that's not true, or you wouldn't be cussing at work."

Brooke laughed in spite of herself. Despite being twenty-three, Cassie was a total prude. Not a prude. Proper. Like what Brooke would be if her mawmaw's Catholic upbringing had stuck. "I know her."

Cassie angled her head in Riley's direction. "Her? The new agent? How? Oh my gosh. Did you sleep with her?"

Why did Cassie assume knowing someone and not liking them meant they'd slept together? Aside, perhaps, from the fact that Riley was exactly the kind of woman she'd sleep with if everything about the situation was different. "Jesus Christ. No. And keep your voice down."

Cassie frowned, although it was hard to know if it stemmed from being scolded or Brooke's use of Jesus Christ in a less than reverent way. "How do you know her?"

Pam was making her way around the room with Riley, doing personal introductions. Riley smiled and shook hands, looking easy and relaxed. There was no way to escape without drawing even more attention to herself. What a fucking disaster.

"Remember the bout last September, the last one of the season?" Cassie had come with her girlfriend at the time. They hadn't lasted, but Audrey had joined their JV squad and was showing real promise.

"The one where that blocker took you out in the final seconds and cost you the whole championship?"

Even though she'd been the one to bring it up, the description still stung. "Yeah. That's the one."

"What about it?"

"She's the one who laid me out." The memory remained as fresh as the day it happened. The bruise on her hip had faded. She wanted to say the same for her ego, but it didn't mean she had any intentions of forgiving or forgetting.

"Oh." Cassie drew the word out, understanding growing with each added second.

"And now she's on my team."

"Wait. What? What do you mean?"

Brooke stole another glance at Riley. She'd either not noticed her or was playing it exceedingly cool. Both possibilities irritated her. "She showed up at practice last night as a transfer. She moved here from Lafayette."

Another "Oh," this one even more drawn out than the first.

"And of all the fucking offices in the entire fucking city, she has to show up at mine."

"Brooke."

Apparently, that was one too many fucks. "Sorry."

"It's okay. I mean, I get why you're mad. I wouldn't want to have to work with her, either."

Understatement of the century. But before she could process it any further, Pam and Riley were right there in front of her. "This is Cassie Sanchez, our rock star receptionist and queen of details, and Brooke Landry, one of our very best agents. Ladies, Riley Fauchet."

Riley shook Cassie's hand before turning her attention to Brooke. Her smile might have been sincere, but it looked to Brooke like a self-satisfied smirk. "Well, hello again."

"I'm sorry. Do you two already know each other?" Pam asked.

"Something like that." Riley extended her hand, all laid-back charm. So infuriating.

Brooke couldn't refuse it without looking rude. "We've met."

"Oh, excellent. Then I'll charge you two with showing Riley around, making sure she has everything she needs to get settled in." Pam turned to Riley. "I'm leaving you in the best possible hands. I'll see you for our meeting at three."

And with that, Pam disappeared back into her office. Brooke tried to summon something to say, but all she came up with was her mama's adage about not having anything nice to say. Seconds, each one feeling like a minute, ticked by.

Cassie, God bless her, picked up on the awkward and took control of the conversation. "So, Riley, are you moving to New Orleans for the first time, or are you moving back?"

"First time. I wanted to be closer to my sister and her kids." Riley smiled as she spoke, which should have earned her some points. Too bad Brooke didn't have any to spare.

"Oh, that's nice. Nothing more important than family."

"Agreed."

The idea that she would uproot her life and career to be closer to family did not jibe with the egotistical, self-absorbed impression Brooke had gotten from their interactions thus far. Not that it mattered. Even assholes could be noble when it came to the one or two things they cared about. "It's a very different market. You're going to have your work cut out for you."

Rather than a snarky comeback, Riley offered an affable smile. "I've been doing my homework."

The friendliness did more to irritate Brooke than snark would have. "If you say so."

Cassie, as if sensing the conversation would only get worse, cleared her throat. "Let me help you get set up in your office, show you where everything is."

"Thanks." Riley grinned at Cassie, then turned her attention to Brooke. "I'm looking forward to working with you."

Brooke couldn't bring herself to agree but knew that disagreeing would be both rude and unprofessional. She settled for a curt nod and retreated to her desk. When Cassie and Riley had disappeared from sight, she indulged in pressing her thumbs to her temples. Really, what were the odds? And more, what had she done to deserve such an unfortunate turn of events?

❖

"So, I hope this isn't too forward or anything, but does she hate everyone? Or just me?" Riley angled her head in Brooke's direction.

Cassie blushed, which was probably all the answer she needed. "What do you mean?"

She shouldn't press. If Cassie had loyalties to Brooke, asking might alienate her and do more harm than good. Unless Brooke was half as frosty at work as she was on the rink, and everyone she worked with knew it. If that was the case, then it would behoove her to learn it sooner rather than later. And whether her bitchiness was reactive or something she went out of her way to inflict on people. "Did she tell you I joined her derby team?"

Cassie hesitated as though unsure she should acknowledge it. Eventually, she nodded. "Yeah."

Either Brooke had told Cassie the whole story and now Cassie was leery of her, or Brooke was an absolute tyrant in every aspect of her life and had Cassie terrified of retribution. Which was more likely? And perhaps more importantly, what did that mean for her?

She could play this a dozen different ways, but direct was her style. And friendly. No matter what Brooke might think or say, she was a nice person. She needed her new colleagues to know that and to give her half a chance. "We might have gotten off on the wrong foot, but I'm really hoping we can get past it."

Cassie smiled, but it seemed more polite than genuine. "I'm sure you will."

Riley offered her most charming smile in return. Not a challenge exactly but maybe a little. "I mean, it looks like we'll be spending quite a bit of time together, so we might as well get along, right?"

"Right."

Okay, this wasn't getting her anywhere. Time to change tactics. "I hear you're the resident expert on how the office runs. I hope you'll tell me everything I need to know."

The change in topics seemed to help Cassie relax. She showed Riley the supply and break rooms, walked her through the quirks of the copier and fax machine, and offered to order whatever she needed to get her office situated. By all accounts, Cassie was competent, warm, and easy to work with. Reserved, maybe, but not set on disliking her. "Is there anything else you need right now?"

"Other than some fairy dust for Brooke, I think I'm good."

Maybe she shouldn't have made the joke, but Cassie snickered. She took that as a good sign. Cassie looked away, but her eyes came back to Riley's quickly enough. "I'm at extension two-two-three if you need anything."

Riley offered another smile. She already liked Cassie and really wanted the feeling to be mutual. "You've already been a lifesaver. I'm sure I'll come running for help before too long."

Cassie blushed, an entirely different kind of blush from the first time. Not that she was looking to collect crushes, but she couldn't help the flash of satisfaction at winning her over, even a little, on her first day. Yes, it boded well for her settling into her new office. Even more, it was much more in line with the reaction she was used to getting from people, women or otherwise.

She took some time arranging her office and setting up the standard-issue laptop. She set out photos and the handful of personal items she'd brought with her and hung her diploma and a couple of certificates on the wall. It might not feel homey, but she didn't anticipate spending all that much time in it. She liked being on the go and meeting clients where they were comfortable. It suited her personality but also served her well in terms of landing and keeping more clients than anyone else at her previous broker.

She launched the MLS and pulled up the listings currently attached to her new office. She'd scoped them out before, but now that she'd met folks, she wanted to get a feel for each agent's niche as well as the number of listings they had in their portfolios. Without hesitating, she pulled up Brooke's listings first.

She might be a bitch, but she was clearly good at her job. She had more listings than any other agent, and they were diverse, both in terms of geography and price point. Riley respected the range more than the number. She'd always believed people with modest homes deserved a great agent as much as those with million-dollar listings.

She worked her way through the rest of the search results, making notes on who seemed to have a territory or a property type. By the time she finished, it was clear that she and Brooke had the most similar styles. Who'd have guessed she and her reticent teammate would have such a thing in common? Maybe there was hope for them after all.

CHAPTER FOUR

For the first time in as long as she could remember, Brooke dreaded going to derby practice. The fact that she was dreading it made her even angrier than she'd been when she learned Riley was now a member of her team. And part of her office.

She shoved equipment into her bag, swearing under her breath and feeling stupid for doing so. It didn't help that Riley was so damned opinionated. She seemed to have an idea about everything—new maneuvers, new drills, new ways of writing listings. Riley was an insidious force that had infiltrated every aspect of her life. Like the Facebook and Google ads she'd suffered through for weeks after accidentally searching camo instead of camis.

There was also the matter of her dreams. More than once, Riley had made an appearance. And they weren't work dreams. Or derby ones. She shuddered at the memory of one particularly vivid encounter her subconscious had cooked up that involved being alone with Riley in the office after hours, the conference table, and her skirt bunched up around her hips.

Angry and now turned on, she drove to the rink the team used for practice. After parking, she cut the engine and sat for a moment. It didn't take long for the temperature to creep into uncomfortable territory. Still, she closed her eyes and took a deep breath. She needed to pull it together.

The knock on her window just about sent her out of her skin. Of course, it was Riley staring through the glass with a stupid grin on her face. Ugh. Could things get any worse?

She opened her door and made to get out only to realize she'd not unbuckled her seatbelt. She did so clumsily, grabbed her bag, and got out. Only the strap of the bag got caught on the gearshift, and she almost wiped out when it jerked her backward.

Apparently, asking if things could get worse ensured they did.

"You okay?"

"I'm fine." Mortified but fine.

Riley chuckled. "I've had those days, where I can't get out of my own way."

Even if it was true, Brooke resented the assertion. It took everything in her not to growl as they walked into the rink.

Half a dozen people were already there, lacing up skates or doing laps. Everyone greeted her and Riley together. Yes, they'd walked in at the same time, but it made it seem like they'd come together or worse, were a couple. At the very least, it made them seem like equals. Even though Brooke had spent the better part of two years building friendships with her teammates, and Riley had strolled in less than a month ago. She was not amused.

She lagged back a step to see where Riley went to set down her things and get ready so she could sit somewhere else. She waited for Riley to start laps so she could position herself opposite her on the rink. It was probably stupid to engage in such an elaborate dance of avoidance, but if she had any chance of not exploding before the end of the night, she needed to keep contact to a minimum.

When Tracy called everyone together to start practice, Brooke moved to the far side of the group. Hits gave her some side eye, but didn't say anything. They started as usual, warm-up drills and some basic walls. Brooke and the other jammers took turns with each group of blockers, working on their own skills while giving the blockers something to defend against.

She wormed her way through or around two groups, but when she came to the third—the one with Riley skating anchor—she found herself foiled. To her credit, Riley didn't taunt her, which was standard practice to help mimic a real bout. After two attempts to squeak through the inside, she tried a more direct approach, shoving her shoulder right into the middle of the wall.

She'd touched Riley before, obviously. It was impossible to practice and not press up against everyone on the team at some point. But this, intentionally pushing her body into Riley's, was different.

It didn't help that they were face-to-face. The contact was electric, sending pulses of heat and something else radiating through her.

Her brain screamed at her to back off, to escape. But she'd been bending over backward avoiding Riley, and it hadn't helped a damn bit. She gritted her teeth and lunged, throwing every ounce of strength and frustration and unwanted attraction against the wall.

Rum Run Her Over stumbled and went down to her knees. The flash of guilt should have been enough to shame her, but it didn't. She ran ahead, looking to put as much distance between herself and Riley as possible.

Tracy's whistle signaled the end of the drill. The shrill sound snapped her back to her senses, and she realized what she'd done. She doubled back to where Riley was hauling Rum to her feet. "Sorry."

Rum laughed. "It's all good. I'm fine. But damn, girl. What's got into you tonight?"

Brooke shook her head and forced a laugh. "The devil, apparently. You sure you're okay?"

She nodded. "Oh, yeah. That said, you try that again and you won't get through."

Rum and Riley exchanged high fives. Brooke skated to the bench to regroup. She needed to get a grip, or she was going to hurt someone. Or herself.

Tracy whistled to have one of the walls reset. Riley raised her hand to get Tracy's attention. "When I was with the Queens, we did an alternating arm lock, and it seemed to hold better. Distributed the force more evenly."

Brooke's jaw clenched, and her own hand went up. "Maybe we shouldn't be changing things we do that already work."

"Maybe we should take pointers from the team that beat us," Cali said without missing a beat.

Brooke waved a hand, not so much ceding the point as knowing better than to start a bickering match in the middle of practice, especially with Cali.

"Let's give it a try." Tracy waited while the blockers arranged themselves and then blew her whistle again.

Brooke grabbed her water bottle in a show of sitting the next one out.

Hits flopped in the seat next to her. "Are you all right?"

"Oh my God. I swear, if one more person asks me that tonight, I'm going to lose it."

Hits merely raised a brow.

"I'm fine. I mean, I'm annoyed, but I'm fine. I just—"

"Want everything to go back to how it was?"

Obviously, the answer was yes. But admitting it would make her sound so petulant. She sighed. "I'm not that pathetic."

Hits patted her hand and gave her a sympathetic look. "It's okay. You can pout. We're all entitled, and you rarely do."

Brooke scowled. "You're not making me feel better."

She shrugged, all innocence. "You're very put upon by it all. I don't know how you manage."

The condescension was worse but ridiculous enough to make her crack a smile. "Okay, that's enough."

Innocence quickly gave way to a smirk. "Really, though. What are you going to do about it?"

Brooke looked over to where Riley stood with three of the blockers. She angled her shoulder, sending her opposite hip jutting out. All three mimicked the move. Brooke rolled her eyes and sighed. "I guess I better get used to it."

Hits patted her hand again and stood. "That's the spirit."

"Leaving already?" Brooke asked.

"Nah." Another shrug. This one had no trace of innocence. She angled her head toward Riley. "I want to learn that technique."

Brooke groaned, then hoisted herself up. Getting used to it was one option. So was learning everything she could from someone with a fresh slate of strategies and experience. She put her helmet back on and skated over to see what all the fuss was about. And figure out how she'd finagle her way past it next time someone tried it on her.

"How was it?" Annie asked.

Riley dropped her bag by the door and scooped Lucas into her arms, accepting his noisy kiss on her cheek and returning it with one just as loud. "Aside from the woman who remains bound and determined to hate me, it was great."

"What do you mean hate you? No one hates you."

She chuckled at the assertion. "This woman does."

Annie set down the spoon and turned away from the stove. "I don't believe it. Tell me everything."

Riley set Lucas down and gave Grace a hug. The kids returned to their activities at the kitchen table, and Riley snagged a Coke from the fridge. She conveyed their initial encounter, how Brooke wouldn't speak to her at the after-party. "And now we work at the same office, and she hardly speaks to me there or at practice."

Annie nodded slowly. "Yeah, she hates you."

Riley rolled her eyes. "Thanks."

"Well, she seems to have come by it naturally."

While that was arguably true, it wasn't how derby worked. She said as much to her sister.

"But you bruised her ego and then invaded her life. That's rough."

"Well, the ego part is dumb. That's how competition works."

Annie didn't say anything. She had this way of waiting Riley out, letting the silence work better than any argument. She'd done it since they were teenagers, but having kids had taken her skills to the next level.

"Are you telling me you're taking her side? I didn't actually do anything. Nothing intentional at least. Or illegal."

Again, she said nothing.

"But I guess I see your point." Damn, she was good at that.

"You have a way, you know."

"What is that supposed to mean?" She sort of knew, but still.

"You have a big personality, magnetic. People are drawn to you."

"Is that a bad thing?" In her experience, it was one of her better qualities.

"No, but it means you take up a lot of oxygen even when you don't mean to."

Riley scowled and tried not to envision herself as some arrogant blowhard. "And that's why she hates me? Because everyone else likes me?"

"Not because people like you, but it probably doesn't help. It makes her feel like the odd one out."

"Huh." She'd not thought of it that way. Or that her presence would feel to Brooke like an invasion of her turf.

"Do you want her to like you?"

She kind of wanted everyone to like her. Not in some obsessive, unhealthy way, but she liked people, and the feeling was reciprocated more often than not. Sure, that wanting was even more pronounced with Brooke, although she'd not analyzed why. "I do."

"Do you want her to like you, like you?"

"Uh." Sure, she found Brooke attractive. It would be hard not to. But was it more than that? And even if it was, would it be a good idea to go there?

"If your immediate reaction isn't no, I think the answer is yes."

Having the hots for a teammate would be dumb. About as dumb as having them for a colleague. A woman who was both, who by all accounts hated her? Abject stupidity. "I—"

"Aunt Riley, will you help me with my spelling tonight?" Grace asked.

She pounced on the distraction. Not that she wouldn't have that conversation; she just didn't need to have it now. "Absolutely. What's on the list this week?"

Grace got up from the table and brought Riley the sheet. Annie shot her a look that said the conversation was very much not over. Riley shrugged and offered a smirk that said she knew Annie had her number.

She took a quick shower before they all sat down to supper, a pasta dish Annie had managed to sneak a few vegetables into. After dinner, she settled at the table to help Grace with her homework while Annie gave Lucas a bath. A far cry from how she'd spent her Saturday nights for the last few years, but she didn't mind in the least. They drilled multiplication tables—the sixes, the sevens, and the eights—before moving on to spelling. "Weird."

"Uh." Grace looked at the ceiling. "W-I-E-R-D."

Riley shook her head. "E-I."

Grace groaned. "It's I before E, except after C."

"Unless it's weird. Or a bunch of other words, actually. But this week, just weird."

"Spelling is dumb."

"It's not."

The answer clearly did not impress. "Don't computers and phones and stuff spell everything for you anyway?"

She'd not been at this long enough to know whether she was supposed to try and reason with her or go the "it's important because

I said so" route. She decided on the former since that was what she would have preferred at Grace's age. "But when words are similar, a computer won't know which one you mean and might put in the wrong one, and then you'd look very silly."

Grace frowned. Riley imagined her trying to craft a comeback, which made her smile. She was saved from a back-and-forth by Lucas bounding into the room in Strawberry Shortcake pajamas, hand-me-downs from his sister, but she appreciated the bending of gender norms nonetheless. "How was your bath?"

He rolled his eyes and groaned as any self-respecting four-year-old would. "Fine."

She glanced at Annie, who came into the kitchen right behind him. She shrugged. "It was a shampoo night."

The horror.

"Can I have a bedtime story?" he asked Riley.

"I can cover spelling," Annie said.

Grace huffed but didn't argue. Riley followed Lucas to his room and let him pick out four books, which was the rule since he was four. Sure, it took him ages to choose, but the arrangement had effectively cut any negotiating, whining, or begging for one more. At least that was her understanding. She'd not experienced life before the four-book rule, but she appreciated the genius of it.

After a food-themed selection involving moose and muffins, pigeons and hot dogs, and a duckling with a cookie, she kissed his forehead and wished him sweet dreams. She helped Grace get ready for bed while Annie tucked Lucas in, and then she and her sister opened beers and flopped on the sofa.

"Mom called today."

Her shoulders tensed involuntarily. "What did she want?"

"Just to chat, see how things were going."

Riley rolled her eyes. "I know she's the last person you'd want here, but I still can't believe she didn't even offer to come."

Annie shrugged. "She could barely handle her own kids. She's not going to help raise someone else's."

"Yeah." Their mother utterly lacked maternal instinct. She wasn't a terrible person, but it left her somewhat estranged from both her daughters. Riley, for some reason, thought having grandkids might change that, bring out a nurturing side that had been deeply buried. It hadn't. Which should have made her feel better, but it broke her heart that Lucas and Grace didn't have a doting mawmaw to spoil them with affection and presents and cookies. She'd actually planned to assume that role herself until recently. But the pseudo-parental figure couldn't also be the spoiler extraordinaire. It bothered her on principle, but she didn't really mind. She was kind of liking the parental role.

"Hey, you okay?"

"Sorry, my mind wandered. I was just thinking how much I was enjoying this arrangement."

Annie regarded her with suspicion. "You don't have to say that."

She smiled. "I mean it. I love spending more time with the kids."

"Even though the rest of your life is turned upside down?"

She thought about her new office, the clients she already had under contract. And her new derby team, including the gorgeous, if frosty, Femme Fatal. She shrugged and offered another smile. "You know, things are falling into place."

CHAPTER FIVE

The problem with thinking things might be falling into place was that it had a tendency to jinx everything. Riley pinched the bridge of her nose. The weekly sales meeting was in full swing, and a dozen agents sat around a conference table discussing the happenings of the week and what they anticipated unfolding over the next month. So far, every single thing she'd had to say was met by a retort or a stony stare from Brooke.

Riley let out a sigh. "Why are you being so difficult?"

"Because what you're suggesting is sketchy at best. Borderline unethical."

It was hard to tell if Brooke really felt that way or if she was just being contrary. Given that she'd dismissed or disagreed with pretty much everything Riley had to say—at work or on the rink—she was inclined to believe the latter. "That's a bit dramatic, don't you think?"

Brooke glared at her before turning her gaze to Pam. "Do you really want us to be the ambulance chasers of the real estate world?"

Pam frowned. "Of course not. But I'm not sure how what Riley is suggesting would make us ambulance chasers."

Brooke squared her shoulders and showed no signs of backing down. "It's desperate, playing to the lowest common denominator."

Riley poked a finger into the table. "It's neither of those things. It's offering people options, people who might feel trapped or otherwise inclined to go it alone."

She'd actually put a lot of effort into researching FSBOs in the last year, both in the Lafayette market and nationally. They were on an upward trend, fueled by sites like Zillow and house-flipping shows on television. People thought they could cut their costs, and boost their profits, by cutting out the professional in the middle.

"But giving those people a discount is basically telling them that our services are overpriced. You're rewarding bad behavior. Not to mention telling our regular clients that they're suckers."

"You make a good point, Brooke." Pam nodded slowly. "But I don't think that means we shouldn't explore Riley's proposal. From what I can tell, no one else in town is doing it, and it could be a great market to tap."

"We're going to get a reputation for being sellouts. I want no part of it." Brooke stood up and walked out of the conference room.

A moment of silence followed, the kind of awkward quiet that always followed someone making a scene. Riley glanced around the table, wondering if the other agents were inclined to follow suit. No one got up, so that was a good sign.

"Riley, can you do some more research on this, maybe draft a modified contract for us to look at? We'll come back to it at the next sales meeting."

"Will do."

"All right. Anything else for the good of the order?" Pam asked.

Dan asked for help planning a photo shoot for a place with few windows, and Kim offered to connect people to a new staging firm she'd found. Pam gave her mini pep talk about turning houses into homes, and the meeting disbanded.

Cassie remained at the table, typing up what Riley assumed were minutes from the meeting. She held back as the other agents filed out of the room. When Cassie stopped typing, Riley shifted into her line of sight. "Hey."

She smiled. "Hey."

"Do you want to have lunch today?"

Her eyes got big, and Riley realized the way her words might have been taken. "Work lunch. I'd love to pick your brain about a few things, and if you let me, the least I can do is buy you lunch."

Her shoulders relaxed. "I would, but I already have plans with Brooke. Tomorrow maybe?"

"I've got a meeting in Slidell. Next week?"

"Completely open."

"Great. You pick the day." She glanced at the door. No one was around. "Any chance you have a few minutes now?"

Cassie nodded. "What's up?"

"I was hoping for some advice about Brooke." On getting her to chill the fuck out.

"Oh."

Riley cringed. "Unless that's weird. I don't want to put you on the spot."

She considered. Riley wished she could read what was going on in her brain. Eventually, she said, "What kind of advice?"

"I get that she doesn't like me, and I might not be able to change that, but I'd like to smooth things over if I could. I hate bad blood, and I'm pretty sure it's stressing her out, too."

"Yeah."

"Yeah, she doesn't like me, or yeah, it's stressing her out?"

Cassie tipped her head slightly. "Yes."

Riley chuckled. "So, short of going away, what can I do?"

She seemed to take the question to heart. "Do you really want to know?"

Not the answer she was expecting. Did she? Yes. She wasn't so rigid or egotistical that she wouldn't take friendly feedback. "I do."

"Maybe you could relax a little."

"Me?" The retort came out more aggressively than she meant. "Sorry. I mean, me? Brooke is the one who's so uptight."

Cassie raised a brow. "Do you want my advice or not?"

She had asked for it. Even if she wasn't crazy about what she was hearing. She liked Cassie and trusted her judgment. "Sorry. Go on."

"You take up a lot of oxygen."

Oh God. That was not the reputation she wanted. The fact that Annie had used the exact same phrase left a knot in the pit of her stomach. "Say more."

"Not like some jerky blowhard or anything."

She rolled her eyes. Was she really that lacking in self-awareness? "Oh, well as long as it's not that."

Cassie was probably close to a decade younger than her, but she fixed Riley with a look sterner than any she'd gotten from a parent or teacher or other authority figure.

"Sorry."

"You have a big personality. It's a nice personality, don't get me wrong. But it's big. And you have lots of ideas. It can be overwhelming for someone like Brooke."

Huh. She really wouldn't have guessed that was the problem. "And what do you mean by 'someone like Brooke,' exactly?"

Another pause. This one longer than the others. Clearly, Cassie liked Brooke and didn't want to say anything that might paint her in a negative light. The hesitation boosted her respect for Cassie considerably. And interestingly, for Brooke. Eventually, she said, "Brooke is an amazing person. She'd go to war for anyone she cares about. But she's a little reserved. Doesn't trust new situations easily. Or new people."

Lack of confidence? That would be the absolute last thing she'd have come up with to describe Brooke.

"I can see you don't believe me."

She chuckled at being so transparent. "You're saying she's timid. It's just not the vibe I get from her."

"Not timid." Cassie shook her head. "Cautious. Like, she's had to work hard, and she's leery when she meets someone who seems to skate through life."

The choice of metaphor wasn't lost on her. "I work hard, too, you know. I just choose not to be uptight about it all."

"You hadn't been in this office one whole afternoon, and you'd made friends with half the sales team."

"I'm friendly." The defensive tone was back. She made a point to rein it in. "Are you saying I should be more aloof?"

"I'm saying things come easy to you. Personally, professionally, probably in derby, too. It's hard to be the person who's been going along, trying hard, doing all the right things and then have someone waltz in and have it handed to them."

If she could get over how much of this conversation made her seem like an absolute tool, she could maybe see where Cassie was coming from. "Do you think I'm an ass?"

"I really don't."

Riley sighed. She always considered herself a people person. This was the first time it might prove to be anything but an asset. "But I'm too much. That's what you're saying."

"Not too much in general. Just too much for Brooke."

It didn't really make sense. Brooke came across as one of the toughest, no-nonsense people she'd ever met. "You're trying to tell me she's sensitive."

"She'd kill me if she heard me use that word about her." Cassie tipped her head back and forth. "Again, cautious. And a rule follower. You're not some crazy rebel, but you don't seem too vested in going by the books."

That, at least, resonated. "Okay. I get where you're going."

"Do you want Brooke to tolerate you or like you?"

Well, that was the heart of it, wasn't it? She did want Brooke to like her, the way she wanted everyone to like her. But she'd be lying if she said there wasn't more to it. She found Brooke insanely attractive, even with the frostiness, and part of her wanted that reciprocated. Not that she could say so to Cassie. "I want her to like me."

"Then go easy. Turn the charm volume down to seven."

"Seven? What is it on now?"

Cassie smirked. "You're at eleven, and you know it."

Ha. Maybe she did. Again, it had never been a liability. Until now. "Point taken."

Of all the arrogant, idiotic ideas she'd had to endure since Riley crashed into her life, this one had to take the cake. Even worse than the idea itself, Pam seemed to think it was worth looking into. And to top it all off, she'd lost her cool and stormed out of the sales meeting like a sulky teenager.

Meg set a pair of dirty martinis on the small table and sat opposite her. "Okay, tell me everything."

She lifted a finger to hold the thought, picked up her glass, and took a sip. The drink was briny and cold, just the way she liked it. She kept her finger up and took another sip before setting the glass down. "I had a shitty day."

Meg nodded. "So I gathered from your text. Give me the details."

She gave a quick rundown of the sales meeting: Riley's ridiculous idea, her less than professional response. Meg nodded slowly, not interrupting. When Brooke finished, she took another sip of her drink and waited for the flow of best friend righteous indignation. Only, it didn't come. Meg sat there, drinking her martini and looking at Brooke like she was some kind of math problem to solve.

Eventually, she set down her glass and said only, "Huh."

"Really? That's all I'm going to get?" Brooke folded her arms and prepared to be indignant on top of agitated.

"Why, exactly, are you so mad?" Meg asked.

Brooke let out a sigh. "I just told you."

Meg tapped a finger on the table. "Yeah, but you deal with annoying people at work all the time."

"I have to deal with her at work and at derby. That makes her twice as annoying."

"Okay. I feel you." Meg nodded, making Brooke think she was ready to concede just how terrible the situation was. "Does it feel like she's trying to antagonize you specifically?"

She wanted to say yes, but it would be a lie. "It's not directed at me per se. If anything, it's like she's trying to be overly friendly."

"Ah. And you hate that because—"

"Because she's waltzed in and is trying to change everything. Literally everything." Like some butch savior swooping in to save the day. She needed a savior even less than she needed a nemesis.

"Uh-huh." Meg nodded, but didn't elaborate.

"And everyone seems to think her ideas are the best thing since sliced bread." Not that everyone thought Brooke's ideas were terrible. But she was careful in putting them out there, making sure she'd thought everything through and had a sound rationale for why people would listen. Riley just opened her mouth, and whatever she was thinking came tumbling out, and people couldn't wait to ooh and ahh over it.

"Sure, sure. Is that all?"

Brooke huffed out a breath. Of course that wasn't all. "And they think she's the best thing since sliced bread, too."

"You already mentioned that." Meg tipped her head back and forth. "But I can see how it might be frustrating."

Meg was baiting her. Even knowing it, Brooke couldn't seem to stop herself. "She's just so charming and easygoing and just does whatever the hell she wants."

"And the fact that she's crazy hot and totally your type doesn't factor in at all." Of course Meg would go there. She should have known better than to think she'd get some straight-up sympathy, even from her best friend.

"She is not my type." Major emphasis on the not. Sex dreams notwithstanding.

Meg raised a brow.

Ugh. Brooke glared at her. "I mean, physically she is, sure. But that's literally it."

"And loves derby."

Technically, that should be a check in the plus column. It took enough of her time that trying to date a woman who didn't get it could prove challenging. "The rivalry cancels that out."

This time, Meg laced her fingers together and said nothing at all.

"We're like sworn enemies."

"Doesn't being enemies with someone have to be mutual?"

"I have enough animosity for the both of us." Brooke shook her head. Meg hadn't even met Riley and yet somehow managed to take her side. How did that happen?

"I'm just saying," she set her laced hands on the table and leaned forward. "If you didn't have the history, if she'd just shown up at practice—"

"And my office," Brooke added.

"And your office. If she'd just shown up and everything else was the same, would you hate her?"

She could say yes, end the conversation, and change the subject. At this point, distraction and cocktails might be her most effective course of action. But she'd called Meg for a reason. Even if she professed to wanting pure commiseration, that wouldn't solve her problem. She needed to solve whatever this was before she did irreparable damage to two of the most important things in her life. "I don't know."

"I think that's the root of all this."

"What? Not knowing?"

Meg's features softened, not quite to pity but alarmingly close. "She's got you all stirred up. I think it's easier to focus on why you're inclined to hate her than the alternative."

Oh God. Was she really going there? It was one thing to joke about Riley being her type. This? This was too much. "I don't know what you mean."

"Yes, you do."

She leaned forward, setting her elbows on the table and pressing her thumbs to her temples. She did. She really, really didn't want to, but she did. "You think I have a thing for her."

Meg grinned, any traces of pity giving way to mischief. "Wasn't it Shakespeare who said it's a fine line between love and hate?"

"No. I'm pretty sure you're making that up."

She shrugged. "Doesn't make it any less true."

"If you quote *Taming of the Shrew* to me right now, so help me—"

Meg lifted both hands defensively. "Never. I was thinking more Benedick and Beatrice."

Brooke groaned. The couple from *Much Ado About Nothing* was one of her favorites, but the idea that she and Riley might be the enemies destined for love was too much. "I can't even respond to that."

"You don't have to respond. Just think on it."

Brooke shook her head, then picked up her drink and drained the glass. Like she had any choice.

CHAPTER SIX

"Is this spot taken?"

Brooke turned, half of a bright red crawfish in each hand. For a split second, Riley thought she might be dismissed. Brooke had eased up on picking fights with her, but they still felt a long way from being friends. But then a hint of a smile crossed Brooke's lips. "All yours."

She set down her beer and took in the spread. She'd been nervous about a New Orleans crawfish boil. Given the city's versions of gumbo and jambalaya, she half expected some kind of fancy sauce or other Creole riff, but no. This looked how a crawfish boil should, crawfish and potatoes and corn, steaming hot and speckled with spice, all dumped onto a long table covered with newspaper. It reminded her of home. "So, is this a Bruisers tradition?"

Brooke's smile grew, reaching all the way to her eyes. "It is. Not always a crawfish boil but something mid-season. Usually after school is out."

Her team had been close, but they never did anything like this. "It's nice."

"After-parties are great, but this feels more like family."

It did. Being at someone's house, music pouring out of a speaker in the window, the sun just starting to set. It reminded her of parties at her aunt and uncle's house out in Breaux Bridge when she was little, ones that lasted well into the night and usually ended with her and Annie in sleeping bags on her cousin's bedroom floor. "Yeah."

Brooke pulled a crawfish tail from its shell and tossed the shell in the bucket. "Speaking of family, how are things with your sister?"

For some reason, it surprised her that Brooke remembered she had a sister. It shouldn't, since she'd put it out there as her reason for moving. Maybe it wasn't the remembering so much as the asking. The question felt more than polite. It felt personal. "She's good. And my niece and nephew are a riot." She hesitated for a moment, weighing whether to continue. "I'm living with them. My sister got divorced a few months ago, and her ex pretty much dropped off the face of the planet."

"Oh." Brooke frowned. "That sucks. I'm sorry."

Riley shrugged. "Don't be. He was kind of an asshole. She was already doing all the parenting on top of working full time."

"Sounds like she's better off with you."

"It's a pretty low bar, but thanks. She could probably manage on her own. She's amazing. But I hated the idea of her doing it alone." And since she had no idea if she'd ever have kids of her own, living two hours away from Lucas and Grace while they grew up didn't sit well.

"And your parents? Are they not in the picture?" Brooke looked at Riley and shook her head. "I'm sorry; that's really personal. You don't have to answer."

Riley smiled, both at Brooke's newfound interest in her life as well as the flash of embarrassment. "No apology needed. My father passed away. My mother means well but isn't really the nurturing type."

Brooke nodded, although Riley couldn't tell if it was from personal resonance or a more general empathy. "Yeah."

"What about you?" she asked, hoping to change the subject. As much as she liked connecting with Brooke, the topic of her family made her oddly self-conscious.

Brooke gave her a funny look. "What? Am I the nurturing type?"

Since she actually didn't have a specific question or direction in mind, she shrugged. "That. Or you could talk about your parents. Nieces and nephews. I'm pretty flexible."

Brooke smirked. "So, you're more uncomfortable than curious."

Being caught in such a weak diversion should have bothered her, but it didn't. "Maybe. Indulge me anyway?"

Brooke seemed to consider for a moment, angling her head and looking up at the sky. "My family is very boring but in a good, reliable sort of way. I'm an only child, and my parents pine for grandchildren. They try not to make me feel bad about it."

"But you do anyway?" Changing the subject might have been her original intent, but genuine curiosity took over.

Brooke peeled and ate a crawfish, then took a sip of her beer. Riley wouldn't have pegged her for moments of hesitation. Or sensitivity, to be honest. But the conversations with both Annie and Cassie echoed in her mind. Maybe they'd been right.

After a long moment, Brooke nodded. "Something like that."

She might not share the experience of wrestling with parental expectations, but she could appreciate that family was complicated. And disappointing people you cared about sucked. "Do you plan to give in one day?"

"Give in?"

"To grandkids." For reasons Riley couldn't explain, she really wanted to know the answer.

Brooke sighed. "Eventually, I imagine."

She couldn't tell if Brooke's tone was wistful or resigned. "That bad, huh?"

Brooke laughed. "Not the kids part. It's more the finding the love of my life part. That feels incredibly daunting."

It was impossible to know if Brooke's frankness had to do with the laid-back vibe of the party or how many beers she'd had. Or maybe she'd finally decided to relax and give Riley a break. She kind of wanted to know, but the warming up felt much more important than the reason, and she didn't want to break the magic of it by asking questions. "I can't disagree with you there."

Brooke gave her a lopsided grin. "Look at us, agreeing on something."

Riley picked up her beer and tapped it lightly to Brooke's. "I'll drink to that."

After sharing the table with Riley, Brooke let herself get pulled into a conversation with Hits's sister about putting her house on the market. Not because she was having a hard time being nice to Riley but because she wasn't. She set up an appointment with Melanie for the next week, then went out of her way to steer clear of Riley. It worked for a while, but then she had another drink and apparently let her guard down and found herself under the carport with Riley and two of her teammates' husbands.

They talked hurricane season and LSU football, who had a new boat and who sold his because his daughter's gymnastics were going to the next level. It wasn't a conversation she'd normally have, but it was kind of fascinating. As was Riley's complete ease with people she'd never met. Since she didn't have the same sort of stake—in the people or the topic—she was able to sit back and observe. Observe and, if she was honest, enjoy.

She drained her drink to have an excuse to leave the conversation. At the makeshift bar, she added ice to her cup, then filled it with Crown and a splash of Sprite. She so rarely had more than one; it was nice to let go a little. Not think about Riley and where they stood and what she was supposed to do about it.

Instead of returning to the carport, she stepped inside the game room at the back of the house. The old air-conditioner in the window chugged away, doing its best to keep the space cool despite the constant opening and closing of the back door. She watched Cali's kids play Mary's in a pretty epic foosball battle. It proved oddly hypnotizing.

Her brain took on the soft edges of a hair too much to drink. She wasn't drunk, really. Buzzed. Relaxed. When was the last time she'd done that? Too long ago. It was kind of nice, actually, especially when the company was so good.

Including Riley.

When the hell had that happened? She'd been so focused on trying to figure Riley out, understand what it all meant. Now, with her edges soft and Riley not trying to run the show, figuring it out didn't seem quite so important. Maybe she could just relax already and stop thinking and worrying for two whole seconds. Of course, there was still the matter of Riley looking sexy as fuck. That remained a problem.

"Can I interest you in a friendly game?"

She hadn't noticed Riley come up behind her, but there was no mistaking her voice. The lilt that was more Cajun than New Orleans, the velvety smoothness she'd imagined against her ear more than once. She turned slowly and found Riley regarding her with curiosity. Curiosity and maybe something else. Desire? Was that possible?

She glanced around the room for a game not in use. "Darts?"

"Yeah." Riley's voice was like whiskey laced with honey.

"Sure." Brooke pushed herself off the railing she'd been leaning against.

Riley stepped to the side so she could go first. It was one of those old-fashioned sort of moves that kind of bugged her when men did it. But with a woman, a butch woman no less, well, that was another matter entirely. She walked up to the board and pulled out the darts. She held both hands toward Riley. "Pick your color."

"I'll take yellow."

When she took the darts from Brooke, their hands brushed. Electricity tingled its way up her arm and sent a ripple of pleasure through her. Far more intense than the contact warranted. Maybe she was drunker than she thought. Brooke gestured toward the board. "After you."

"Oh, no. I insist."

Her words seemed to carry meaning beyond the game, but Brooke couldn't be sure. Probably better not to try. She stepped to the line and took her aim. The dart lodged in the cork but barely. Shit. She was about to embarrass herself. She took a deep breath and told herself to focus. The next two fared better and left her with an eleven and a fifteen. Nothing to write home about, but enough.

"Not bad."

She reclaimed her darts and noted the score on the chalkboard. "You don't have to humor me."

"I'm not. That's a very respectable start."

Brooke's thoughts were anything but respectable, but no one had to know that but her. "You're about to hustle me, aren't you?"

"I have no idea what you mean." Riley took the spot Brooke had vacated and proceeded to hit a bull's-eye, an eighteen, and a twenty.

"You were saying?"

Riley lifted both hands. "Luck, I swear. I'm not that good."

It turned out she wasn't completely lying. Riley won in the end, but the game took forever to finish. Weirdly, Brooke didn't mind the loss or the time spent in Riley's company.

"Can I offer you a ride home?"

"Uh." She'd planned to bum one off Hits, but she technically lived in the opposite direction.

"I mean, I don't want to be the one to tell you that you shouldn't drive home, but—"

"Oh, no. I know I shouldn't drive home."

Riley offered a half-smile. "You just don't want me to be the one to drive you."

She said it kindly, but it made Brooke feel small nonetheless. She couldn't admit her hesitation had little to do with not liking Riley and everything to do with the fear that maybe she was starting to like her a little too much. "Hits and I usually DD for each other, but she lives in Slidell."

"That's silly, then. I'm in Metarie."

It did make a whole lot more sense. And Hits was looking awfully chummy with a woman Cali had brought with her. She'd hate to interfere if there might be a connection brewing. "That would be great. Thanks."

Riley's smile went all the way to her eyes. "Just let me know when you're ready."

Brooke shrugged. "Whenever you are, but I'm in no rush."

"We could play one more game of darts?"

"So you can kick my ass again? No thanks." She poked Riley lightly in the chest to make it clear she was teasing.

"Pool?"

Now they were talking. "You're on."

Before starting, Brooke decided to make herself one more Crown and Sprite. Might as well enjoy this state as long as possible. "Can I fix you something?" she asked Riley.

"I'll take a plain Sprite."

She filled a second cup with ice and poured both drinks. The pool game took even longer than darts had. By the time Brooke eked out a win, she was tipsy and bordering on silly. Definitely her cue to call it a night. Riley didn't seem to mind heading out, reminding Brooke that she lived with two little kids who woke up very early, and they made their good-byes.

At a red light, Riley sneaked a glance at Brooke only to find Brooke already staring at her. Unlike the stares she'd become accustomed to, this one held no animosity. If she didn't know better, she might say it was a look of desire. "What?"

Brooke shook her head slowly. "You're really attractive, you know that?"

She chuckled. Good to know her instincts weren't totally off. "How drunk are you?"

Brooke laughed. "I'm not. I don't have to be drunk to pay you a compliment."

Riley raised a brow.

"I'm sorry I've been a bitch to you."

She knew better than to say it, but she kind of liked drunk Brooke. "You haven't been."

"Yes, I have, and we both know it."

"All right, let me rephrase. I get why you have."

"Still, that doesn't make it okay."

The olive branch was more than she would have hoped for, drunk or sober. She didn't want to waste it. "What if we called a truce? Or started over? Or something like that?"

"Really?"

"I sort of have a vested interest in us getting along." One that had nothing to do with the attraction she couldn't seem to shake.

Brooke smiled, a conciliatory smile that gave Riley even more hope than the apology. "That would be nice."

She pulled into the driveway Brooke indicated and cut the engine. She got out to open the door for Brooke, who was definitely moving a bit slow, and grabbed her bag.

"Are you always so chivalrous?"

A loaded question if she ever heard one. "Does it bother you?"

Brooke closed her eyes and shook her head slowly. "No."

Riley smiled. "Then yes."

That earned her another laugh. God, she loved Brooke's laugh. Even more, she loved being the one to inspire it. Which was probably dangerous territory, but she couldn't bring herself to care.

"I'm not a fan of needing to be rescued."

"You're highly capable. Surely, you never doubt that."

Instead of answering, Brooke focused on taking out her keys and unlocking her door. Riley followed her inside. She flipped on a light and motioned to the floor. "You can leave that there. Thank you for bringing it in and for the ride."

"Happy to. I mean it."

Brooke turned and looked right into her eyes. "I believe you."

Unlike the comment about being chivalrous, the statement felt like an unequivocal compliment. It kicked her already elevated heart rate up a notch. "Be sure to have a couple ibuprofen and a big glass of water before you go to bed."

"I will."

Brooke moved toward the door, and Riley took it as her cue to leave. Only Brooke stopped short, right in front of her. As unlikely as it seemed, it felt like Brooke was about to kiss her.

And then she did.

She put one hand on Riley's shoulder. Riley could feel her shift onto her tiptoes. The hem of Brooke's sundress brushed against her knees. And then her mouth, warm and soft and sweet, was on Riley's.

Unable to resist, Riley threaded both hands into her hair. A little sound of pleasure escaped Brooke's mouth. It was all the invitation she needed to take the kiss deeper. She angled her head, nipped Brooke's bottom lip gently. Another hum and Brooke's tongue found hers.

Blood roared in her ears, and all the desire she'd been trying to talk herself out of for weeks came flooding back. Wanting to drag Brooke to bed warred with knowing she shouldn't, not like this. She reluctantly pulled away, at least long enough to decipher Brooke's intent.

"Shit." Brooke blinked at her, a complete lack of intent evident on her face.

"That bad, huh?" Maybe if she lightened the mood, it would help.

Brooke slowly shook her head. "Not bad at all."

"Oh, so more of a wow, then." Riley grinned. That was the word she'd come up with.

"But this is a terrible idea."

Riley's heart sank. Even if she knew it was true, it didn't make it suck any less. "Yeah."

"You agree?"

What an impossible question. "It probably isn't the best thing to do in this moment."

Though, God, did she want to keep doing it. Kissing and so very much more.

CHAPTER SEVEN

Brooke rarely had hangovers, not because she was immune but because she was an adult and practiced restraint. She'd lapsed on both those fronts. And if the hangover wasn't bad enough, she had the heavy mantle of regret to drag her down. What had she been thinking?

She hadn't. That was the problem. Too much alcohol paired with her absolute exhaustion over Riley and what to do with her had rendered her good judgment null and void.

Could she merely have made a general fool of herself? No, of course not. She had to go for the jugular of self-inflicted humiliation and throw herself at Riley. And Riley couldn't just push her away or call her out for being drunk and stupid; she had to be calm and rational and the grown-up of the whole thing. Which maybe shouldn't have made it worse, but it totally did.

Riley had even sent her a text the next morning asking if she was okay. Ugh.

Brooke had managed to avoid her at the office for most of the week, but tonight was practice, and there was no getting out of it. Her dread was made even worse by the fact that she seriously considered skipping. She never skipped. Besides, skipping would only prolong the inevitable.

She slogged through the day, grumpy and snippy and hating herself for it. She grabbed an early dinner with Meg, who sensed the depths of her frustration and didn't tease her too terribly. She insisted on a blow-by-blow, though, as her best friend prerogative.

"It sounds to me like she regrets stopping more than you kissing her in the first place." Meg took a bite of her Cobb salad and pointed at Brooke with her fork. "What exactly did she say again?"

Brooke closed her eyes and tried to summon the precise words from her whiskey-addled memory. "'It probably isn't the best idea.' I'm pretty sure that's it. Oh, and 'in this moment.' She said, 'in this moment.'"

"Uh-huh. She definitely wanted to hook up with you."

"Stop." She'd not allowed her brain to go there, and she certainly didn't want to now.

"I'm serious." Meg pointed again with her fork. "She offered you a ride home, she walked you to your door. And unless you're lying to me, she didn't try to stop you from kissing her."

"Ugh. I wish she had."

Meg took a deep breath, and Brooke felt a pep talk coming on. Meg, a director of social work at a hospital, was really good at pep talks. Especially when they might be needed but weren't really wanted. "What if you hadn't stopped?"

"I could regret sleeping with her instead?"

Meg frowned, clearly unimpressed with Brooke's answer. "Did you want to sleep with her?"

The regret would be bigger for sure, but she couldn't help wondering what it might be like. "I—"

She lifted a finger. "Not in hindsight with all the layers of whatever psychological bullshit you've got going on right now. In the moment, did you want to sleep with her?"

Lying wouldn't get her anywhere and would insult Meg's intelligence. "Yes."

Meg sat back, a look of satisfaction on her face. "See? Was that so hard?"

"Yes." She stabbed at her salad and took a large bite.

"What if all of this is foreplay?"

Brooke set down her fork and crossed her arms. "Are you kidding me right now? I thought you'd let that go?"

"Well." She let the word drag out. "That was before you made out with her."

"We didn't make out."

Meg took a very slow sip of her Diet Coke. "Uh-huh."

"Ugh." She'd used the word so much she was starting to get on her own nerves.

They finished eating, and Meg insisted on paying after giving Brooke such a hard time. On the drive to the rink, Brooke mulled over Meg's theory. Although, if she was being honest, stewed might be a more accurate description.

❖

Riley had been disappointed when Brooke halted their all too brief kiss. She'd been slightly worried when Brooke hadn't returned her text the next day and annoyed when Brooke avoided her at work. Now that practice had rolled around and there'd be no avoiding each other, she found herself with an unpleasant mixture of the three.

It was flat-out rude to ignore a friendly check-in. And even if Brooke regretted the kiss, she'd been the one to initiate it. Basic make-out etiquette demanded that she at least acknowledge what happened. A little *it's not you, it's me* wouldn't hurt either. But no. Nothing. Nada.

She walked into the rink, half expecting Brooke to have bailed on practice. She was there, though, already skating laps and looking fierce and gorgeous and completely disinterested. Riley laced up her skates and joined the pack, stealing glances at Brooke but not initiating conversation. Not a test per se, but kind of.

Not a word during warm-ups. Not a flash of eye contact. Not so much as an acknowledgment of her existence. By the time they got to mock jams, Riley was pissed. It was as if they were back to square one. Hell, worse than square one because Riley now knew what Brooke's mouth felt like under hers. How she tasted. That little noise she made before her defenses went up.

The distraction of it was enough to throw her off her game. She let jammers through; she missed cues from her fellow blockers. She even tripped over her own feet a couple of times. By the time Tracy blew the final whistle, she felt more defeated than angry.

Brooke left practice like she'd spent the rest of it—without saying a word. At least, without saying a word to Riley. She chatted with other members of the team like it was any other practice. She wasn't subtle in her snubbing of Riley, though, and Riley caught more than a couple of questioning looks before things broke up for the night.

She considered ducking out herself before anyone had a chance to ask questions she didn't want to answer, but Hits made a beeline for her before she could pull off her skates. "What the hell was going on with you and Femme tonight?"

She could play dumb. These women had become her friends, but they were Brooke's friends first. But she wasn't a liar or a coward. "I think Brooke is pissed at me."

"I thought that was old news. Y'all seemed almost chummy at the crawfish boil."

Chummy. "Ha."

"So, what happened?"

While she might have been inclined to respect Brooke's privacy before, all bets were off at this point. "I drove her home after, and she kissed me."

"Oh." Hits's expression remained calm, but her eyes were anything but.

"She'd had a bit to drink, and we both sort of agreed it wasn't a good idea, but now she's acting like I ran over her mawmaw with my car." And as much as that irritated her, the underlying hurt of it was way worse.

"Did she say it was a bad idea, or did you?"

"Does it matter?"

Hits raised an eyebrow that confirmed what Riley already knew. Of course it mattered.

"She did, actually. I agreed reluctantly but with total respect for her saying no."

"Okay. All right." Hits nodded like she was solving a puzzle. "And do you like her, or do you just want to get in her pants?"

Even though they'd only known each other a couple of months, Riley didn't balk at the question. Derby had a way of building intimacy. And while it was known to have its share of drama—tied to hookups as often as egos or anything else—she didn't get the feeling Hits was fishing for gossip. "A little of both?"

The comment earned her a punch in the arm. It seemed as much commiseration as judgment, though, so she didn't take offense.

"I thought we were cool, but now she won't even talk to me."

Hits nodded. "Yeah."

"Really? That's what you got? You're a whole lot of no help."

"Sorry, bruh. That really sucks." She offered a shrug.

Not much better. "What am I supposed to do? You're friends. Give me something I can work with."

"Femme is sort of a tough nut."

Yeah, not the word she would have used. But interestingly, this conversation felt similar to the one she had with Cassie. Not the part about her taking up all the oxygen. The one about Brooke being pricklier than a cartoon cactus. "Go on."

"She gives the impression of being super uptight."

"Impression?"

Hits conceded the point with a wave of her hand. "Okay, she has a tendency to be really uptight. But she's also a really great person."

"I didn't think I needed convincing of that. I could handle cool. It made sense. This, this hot and cold business? I don't think so."

"Her feelings run deep, and I think that scares her sometimes."

The assessment hit Riley like a punch to the gut instead of the arm. She pressed a thumb to the space between her eyebrows. "Are you sure she doesn't just hate me?"

"Brooke doesn't hate anyone. That I can say unequivocally."

Her use of Brooke's name and not her derby moniker did as much to drive home the point as her words. Riley nodded. "Okay."

"So, you need to figure out what you want to do with that."

"Well, for starters, I'm not going to pick a fight with her."

Hits offered an empathetic smile. "It's a good start."

"Yeah." It might be. The problem was, beyond that, she had absolutely no idea.

CHAPTER EIGHT

The second Brooke heard the shrill whistle, she knew it was for her. The ref called out her number and offense, sending her to the penalty box with a jerk of his thumb. She skated off the rink and took a seat, swearing under her breath.

"What the hell's gotten into you, Femme?" Tracy glared at her from the bench.

She knew exactly what the hell had gotten into her, but she sure as hell wasn't about to own it. It was one thing to let the opposing team get under her skin. A member of her own? Humiliating. And that's exactly what was going on. Riley and her smug confidence. Riley and her new ideas and playing fast and loose with the rules. Riley and her gorgeous mouth that tasted even better than it looked. Riley and—

"Femme."

And now she'd been so busy sulking, she looked like a space cadet. Great. "What?"

"That's six penalties. One more and you're out."

She knew that was six. She wasn't an idiot. She glowered at Tracy, throwing in an eye roll for good measure.

"I'm not pulling you out, but we've got close to ten minutes left. Get it together, will you?"

The official signaled the end of her time in the penalty box. She launched herself from the bench and rejoined the jam, jockeying for position and trying to make up for the precious seconds lost. She shouldered her way through the pack, then picked up speed, looping the rink to start the process again. She'd just strategized her next move—

one that wouldn't require close proximity to Riley—when Riley spun around to hip check a blocker from the opposing team.

The move created the perfect opening. She couldn't not take it. She leaned in and darted forward before the pack shifted, and the space closed. Just as she slipped through, she could make out Riley's voice behind her. "You're welcome."

She careened into the opposing team's jammer, needing somewhere to channel the flare of agitation. The sound of the whistle once more made her stomach sink. She didn't bother keeping the swearing under her breath as she moved off the field of play. Since she was officially ejected from the match, she didn't even bother with the penalty box, skating instead to her own bench. She yanked the panty off her helmet and handed it to Tracy but refused to make eye contact.

The rest of the bout passed in a blur of her own self-loathing. Although tempted to skip the after-party altogether, it was a line of bitchiness she wasn't willing to cross. Or maybe cowardice. Either way, she didn't want her teammates to think she'd sunk so low.

On the short drive to the bar, she alternated between giving herself a pep talk—it wasn't as if she was the first of the Bruisers to get ejected on penalties—and a stern directive to get a grip. Riley showed no signs of going anywhere, and unless she wanted to remove herself from the equation, she was going to have to find a way to get along. Ill-advised kiss notwithstanding.

The question was, could she do it?

She could. She'd been nice to bigger jerks at work. Even a couple of former teammates had been more obnoxious than Riley, and she'd always managed to keep her cool. There was no logical reason for Riley to continue getting under her skin the way she did. Even though Brooke couldn't stop thinking about kissing her, and Riley, by her observation, couldn't care less.

Brooke got out of her car and squared her shoulders. She could do this. She walked into the bar. Even if the sting of such a stupid loss was still fresh. Even if she still hated herself for getting ejected for the first time in her derby career. Even if she had this low-grade urge to hip check Riley into the middle of next week.

Inside, conversations were going, and no one seemed bothered by the loss the Bruisers had just endured. That was good, she supposed.

Hits came over and slung her arm around Brooke's shoulder. "Do you want to talk about it?"

Brooke shook her head. "Nope."

"Let me buy you a drink. Beer or something stronger?"

She considered for only a second. "Crown and Sprite."

"That bad, huh?"

She let out a sigh laced with a trace of growl. "That bad."

Hits headed to the bar and returned a minute later with a pair of matching drinks. She handed one to Brooke. "Cheers."

Brooke shook her head. "What could we possibly be toasting?"

"Come on. It wasn't that terrible."

Brooke downed half her drink before raising a brow. "We lost to a team we've obliterated the last three years running."

Hits shrugged. "Yeah, but no one got hurt. It's our first loss of the season. And we're here drinking cocktails. Life's still pretty good in my book."

For as tough a blocker as Hits was, she had a surprisingly easygoing approach to derby. Not entirely unlike Riley, but in a much less annoying way. "You have a point, I suppose."

"We all have shit nights, Femme. No one is holding this against you but you."

Rationally, she knew that. And if she'd been distracted by work or a family thing or, God, anything but Riley, she might be able to let it go. The fact that it wasn't anything like that, or anything remotely important in the grand scheme of things, was what got her. She'd let Riley's presence completely derail her and ruin one of her absolute favorite things. That was what she resented, far more than the humiliating defeat or Riley's instant popularity with people she'd taken months to become easy with.

"Are you sure you don't want to talk about it?"

She let out a full growl this time. "I'm sure."

Tracy joined them and started talking about a job interview she had coming up. It proved the perfect distraction. And giving Tracy a pep talk meant Hits was no longer trying to give her one. She actually started to forget about what a shit night she'd been having and even took Hits up on her offer of a second drink. It was all going well until she turned and found herself face-to-face with Riley.

Brooke looked around in search of an escape, but there was none to be had. At least none that didn't involve completely abandoning her resolution to make nice. Great.

"Hey." Riley smiled. She'd been wanting to get Brooke alone all night. Well, not alone. Even if she had the occasional fantasy of getting Brooke alone in a very different way, she knew she'd be barking up the wrong tree. That ship had sailed, and she was more determined than ever to be friends. It was their best chance for making it through in one piece.

"Hey." Brooke's surliness came through, but it was laced with something akin to sadness that made Riley want to hug her.

"Are you okay?"

"I'm fine."

Riley raised a brow. "You're not a very good liar, are you?"

Brooke closed her eyes for a second, and Riley couldn't decide if she was on the verge of tears or trying not to throat punch her. "Fine. I'm not great, but I really don't want to talk about it."

At least she could empathize on that front. "We all have shitty bouts. It happens."

Brooke glowered. "I don't."

She could have taken the statement as ego. It might have been easier if she had. It would keep Brooke in a tidy box of all-around bitch. But her conversation with Hits echoed in her mind, and Riley could tell it wasn't actually ego at all. Brooke seemed, what? Defeated. "You might expect perfection of yourself, but no one else does."

"Look, I get that you're trying to be nice, but I'm not interested in a pep talk."

Riley couldn't help but chuckle. This conversation felt oddly similar to one she'd had with Grace only a few nights before. She knew better than to say so, but it might not hurt to apply some of the same principles. "Would you feel better if you hit me?"

"What?" Brooke looked at her with apparent confusion, although Riley got the sense part of her wanted very much to coldcock her.

"It's obvious that I'm what's bugging you so much. I'll be honest, it feels like a whole lot more than the fact that I shoulder checked you in a bout almost a year ago. But I'll be damned if I know what it is."

Brooke opened her mouth, then closed it. She didn't speak.

Riley considered her options. The most reasonable would be to walk away. Brooke had rejected all of her attempts to make nice. Even offering herself up as a punching bag hadn't cracked her. It wasn't as if they needed to like each other to play on the same team. She could step back and leave Brooke's friends to commiserate with her or cheer her up or whatever they did to pull her out of a funk.

The problem was, she didn't want to do that.

For whatever reason, she liked Brooke, and she wanted Brooke to like her. Part of it was her own ego. Everyone liked her. Brooke was like this puzzle she needed to solve or, perhaps more accurately, a dare she couldn't seem to resist. There was also the matter of Brooke being off her game. If the Bruisers had any hope of finishing a winning season, Brooke needed to be in top form. None of their other jammers came close to her in terms of stamina or finesse.

But even as she told herself these things, she knew it was a whole lot more than that. For some inexplicable reason, she had feelings for Brooke. Sexual attraction laced with something romantic and protective and completely out of her comfort zone. She'd spent a month denying it and another trying to distract, divert, or otherwise talk herself out of it. And all she'd managed to do was make it stronger.

Brooke Landry had gotten into her system and showed no signs of going anywhere.

"The way I see it, there's this weird tension between us. Ignoring it is only making it stronger, so I think we need to blow it wide open."

Brooke angled her head and seemed to consider the offer. "And you think me decking you will do the trick."

She decided to take a chance. "Well, it's either that or we go to bed together, and I'm guessing you're far more inclined to punch me than sleep with me."

She didn't know what she expected, but it sure as hell wasn't for Brooke to bust out laughing. But that's exactly what happened. Not just a laugh, either. She leaned forward, braced a hand on one of her knees, and really laughed.

Riley waited her out. It took a while. During that time, she tried not to take it personally that the idea of sex with her proved so hilarious. When Brooke finally stopped, there were tears in her eyes. "Oh my God."

"I mean, I figured you wouldn't want to; that's why I led with the hitting."

Brooke pressed her lips together and wiped her eyes. "I don't want to hit you."

Riley raised a brow. "Does that mean you do want to go to bed with me?" She was seriously pressing her luck at this point, but whatever.

"I do not."

That was a shame. Not that she expected Brooke to say yes, but it stung to be dismissed so readily. In general but even more so by Brooke. And after what had been, in her book, a pretty spectacular kiss.

Brooke smiled and blew a strand of hair out of her eyes. "I'm going to go home now."

If she didn't know better, she could close one eye and think they were flirting. "Was it something I said?"

Whatever moment they'd shared passed. Brooke's eyes cooled, and she glanced toward the door. "It's been a long day, and clearly, I'm not fit for conversation."

"I think you're doing okay." Riley couldn't put her finger on it, but it felt like maybe Brooke's shell might be starting to crack, and she didn't want to let her leave. Like letting her go would put them back to being enemies.

"You don't need to lie." Brooke sighed. She looked exhausted all of a sudden. "Besides, I have an open house tomorrow, and I need to be ready for it."

And just like that, the cracks closed. The flash of anger was gone but so was the humor. Riley was left with cool, aloof Brooke. She shouldn't but she'd almost prefer the flash of defiance to this detached disinterest. She let out a sigh of her own. "All right. I hope it goes well tomorrow."

"Thanks." Brooke turned to leave but paused. "I'm sorry about earlier."

Riley opened her mouth to ask what earlier Brooke was referring to, but she didn't have the chance. Brooke made a beeline to the door, pausing for only a second to say something to Hits. And then she was gone.

Riley stared at the exit for a moment as though she might will her to come back. She didn't, of course. Riley shook her head and turned her attention to her other teammates. She talked and laughed, made plans to catch up with a couple of people for lunch on Sunday. But a part of her mind remained on Brooke. The unexpected laughter, which turned her on more than she'd care to admit, and the cryptic apology.

If she was smart, she'd wash her hands of Brooke Landry and not look back. Because even if they found some sort of peace, everything about Brooke screamed prickly, mercurial, and impossible to please. Chasing after her could only lead to disaster.

And yet. And yet, chasing after her was exactly what Riley wanted to do.

CHAPTER NINE

Brooke stepped through the front door, and her mouth fell open. Not figuratively either. The chaos around her was so bad, so unexpected, her jaw dropped. She closed her eyes and counted to ten. When she reopened them, the initial shock was gone, but the chaos remained.

How the hell was she supposed to run an open house in two hours when the house in question looked like a tornado had blown through?

First things first. She pulled out her phone and called the sellers. The wife, since that was who she'd spoken with most.

"Hey, Brooke." Jody drawled her name as though they were long-lost friends. "What's up?"

"I just got to your place for the open house today."

"Oh God. That's today?"

Brooke closed her eyes again. "Yes, it's today. This is what we agreed on last month."

"But the house is a mess."

Well, at least she wasn't in denial of it. "I know. I'm here."

"We're in Gulf Shores."

Funny how quickly a day could go from bad to worse. "Uh."

"I'm so sorry. I thought it was next weekend. I actually meant to call and tell you not to do any showings this weekend because we left in such a rush." She sighed. "I forgot that, too."

If Jody and Marc had been jerks, it would have been easy to cancel the open house and tell them to call her when they were serious about selling their house. They weren't jerks, though. They were sweet, well-meaning flakes. "Do you mind if I touch your stuff?"

Jody gasped. "You would do that? Oh, Brooke, you're an absolute lifesaver."

"I'll try not to break anything, but I'm not going to be delicate about it."

"You do whatever you need to do. I promise I'll make it up to you when we get home."

The nice thing was that Brooke believed her. She'd already been gifted a nice bottle of wine after taking photos for the listing, even though that was part of her job. "Okay. I'm going to hang up now so I can get started."

"Right, right. You are the best. I'm going to recommend you to everyone I know."

"I'll take it." She would, too. She didn't make a point of targeting high-end listings, but she wasn't about to turn her nose up at them, either. A handful of sales like this one could make for a nice little bump in her earnings.

"Thank you, thank you, thank you."

She ended the call and took a few seconds to strategize. First up, see if she could snag a second pair of hands. She called the main office and crossed her fingers that someone might be available and inclined to do her a favor.

"Edelman Real Estate, this is Cassie."

"Hey, Cassie. It's Brooke." She took a minute to explain her situation and the resulting desperation. "Is there anyone around?"

"Um, Riley's here."

She rolled her eyes. Of course Riley would be there. "No one else?"

"Sorry. A bunch of open houses today."

Yeah. It was a good day for them. She shook her head. "All right. Could I talk with Riley?"

"Sure. Hold just a second. Wait, do you want me to tell her what's going on and ask her for you?"

It would be pretty chickenshit to do that, but every second she spent on the phone was one she couldn't spend cleaning up. "Would you mind? That way I can get started here. Just text me with her answer."

"You got it. Good luck, girl."

"Thanks." She was going to need it.

Brooke ended the call and set her phone and purse on the coffee table. Then she got to work and tried not to think about what would be worse, Riley saying yes or saying no.

She tackled the living room first since that was the first thing potential buyers would see when they walked in. Fortunately, there was a large ottoman with storage and a generous coat closet. She picked up toys and books and random articles of clothing and shoved them anywhere they'd fit. The room needed a vacuum, but she should see how bad the rest of the house was first.

She did a quick tour, relieved Jody wasn't the type to leave dirty dishes in the sink when she went away for the weekend. The bathrooms weren't a disaster, either. Probably because they had cleaners every week. Her phone pinged just as she came down the stairs with a text from Cassie.

Riley will be there in fifteen. I gave her the info.

Her annoyance at having to see and interact with Riley paled in comparison to her relief. Yes, she'd owe Riley one, and that would suck, but salvaging the open house mattered more. At least today. She might feel differently tomorrow, but she'd cross that bridge when she got there.

She cleared off the dining room table, made haphazard piles of the papers and books and magazines strewn about the office, and was just about to head upstairs when the doorbell rang. *Please, please, please be Riley.*

Brooke shook her head at the absurdity of that and opened the door. Sure enough, Riley stood on the other side. She wore jeans and a short-sleeved shirt with deck shoes and had a large shopping bag in one hand. She offered a playful smile. "How bad is it?"

"Not as bad as I thought. More cluttered than dirty. I'm really grateful for the help, though." She forced herself to make eye contact. "Thank you for coming."

Riley set down the bag and looked around. "We're colleagues. More than colleagues, technically. I'm sure you'd do the same for me."

She said the last part with a wink that left Brooke wondering if she was teasing or calling her out. Great. "Well, I owe you one now, so feel free to call it in anytime."

It was the best she could come up with, and it got a chuckle out of Riley, so she'd take it. "Okay, what do you need? I'll take directions."

Brooke couldn't help but smirk at that.

"Don't get used to it." Riley returned the smirk.

"How do you feel about making beds?" If the circumstances were different, she might take some satisfaction in telling Riley what to do. At this point, all she felt was relief.

Riley angled her head. "I'm an expert bed maker. On it."

Without another word, she headed upstairs. Brooke watched her go, unsure what to make of the interaction. She looked over at the bag but resisted the urge to peer in. It was none of her business. Riley could have brought whatever it was inside to keep it from sitting in her hot car.

Realizing she was wasting precious time, Brooke squared her shoulders and continued working her way through the downstairs, decluttering as much as possible. There wasn't much in the way of dust, so she pulled out the vacuum and did a quick job of the rug in the living room and entryway. She tucked it away and started opening shades and flipping on lights to make sure the spaces were as bright and inviting as possible.

Satisfied with the downstairs and with a half hour to spare, she headed to check on Riley only to find her bounding down toward her. "All set upstairs."

"Really?" That was quick.

"Beds made. Crap thrown in closets. Candles going in the bathrooms. Lights on."

She didn't want to be impressed, but she was. "Wow. Thanks."

Riley lifted the bag, gave it a little shake. "I brought cookie dough."

Brooke narrowed her eyes. Is that seriously what was in there? "Excuse me?"

"Cookie dough. To bake. For the potential buyers."

"I picked up some cookies from La Madeleine. I was prepared until I got here." She hated the defensiveness in her voice but whatever.

"Yeah, but those won't make the whole house smell amazing."

She knew of agents who did that, tried to create some Pavlovian positive reinforcement with the aroma of fresh-baked treats. She'd always considered it a rather cheap ploy, meant to distract from things about the house that left something to be desired. "That's really not necessary."

"Of course it's not. Neither is showing a clean house, but we do what we can, right?"

Brooke frowned. "I feel weird using their oven."

"I just picked up their underwear. I think the line of good boundaries has been crossed."

She laughed in spite of herself. "Fine."

Riley waved a hand, essentially dismissing her. "You go do your thing. I'll handle things in the kitchen."

Even if she didn't like it, she wasn't about to argue with the person who just saved her ass. And people would be arriving soon. She took a deep breath and mustered a smile. "Thank you."

Riley disappeared into the kitchen, and Brooke bustled around, setting out packets of information and business cards. She went to her car and pulled out the open house sign and balloons, setting them up in the front yard. When she walked back into the house, the aroma of chocolate chip cookies hit her first thing. Damn it to hell if Riley wasn't right. She went to the kitchen and found her moving cookies from a sheet pan to a large plate like she'd done it a million times before. It was annoying just how confident and relaxed she looked doing it. And if she was being honest, how hot she looked, too.

"Do you always do this?"

Riley glanced up and smiled. "Bake for an open house? Always. Usually from scratch, though. I think you can really tell the difference. But you know, beggars can't be choosers."

Brooke bit her lip. "I don't suppose I can argue with that last part."

"Hey, it's cool. I'm happy to help."

She really sounded like she meant it. Brooke didn't know what to do with that. Or with the weird fluttery sensation she got when Riley smiled at her. Everything about this day had gone so far sideways, she didn't even know where to start. "Still. Thank you."

"I'll clean up in here. Is there anything else you need? I can stick around, but I'm not really dressed for an open house."

Again, she sounded as if she meant it. And not in a *you owe me big-time* sort of way. It was so weird. "I think I'm okay. I really can't thank you enough."

"Oh, don't worry. I'll think of something you can do to pay me back."

If she didn't know better, she'd swear Riley Fauchet was flirting with her. Which was absolutely insane. And clearly some warped figment of her imagination. Must be the stress. Or the heat. Or something. She opened her mouth to reply—although she had no clue what to say—but was spared having to by the front door.

Riley tipped her head. "That's your cue. Knock 'em dead."

"Uh, thanks." She escaped the kitchen and headed to the front of the house to greet the first guests. She smiled and introduced herself, delivered her pitch, and invited the couple to look around. Before she finished her spiel, two more families walked in.

The turnout was better than she'd hoped for, which made her all the more grateful she hadn't had to cancel. During a brief lull, she poked her head in the kitchen. No sign of Riley, but the cookies were more than half devoured. She was going to have to add baking to her open house checklist. It annoyed her, not because she disliked baking, but conceding that Riley was right about something remained annoying.

She didn't dwell on it for long. A couple of agents she knew from another broker stopped in. They chatted about the house but talked shop in general. Both of them complimented her on the fresh-baked cookies before leaving.

By the time things wound down, close to fifty people had passed through. A few were casual gawkers, but she wouldn't be surprised if an offer or two materialized in the next few days. Despite the couple hours of panic, it had been a very successful showing.

When the last family left, she took down the sign and picked up her materials from the house. She sent a text to Jody, letting her know things had gone well, only to get effusive thanks in return. She texted Cassie as well with an assurance that things had worked out. She finished cleaning up and let herself out.

Only after climbing into her car did she realize how exhausted she was. The three hours she'd expected to spend on her feet had been closer to five. Added to that, the stress of how things started. And Riley. Having her show up had gone better than she could have hoped, which was disconcerting.

She needed to come to terms with knowing she might not be able to dislike Riley any longer. Brooke started the engine, cranked the AC, and sighed. No, there was no might at this point. She liked Riley, plain and simple. Which would be fine if she didn't find her sexy as fuck on top of it.

CHAPTER TEN

After the open house, something in Brooke softened. Not quite to the point of being friends, maybe, but friendly. And if Riley wasn't so focused on how much she wanted Brooke, way beyond friendship, she might have been able to enjoy it. The problem was that she did want Brooke. She wanted her badly.

It wasn't just physical, either. That would have been aggravating, but she'd know what to do with it, how to manage it. No, this was worse. It was like having a serious and seriously unrequited crush. She'd not been in that boat since college. Only this was worse because she knew what it felt like to kiss Brooke, and of course, it had to go and be even better than she'd imagined.

At least things were clicking on the rink. They'd won the last bout handily and were poised to do so again against the Biloxi Betties, the number one team in Mississippi. Just a few more minutes of holding a decent, if not comfortable, lead. They'd have the win and would seal their spot in the playoffs.

Brooke called off the jam, and Tracy called a time-out. They gathered into a huddle. Riley had some water and, as she'd taken to doing, kept her mouth shut. She'd been hesitant to take that advice, but it seemed to be working. It might not be the reason Brooke had softened, but she figured it couldn't hurt.

"How's everyone feeling?" Tracy asked.

They were down a couple of people thanks to the first week of school, and the starting lineup had stayed in more than usual. Riley glanced around, but no one looked as if they'd hit their limit. If anything, holding steady against such a formidable opponent seemed to energize them. Everyone nodded or voiced their desire to stay in.

"Okay. Next jam, I was thinking we could do the reverse wall and sneak Femme around the inside."

Everyone nodded but Brooke. Riley opened her mouth, then bit her tongue. When Tracy gave Brooke an expectant look, she smiled. "I think we should do Riley's backward lock."

It was a good thing she was biting her tongue because otherwise, her mouth would have fallen open. It was the move she'd introduced shortly after joining the Bruisers. The one Brooke had no use for and that had started one of their many sparring matches.

She was saved from being the incredulous one when Hits said, "Really?"

Brooke rolled her eyes but smiled. "The Betties haven't seen it yet, and it's a really good move."

"But it means you taking the outside. You hate the outside." Again, Hits saved her having to say what she was thinking. The outside made Brooke vulnerable to the kind of move Riley had used on her way back when and to being taken out more generally. Brooke hated being vulnerable.

"But they won't expect it, and we'll be able to lock this down on the next jam."

No one argued. Tracy made quick eye contact with everyone. "Agreed?"

They broke the huddle and headed to the line. Riley grabbed her hand. "Why are you pushing for this?"

Brooke shot her a disapproving look. "Seriously?"

"I am serious. It's just a game. What difference does it make?"

Brooke took her spot, not breaking eye contact with Riley. She lifted a brow. "The difference is, I'd like to kick some ass."

In that moment, things between them changed. Riley could feel it. She wanted to unpack it, explore it, drag Brooke to some quiet spot and see what might unfold. But first, they had a bout to win. She took her place with the other blockers behind the line. The whistle blew, and everyone moved seamlessly into position. Riley and the other blockers held firm, and Brooke squeaked past them and the Betties blockers almost as if everyone was in on it.

Brooke snagged the lead jammer slot, the move seeming to give her an extra boost of speed. She went in again and again managed to squeeze through, maybe not as gracefully as the first time, but it hardly mattered. In the end, she managed three loops, essentially sealing their victory. When Brooke called off the jam, she looked right at Riley and offered a wink that seemed to say a hell of a lot more than "good job."

The Betties took the loss graciously. The post-bout pictures and awards were spirited and full of props, including unicorn tiaras for Brooke and the Betties pivot as MVPs. For the second time that night, Riley wanted to snag Brooke and steal away. She couldn't, of course, but every minute that passed made her question whether she'd imagined the shift, conjured it from her desire for Brooke and her desire for things between them to be different.

By the time everything was packed up and she was on her way to the after-party, she'd changed her mind at least half a dozen times. And by the time she walked into the bar, she'd worked herself into a state of complete indecision over whether she wanted a moment alone with Brooke or not.

❖

"See what happens when we all work together?" Tracy slung an arm around each of their shoulders.

Riley nodded, but Brooke gave her a bland look. "You say that like we've never won before."

Tracy elbowed her in the ribs. "Do I need to start teasing you about fouling out, young lady?"

Brooke elbowed her back with what appeared to be considerably more force than she'd gotten. "No. And don't call me young lady."

"Yes, ma'am." Tracy pulled her arms back and slipped away before Brooke could elbow her again.

"She's not wrong, you know," Riley said after taking a sip of her beer.

"Yeah, yeah." Brooke didn't seem mad, but her face took a serious turn. "I need to tell you something."

The intensity of her tone, the look on her face, gave Riley pause. "What's that?"

"The night of the crawfish boil? When you drove me home? I wasn't that drunk."

Riley narrowed her eyes, trying to suss the underlying meaning. "To drive, you mean?"

"Oh, no, it was good I didn't drive. But by the time we got to my house, I wasn't really. When I kissed you, I knew what I was doing."

The words sank in, making her brain recalibrate what happened, what it meant. On top of the fact she was bringing it up now. "Why are you telling me this?"

"Because it was chickenshit of me to play it off as the Crown talking. Because you deserve to know the truth." She looked down, then back up and right into Riley's eyes. "Because I want to do it again, and I don't want you to mistake my intentions."

"You want to kiss me again?" Such a weak response, but it was the best she could manage with her brain so scrambled.

Brooke cocked a brow. "I'd like to do a lot more than kiss you."

Confidence was one of the things Riley found sexiest about Brooke. To have it directed at her in the form of a come-on was enough to short-circuit her whole system. "You do?"

"If the feeling isn't mutual, no harm, no foul." Brooke's tone was light, but her eyes had cooled.

"It's mutual. It's absolutely one hundred percent mutual. I'm just having a hard time forming sentences." She lifted a shoulder and hoped Brooke believed her.

The smile was slow, sultry, and satisfied. "You want to get out of here?"

Even her half-baked sentences abandoned her. Riley nodded. "Good."

Brooke took her hand and led her through the bar. She was pretty sure people were staring at their joined hands or at them leaving together barely an hour into the party. She didn't even care. She was pretty much on board with anything Brooke had in mind, and she wasn't about to blow the chance to see where things might go.

Outside, the air remained oppressive and sticky. The parking lot was packed, and more cars crept up the lane, looking for a spot. Brooke didn't stop walking. "You okay going to my place?"

"Yep."

She glanced over her shoulder. "You okay if I drive?"

Aside from wanting to press her against the nearest car and kiss her, it was the best idea she'd heard all night. "Yep."

A flash of headlights announced they'd arrived at Brooke's car. Riley slid into the passenger seat and closed her eyes for a second. Were they really doing this?

"Having second thoughts?" Brooke regarded her with something resembling concern.

Riley turned as much as her seat belt and the confined space would allow. "I've wanted you from the moment I first laid eyes on you."

Concern morphed into disbelief. "That was almost a year ago."

"Yep."

"The same day you shoulder checked me halfway to Texas."

"Yep." Riley grinned and decided to take a chance. "Those things aren't mutually exclusive, you know. All's fair in love and derby."

Brooke nodded slowly. "I heard that once."

"Yeah, so, as long as it's not a deal breaker for you—"

"It's not." She put her car in gear and started to drive.

CHAPTER ELEVEN

When Brooke pulled into the driveway, Riley surveyed the house. A tidy little ranch she'd guess was built in the fifties. She hadn't paid much attention the night she dropped Brooke off. "You have a cute place."

Brooke smiled at her. "Thanks."

"I'm still staying with my sister." She hoped that would change before winter, but she'd delayed putting her place in Lafayette on the market and wanted that sale to be final before she made the investment here.

"I forget you're living with her."

"Not for too much longer, I hope."

Brooke regarded her with curiosity. "Are you getting a place of your own or going back to Lafayette?"

Riley chuckled. "You trying to get rid of me, Femme?"

"If I was trying to get rid of you, I wouldn't be trying to get you in my bed."

"That's good because I'm not going anywhere. Except, for the moment, your bed."

Brooke cut the engine and climbed out. Riley followed, standing behind her as she unlocked the front door. She resisted that recurring urge to push Brooke up against it and kiss her but allowed one of her hands to go to Brooke's hip.

The door opened, and Brooke pulled her inside. She closed it behind them, and then it was Brooke pushing her up against the door and kissing her senseless. An absolutely perfect turn of the tables as far as she was concerned.

When Brooke broke the kiss and leaned back, her eyes were dark with desire. "You're a really good kisser."

The playful declaration made Riley smile. "Thanks."

"This probably sounds weird, but I could really use a shower first."

Riley let her gaze travel down Brooke's body and back up: the fishnets, the tight black shorts, the tank top with the Bruisers logo splashed across the front. Her brain needed no other prompting to imagine Brooke's body naked and wet and slicked with soap. "And if I said I agreed?"

"I'd say we should start there."

Without another word, Brooke led them through the living room and down a short hall to a surprisingly spacious bathroom. "Nice."

"Thanks. I had some work done when I bought it. Sacrificed a tiny fourth bedroom to make a bigger bathroom and walk-in closet."

"It's funny how losing a bedroom isn't a cardinal sin anymore."

"Quality over quantity, right?" Brooke smiled and, without ceremony, pulled her shirt over her head.

Even in the decidedly unsexy sports bra, the sight of her skin kicked Riley's pulse up a few notches. "You're really beautiful."

Brooke rolled her eyes. "I'm a sweaty, smelly mess."

"Who is absolutely stunning."

"Stop plying me with compliments and take your clothes off."

The command did more to her libido than even the sight of Brooke's body. "Yes, ma'am."

Brooke turned on the water and glanced over her shoulder. "Don't ever call me ma'am."

Riley snickered and followed her into the shower. The second the water hit her, all traces of humor vanished. She let out an expletive. "Damn, woman. You could make it a tiny bit warm."

"Sorry." Brooke smirked like she wasn't the least bit sorry, then reached around and adjusted the handle. "Better?"

The water warmed slightly. "I'll take it. Do you always take frigid showers?"

Brooke, who'd dunked her head under the spray, opened her eyes and raised a brow. "Usually."

Riley had a joke about her being frosty on the tip of her tongue, but she swallowed it. They weren't in teasing territory, at least not yet. "I admire your fortitude."

Brooke chuckled and picked up a shampoo bottle. She squirted a blob into her hand and lifted it. Riley accepted a smaller sized dollop and worked it into her hair. They took turns washing and rinsing. It should have been weird to be naked and soapy together, but it wasn't. She couldn't decide if it was having spent so much time together or the physical nature of a lot of that time. Whatever it was, it worked. In a matter of minutes, they were toweling off. The sexual tension hadn't abated, yet she'd managed to keep herself in check and not have their first time be in the shower. Not that there was anything wrong with shower sex.

"You know, I think that's the first time I've showered with a woman before sleeping with her."

Brooke rubbed at her hair with a towel. "Are you complaining?"

She let her gaze travel down to Brooke's towel-clad body, complete with droplets of water still clinging to her shoulders. "Not in the least."

"Good, because I'd hate not to have sex at this point."

Brooke grabbed Riley's hand and pulled her into the bedroom. Riley opened her mouth to say something clever, but she had no words. And before she could find any, Brooke dropped her towel. With a flick of her finger, she undid Riley's, too, leaving them both in a pile on the floor.

She'd literally just seen Brooke naked. Touched her, even. But the sight of Brooke's body—golden skin, the juxtaposition of her muscular arms with the soft swell of her breasts—fogged her brain and left her breathless. She shook her head in an attempt to clear it. Not the time to come across like some gawking idiot who'd never been with a woman before.

"Not changing your mind, are you?"

Riley shook her head again. "Oh, no. I'm just wondering what I did to get so lucky."

Brooke angled her head like she was contemplating a serious answer to the question. When she smiled, Riley expected a snarky comeback. But then she said, "I'm lucky you didn't write me off by now."

Riley shrugged, determined to play it cool. "Well, you're pretty hot."

Brooke chuckled, but then she frowned. "I don't want to kill the mood or anything, but I'm kind of serious. I was pretty horrible to you."

"What can I say? I like you." It was Riley's turn to smile. "And I like a challenge."

Brooke nodded slowly. It was a perfect answer, really. Not too syrupy, it walked the line between taking her to task and letting her off the hook. And whether Riley meant it that way or not, it hinted at the fact that getting Brooke into bed was a win of sorts. Rather than resenting the implication, she appreciated it. It made her feel like they were evenly matched.

Instead of a verbal reply, she put a hand on either side of Riley's face and pulled her into a kiss. Like the banter, it wasn't a matter of her taking charge or ceding control. Riley's lips covered hers, their tongues danced over each other, a sensuous back and forth that reminded her of the last few months.

Riley broke the kiss and brought her mouth to Brooke's neck, sucking and nipping and driving Brooke absolutely nuts. "Is there anything you love? Anything you absolutely hate?"

The questions murmured against her ear should have felt jarring, the awkward but obligatory negotiation of being with someone the first time. But rather than pulling her out of the mood, making her self-conscious, it turned her on. Maybe because Riley seemed genuinely interested in her answer, her pleasure. "I like hands," she said softly, barely pulling her mouth from Riley's neck. She hesitated for a moment, then added, "I like it a little rough."

Riley pulled away.

Her cheeks flushed, but she offered a playful shrug. "Don't tell me you're surprised."

The intensity of Riley's stare raised her temperature several degrees. "Not surprising. Just really fucking sexy."

If she'd been turned on before, Riley's comment kicked her arousal into overdrive. Before she could say as much, Riley nudged her onto the bed. Not a shove, exactly, but it was close. And it was sexy as hell.

The next thing she knew, Riley was on top of her, pressing into her. She ran her hands up Riley's arms, felt the muscles bunch under her hands. "You're pretty fucking sexy yourself."

Riley's answer was to take one of Brooke's nipples between her teeth. Assertive, confident, and just the right amount of pressure. She could have come from that alone, but where was the fun in that? She raked her fingernails down Riley's back, eliciting a hiss of pleasure that made her smile.

Riley moved from one breast to the other. Not rushed but not lazy either. Deliberate. Considering the last three months had, in fact, been like extended foreplay, she welcomed the pace. "You should fuck me now."

Without hesitation, Riley slid two fingers through her wetness and plunged into her. Brooke arched off the bed, pleasure laced with surprise. "Fuck."

Once again, Riley's mouth was at her neck. She held her hand still. "Is this not what you had in mind?"

A ragged chuckle escaped Brooke's lips. "Oh, no. It's perfect."

Riley pulled out, then filled her again. "Like this?"

"Yes." She swallowed. So damned perfect. "Just like that."

Riley placed a hand on her sternum, not technically holding her down but sort of. Just the right amount of constraint. Brooke raised her hips again, rising to meet each thrust of Riley's hand. Riley didn't hold back. She fucked Brooke with confidence and skill. Brooke closed her eyes and gave herself over to the sensations coursing through her body.

"Look at me." Riley's command caught her off guard. But much like the assertiveness, a total turn-on.

Brooke complied and looked right into her eyes. Riley's gaze was intense, possessive. It sent a shiver of ecstasy through her. She didn't blink, didn't look away. She continued to rise to meet Riley's hand, and Riley continued to fuck her like she'd not been fucked in a very long time.

She closed her eyes when the quiver started slow, deep in her belly. But like a fire engulfing a pile of dry kindling, the orgasm tore through her, leaving her singed and sweaty. "Oh my God."

"Yeah." Riley mumbled the word with something that felt like reverence.

Brooke opened one eye, then the other, almost afraid of what she might find. But instead of reverent or sentimental, Riley looked at her with a satisfied smile. The smugness should have irritated her, but it didn't. No, if anything, it turned her on even more. And it absolutely, one hundred percent, made her want to reciprocate.

She sat up and placed a hand on each of Riley's shoulders. They were even more muscular than she'd have expected, which made her smile. She nipped one of those shoulders, then used her position to nudge Riley onto her back. Again, not a shove, but something close.

She straddled Riley's thighs, enjoying the groan that escaped her lips, then leaned forward, bringing her own mouth close to Riley's ear. "And you? Is there anything you don't like, anything you absolutely love?"

Riley chuckled. "I'm pretty easy."

Brooke pulled just far enough away to look into her eyes. "Really? You're going to be coy with me now?"

Riley shook her head. "I'm not being coy."

Brooke squirmed a little on top of her, taking immense pleasure from the way her eyes rolled back in pleasure. When she stopped, Riley opened her eyes and looked into Brooke's. "I like it when a woman does what she likes. It really turns me on."

"A very diplomatic answer." Brooke leaned in again and kissed Riley's mouth. Then her jaw. Earlobe and neck were next. She worked her way down, tracing her tongue over the lines of Riley's body. She relished the way Riley's skin smelled like her soap but had a taste completely her own.

"See? I wouldn't have asked for that, but it feels amazing."

"Mmm-hmm." Brooke continued to work her way down Riley's torso. She wasn't about to protest being told to do whatever she wanted. She settled herself between Riley's thighs, pausing for just a moment to process just how perfectly she fit, just how right it felt. When she pressed her tongue into Riley, heard her sharp intake of breath, she couldn't help but smile.

She took her time, enjoying the way Riley tasted, the way she moved. Uninhibited, yes. But also letting Brooke set the pace and the intensity. After taking control a moment ago, it was a sexy shift.

Riley touched her hair, made these incredibly sexy sounds. When they pitched higher and her breathing became irregular, Brooke increased her pace. Riley kept up, moving with Brooke in a way that had her turned on again.

The muscles in Riley's legs started to tremble. And then she froze, her whole body taut. Brooke opened her eyes and watched her tumble over the edge. She was stunning.

"Holy crap."

Brooke chuckled at the declaration, delivered in a raspy voice. Riley accompanied it with a feeble pat on Brooke's head. Knowing she'd put Riley in that state made her smile. "You okay?"

"I am so fucking okay." Riley lifted her head, looked at her briefly, then let it fall back on the pillow. "That was amazing."

"Agreed." She crawled up the bed and draped herself over Riley. Riley ran fingers through her hair. "That's what you like, huh?"

Brooke lifted her head. "I really, really do."

"Then I feel really, really lucky."

Brooke rested her head on Riley's chest. Riley resumed playing with her hair. It was sort of hypnotic, something she loved more than she admitted. "I kind of can't believe we just did that."

Riley's hand stilled. "You're not regretting it, are you?"

"No regret, not even a little."

"But?"

"But I'm not sure what to make of it, I guess. I'm not sure where it leaves us."

The fingers stroked through her hair once again. "Do we need to figure that out now?"

She sighed. "No. And I'm sorry for overthinking. It's kind of my thing."

Riley's lips pressed to the top of her head. "Don't apologize. I sometimes don't think enough."

The confession made her smile as much as the sentiment did. "An unlikely pair we are."

"Or maybe perfectly complementary."

Huh. She'd not have thought of it that way. Not that they were a couple or contemplating the future, but the idea of being yin and yang proved reassuring. The idea this wasn't some problem she needed to solve.

"We'll figure it out, you know. It'll all be fine."

Rather than making a comment about famous last words, Brooke let herself believe it. Trouble would make itself known soon enough. She lifted her head again and pressed her lips to Riley's. "It will."

Riley's arms came around her and she rolled over, flipping their positions. "In the meantime, I think you should relax and let me do whatever I want to you."

She lifted her chin. "Oh, yeah? What did you have in mind?"

Riley kissed her. Just as Brooke had done, she kissed her way down Brooke's body. "Tell me, if I promise to use my hands, can I put my mouth on you?"

The request sent her arousal racing. "I think you should do whatever you want."

Riley raised her head and made eye contact. "I like the sound of that very much."

Chapter Twelve

B rooke half expected things to be awkward the next morning, but they weren't. They weren't awkward at the office, and they weren't awkward at practice. Riley made a quiet comment about hoping they could get together again, but otherwise she acted as if nothing between them had changed. It made it easy to make plans with her for dinner on a night they didn't have derby, to invite her home after. And to do it again a week later.

The derby season wound down, or in this case, wound up. Just like last year, the Big Easy Bruisers found themselves in contention for the state title. And just like last year, they were going up against the Cajun Queens.

The lead-up to the bout brought a fair amount of ribbing about Riley's defection and her loyalties. What would have made Brooke angry or anxious or otherwise stressed out a few months prior no longer bothered her. Not that she didn't want to win. But she'd settled into her team in a way she never had before, like she no longer had something to prove.

The night of the bout arrived. The team carpooled to Lafayette, prepared to take on the Queens on their home turf. Since Riley's sister and her kids were going, too, Riley rode with them, and Brooke drove herself, Meg, and Cassie.

During warm-ups, Riley skated over to chat with her former teammates. Brooke's first reaction was a flash of panic, fueled by a flashback to the year before. What if Riley's loyalties remained with the Queens all along? What if she was plotting with them right this second to throw the bout and give the Queens back-to-back titles?

"Why do you look so nervous?" Hits came to a T-stop in front of where Brooke was stretching.

"I'm not nervous." She wasn't sure why she lied. She never managed to be convincing.

Hits gave the incredulous look that said just what she'd been thinking.

"It's a big bout even without the promise of vindication. I'd be worried if I wasn't nervous." While not the cause of the churning in her stomach, at least it was true.

Hits laughed. "Always the serious one. Just relax and enjoy it."

Brooke frowned. She always had been serious. Most of the time, it served her well. Yes, making friends took longer than she wished. Yes, it had made things infinitely harder with Riley. She looked over at Riley, who had her arm draped over one of their opponents' shoulders. She laughed as if there wasn't a thing in the world at stake. And instead of bristling, of feeling insecure and impatient, she smiled. "You're right."

In that moment, everything clicked into place. Things didn't feel hard or messy. They just felt good.

Riley returned to the Bruisers bench, and they finished warming up. Tracy gave her pep talk, and they were off.

The first half passed in a blur. The Queens were as fierce as she remembered, perhaps even more so. But the Bruisers were on fire. When they skated into the locker room for halftime, they were up by close to forty points.

"You, my dear, are on fire." Riley pressed a kiss to her temple.

"Same to you." She gave Riley a friendly hip bump.

"Okay, okay." Cali made a show of coming between them. "Let's save the kissy kissy for after the bout."

Just a few months ago, that kind of comment would have mortified her. Now, she gave Cali an elbow to the ribs. "You're just jealous."

"You bet your ass I am."

At the start of the second half, Brooke couldn't remember a time she felt happier or more alive. And not that she didn't always love being in the rink, but something about really letting loose made it even better.

She might not need to win, but it didn't make the victory any less sweet.

❖

By the time Riley pulled into Brooke's driveway, it was after midnight. At this point, they'd spent over a dozen nights like this, although rarely did they start so late. Gone was the initial apprehension, the wondering if Brooke actually liked her. The anticipation, however, remained. The thrill of seeing Brooke, of kissing her and touching her and falling asleep with her, was just as powerful as that first night. But with it came a comfort, and the hope that there might be a lifetime of such nights. They hadn't had that conversation, but Brooke had commented about being together at New Year's, of starting the next season as those other kind of derby wives.

Brooke opened the door before she had the chance to knock. "I waited for you to shower."

Riley smiled. It had become a bit of a thing, showering together, especially after practice or a bout. There was something appealing about getting clean before getting an entirely different kind of dirty. "I'm glad."

They undressed each other, the process sensual but not frantic. Riley, having learned her lesson, turned on the water and adjusted the temperature. In truth, they'd come to a very friendly compromise on the matter. Like so many others.

It was still hard to believe they'd come so far.

"I love you, you know."

Brooke, who'd been rinsing shampoo from her hair, wiped her eyes and blinked them open. "What?"

She'd not meant to say it, at least not like this. But she couldn't bring herself to take it back. "I said I love you. But I get that the timing is weird. I'm sorry about that."

Brooke searched her face but didn't answer right away. Riley did her best not to panic. It didn't help when Brooke started to shake her head. But eventually—eventually—she said, "Don't apologize."

Riley nodded. Not exactly the response she wanted, but not terrible.

"I love you, too, for the record."

It was Riley's turn to shake her head. "Don't feel like you have to say it back."

"I don't. I was just waiting for the right time." She offered a playful shrug.

Riley threaded her arms around Brooke and pulled their bodies close. She kissed Brooke long and slow, letting the water stream over them. When she finally pulled back, she tipped her head ever so slightly. "Let's just remember who said it first."

CLOSED DOOR POLICY

Erin Zak

CHAPTER ONE

"So, an emergency room nurse from Chicago…"

Caroline Stevens looked up from the vodka and cranberry juice she was pouring. Bartending was definitely a departure from the insane intensity of the busy emergency room at Christ Hospital, but she was enjoying it. A newbie to Sedona, Arizona, she knew she needed to get a job and get one quick, one to help pay her bills, pay her daughter some rent money, and hopefully not cause her to go crazy in the meantime. When she had found the bartending position, she didn't think the owner would hire her. But he had called her back, and she started training a day later. She was thankful now to have something to focus her energy on. And oddly enough, she was picking it up a lot quicker than she imagined. She placed the drink in front of one of the bar's regular customers, a young woman named Kelli. "For my whole career," she added with a smile and a shrug. "Until now, of course."

"Tell us why you're tending bar then? In Sedona, of all places. Like, what'd you do, throw a dart at a map?"

"I think, as the bartender, I'm the one who's supposed to listen to you, not the other way around."

Kelli laughed while her other friends, Kate and Michael rolled their eyes. From what Caroline gathered from their drunken conversations over the past couple of weeks, they were all home for the summer from Arizona State University. She hated to admit it, but at first she hated the company. They were so much younger, and it was sad how much it reminded her how old she'd gotten in the last ten years. Wrinkles, extra weight, creaky bones…not to mention the extra baggage she seemed to be carrying around these days.

Caroline leaned forward, hands on the bar top, and lowered her voice. "Oh, is that not how it works in college when you have a fake ID? Don't want to get too close to the bartender?"

Kate let out a nervous laugh as she fumbled putting her black hair into a ponytail. "How would you know if we have fake IDs? These are our real IDs."

"Do you think I'm stupid?" Caroline placed the drink on a coaster in front of Kelli.

"Hey," Kate said while holding her hand in the air. She had a birthmark above her lip, and it really suited her. "I am legit twenty-one." She paused and waited a beat, then two, before she added, "Now."

Caroline couldn't hold back her laughter. "Exactly what I thought."

"This is my ID," Kelli said as she shoved it across the bar top. "I promise it's not a fake."

"I know, I know." Caroline pushed the ID back toward Kelli. "I know how to spot a fake."

"Is it because you have a fake ID?" Michael asked with an adorable smile. He had a Chicago Cubs hat on backward as well the start of a dark beard. He rubbed his hand over his cheek, chin, then other cheek before he finished with, "I mean, you can't be more than twenty."

Caroline let out a laugh. "Are you flirting with me?"

He waggled his dark eyebrows and flashed another grin.

"I am old enough to be your mother."

"Totally fine. I like 'em older." He took a drink of Guinness while he kept constant eye contact with her.

The head on top of the dark beer left a foam mustache on his upper lip, and Caroline raised her eyebrows. "I like your 'stache." She couldn't hold back the laughter.

"She's flirting back, guys." Michael laughed after he hurried to wipe the foam away. "Watch out."

Kate laughed, and Kelli joined in. "You wish." Kelli shook her head.

"Seriously, Caroline, are you gonna tell us why you're here? I am literally going to school for nursing. If you tell me it's not all it's cracked up to be, I'll be so depressed." Kelli heaved a giant sigh.

"You'd better tell her," Kate said with a laugh. "She's gonna need CPR if you don't."

"Listen, kids, I needed a change."

"Was it because of the dead bodies?" Kate seemed close to having a breakdown.

"Yeah, like, how many dead bodies have you seen?" Kelli shrugged. "Like, ten? A hundred? I mean, it has to be a lot."

"You get used to the dead bodies."

"Are you sure?" Kelli asked. "I'm so scared of the dead bodies."

"As long as you're okay with blood."

"Oh God." Kate laughed. "She gets woozy when she sees blood."

"Only my own." Kelli waved her hands around. "I swear."

Caroline laughed as she did a quick once-over around the Mission Pub. The normally busy bar was far too empty for a Friday afternoon, especially at the end of May. She needed more customers so she could escape these questions. "Okay, fine." She leaned closer. They huddled as if she was going to tell them the secrets to the world. She pushed the strands of hair from her ponytail behind her ears. She sighed. "I killed a man."

Kelli gasped, and her mouth fell open.

Kate's eyes were so wide, they looked as if they might pop out of her head.

Michael smiled, cocked an eyebrow, and pointed at Caroline. "You're lying."

She laughed. "Yes, I'm lying."

Kate and Kelli both let out a breath and clutched at their hearts. "You are horrible. We thought you were serious."

She laughed at how gullible they were. "Seriously? There was an incident with a gun. And after it happened…" She took a deep breath and let it out as she started to wipe down the area behind the bar top. "I needed a change."

"An incident with a gun?" Michael laughed. "That's all you're gonna say?"

"Come on, Michael, don't push it."

"What? Were you shot or something?"

Caroline watched in the mirror behind the bar as Kelli smacked Michael across the arm. "Stop," Kelli whispered.

"Okay, here's the story." She shook her head and turned. Her therapist had told her a hundred times, talking about it might help her heal. Maybe her therapist was right? Didn't hurt to try. "I was the charge nurse one night in the middle of January. We had multiple GSW's roll in and—"

"GSW?" Kate scrunched her face.

"Gunshot wound," Kelli whispered.

She chuckled. "Yes, gunshot wound. So, beginning of January, cold as hell, multiple shots fired on Cicero Avenue, super close to Christ Hospital where I worked. The patients rolled in, and we worked our asses off to get them stabilized."

"See? This is the shit I love," Kelli whispered as she leaned even closer over the bar. "Sorry. Keep going."

"The night stretched on for what felt like days. Every time we turned around, another trauma rolled in. The very definition of a 'rough night.'" Caroline licked her lips. Her heart was starting to beat faster and faster. "So, we're wheeling patient number one to the elevator to head to surgery when a man comes flying in through the doors. He's waving a gun." Typically, the story wouldn't let itself be told after she said those words. Now, for some reason, she didn't want to stop. She bit down on the inside of her cheek. *You can do this.* "He was high on something. Meth or crack or something awful." Caroline took a deep breath. Kate and Kelli both had their hands over their mouths. Michael looked as if he'd seen a ghost. "I tried to calm him down, and the police officers all had their weapons pulled, ready to shoot him if he didn't drop his gun, but…" Her mind was rolling the footage of the night, complete with the frigid temperatures, the wind whipping in the ER doors, and the police officers yelling. "He didn't listen, and when he spun around, gun aimed, the officers shot him, but he still pulled the trigger on his gun and—" Caroline took a step back from the bar and lifted the edge of her shirt to reveal a scar on her stomach. "Now I live with this extra-special scar."

"Holy shit." Kelli leaned back in her chair. "Spleen?"

"Nicked it. Yes." She adjusted her shirt and shrugged. "So, there's the story. Okay? No more questions."

"One more question," Kelli said with her hand held out. "Just one."

"Fine."

"Was it worth it?"

Caroline forced herself to smile because it wasn't worth it. She lost everything. Her husband. Her mind. Her career. "Ask me in a couple months," she finally said and watched the look of compromise pass over Kelli's face, who seemed okay with her answer. Thank God, because complete honesty might have ended poorly.

"So, now what?" Kate's voice was hopeful and it suited her with her bright eyes and clear complexion. She adjusted her glasses. "I mean, not that you're not an awesome bartender."

"I'm enrolled to take some classes at the extension campus this summer." Caroline shrugged. "I was thinking maybe I could teach? I used to love teaching the Advanced Cardiac Life Support class at the hospital."

"Hold up." Kate picked her phone up and quickly pulled up a website. "Yep, I was right." She held her phone out to Caroline. "They're hiring a nursing instructor for the career center at the high school. You could apply and get it."

Caroline read through the ad on the career center website. *Must have nursing experience. Must have a teaching certificate or be taking classes toward the completion of one. Must be available to start at the start of September.* "This sounds awesome."

"And Kate's dad is the career center director." Michael raised his beer in a mock cheers. "I'm sure she'd put in a good word for you... especially if you don't tell him about the fake IDs."

Kelli leaned her head down and placed her forehead on the bar. She let out a groan that could have woken the dead. "Please don't tell our parents."

Thank God it wasn't busy, or Caroline's laughter would have been inappropriate.

CHAPTER TWO

"The semester starts in one week." Dr. Thomas Brady leaned back in his chair and looked around the conference room table. "I need to know who wants to be a part of the faculty-student mentor program, and who wants to be coerced into being a part of the program."

The faculty members around the table all started to murmur to those sitting near them. Dr. Atlanta Morris kept her arms folded tightly across her chest. There was no way she was going to volunteer, and hopefully, she wouldn't be approached at all. The last thing she needed was to be strapped down to mentoring a student, especially with a loaded schedule and helping to oversee the new program for a quick teaching certificate. She wasn't super happy about giving up her entire summer, but it would look really good for her if the program went well.

Dr. Brady continued to scan the room after hearing a couple professors volunteer their help.

"Atlanta?"

Fuck. "Yes, Dr. Brady?"

"You're spearheading the programs at the new Sedona extension campus?"

She suppressed an eye roll. "Yes, sir."

"Are you already settled in Sedona, then?"

And another thing she wasn't thrilled about was having to move. To Sedona, of all places. Thank fucking Christ they compensated her well and also paid for her rental. "I am. I am headed back up there after this. I think I have a full roster for the four classes we will be running up there. Twenty-two students."

"I think it's going to be a great extension," Sheri Higgins said with a smile as she nudged Atlanta with her elbow. Sheri's shoulder-length blond hair was pulled back into a ponytail at the base of her neck. She was working to grow it out, and Atlanta knew she would get sick of it in about a month and cut it off. Sheri was quite a bit older than Atlanta, and while she was only a continuing lecturer, she was a hell of a professor who inspired her students. Atlanta admired her dedication to the students. They had an amazing friendship, so it didn't take much for Atlanta to ask Sheri to help launch the extension. They worked so well together, and Sheri was the only person Atlanta ever listened to, especially about how to navigate the faculty and campus politics. "I'm teaching the communications course."

"Interpersonal Communications?" Dr. Brady asked, and when Sheri nodded, he said, "Atlanta, you realize if this extension expansion goes well, it'll be a major win for us with the state for funding?"

Atlanta smiled. Yes, she fucking knew it, and she also knew most of the other professors were rooting for her to screw up. As the newest tenured professor, as well as the youngest the university ever had, she was constantly under scrutiny. Her teaching tactics were often questioned, and every now and then, some asshole would bring up her indiscretion from grad school. Almost fucking around with a student was going to haunt her for the rest of her career. Sweeping it under the rug only worked for so long before someone brought it up, and the ridicule would start all over again. She'd worked her ass off to get to where she was. Even though she was one of the most difficult professors, she was always voted the favorite by the students. So, she had to make sure the program went well, or the older male professors would start the proceedings to get her tenure removed. She'd already heard the rumblings. News traveled fast around a college campus. "I heard the news, yes. Thank goodness I have the help of Sheri and Molly Wright."

"And Jorge Mendez," Sheri added. "He's teaching the foreign language class."

"Sounds like you have a great group up there." Dr. Brady paused and rubbed his hands over his large belly. "I'll let you all decide who is mentoring which students up there. I don't want those students to miss out on your years and years of experience."

Atlanta heard a snicker from one of the male professors at the end of the table. She leaned forward and turned her head to glare, but Sheri nudged her again. "You're right. My group has a lot to offer. Too bad not everyone does."

Sheri groaned softly. "We're all excited to get started," she quickly said, probably to divert the attention away from Atlanta's snide remark.

"That concludes our meeting. Please be back for the summer wrap-up meeting at the beginning of August." Dr. Brady held his hand up as everyone around the table started to push their chairs out. "I'll be visiting classrooms and speaking with your students, as well. We want to make sure we are staying on top of this mentor program."

Atlanta quickly stood and rushed out of the room, Sheri speed walking behind her to catch up. "Jesus Christ, I hate that giant asshole of a man so much," Atlanta said under her breath as she waited to board the elevator to the second floor.

"Oh, I couldn't tell." Sheri rolled her eyes. "You know you're going to get canned if you keep it up."

"No, I won't. I'm the professor of the year for the past five years. There's no way the chancellor would allow it."

"Don't be so sure. They fired Beth Rudnick for less than what you're doing." The elevator doors slid closed, and Sheri turned her entire body so she was facing Atlanta. "You are too important to me to let you get fired. You hear me?"

"Gee, thanks, *Mom*."

"Someone needs to be your mom, Atlanta. You act like an asshole sometimes. Keep your mouth shut and your head down. Teach. You're good at it." Sheri sighed. "I'm not moving my husband to Sedona for two months for shits and giggles. We are going to knock the socks off this extension implementation, you hear me?"

Atlanta raised her eyebrows and tilted her head. "Loud and clear."

"Thank you." Sheri turned and waited for the elevator to open after the ding sounded. "Besides, I'd really love to be able to punch the fucking smirk off Brady's face when our program goes state-wide."

Atlanta laughed as they exited the elevator together and turned down the hallway toward Sheri's office. When they were safely behind a closed door, Sheri handed a folder across her desk. "What's this?"

"The calendar for the semester. Also, I made sure we all had a paper copy of the syllabi for the four classes. Oh, and I worked with Jorge and Molly to make sure the schedule for classrooms made sense."

"Oh, yes. Apparently, we have to share the community center with a couple other groups during Thursdays and Fridays. You made sure the class schedule leaves those days open?"

"Yes, ma'am," Sheri said.

Atlanta looked up from the schedule and glared at Sheri across the desk. "You're the ma'am. Not me."

Sheri chuckled. "You always point out I'm older and wiser. Thank you."

"Wiser? Hardly." Atlanta continued to skim through the folder.

"I want you to read over everything, and if you need to, make changes on the Dropbox. I know how you love paper copies, though. You shouldn't have to change a thing. I've been over the entire packet backward and forward. Three times." Sheri smiled. "Actually, more like six times."

"You're so thorough for a senior citizen."

"You're going to get my foot up your ass."

Atlanta laughed. "Thank you for doing all of this. Seriously."

"You're welcome," Sheri said with a smile. "Oh, one other thing. Your syllabus doesn't have office hours on it."

"I don't do office hours." Atlanta shrugged. "So, that'll be easy."

"What? Since when? You have to have office hours. They're part of our contracts."

"Not mine. I had the office hours part taken out. If a student needs me, they have to make an appointment. Period. I hate office hours. I don't work well with those demands."

"Explain to me how no office hours will go over with the students you need to mentor."

"Um, no." Atlanta shook her head as she flipped through the rest of the papers in the folder. "I am not mentoring students. No way. You three can handle the twenty-two students. I don't mentor."

"You are out of your goddamn mind. You are helping us."

Atlanta looked up at Sheri. If it wasn't for the life-threatening death stare Sheri had plastered across her face, she would have argued. She swallowed once, then twice because if there was one thing she knew she should never do, it was piss off Sheri Higgins. "We'll see," she said softly and looked back down at the folder.

Sheri laughed. "You're such a pain in my ass."

"Yeah, well, I do what I can." Atlanta closed the folder and leaned back. "I was thinking about calling my no office hours thing the 'Closed Door Policy.' Has a nice ring to it, doesn't it?"

"Oh my God. Are you really going to say 'Closed Door Policy' to your class? You sound like a bitch."

"You seem to forget. I *am* a bitch."

Sheri rolled her eyes. "No, you aren't. You need to stop trying to keep that mean front up because it doesn't really work. Look at how many teaching awards you have."

"I get them to respect me. Exactly how you taught me."

"Oh, I know. I also taught you about how geese communicate, and why they fly in a V formation, but you didn't care about the lesson. In fact, you made fun of me."

Atlanta laughed as her mind flashed back to the first time she had class with Sheri Higgins. Now, she was a professor with her, and they were starting a new program together. Even though Atlanta wasn't exactly happy about the reason behind organizing the program, she had to admit, it felt kind of good. She was sort of looking forward to getting out of Phoenix and heading to Sedona later in the afternoon. She needed a change of pace, and she needed to stop fearing her fellow faculty members so much. Maybe being away from the worst of them would be freeing. She could hope.

CHAPTER THREE

"Mom, do you want breakfast?"

"I'm fifty-five years old, Samantha. Do you really think you need to make me breakfast?" Caroline shouted the words up the stairs at Samantha, who was holding her nine-month-old on her hip. Little Oden was awake, giggling and pulling on Samantha's long blond hair, which she refused to cut. Caroline couldn't blame her, though. One of her biggest regrets was chopping her hair off when she had Samantha. And it had taken years and years for it to grow back to the length she loved.

"You're hilarious." Samantha tilted her head while smiling. "You know I didn't make it; Andrew did."

"Honey." Caroline paused and leaned against the wall, still at the bottom of the stairs leading to her basement apartment. "Living with you doesn't mean you and Andrew have to take care of me."

Samantha sighed, and Oden giggled as he reached both hands for Caroline. "Just get up here and eat the damn eggs." She turned on her heel and marched up the other set of stairs.

Caroline laughed because, of course, her daughter inherited her temper. And her use of swear words. She tied the sash on her robe and climbed the stairs to the main living area. When Samantha sprang the news that she was moving to Sedona with her new husband, Caroline had a difficult time. Then Samantha got pregnant, which was even harder for Caroline to deal with. She wanted to be a grandma and love on her new grandchild, but her ex-husband was not a fan of traveling. He wasn't a fan of anything really, including Caroline, it seemed.

"Ooh, what do we have here?" Caroline pulled out a chair next to where Oden was strapped in his highchair. He was so excited when she leaned down, captured his sweet cheeks in both hands, and squeezed gently. "Hello there, little Oden. How is Grammy's boy this morning?" He giggled and yammered away, enjoying his scrambled eggs and bananas. After she sat, she sipped her coffee and sighed deeply because it was delicious. Samantha had learned how to make a great cup of coffee. Thank goodness because she wasn't much of a cook otherwise. Probably best Andrew was the stay-at-home dad and Samantha was the breadwinner.

"Since it's your first day of school, we figured we needed to get your brain fueled to learn." Samantha's grin was mostly proud, but there was also something else there. Was it sarcasm? "And I can take you to school on my way to work." Samantha winked before she took a drink of coffee.

Sarcasm indeed. "Ha ha." Caroline rolled her eyes. "I'll try to not be a holy terror like you were in college. Sound good?"

"She was a holy terror in college?" Andrew came rushing into the kitchen wearing an apron with a towel thrown over his shoulder. "I'm shocked."

"Literally, the worst."

"I was not."

"You flunked out your first year." Caroline cocked an eyebrow. "Don't even make me recount the tales of your horrendous partying."

"Mom, you know we let you live here for free?"

Caroline laughed. "Oh, how the tables have turned. You lived with me for free your entire life."

"So," Andrew started, sliding over a plate with eggs over medium, hash browns, and two sausage links on it. "How many classes do you have today?"

"Two, a communication class and an English class. I heard the English professor is very difficult."

"Is it all day?" Samantha sat on the other side of Oden's highchair and helped him with his food.

"Yes, ten to noon for the first class, one to four for the second one. This will be my long day. Tuesdays and Wednesdays I have one class apiece. I'm only taking three total." Caroline smiled when Samantha opened her mouth to say something. She raised her hand. "Don't worry. I'll write it on the calendar."

"Oh, whew. Thank you."

"Are you nervous?" Andrew was standing at the massive island in their beautiful French country kitchen. He was such a nice-looking man. He had sandy-colored hair with incredibly green eyes he'd passed on to Oden. He was attempting to grow a beard, but it was coming in very patchy, and it made him look about ten years younger than he really was. She wasn't allowed to comment on the beard, per Samantha, who said he was self-conscious about it. Samantha joked about it, though, especially when she got a glass or two of wine in her. She was helplessly in love with him. Caroline was so thrilled Samantha had found someone to spend the rest of her life with, especially someone who understood how stressful her position as a chief financial officer was.

"I am insanely nervous." Caroline took a deep breath. "I don't think I've ever been this nervous in my entire life."

"Well, don't worry." Samantha placed her hand on her mother's and smiled. "You're going to be so awesome. And when you get the job, those high school kids are going to love learning from you. You're an amazing teacher."

"Oh, please. How would you know?"

"Um, because you taught me everything I know." Samantha grinned. "Duh."

"Oh, Sammie, you're gonna make me cry."

"Well played, babe," Andrew said with a laugh from across the kitchen.

Samantha squeezed Caroline's hand. "Don't worry about anything, okay? Especially about Dad. You're going to come out of this much happier."

"I know, I know." Caroline took another drink of coffee and set it on the table. "Have you heard from him?" She rarely asked, but every now and then, her curiosity got the best of her.

"Once."

"In three months, you've only heard from him once?" Caroline shook her head. "He's ridiculous."

Samantha shrugged. "Nicole is his new priority."

"Yeah, yeah. Must be hard caring for a twelve-year-old."

Andrew let out a laugh. "She really is awful, isn't she?"

Caroline nodded. Jason leaving her after the whole hospital

incident was bad enough, but finding out he was seeing a woman half his age before the divorce was final was worse. Every day it got a little easier, but in the end, she still wondered if she would ever truly be happy again.

She was hoping this college program would help. Even though a part of her was dreading it, she was still trying to remain positive. She needed to move on from the gunshot wound, she needed to find peace, and she needed to find happiness again before it was too late.

❖

First day of the program and Atlanta was pumped. Well, as pumped as she could be given how incredibly nervous she felt. After checking in with Sheri, Molly, and Jorge, she found the roster had shrunk by three students. They were facing criticism already. Dr. Brady and the rest of his followers were never going to let them live it down if admission and enrollment rates weren't stellar.

Sheri tried to calm Atlanta down by reminding her that, at the end of the day, the only thing of importance was making sure the students learned. "*Inspire Them to Fly*. Remember?" Sheri always referenced the damn sign she kept hanging in her office. Atlanta knew she was right, but it still worried her.

As she stood behind the podium in her classroom watching the students coming back from lunch, she tried to calm herself. She was never nervous to teach. She was a great teacher, and creative writing was her forte as well as her favorite class to teach. Even though most students hated her at first, they ended up liking what they learned in the class. She wasn't there to be liked. She was there to get passion out of the students' heads and onto the paper, and she succeeded. Always. She rarely gave As, but the five or six students who received them also went on to be published authors. She pushed her students, and in the end, they respected her.

She didn't start off thinking she'd be one of those professors who kept things hard all the time. She figured she'd be likable and personable, someone the students wanted to get to know. Having a laid-back persona only got her into trouble, though. Atlanta learned right away that beautiful girls with broken hearts were all too eager to bleed all over the page, and she was all too eager to fix those beautiful girls. Especially one in particular, and the girl almost ended Atlanta's career before it started.

Thankfully, it was during a time when a slap on the wrist was all the college was handing out for indiscretions such as hers. Unfortunately, Dr. Brady didn't feel the same way as the former dean of students. And Atlanta spent most of her time as a professor at Arizona State being the evil stepchild no one liked. Being tenured didn't help, either. All it did was make the target on her back even bigger.

She knew she needed to do what Sheri always told her to do: Keep her mouth shut and her head down. Teach. Do what she was good at.

"Okay, class, I'm Dr. Morris. I'll be your creative writing professor." Atlanta scribbled her name across the whiteboard and put a lid on the nerves bubbling in her chest. She turned and looked around the room. The stadium seating did nothing for her teaching style. She wanted the students close so she could see their expressions. Not squint at them in the back of the room. "First things first. Everyone move closer. Especially in the back row." Atlanta watched as the students started to move, slowly, and she shook her head when she heard them moaning and groaning. "Seriously? This should not be a big deal. I don't want to shout when there are so few of us. Let's do the first three rows, then get out paper and a writing implement." The students started to find seats in the first three rows as instructed. Atlanta made sure to study the students as they pulled out writing supplies. "Okay, ready?" They all nodded. "I want everyone to write their name, one interesting thing about themselves, and one paragraph about why you're here. You have ten minutes. Go."

Atlanta moved from behind the podium to a wooden table standing in front of where the students were seated. She sat on the table and watched as they wrote, taking mental notes about how they held their pens and pencils, how their paper was positioned, their expressions, and even the way they sat. The class consisted of almost equal numbers men and women. The bulk of them were traditional-aged. Most were probably there to get extra credit to get ahead in their programs at the main campus or make up credits from a semester's worth of partying.

Atlanta scanned the room again, and this time her eyes landed on an older woman in the third row on the right. She was writing a lot; her entire page was covered with scribbles. Atlanta's stomach filled with butterflies. She felt the familiar tug of her heart as her eyes roamed over the woman's features. Her blond hair was pulled halfway up with a barrette, and she was bobbing her foot up and down as she wrote. As she sat there in her black, V-neck T-shirt and light blue jeans, Atlanta wondered what her story was.

The woman stopped writing and looked at the ceiling as if to gather her thoughts. Atlanta tried to be nonchalant as she intently watched the woman move her side-swept bangs from her forehead with the hand holding the pen. She adjusted her dark-framed glasses, thankfully never noticing Atlanta staring. When she nibbled on the end of her pen, it finally hit Atlanta why this woman made her feel so strange.

Aside from being gorgeous, she was absolutely not at all what Atlanta expected from this group of students. She was older, and it was definitely not a bad thing. In fact, from the couple of times Atlanta had nontraditional students in class, she made the assumption that the woman was going to take the classes seriously. And from the way she was writing, with the pensive look and intense concentration, she was taking this ten-minute icebreaker far more seriously than any of the other students, who were all finished and pretending not to be on their cell phones.

She finally pulled her gaze from the woman when the realization slammed into her; those butterflies in her stomach and the tug in her heart meant one thing and one thing only: she was going to have to be the bitch everyone knew her for.

Because if she was nice to this woman…

If she started liking what this woman had to say or write…

God.

She could taste the bile in the back of her throat. She was going to vomit if she kept analyzing the situation.

"Okay, everyone. Writing implements down. I know you're going to be thrilled about this. I want you all to read them out loud to the rest of the class." A collective groan echoed throughout the class and she smiled. "Perfect. If it makes you squirm, it makes me happy, so get to it. We'll start with you in the front."

❖

Caroline waited patiently for the students to read their paragraphs of why they were here. She wasn't as nervous as she thought she was going to be. She wasn't sure why, either. Maybe it was because the professor looked young enough to be her daughter. Except her daughter would have never come home with a nose ring like Dr. Morris's. She was wearing light blue skinny jeans with a white button-down. Her sleeves were rolled to her elbows, and she had a few bangle bracelets on one wrist and a bunch of braided bracelets on the other. She had a silver watch that was far too big, and when she spoke, she'd push it up her forearm until it was snug against her skin. She also had tattoos on her arms; three Caroline could count. A colorful hummingbird and a bunch of indecipherable writing on one forearm and a single word on the other. Caroline couldn't read what it said, which was sort of driving her nuts.

The good thing about Dr. Morris was she was very into what the other students wrote. She'd ask a question after each student read, and she took notes the entire time. She was sitting on top of the wooden table with her legs crossed, barefoot, her Birkenstocks on the floor in front of the table. Caroline was completely bowled over by how laid-back she seemed, especially because her regulars at the bar said they'd heard Dr. Morris was a raging bitch.

"Don't piss her off," Michael had said as she poured drinks at the bar the night before. "She once kicked a student out of class because the girl didn't turn off her cell phone."

"Well, yeah, being on your cell phone during class is rude. I don't blame her," Caroline commented.

"Um, her dad was sick and in the hospital. They called her to tell her he had passed away." Kelli was shaking her head. "She's horrible. At least she was to my class."

Caroline swallowed. "Wow. Okay, then."

"So, what's the moral of the story?" Kate laughed, looking from Michael, Kelli, then at Caroline. "Jesus. You guys are slow learners. Turn your fucking cell phones off. Or better yet, leave it in your car. Thank God I'm in the class with you, Caroline."

Caroline shifted in her seat as she pulled her attention back to the class. She glanced at Kate, who was sitting next to her, bolt upright. Kate was up next, and unfortunately, the nerves were starting to creep up. She took a couple deep breaths and tried to not focus on the facts:

this professor was so intriguing, and as good as she was in class, the professor wasn't going to be easy. She had suffered through her fair share of mean profs when she went through nursing school. Hell, most of the doctors she encountered were total assholes, too. She could totally handle when people were mean to her. So, if this professor wanted to be mean, bring it on. She would stand her ground. She was smart and strong. And if she had to, she'd be mean right back.

But something about this professor was already causing her to question her abilities. Everything about Dr. Morris was captivating, even her hair, which was lovely and long, a beautiful auburn color, and fell in large natural curls over her shoulders as she sat there scribbling notes, left-handed, in a notebook.

Caroline felt her mouth go dry when Kate finished and sat. Dr. Morris's eyes landed on her, eyebrows raised and a pissed-off expression plastered on her face. There went her capacity to be strong, right out the door. Her palms started to sweat, and her knees began to shake. When she stood, everyone turned in their seats and stared as if she were on trial for some heinous crime. "My name is Caroline Stevens." Her voice was shaking. *Great.* She took a deep breath and licked her lips. "I'm obviously older than most of the people in this room. Our professor included." The students all laughed. Dr. Morris, on the other hand, did not even crack a smile. *Shit.* "I was an emergency room nurse on the south side of Chicago for more than half my life, and after…" Caroline paused. She didn't know if she should read what she really wrote about her trauma from the gunshot wound from a gangster, then being left by her husband because she couldn't deal with said trauma and he couldn't deal with the PTSD. She didn't think she'd be reading this out loud. She thought she'd hand it in and never see it again. She took a deep breath and decided to take the easy route. "After a lot of soul searching, I decided to make a career change." She looked up at Dr. Morris before she sat and waited for a question or a comment, but Dr. Morris said nothing. She sat there with no expression on her face at all until she finally broke eye contact with Caroline and looked at the rest of the class.

"Thank you, everyone. Class is finished for today. Don't get your hopes up, though. This will be the only time we let out early. Please leave your papers on the table before you leave, and I'll see you all next Monday."

What the hell? Caroline was instantly upset.

"Did you not write about why you really left your job?" Kate whispered while she shoved her notebook into her backpack.

Caroline shook her head as she felt tears welling. How had she let this stupid professor get under her skin? She wanted to know what she did to get treated differently, but she also didn't want to stick around long enough to find out. Her first day of class had gone so well until then. She quickly stood when Kate grabbed her arm. They rushed down the steps of the classroom and placed their papers, facedown, on the table. She flew out of the classroom as fast as she could leaving Kate in her dust.

Chapter Four

I can handle this. I can totally handle this.

Atlanta rolled a chair across the linoleum in the classroom until it was next to the podium. She gathered her papers, sat on the chair, took a deep breath, and glanced at the clock. Four minutes before class started.

Four.

Minutes.

Until Caroline Stevens.

And her blond hair.

And really smooth voice.

Stop. Stop. Stop.

Atlanta wasn't stupid. She knew she needed to keep a handle on her emotions. She didn't leave Phoenix for Sedona to clutter up her heart with yet another mistake. She didn't need the drama. Truthfully, it was easier to not deal with matters of the heart during the semester. Nine times out of ten, she was way too tired to do anything after teaching all day. Especially entertaining a significant other. She couldn't find the emotions she needed to be able to want to spend the rest of her life with another person. She liked to keep to herself, and occasionally obsess a little about unattainable women *who weren't students*. Life was easier then. She'd never get hurt. So, letting her feelings get out of control for Caroline couldn't happen. Not now. Not ever.

After reading Caroline's paper from the last class, Atlanta felt even worse about being mean. Caroline had skipped over most of what she wrote. She understood Caroline's decision to make a career change. Stress that stemmed from post-traumatic stress and divorce couldn't be easy to deal with. She was not equipped to handle a student who was attractive *and* broken. She wasn't sure why, but learning so much about Caroline in such a short amount of time made the need for her self-imposed cold front even stronger.

And being mean would surely wreak more havoc on Caroline's soul and spirit.

Her soul and spirit? Jesus. Come on, Atlanta. Get your shit together.

Having a soft spot for Caroline would do neither of them any good. She needed to remember that, to focus on the bad parts of her. Caroline's issues would be no match for Atlanta's inability to connect emotionally. Even if Caroline was gorgeous with a breathtaking smile, luxurious hair, and a curvaceous body Atlanta had spent entirely too much time thinking about. Caroline was, quite literally, haunting her every thought. Her imagination was running wild, and she was fantasizing about Caroline in all sorts of ways, in all sorts of positions.

In one scenario, across a table, drinking coffee, and then in the next bent over the same table, naked, begging for release...

Atlanta shook her head, snapping her attention back on the clock. Two more minutes trapped with her thoughts of Caroline...of her hands and her neck and her jawline...

Jesus, I need to get laid...

Finally, students started to enter and find their seats, softly talking to each other.

One by one, the first three rows started to fill. Atlanta glanced at the door, hating herself a tiny bit because she was actually eager to see Caroline. She was getting more and more antsy, assuming Caroline wasn't going to show up. Maybe she dropped the class. Atlanta wouldn't see her anymore, possibly ever again. The thought made her stomach twist.

How had this gotten so out of control in such a short amount of time? Especially when she was trying, albeit not her hardest, to not let herself go there. As her brain started to construct a plan to beat herself up for letting her emotions get the best of her, Caroline walked through the door with Kate.

Atlanta's pulse quickened, her stomach tied into a knot, and her palms began to sweat. She had it bad, and absolutely not in a good way.

The pair was laughing about something, and the way Caroline's face lit up when she smiled made it so very difficult to look away. Caroline was wearing a jean jacket over the top of a black dress that fell right above her knees. She had on black, strappy sandals, and Atlanta made herself pull her gaze away from Caroline's bare calves. She rolled her eyes as she focused on the graded papers on her lap. She needed to get her shit together and fast.

❖

Caroline stood and cleared her throat. Her entire notebook was shaking as she held it in front of her. She steadied herself with a deep breath in through her nose.

"I was seventeen the first time I saw a dead body." She took another deep breath. "I remember every detail as if it was yesterday. The color of the sky, the way the humidity hung frozen in the air, the smell of the burned rubber from the tires on the icy pavement. Even now, I can taste the sourness in the back of my throat as I recall the memory. February in Chicago, and winter finally arrived with a vengeance, bringing the ice storm of the century with it. The storm would be happening in a few short hours. I was sent to pick up bread, milk, and a bag of flour. The store was down the street from our home on the north side of the city. My mom let me walk there all the time. I was seventeen, I could handle it, I was an adult." She closed her eyes, then slowly opened them as she continued. "The store owner remembered me by name, and I was so embarrassed because I didn't have enough money. I must have dropped it on the way. Some adult I was."

A few of her classmates chuckled. "But he ushered me to the side of the line, told me he'd cover the leftover, and made sure he double bagged my groceries. I'm not going to lie, a bag of cookies from the deli ended up in my basket somehow. Which may have been why I didn't have enough money, but I was not about to admit it. Especially to him and especially to you all."

Another laugh moved through the students. "I left the store quickly. I noticed the drop in temperature from the few short minutes I was in the store. Oddly enough, though, I don't remember much except when I turned the corner, a driver jumped the curb, narrowly missing me."

The entire class was silent.

"There was something behind me, and when I turned, I saw it."

She looked up from her paper and caught the gaze of Dr. Morris, who looked away. She brought her paper up again and finished reading. "Jack Murphy died instantly. He left behind three daughters and a wife, a mom and a dad, and a brother named Fritz. He was our neighbor. He was dead, and I was alive."

When she sat, the students all started to clap. A few even shouted at her, telling her how amazing it was. Kate leaned over. "I have chills all over. Look at my arms, goose bumps."

Caroline smiled. "All the truth," she whispered, her eyes never leaving Dr. Morris as she sat stoically on the table.

"Okay, so what do we think about each memory we've heard?" Dr. Morris glanced around the class.

There was something about Dr. Morris's voice, her posture, how she was sitting there...Caroline wanted to answer, if only so she would look at her, so she raised her hand. Dr. Morris called on another student in the front row.

"They were all very vivid. Especially Caroline's. So crazy."

"Okay, but what else?"

Caroline kept her hand in the air, but Dr. Morris, again, didn't call on her.

"They made you feel things. Despair. Heartache."

"Good," Dr. Morris said as she stood and turned toward the whiteboard, completely ignoring Caroline's raised hand, which she slowly retracted. Kate glanced at her and shrugged. Caroline tried to not let it bother her, but it was too late. "I want you all to write about someone in your life who has been a great teacher and taught you one of the best lessons."

"What if it's some*thing*? And not a someone."

Dr. Morris flipped around, and Caroline immediately regretted letting herself ask the question. "What do you mean?"

Caroline swallowed. Dr. Morris's tone of voice was enough to make her want to crawl under the small tabletops in front of their chairs. "Um—"

"A teacher." Her voice was so firm. "A person. A lesson. Period." Dr. Morris shook her head. "Is it really hard to understand?"

She went to open her mouth to answer or to protest Dr. Morris's bullshit response, but she felt Kate's hand on her thigh above her knee. Kate squeezed her gently, so she took the hint and shut up.

"I want you all to read your pieces out loud next class, and we will critique them as a group. Print out enough copies for everyone. This class isn't only writing creatively. We also need to learn how to critique and help others write better."

She swallowed. She watched as Dr. Morris scribbled notes about critiquing papers on the white board. She went into detail about editing for grammar, spelling errors, and content.

Blah, blah, fucking, blah.

All she could think about was how she wanted to throw up. On Dr. Morris. Why was this woman such an awful person, and why did she have to humiliate Caroline? Her question was valid. And to be treated as if she were an imbecile was horrifying. Dr. Morris acting as if Caroline was too stupid to matter was making her want to drop the class. And dropping the class would set her even further behind.

She was making great money at the pub, so would it really matter? She was also in no hurry to move out of her daughter's when she got to see little Oden so often. He was a bright light in her dreary, school-filled days.

Caroline glanced up as Dr. Morris continued to talk about writing, papers, and a lot of other things she should have been taking notes on, but all she could think about was why Dr. Morris hated her so much. What had she done? She was putting in so much effort already, and it was only the second class. She was engaging, she was participating, she was trying her hardest to impress, and all she was doing was clearly irritating Dr. Morris. Caroline pinched her top lip, a common thing she did to make sure she didn't start crying.

When the class was finally dismissed, she quickly gathered her books and headed out of the class, Kate two steps behind her.

"What the hell?" Kate asked as she pushed a hand through her hair. "Why the frick does Dr. Morris hate you?"

"Beats me." They were on their way to the parking lot when Caroline stopped in her tracks and looked back at Kate. "I do not deserve to be treated like I've done something wrong when I haven't. I am a good student. I haven't even had time to screw up."

"You are the best writer in the class. I wouldn't worry too much about screwing up."

"Oh, yeah?" Caroline asked as she started to fish through her messenger bag. She pulled out a wadded up piece of paper and shoved it at Kate. "Read this."

Kate pulled the paper out of the ball and started to read. "This is our first assignment..." She kept reading. "Wait." She looked up from the paper and narrowed her eyes. "Your husband *left* you?" She didn't wait for a response before she continued on but stopped again. "Why didn't you read this out loud? This is *really* good."

"Because. I didn't feel comfortable." She reached around and pointed at the writing on the paper. "What does the comment say?"

"*No points awarded. You should have read this out loud.*" Kate sighed as she looked up. "Okay, yeah, she has it out for you."

"If I don't pass this class, I'll have to apply for the position without the certificate. They'll never hire me."

"Hey, I'll talk to my dad, okay? I'll make sure he knows how awesome you are if for some reason you don't get through it." Kate smiled as she placed a hand on Caroline's arm. "Don't worry. You can always complain about Dr. Morris if you really want to."

"Yeah, right. When has complaining ever helped? She'd probably crucify me." Caroline and Kate approached their cars. "I'll have to buckle down and figure it out."

"Exactly, that's the spirit."

She rolled her eyes as she opened her car door and climbed in. "You're not helping."

Kate laughed and did the same, starting her own car. "I think I should probably not be associated with you. The black sheep of our class."

She held her hand out the window, her middle finger in the air. "You're a dick!" Kate laughed as she pulled away, leaving Caroline in the parking lot wishing she'd never left Chicago.

CHAPTER FIVE

Y ou guys, it has been awful. Seriously."

"Oh, come on, it can't be as bad as you think." Kelli reached across the table and dipped her tortilla chip into a bowl of salsa. When she brought it to her mouth, a dollop of salsa landed on her shirt, right between her breasts. "Jesus. I can't eat without dropping shit on my tits. What the hell?"

"Probably because they're giant." Kate started to laugh, and it caused Michael to laugh.

"They really are." Michael dodged Kelli's backhand. "What? I'm just saying."

Instead of meeting for drinks at the pub on Friday, they coerced Caroline into meeting them after her shift. Nine at night, and Caroline was eating chips and salsa, waiting on a burrito, and savoring her third margarita as if it were a lifeline. She felt like a twenty-one-year-old, and it was *amazing*.

"Listen," Kate said as she held her hand in the air. She did the move often when she wanted the microphone. "Caroline, I think it's going to get easier. You're doing so well in the other classes you had to take."

"I don't know." Caroline sighed. "These last couple of weeks have made me realize how out of practice I am."

"Out of practice? At what?" Michael leaned forward, arms folded on the table, and smiled. "At being a millennial?"

Caroline shook her head. "I hate you all. Why do I even speak to you guys?"

"Oh, come on. You love us. We keep you young." Kelli let out a boisterous laugh. "And don't worry. You're catching on fine. You're drinking and stuffing your face with us like a professional."

Michael leaned in until he got Caroline to look at him. "Seriously, though. College isn't supposed to be easy. We don't want Joe Schmoe over there," he motioned toward a very inebriated customer at the bar, "teaching the youth of America."

"Wait, isn't that Mr. Green? Our history teacher from high school?" Kelli raised her eyebrows before eating another chip.

"Listen to me, Caroline." Kate placed her hand on Caroline's wrist and pulled on her gently. "You cannot let Dr. Morris get you down."

"I told you she was a bitch." Michael drank from his beer and shrugged.

"Yeah, you weren't wrong." Caroline lowered her eyes and sighed. She could not stop thinking about the way Dr. Morris made her feel. And the thoughts were infuriating.

"Okay," Kelli started and smiled. "You are so likable. Dr. Morris will come around, and you'll be the teacher's pet in no time flat."

Caroline picked her margarita up and took a large gulp of the too-sour-for-her-liking drink. Her lips smacked together, the lime flavor hitting her on the back of the tongue. The liquor, thankfully, was hitting all the right spots. "So, I need to stick it out?"

"Kill her with kindness?" Kate offered.

Kelli smiled. "You're gonna be fine, I promise."

Caroline sat back in her chair. As the three of them started to talk about their weeks, her mind began to wander. After class let out on Monday, instead of obsessing about things she couldn't control, she immersed herself in research. Not just any research, but the kind that consisted of googling one Dr. Atlanta Morris, who was, apparently, a damn prodigy. She received her doctorate in creative writing from the University of Denver when she was only twenty-seven. She started undergrad at the age of sixteen and managed to graduate with honors in every program she went through. She was one of the youngest professors in the English department at Arizona State.

Her Facebook page was on severe lockdown, except for a few profile and cover photos. One of the profile pictures had to be from when Dr. Morris first set up the page because her hair was shorter and she was without her signature nose ring.

Everything about this woman was intriguing on a level Caroline had never encountered before. She knew part of the reason she couldn't stop thinking about Dr. Morris was because she couldn't stand when someone didn't like her. She wanted to get to the bottom of it, but how? If it meant dedicating every spare moment to writing, researching, and obsessing about Dr. Morris, then so be it.

❖

Frank Higgins was one of the kindest people Atlanta had ever met in her entire life. He was so wonderful, and he treated Sheri like the queen she thought she was, and it made him even more amazing. So, when the two of them kidnapped her from her front porch on Friday night, she didn't really put up a fight. Besides, he'd always foot the bill for whatever they ate and drank. Being a successful financial planner had its advantages.

The downtown scene in Sedona was great. There were a lot of different shops and restaurants that catered to the tourists, of course, but most of the restaurants even had local followers. After a certain time of day, the tourists would retire, and the locals would come out of the woodwork.

When they rolled into the Mission Pub, Atlanta fell in love with the ambience. Everything about the environment was perfect and put her at ease. Mission was absolutely her kind of joint. Trendy, great music, microbrews from the area, and a dartboard.

"That is your fourth bull's-eye this round," Frank said with a whiny voice. "Not fair. I think you're a dart shark."

Atlanta shrugged. "You're the one who wanted to play."

"And you thought you could beat her, even though I told you it was not gonna happen," Sheri added.

Frank sighed. "You two are hustling me, aren't you?"

"I'm pushing sixty, Frank. I do not hustle."

"I am most certainly hustling you. For. Sure." Atlanta grinned.

Frank laughed a hearty laugh and lined up to throw. He hit a triple twenty and wiped his brow. "Thank God. You were gonna score on me all night if I didn't close twenty."

"She'll still win," Sheri said while shaking her head.

Atlanta smiled as she lined up and threw another bull's-eye, followed by a triple eighteen and another sixteen, closing out the board.

She peered at her score, pulling her clear-framed glasses down her nose. "Looks like I won, buddy."

"Best two out of three."

"Frank," Sheri whined, her voice laced with irritation.

"Okay, fine. You've won one game. I want a rematch."

Sheri held her hands up. "No, I want to sit and talk. You can have a rematch later."

"The boss has spoken," Atlanta whispered as she leaned into Frank's shoulder. "I'll kick your ass in a while." She chuckled as he rolled his eyes and playfully slammed the darts on the table. When she slid into the booth across from Sheri, she pulled her beer along the table, careful to not spill it. Avery White Rascal ale was her favorite beer, and it reminded her of Denver. As well as other things, which sometimes hurt but needed to be remembered.

"So, tell me about your class, Atlanta," Frank said as he lifted his beer to his mouth.

"I think it's gonna be good. I don't know."

"I think you have some potential in there." Sheri paused. "Of course, there are a couple students who could be lost hopes…"

"What about Jorge? Is he cool?"

"Yes, actually, he's super awesome." Sheri pushed her hair behind her ears. "He's going to meet us later, I think. Molly is out, though. She said she had a headache. But we all know what a headache is code for—"

Atlanta chuckled as she raised her eyebrows. "She's getting laid."

"Yep."

"They're so weird. Tony and her are the most interesting couple ever."

"Why? 'Cause he's so much older than her?"

"No, because…well, yeah." Atlanta started to laugh. "I don't have anything against age gaps, but it's just strange. Thinking about them having sex? Ugh. I don't want to think about you two banging either."

Frank and Sheri both descended into laughter as Frank said, "Well then, don't ask what we did before we picked you up."

"Jesus *Christ*." Atlanta scrunched her face and rolled her eyes.

"So," Sheri started after she took a sip of her merlot. "What do you think about the nontraditional student?"

"Caroline? Wait…who?" *Welp, fucked that up.* Atlanta pulled a breath in quickly. "I mean, I don't even know who you're speaking of."

Sheri arched an eyebrow. "Sure."

"She's insignificant."

"Sure."

Atlanta rolled her eyes and shook her head. "Insignificant."

"I *know* your type."

"My type is *no students.*"

Sheri let out a puff of air, and Frank smiled. "Now I want to know about this 'older lady.'"

Atlanta hated how Frank always wanted to be one of the girls. "She's not someone we need to talk about."

Sheri leaned forward. The way the wineglass magnified her mouth made Atlanta chuckle despite herself. "You aren't telling the truth right now." Sheri pointed at Atlanta. "If this older lady wasn't catching your attention, you wouldn't be so freaking shitty to her."

"What the fuck? How the hell would you know I've been shitty to her?" Atlanta caught herself. "I mean, how have I been shitty? I haven't been shitty. Goddammit."

Sheri tilted her head. "Oh really?" She looked at Frank. "I peeked into her class the other day. This woman, who, by the way, wrote this awesome story about a memory that changed her life, had a question about another writing assignment. And Miss Priss over here," Sheri waved her hand at Atlanta, "barely answered it and kept her head down in her notebook the entire fucking time. Her actions were rude and uncalled for, in my opinion. Of course, we all know my opinion doesn't count for much when it comes to Atlanta."

Atlanta wanted to reach across the table and pull her hair, or something equally dramatic, to shut her up, but she also knew Sheri was absolutely right.

Sheri looked back at Atlanta. "Tell me I'm wrong."

"You're wrong."

"Ha!"

Atlanta brought her beer to her lips, but before she drank, she said softly, "You're not wrong."

"See? I knew it."

"Stop, please."

"Why are you treating her poorly? You are the one who needs to stop."

"You know why." Atlanta positioned herself in the booth so she was sitting on her legs. She towered over the table, and she leaned across to stare directly at Sheri. "I cannot even entertain the idea." She looked at Frank. "Or discuss it." She pulled herself out of attack mode and cleared her throat. "So, why even bring it up?"

"Okay, wait." Frank glanced at his wife and then back across the table. "Didn't you do something with a student once?"

"Jesus." Sheri smacked Frank on the arm. "Do you have any couth?"

"What?"

Sheri made eye contact with Atlanta and smoothed her hand across the table until she was close to Atlanta's balled-up fist. "I have never told him the details. I promise."

Atlanta took a very deep breath and slowly let it out. She waited one second, two, then three, before she softly answered Frank's blunt question with a simple nod.

Frank sighed.

Sheri sighed.

"The incident happened in grad school. So I didn't get in a huge amount of trouble. Yet the whole goddamn ASU faculty somehow knows about it. Now I'm a target. As if those old men never diddled a needy student before."

"Diddled?" Sheri smiled. "Really?"

Atlanta couldn't hold back her laughter as she repositioned herself in the booth. "Listen," she started and looked at the ceiling. "There is absolutely no way I can let my guard down."

"I understand." Sheri reached across the table again and this time hooked Atlanta's index finger with her own. "I really do, but you can't treat her differently than everyone else."

"Um, aside from the obvious, why can't I?"

"Because." Sheri closed her eyes and clenched her jaw while still holding on to Atlanta's finger. When she relaxed and opened her eyes, she said softly, "You know how it feels to be treated differently. Don't you?"

Atlanta rolled her eyes. "Not the same."

"Yes, it is the same. You've complained a million times about how these 'old man' profs treat you differently. And now you're going to do the very same thing to a student? I don't think you're being fair."

"Whatever."

"You know I'm right."

"Okay. Fine."

"And also…"

Atlanta watched Sheri's eyebrows knit together. "What?" No answer. "Sheri Higgins. What aren't you telling me?"

"So, um, you might, just a little bit, uh…be, y'know…her mentor."

Atlanta was pretty sure she heard correctly, but Sheri mumbled the last couple of words. Did she say mentor? *What the*— "Did you say what I think you said?"

"Look," Sheri started. She pulled her hand from Atlanta's and started to list things on her fingers. "One, Jorge was in charge of the mentor list. You gave him the task to do, and he did it. Two, you're so good with nontraditional students. I don't know why, but you are. Three, Molly had five students she wanted already. Four, we all knew you didn't want a full list of students. Caroline and one other student are all you have."

Atlanta's stomach was sitting on the floor next to the booth. She looked around the pub. Business was starting to pick up. Thank goodness because she was ready to start crying, and the only thing stopping her was the idea of being seen by random strangers.

"Hey, you guys," came Jorge's voice, breaking through her freak-out. She blinked a few times as she continued to stare at Sheri.

"How's it going? Is everything all right? You look like you've seen a ghost, Atlanta." Jorge nudged her with his elbow.

"She's fine."

"Oh shit." Jorge looked from each person until he landed on Sheri. "You told her about the mentor thing, didn't you?"

Sheri nodded.

"Look, you can have one of mine if you really want more students. We were trying to make sure you had time since you're teaching a full load next semester and have to make sure all the proper paperwork is turned in for the extension expansion…"

Atlanta heard his voice trail off, and she looked over. "It's really okay, Jorge. I promise. I was surprised you did it without me. No worries."

"We thought it'd take some pressure off." Jorge shrugged. "You can blame Molly because she told me you'd be fine with me assigning the students."

"I will absolutely blame her," Atlanta said, as she forced herself to settle down. Jorge launched into a story about his rental and the people who were living next to him. Atlanta focused on her beer. She was going to have to buckle down. Buckle everything down. Her rage, her feelings, and her heart.

CHAPTER SIX

There is not one bone in my body that wants to go to this session."
Caroline leaned against the wall of the community center lobby. "I
don't understand why these sessions are necessary. None of this makes
any sense whatsoever." She sighed as she held her phone against her
ear and listened to Kate getting the children she nannied ready for the
day.

"I kind of agree with you. Meetings with mentors are a pain in the
ass." Kate groaned. "No, Jack, you can't say that word." She let out
an exasperated sigh followed by a chuckle. "He said 'ass' because he
heard me say it. Perfect."

"You're a wonderful role model, dear. Don't forget it."

"I learned it from you," Kate said, and her laughter from the other
end of the phone was perfect. "So, what are you going to do? You can't
drop the class, and it'll be real hard getting out of the mentor sessions."

"I have no idea. I guess deal with it? I wish my English credits
from my bachelor's degree would have been good enough. English is
English. Why would they be too old?"

Kate chuckled. "I always forget you're, like, so much older than
me."

"What the hell, Kate?" Caroline echoed her laughter.

"I know you're freaking out, but try to go with the flow. Dr. Morris
will eventually drop her bitchy demeanor."

"I certainly hope so."

"What do you have to bring to this meeting? The paper about an
amazing teacher?"

"Yes, because I wrote about time being a teacher instead of an actual person." Caroline shook her head and sighed. "So stupid. I don't even understand what the big deal is."

"Why don't you go on and meet with her, then let us know how it goes when we're together again. Tonight is trivia night at the pub. Do you work?"

"I do, but I get off at nine again, I can join in after."

"Sounds perfect. Go. Keep your head up. Don't let the haters get you down. You're old but mighty."

"I'm literally going to kick your ass the next time I see you."

Kate laughed. "Okay, *Mom*. I'll talk to you later."

Caroline gasped, and Kate's laughter continued until the line went dead. "That bitch," Caroline said under her breath. She slid her phone into the outside pocket of her messenger bag as she turned down the hallway toward the office of Dr. Morris. Caroline's heart was in her throat when she approached door number seventy-four. Seeing the closed door only led to more erratic heart beating as Caroline raised her hand and knocked softly.

"Come in," she heard. The sound of her turning the doorknob was so loud, it seemed to echo off the empty hallway.

She poked her head into the office and forced herself to smile. "Hi, I'm a couple minutes early."

Dr. Morris didn't look up from her MacBook. "Have a seat." She barely motioned to an empty chair across from the completely uncluttered desk. Next to Dr. Morris's computer and notebook sat Caroline's paper. There was an angry, red F on the top.

Caroline sat, pulling her bag up and over her head to set on the floor. She could feel her hands shaking, so she clasped them together and rested them in her lap. The office was quite a bit warmer than the hallway had been. Beads of perspiration formed along her hairline. She thanked God she actually did her bangs today and hadn't pulled them back in the spirit of being lazy. She did a once-over of the office as Dr. Morris continued to type furiously on the keyboard, the clicking loud in the confined space. The overhead lights were off, and two lamps provided soft ambience. The environment would have seemed calming if it wasn't for Dr. Morris clearly having it out for her and trying to ruin any chance of her getting her teaching certificate.

There were a few items hanging on a bulletin board behind the desk. An ASU Sun Devils pennant, a University of Denver sticker, and a Golden Girls poster with "#SQUADGOALS" on it. The office smelled like lavender. Clean and fresh, no hints of vanilla, no bergamot, only lavender.

The smell was amazing and so what she expected. She pulled her focus from the scent and glanced at Dr. Morris and her auburn hair. How easy it was for her attention to zero in on the way Dr. Morris's hair flowed so beautifully over her shoulders. She was wearing a different pair of glasses, tortoiseshell plastic on the top of the frames and wire along the bottom. They were totally an old-school style. Caroline loved how the arms of the glasses were actually a salmon color that matched Dr. Morris's button-down shirt. She had the sleeves rolled up again, and when she moved her arm, Caroline could finally make out that the simple tattoo was actually Roman numerals. *XI.X.XI.* Was it a date? What did it mean?

And why were they sitting in silence? Was this some sort of punishment? For what, she didn't know. Maybe for being such a good fucking person for her entire life. Bad people never got punished. Bad people who left their wives during moments of need and desperation never got punished. But Caroline? Good, kind, wonderful Caroline who helped save lives for twenty-seven years, was being punished.

This was bullshit. She didn't need to give up her entire Thursday afternoon before work to sit and watch this mean woman type. Even if it was strangely calming in a weird, almost peeping Tom, kind of way.

Caroline cleared her throat, hoping Dr. Morris would look up from her computer, to no avail. Dammit. She didn't know what else to do besides actually saying something to this insufferable woman. "Look," she finally gathered the courage to say. Dr. Morris continued to type. Of course she fucking did. "If this is all this is going to consist of, we can say we did it, and I'll go."

"I'm almost done."

Caroline sighed, but it came out as a groan, and Dr. Morris finally glanced up. The eye contact almost stopped her heart. She instantly sat straighter in her chair. "Sorry."

Dr. Morris typed a few more words or sentences. Shit, *paragraphs*, with how fast she was typing. She closed her laptop and pushed it to the side before she clasped her hands together and leaned forward. "So, Ms. Stevens."

"You can call me Caroline."

"Ms. Stevens, tell me," Dr. Morris started.

She was wearing dangly gold earrings with gold feathers on them, and the way they were mingling with her hair made Caroline's mind short-circuit for a brief second. Dr. Morris was looking at her hands, though, not at Caroline. The lack of eye contact was driving her nuts. She wasn't a top-notch communicator by any stretch of the imagination, but goddammit, a little eye contact never hurt anyone.

"Tell you what?" Caroline's words came out a lot more irritated than she planned, but the tone got Dr. Morris to finally make eye contact.

Atlanta tried to soothe the butterflies in her stomach, but all they did when her eyes locked on to Caroline's was beat their wings harder and faster. "What are you expecting to get out of this program?"

Caroline's left eyebrow arched. This was the first time Atlanta had been close enough to see the fine lines around Caroline's eyes and on her forehead above the arched eyebrow. "You mean aside from a teaching certificate?"

Atlanta nodded and squeezed her hands together as hard as she could. Her thumb knuckle popped. The loud crack embarrassed her.

"Well, you read my paper. The one you didn't give me any points on."

"Yes, you should have read it out loud, but for some reason—"

"*Some* reason?" Caroline didn't seem to care that she cut her off. "I didn't read it out loud because I didn't know we'd have to, and I also didn't want to tell my backstory to a class full of kids who are younger than my daughter." Caroline furrowed her brow. "I didn't think it was their business. And frankly, it's not yours."

Atlanta was so insanely turned on by Caroline's outburst, she had to take a deep breath. This wasn't working. None of this was working. "Then why did you write it down?"

"I don't know." Caroline's shoulders fell as she retreated from attack position. "I just…started writing, I guess. And it poured onto the paper."

Atlanta, against the best judgment she had, felt herself smiling. "That's not a bad thing."

Caroline shrugged. "Listen, Dr. Morris, I don't really want to do these mentoring sessions. At all. And especially with you."

Well, hearing those words stung. Even though Atlanta knew she deserved them, they still stung. "Unfortunately, our commitment to student success at all campuses, but especially the extension campuses, begins and ends with our mentor program. Mentor sessions are a requirement, but we can switch you to another professor if you would rather." Atlanta watched the idea wash across Caroline's face. She was absolutely considering it. "If it makes you feel any better, I wanted to talk to you a little more in depth about your writing."

Caroline let out a puff of air. "Oh really?" She reached across the desk and picked up her paper Atlanta had hastily graded the night before in a fit of lust-filled rage. "You mean the writing you think must be pretty shitty if you give it an F?"

Atlanta eyed the paper as Caroline looked at it. "I can explain."

"Explain what?" Caroline laughed. The sound was borderline maniacal, but she was somehow holding it together. Must have been the years of trauma experience in the emergency room. "Explain why you hate me? Because that's what you should be fucking explaining." Her eyes went wide, and she once again let her shoulders fall. "I'm sorry. I shouldn't cuss."

"No. It's okay."

Caroline leaned back in her chair. Atlanta tried her very hardest to not let her eyes wander to Caroline's chest, but it was too late. She looked, and how had she not noticed this woman's breasts before? They were…

Caroline cleared her throat, and Atlanta quickly adjusted her gaze. *Fuck. Busted.*

"I don't want a different mentor," she said softly. "I don't want to be treated differently."

"Done." Atlanta heard herself say the word before she could even think about it. She was so mad at herself. This was a perfect opportunity to let this go, to move on, to not back herself into a corner that had only one way out.

"So…"

Atlanta watched Caroline as a smile began to form on her dark pink lips. They were plump but not overly, and she had to be wearing lipstick. There was no way the color was natural.

"An F?" She flipped the paper around so Atlanta could see it. "I mean, I realize I went against your very specific instructions, but…" Her voice was layered with sarcasm and *wait. Was she flirting?* "I think it's actually pretty good."

Atlanta pushed away from the desk and stood. She had completely done a one-eighty in the span of about three minutes, and it was absolutely unacceptable. She paced three steps to the left, then three steps back in her small office and rubbed her hands on her jeans. "It's not bad." She laughed. Nervously. "It's not good. But it's not bad."

Caroline chuckled, shook her head, then sighed loudly. "You know it's good, and it wouldn't kill you to pass out the compliment."

"I'll let you know." She paused, stopped, and turned toward Caroline. "When something you write is good. Until then, it's not bad." She held her hands in the air at her sides. "Okay?"

Caroline smiled.

And she was gorgeous. The air in the room was thick, almost heavy, and Atlanta wondered if she was feeling woozy or if she was overreacting. When she didn't think it could get worse, Caroline bent down and pulled a pair of glasses from her bag, making a direct line of sight for Atlanta to stare down the front of her dark purple blouse. Caroline sat upright and slid the glasses onto her face before she looked at the paper.

"Time is the only teacher I have ever had that never changes but always teaches me something new," she read with her smooth voice. "Time hurts, it heals, it kills, it survives."

Atlanta leaned against her desk to steady herself and closed her eyes so she didn't have to keep staring at Caroline as she read.

"The time between heartbeats, the time between souls, the time between a crisis and a savior. It's time that stays. It's time that changes. We learn. We grow. We live. We die." She took a breath.

"The heartache caused by time crawling, by time speeding, by time in and of itself, is the only lesson I've ever learned that makes sense to me. Time is the greatest teacher. For without time, would any of us really feel or learn anything?"

The paper crumpled softly, indicating maybe Caroline was done. Atlanta opened her eyes and found Caroline was standing now.

"Time's up on our mentoring session," Caroline said quietly.

Atlanta cleared her throat when Caroline handed her paper back.

"You're right. It's not good at all." She opened the door and left before Atlanta was able to say another word.

CHAPTER SEVEN

"I cannot believe there's a tiebreaker. What a crock. We worked our asses off to win tonight, and those dick holes over there think they're gonna win? Over my dead body."

"Kelli, honey, you gotta settle down." Michael laughed. "We'll pull a win out in the end."

"We have a half hour to wait before they do the tiebreaker. I don't know if I'll be able to make it. I'm so tired." Kate rubbed her eyes with the heels of her palms.

"And *I'm* the old lady?"

"Oh, shut up." Kate waved her hand at Caroline as she yawned.

"Tell us about the mentoring session." Kelli grabbed a soft pretzel stick and munched away happily. "Did it go as expected?"

Caroline did the same, dipping the pretzel in beer cheese before taking a bite. "Um…" She bit down into the salty bread, chewed and chewed before finally mumbling, "I guess it was okay." She covered her mouth lightly with her hand. "She did a complete turnaround and was sort of being nice to me by the end of it."

"That's good, isn't it?"

"Yeah, well, I don't know, Kate. I don't trust her." Caroline took another bite, chewed, and swallowed. "I don't need her to like me. I want her to not treat me poorly. Or hate me."

"Sort of the same thing." Michael tilted his head. "I mean, right?"

"Absolutely not." Caroline turned a bit toward Michael. "There was this doctor in the ER who would constantly belittle me and my nursing staff. He was such a giant asshole. He thought his shit didn't stink. He was young and cocky."

"Sounds like my type," Kate said, followed by a dreamy sigh, making them all laugh.

"I put him in his place, finally, because one of my best nurses ended up filing a grievance. I asked him why he hated us, and why he was so nasty to us all. He changed his tune, but it took pointing out his behavior multiple times before he finally did something about it. He didn't like me for putting him in his place, but he certainly treated me a lot nicer after the confrontation."

"Did you put Morris in her place, then?"

"Not necessarily, but I did say the f-word in front of her."

"Ooh, you cussed in front of her? You should be happy she couldn't send you to the principal." Kelli playfully pushed her shoulder.

"It worked. She changed her tune." Caroline took a drink of sauvignon blanc. "I don't know what it is about her, but I cannot stop…" Caroline let her words trail off as she tried to gather her thoughts. It was way too soon to make a confession detailing how she couldn't stop thinking about Dr. Morris. Bringing up the vivid fantasies about her professor in some very compromising positions was not something she should do, even though part of her was dying to come clean and talk about the emotions swirling inside her. Everything happening was so insanely out of character for Caroline. She was confused, but the feelings were also starting to frighten the hell out of her.

"Cannot stop what?" Kate's eyes were wide.

"Oh, nothing."

"Yeah, no." Kate looked at Kelli, then Caroline. She was sitting at attention, her elbows on the table, her eyes wild. The idea of getting a juicy tidbit certainly perked her tired ass up. "You need to finish your sentence. Cannot stop *what*?"

"And now it's time for the tiebreaker question. Listen up, teams. You will have to get the entire question right in order to win. Did you all hear me?"

Kate groaned. "What the fuck? I don't even want to play anymore."

"For real." Kelli pointed at Caroline. "You're not getting out of this one."

Caroline had never been happier to be saved by a man interrupting her. The temperature in the pub felt as if it rose at least ten degrees as she sat there, on the one hand thanking God for the interruption, but on the other wishing she could understand what was going on in her mind. Maybe talking about it to her new, hip friends would be beneficial? Maybe they'd help her work through this confusion.

"And the question is: What are the seven different meals for a Hobbit and at what times are the meals consumed?"

Michael's eyes went wide, and he started to laugh. "Are you *fucking* kidding me?"

"Michael, come on." Kelli huffed. "You have got to know this. You're the biggest nerd I know."

"First of all, I am not a nerd. I am a geek. Big fucking difference." Michael pushed his hand through his hair. "And second, the last time I read the entire *Lord of the Rings* series, I was in middle school."

Caroline stifled a chuckle. "Okay, yeah, totally means you were a nerd."

"Okay, well, fuck you." Michael flipped Caroline off as he laughed with her.

"This is the last question, you guys. If we get this right, we win and go home." Kate clenched her jaw together. "Come on. Do not chump out on me now. I want to win."

Caroline laughed again but abruptly stopped when she felt a hand on her back and heard a chair being pulled out from the table.

"I know the answer to this. Can I join late?"

Caroline looked over at Dr. Morris standing next to her, a grin plastered on her face.

"Um…"

She sat, tossed her hair over her shoulder, and her scent filled the air. All Caroline could do was stare. At her glasses, nose ring, at the eye shadow she was wearing, the eyeliner, and holy fuck, she was sitting right at their table. "I know the answer. Do you want it or not?"

"Well, shit," Michael said frantically as he grabbed the paper and pencil. "Go."

"Breakfast is at seven in the morning, then second breakfast at nine. Elevenses is obviously at eleven, then luncheon is, I think, at one in the afternoon. Then afternoon tea at four. Dinner at six, supper at eight. There."

Caroline blinked once, twice, then three times. "What the hell? How do you know that?"

"*Lord of the Rings* is one of my favorite series ever. I did my doctoral dissertation on the importance of Tolkien in college society and culture."

"You're joking, right?" Kelli asked.

Dr. Morris laughed as she held out a hand to her. "I've had you in class before, haven't I?"

Kelli pushed out a laugh. "I think so, yes."

"And you, too," Dr. Morris said, pointing at Michael. "I seem to recall you falling asleep."

"Oh," Kate whispered. "Awkward…"

Dr. Morris laughed before she stood. "I thought I'd come over and say hi. I'll let you all go."

And just as quickly as she breezed into Caroline's area, Dr. Morris stood and retreated to a table with Professor Higgins and Dr. Wright. Kelli leaned across the table and latched on to Caroline's wrist, making Caroline finally look away from Dr. Morris's table.

"What. The fuck. Was that?"

"That was—"

"So weird," Kate said with a grin. "Because now I know what you cannot stop. You cannot stop thinking about her, can you?"

Speak. Caroline. Speak. Now. Tell them. "No," Caroline lied.

"Caroline, honey," Michael said as he left money on the table. "You are a horrible liar. Anyone ever tell you that before?" He stood, a smile on his lips, then leaned down to kiss Caroline on the cheek. "Have a good night, Mom. Come on, you two."

"I'm not leaving!"

"Kate, two seconds ago, you were ready to go home. We're leaving. Let's go."

"Well, I'm leaving, too," Caroline said as she started to stand.

Kelli put her hands on Caroline's shoulders. "No, you aren't. Have a good night." Then Kelli left, pulling Kate by the arm. They stopped at the table where Dr. Morris was sitting, and before Caroline knew it, Dr. Morris was on her way over to the table in her black skinny jeans, sandals, and tight red tank top that was absolutely showing off her arms and her curves and…

Caroline pulled her gaze from the approaching Dr. Morris and grabbed her wine. She swirled what was left in the glass, thanked God it was almost empty, and started to devise an escape plan. She needed to get the hell out of there and get home. Fast.

Because the ache between her thighs?

Yeah, it was not going to cure itself.

Jesus, what is happening to me?

❖

Atlanta sat across the table from Caroline. She placed her beer on the already used cardboard coaster before she made eye contact. Caroline's mouth was hanging open a bit, and the pure shocked expression made Atlanta smile. "You okay?"

Caroline blinked rapidly and shook her head as if she was shaking herself out of a daze. "Yep. I'm good."

"Good." Atlanta reached up, pushed her hair away from her face, and tucked the unruly pieces behind her ears. She glanced around the bar. "So, what happened?"

"I'm sorry?"

"With the trivia. Did you win?"

Caroline pursed her lips. "Y'know, I don't think Michael even turned our answer in." She chuckled, defeated, and shrugged. "I didn't hear them announce anything, either. Did you?"

Was this really what they were going to talk about? "Nope."

"Hmph."

Atlanta took a drink of beer as she studied Caroline over the top of the glass. She was wearing a T-shirt with the bar's emblem on it. "You must be a fan of this place?"

Her eyebrow arched as if she didn't understand the question. Then it seemed to hit her because she let out a girlish giggle which, in another circumstance, would have sounded way out of place. "Oh, you mean because of my shirt?" Caroline smoothed her hands over the T-shirt, and when she did so, the slope of her breasts caught Atlanta's attention. "I work here. This is my uniform. My shift ended about an hour ago."

"*You* work *here*?"

Caroline giggled again. And the sound was delightful enough for Atlanta to wish she could hear it as often as possible. "Yes, I work here."

"Wow."

"Are you shocked because I'm too old to be working here?" Caroline's tone made it clear she was putting her defenses up.

"Whoa there. That's not at all why I'm shocked. And I'm not shocked."

"Sure sounded shocked."

"Whatever." Atlanta waved her hand. This conversation was awful.

Caroline leaned a little closer. "Do you really think this is necessary? Us? Talking? I mean, if you're doing it for my benefit so I don't continue to think you hate me, I promise you, I'm fine."

Atlanta didn't want to admit it, but she absolutely loved how blunt Caroline was. She didn't beat around the bush. The bluntness was refreshing since the majority of people in Atlanta's life were always eager to sugarcoat things. As if she had a fragile ego or something. "Well, thank you for letting me off the hook." Atlanta squinted and propped her arms on the table. "But I genuinely wanted to come over and talk to you. Is that really hard to believe?"

"A little, yes."

"I really did a number on you, didn't I?"

Caroline opened her mouth, then closed it. She was obviously going to say something but decided not to. She looked over at the bar and motioned for another glass of wine. Her hair was in a French braid, and her bangs were pulled away from her face, held back with a bobby pin. She must have been pretty busy at one point because her hairline, along the back of her head, was damp with sweat. The baby hairs were in ringlets, and Atlanta wondered if her hair had a natural curl to it. Caroline accepted the glass of wine from her coworker and looked at Atlanta. "You didn't correct me," she said before drinking.

"On what?"

"I said you hate me. You didn't correct me."

Atlanta nodded. "Ah yes." She watched as Caroline mimicked her seated position and posture with her arms on the table. "I don't hate you, obviously." Atlanta let her eyes wander over Caroline's facial features, her slender nose, high cheekbones...her pink lips. "I try hard to maintain a certain level of bitchiness toward all my students."

"You're kidding me, right?"

"I wish I was."

"Well, congratulations, because you have been exceptionally bitchy toward me. Just letting you know."

Oh, I know. "Really?"

"Yes." Caroline smiled. Her teeth were perfect—from braces or good genes, Atlanta wasn't sure—and she wondered if everything about this woman was going to be without flaws. Because if that was the case, Atlanta really was screwed. "Really."

"Well, I apologize. I'll try to make sure everyone else receives the same treatment from now on."

Caroline laughed. "Yes, please. Every student in class should feel your wrath. Like they're disliked for breathing." She breathed a very shaky breath, as if realizing how ironic it was considering her previous statement. "Like they don't matter at all."

Atlanta was trudging into territory she didn't want to be in, going against everything she believed in, but all of her self-imposed warnings were a distant memory. She wished she could say it was because she was strong, self-aware, and didn't need to keep her walls built as high around Caroline, but she would have been lying. Atlanta watched Caroline lick her lips. She let her eyes follow Caroline's fingers, her dark, cherry painted nails, as she scratched her jaw. She ran those nails across her collarbone and looped her index finger into the self-made V-neck of her T-shirt. Everything about Caroline was pulling Atlanta further and further in, and for reasons out of her control, she wasn't applying the brakes. "Can I ask you a question?" Atlanta waited for Caroline to answer, but she didn't speak, only raised her chin and widened her eyes. "Why Sedona?"

"Um." Caroline peered upward, pulled her bottom lip into her mouth, and tilted her head. "I guess the main reason is because my daughter lives here, but, I mean…" She looked straight into Atlanta's eyes. "The views are pretty remarkable."

Yes, they sure are. "I can't argue."

"I'm not one to believe in spiritual mumbo-jumbo, either. Like, you know how people say Sedona is a vortex?" Caroline smiled as she stared into the distance. "I feel good here. Maybe there's some truth to the spiritual energy. And that's big coming from me. You probably don't care, but I haven't felt at peace in a long time."

Atlanta cringed. She shouldn't care, but she did. Almost too much, considering… "Do you mean because of the incident at the hospital?"

"You mean when I got shot?" Caroline chuckled when Atlanta did. "By the way…" She cleared her throat. "You have a knack for retelling a traumatic experience."

"Oh, well, thanks. Sure wish the professor would have thought that." Caroline smacked the table lightly. "Wait…You're the professor. And I didn't get any points on it. Hmph." Caroline's tone for the snide comment was not missed.

"Well, then," she said as she rubbed her palms on her jeans. She had stepped so far out of her comfort zone with this woman, she was now allowing her to be the icy one, and that simply was not allowed. She stood and maneuvered around the table. "You have a nice night, Ms. Stevens." She dropped the words with a bit of an attitude and a dash of the same demeanor she had used on Caroline to start with. She headed back to the table where Sheri and Molly were seated. She regretted leaving, but she needed to repair the brake line in the runaway car she was driving. No good would come from befriending Caroline. Absolutely no good would come from falling into bed with her, either, which was exactly where she'd be heading if Caroline arched her eyebrow one more time, bit her lip again, ran her finger along the neck of her T-shirt…or breathed.

Sheri cleared her throat when Atlanta slid into the booth. She motioned toward Caroline with a gentle tilt of her head. "What's going on over there?"

"Nothing." Atlanta knew her answer was laced with irritation and anger. No, not at Caroline. She was more upset with herself for trying, for thinking it was a good idea, for all of it. "Don't worry about it."

"Atlanta," Molly said, low, followed by a sigh. She pushed a hand through her short gray hair. "You better be careful."

Atlanta took offense even though Molly and Sheri both had every right to remind her. "Why does everyone act like I'm constantly sleeping with students?" She moved her icy stare from Molly to Sheri, then back to Molly. "Seriously. Why? I almost did it once. Once. You both realize I haven't fucked up again, correct?" They nodded. "Then stop, please. I'm not going to do anything."

"What *are* you doing?" Sheri whispered her question, and all Atlanta wanted to do was say she had no idea because she really didn't. Instead, she took a deep breath and gathered words to formulate a lie. "I wanted to apologize for being so mean to her and singling her out. You said I was rude, Sheri, and I felt bad. The end. Okay?"

"Mm-hmm."

"Okay, okay." Molly leaned her shoulder into Atlanta's. "If it makes you feel any better, she left."

The truth was, no, Caroline leaving didn't make Atlanta feel any better. In fact, it made her want to throw up. And that was not the ending she was going for.

CHAPTER EIGHT

Four whole weeks managed to fly by in the blink of an eye, and Caroline, shockingly, wasn't "the old lady struggling in class." Three of the four classes were going exceptionally well, especially the communications course. Caroline wished she had learned about understanding body language years ago. "No, seriously," she started with a laugh. She peered at Kate over the top of her reading glasses as they sat in the lobby area of the community center. "My husband used to say I was a horrible communicator."

Kate's brow furrowed. "Ex-husband you mean?" She placed the flash cards she was studying on the table and ran her fingers through her short hair.

"Oh, shit, yes. My ex-husband." Caroline shook her head and started to highlight portions of her notes. She passed out copies of two sheets of practice test questions.

"Let the fucker go." Kate let out a puff of air. "He doesn't deserve your awesomeness."

Caroline felt a sense of self-love bubbling inside of her. "Wow. Thank you, Kate."

"I'm being serious. What a piece of shit. Leaving you with no warning? Ugh. I can't even with how much I don't like him."

"Please, don't sugarcoat anything." Caroline laughed as Michael and Kelli joined them. Study session for the communications test was about to begin, and they had all asked Caroline for help. She felt honored instead of old, which was a good step in the right direction.

"What's so funny?" Kelli pulled out a notebook from her backpack, then dropped her bag on the floor with a thud.

"Oh, nothing. Just Kate being brutally honest with me." Caroline shook her head. "Okay, everyone start working on these flash cards Kate has been going through. I am going to work on finding the answers to the next round of questions."

"Man, Caroline, I'm so happy you're in this class with us. Actually, my mom is so happy you're here." Kelli swirled her Starbucks Frappuccino in its glass jar and laughed. "I would have flunked both tests without our study groups. She actually said she wants to meet you."

"Your mom?"

"Mm-hmm," Kelli nodded. "She said, 'This Caroline woman may make it possible for you to graduate and get a job. I need to meet her.'"

"My God," Caroline breathed as realization slammed into her. "I'm a legit college student. I even live with my daughter."

"Not the same," Michael said with a wave. "You raised her. She owes you."

"Oh, is that it?"

All three of them nodded and said, "Yes," enthusiastically. Caroline chuckled at her friends.

Friends.

The word stuck awkwardly in her throat. She never imagined her life taking the turn it had, but she was finding her groove again with her newfound friends, even though all three were significantly younger than her. Instead of making her feel inferior, their age difference was helping her in ways she didn't anticipate. She rediscovered the vein of confidence within herself she had no idea vanished. She found it strange considering how assertive she always needed to be in her old life. Surviving the entire ordeal, from being shot to being left by her husband, she never realized how deeply she buried a very important part of herself. Her new friends helped her find the part of herself that helped her survive in the first place.

She also knew, regardless of their age difference, they were all equals in the classroom. That part alone was reason enough to get their respect, and in turn, their admiration. Even if it was only because she was helping them get As, Caroline didn't care. She was finally enjoying life again, and school again, after struggling to find her footing. Knowing she'd figured everything out felt fantastic.

Well, almost everything. Not the damn writing class.

"I mean, I'm really glad we don't need help with writing, though." Kate nudged Caroline's elbow, a teasing smile displayed. "If you let me help you, maybe you'd be okay?"

Caroline sighed. "I don't think anything is going to help me. I'm actually planning on dropping it and retaking it next semester with a different prof."

"Oh no, Caroline, don't drop it. I think you can still pull out a great grade." Kate's pout was almost cute. "You're not doing bad."

"I have a D. You have a B. I'm doing awful. And, not to sound like a horrible person, but I really don't understand how you're getting a better grade than me."

"Are you saying I'm stupid?" Kate's mouth fell open.

"Stop." Caroline rolled her eyes. "You know what I mean."

"Well, it's probably because…" Michael's voice trailed off, and he glanced around the lobby where they were studying. The floor-to-ceiling windows were facing the Red Rock Mountains and, more specifically, the peak called Snoopy Rock. The formation was hard to see unless you really looked, but the outline looked like Snoopy lying on his back. The peak was one of Caroline's favorites for no other reason than she loved *Peanuts* as a child. Snoopy Rock made her feel as if she was coming home, even though her home was almost seventeen hundred miles away.

"Because what?" Kate was holding the very worn flash cards again. "Spit it out."

"I'm making sure we're alone." Michael whispered. He shifted in his chair, leaned forward, and looked at each of them for one whole second before settling his dark eyes on Caroline. "I did some recon and…she basically slept with a student before."

Kate let out a laugh that echoed throughout the empty lobby. Caroline felt her stomach drop.

"No way," Kelli whispered.

"Yeah, no way," Caroline echoed even though her brain was already believing it. "How do you 'basically' sleep with someone, first of all?"

Michael shrugged.

"I mean, what does that even mean?"

"I don't know, but I swear. I heard it was while she was in grad school as a TA. But it happened. My source confirmed it."

"Who is your source?"

"Well, interestingly enough, the pitching coach." Michael pushed his hair away from his face and sat back in his chair as if proud he had this knowledge and was imparting his wisdom upon them. "I asked him about her, because, well..." He cleared his throat. "She's kinda hot."

"Jesus." Caroline rolled her eyes. "Seriously?"

His indignant look was quite comical. "Yes. God. Either way, I'm telling you, he wasn't lying. He said she's a total hard-ass because if she messes up, she'll get her tenure reviewed. One of the old school profs can't stand her, I guess. He's always trying to bury her." Michael shrugged and picked his pencil up. He twirled it and flipped it over each of his fingers with ease. He drummed out a quick beat on the table before he finished with, "So, now you know why she treats you differently."

"I'm confused." Caroline glared at him. "Explain."

"I think he's saying she wants to fuck you."

Caroline gasped as she snapped her head toward Kelli, who was seated on her right. "What the hell are you talking about?" If they were right, everything made sense. Every exchange. Every poor grade. Every negative comment. Every caught glance. Every. Single. Thing.

"That is what I'm saying." Michael shrugged and drummed his pencil on the table again, this time beatboxing in unison.

"No." Caroline checked over each shoulder before she cut through the air with both hands. "We are not talking about this any longer. You all are going to flunk the communications test tomorrow, and I won't even care."

Michael flashed his megawatt smile. "You think any of us care about the damn test? I, for one, want to discuss your apparent disgust over a woman wanting to fuck you." He leaned forward, waggling his eyebrows. "Care to elaborate?"

"Absolutely not."

"Come on, Caroline." Kate pushed the forgotten flash cards to the side. "Let's talk."

"You all can kiss my ass." Caroline did a sweeping gesture and pointed at each of them.

Kate let out a small "Even me?"

"Yes, especially you."

"Harsh," she whispered but smiled as she leaned forward. "Is it because she's a woman?"

"I am not talking about this."

"Or is it because she's a dick to you?" Kate propped her chin on her palm. She pushed her glasses to the top of her head.

Caroline couldn't suppress her exasperated groan. "You all are worse than children." She watched as they nodded. Michael and Kelli copied Kate's posture, the palms of their hands wedged under their chins, dreamy smiles on all three of their faces. "She is purposely rude to me." Caroline sighed. "Even after our mentoring session, when she seemed like maybe she was going to turn a corner, she was rude to me at the pub. I don't know how to handle her—" She pulled a breath into her mouth. "I mean, I don't know how to handle this. All of this, which really isn't worth talking about." She found herself not able to tear her eyes away from the spiral binding on her notebook, dwelling on the way she'd felt when Dr. Morris stood and left her sitting at the table in the pub. The whole scene devastated her even though she'd provoked every single thing. She was not a quitter, at all, but after the other night, she wanted to drop all her classes and never go back.

"Oh shit."

"Yeah, oh shit. Perfect reaction." Caroline swallowed the lump which had formed.

"No," Kate whispered. "No."

"What?"

"Shut up."

"What are you talking about?" Caroline looked over to where Kate's eyes were focused, and her stomach once again fell to the floor. "Oh *shit*."

Michael and Kelli looked, and their "oh shit" responses were whispered as they all looked back at their notebooks. "Act busy. Act busy." Michael hurried and picked up his highlighter but lost his grip and flung it across the room. Caroline watched as it flew across the lobby and slid across the floor to stop right in front of Dr. Morris and Professor Higgins as they stood and finished a conversation.

"Ass," Caroline hissed as she glared at Michael. He snickered while Kate and Kelli held back laughter. Michael's head was bent, and he was acting as though his notes held the secrets to the world.

"Mr. Jones, your highlighter." The very sound of Dr. Morris's voice slicing through the snickers of her classmates was enough to make the hairs on the back of Caroline's neck stand. Her entire body erupted in chills. She refused to make eye contact, afraid she'd crack under Dr. Morris's icy stare. Everything was starting to make sense as to why this professor made her feel as if she was a teenager again. The very thought of Dr. Morris being mean to her because she was protecting herself was making it harder and harder for Caroline to continue to hate her. Even though the last exchange she'd had with Dr. Morris in class on Monday was enough to make her shut up and not ask another question for the remainder of the program, she still felt a pull to the cold professor. She was so confused. She was starting to question her very existence.

Michael grabbed the highlighter. "Thank you. Sorry, it slipped."

"It's fine." Dr. Morris's words were so succinct.

"Are you all studying for my test tomorrow?" Professor Higgins seemed ecstatic. "I'm so happy to see you taking it so seriously, especially you, Caroline. You're doing so well in class."

Caroline felt Professor Higgins's hand on her shoulder, so she glanced up at her. "It's a really great class. I'm enjoying it immensely."

"I'm glad. Not as much as Dr. Morris's class, I'm sure." Professor Higgins smiled. "I've heard you're quite the writer, Caroline."

Caroline's eyes snapped back to Professor Higgins. "What?"

"Yep, Dr. Morris here has showed me some of your work."

Caroline felt her brow furrowing as she focused a glare on Dr. Morris. "Oh really?"

Professor Higgins cleared her throat. "She sure has." Caroline saw the way Professor Higgins looked at Dr. Morris, the emotion in her eyes, the small smile on her lips. "She's a tough grader, though."

"Yeah, she really is." Caroline kept her eyes locked on Dr. Morris, who clearly couldn't handle how Professor Higgins was throwing her under the bus.

"Okay, well, we'll leave you kids to it." Dr. Morris looped her arm through the crook of Professor Higgins's and started to walk away, pulling the entire time.

"Kids?" Caroline asked when Dr. Morris was out of earshot. She looked at her classmates. "*Kids?*"

Michael laughed. He tossed his highlighter into the air and caught it expertly. "I'm so smooth."

"You did that on purpose, didn't you?"

He nodded and grinned, his straight teeth sparkling.

"You fucker."

Kelli let out a laugh. "Bro, you're awesome."

"Bro?" Caroline shook her head. "I hate you all."

"Even me?" Kate asked again, this time holding back laughter.

"Especially you."

Kate leaned over to Caroline and laid her head on her arm. "I love you, though."

"You still suck." Caroline let herself find the humor in the situation as they all started to pack their bags. She was trying to not focus on the new information she'd discovered. There was too much truth to handle right now. As she said her good-byes to her classmates and started the drive toward her daughter's house, she found her mind wandering.

What if the rumor was true about Dr. Morris?

Caroline knew she needed to keep her distance. Get through the next four weeks and hope she passed the class with a C.

Or...

She could get the A she deserved.

In whatever way possible.

CHAPTER NINE

"The trivia guy canceled tonight." Caroline placed a glass in front of a customer at the bar. "He said he had something come up. I don't know."

"Aw man, that stinks." The guy slapped the bar top after his whiney comment. "We were so excited. We're visiting from out of state and wanted to do something fun."

"Yeah, you're like the fifteenth person who's upset. I'm really sorry. Will be you around next Thursday?"

"Unfortunately, no." The guy's wife sighed. "We wish we could stay forever."

"Yeah, Sedona sort of gets under your skin. The people, the mountains, everything." Caroline wiped the bar with a wet rag and moved to the next customer. "What can I get you?" She listened to the woman's order, then typed it into the computer. She heard someone pull out a stool at the end of the bar where no one was sitting. When she saw it was none other than Dr. Morris, her stomach plummeted to the floor.

She looked back at the computer screen as quickly as possible, hoping it wasn't obvious that Dr. Morris's presence took her breath away. As busy as the bar got sometimes, this was the only moment she wished she had a partner to help because the last thing she wanted to do was be cordial to her professor. A professor who continued to treat her terribly. So terribly that instead of putting herself through the uncomfortable mentoring session earlier in the day, Caroline had skipped it altogether. She didn't call; she didn't email. The words "fuck it" rolled around her brain more than a couple times, but all of her courage and pigheadedness was insignificant considering the fear she felt in the moment.

She raised a finger at Dr. Morris and started to pour the other customer's merlot. The sound of the wine slugging into the glass wasn't nearly loud enough to drown out her heart beating in her eardrums. The impending doom at the other end of the bar was causing her hands to shake. Caroline slid the glass in front of the woman, spun expertly toward Dr. Morris, and plastered on the fakest smile she'd ever had to muster. "What can I get you?"

"A vodka soda with a lime." Caroline nodded, but before she could turn and escape, Dr. Morris also said, "And an explanation as to why you skipped our mentoring session today."

Caroline froze, but her wheels were turning. "I had to cover for my coworker last minute." Years of having to think on her feet as a trauma nurse helped tremendously when it came to being put on the spot. "Dog was sick."

"Oh really?" Dr. Morris's eyebrow arched, and her eyes seemed to almost sparkle behind her glasses. This pair was made of clear plastic and looked even better on her than the other two. Why, oh why, did everything about this unbearable woman affect Caroline so intensely?

Caroline nodded, offered a gentle "mm-hmm" and hurried away. She made the drink as fast as she could, squeezed the lime, then anchored it on the side of the glass. She set the glass on the bar top along with the folded receipt.

"Assuming that's all I'm going to drink? Doesn't seem like a good business strategy."

Caroline felt herself glaring, so she relaxed her forehead and shrugged. "I'm not assuming. It's all I'm allowing you to drink."

Dr. Morris's mouth fell open the tiniest of bits, and Caroline felt a sense of accomplishment. But it was short-lived when her eyes caught the pub owner walking in. He strutted over to Dr. Morris and smacked his burly hand on her shoulder.

"Atlanta Morris. What the hell are you doing here?"

The stunned look on Dr. Morris's face was child's play compared to the look Caroline imagined was on her own. *Are you fucking kidding me? What are the odds?*

"Holy shit, Todd, how the hell have you been?" Dr. Morris stood and hugged Todd. Their loud smacks on each other's backs were enough to make Caroline wonder if Dr. Morris would throw her under the bus for not being very hospitable. She'd get fired for sure. Todd was a great boss, but his one rule was "always treat the customers as if they are family." The more she thought about it, though, collecting unemployment didn't sound all bad. She'd have more time to study. *Go on, Dr. Morris, rev up the bus engine.*

She walked away from them but not before Todd held his hand out and said, "You've met my newest bartender? Caroline, all the way from Chicago. The Windy City. She's amazing, isn't she? Can you believe she's never bartended before?" He smiled. "Caroline, you're doing great. I was talking to Max, and he said he's never been happier with one of our hires."

Caroline laughed. "Are you serious?"

"I am." The sound of Todd's boisterous laugh shot a bolt of fear straight into Caroline's gut. Who was she trying to kid? She needed this job. If Dr. Morris ruined this… Caroline moved her gaze from Todd to Dr. Morris and waited for her answer.

"We have met, actually. She's definitely a keeper."

Whoa, whoa, whoa. What was that now?

"She's way better than a few of those guys you have down at the Culinary Dropout in Phoenix."

Todd laughed again. "Jesus fucking Christ, tell me about it. I swear."

"How do you two know—"

"College, Denver; she was going through all her TA bullshit, and I was young and in need of older gay friends."

"Oh, so you knew Dr. Morris when she was actually a nice person?" Caroline heard the words come out of her mouth and felt instant regret. *Here comes the bus, full speed ahead…thump, thump.* Until she saw the hint of a smile on Dr. Morris's face, she didn't think she was going to survive whatever was going to happen.

"Joke's on you." Dr. Morris raised her glass, sipped, then pointed at Caroline. "I have never been a nice person."

"I'm shocked."

"So." Todd paused and cleared his throat. "You two know each other well?"

Dr. Morris never took her eyes from Caroline's face. "She's in my English class this summer at the community center."

"Ah." Todd looked at Dr. Morris, then back at Caroline. As if a lightbulb went off over his head, he widened his eyes and said, "Oh!" He slid a barstool out and sat next to Dr. Morris. "I'll take a Great White ale, Caroline, and keep them coming, please."

Caroline couldn't help but chuckle. She knew what the lightbulb meant. Dr. Morris was going to get questioned. And it was going to be very fun to watch from afar.

❖

"Okay, now can we talk?" Atlanta waited for Caroline to look up from wiping down the bar top. "Did you hear me?" She slid onto a new stool closer to the middle of the bar. Todd had finally stopped talking Atlanta's ears off and left, mumbling something about finding a Lyft on his way out. The bar had cleared out, leaving only two other customers seated at a booth far enough away that it had to be annoying for Caroline. She kept up the great service, though, and never seemed to get angry or flustered. Not even when they spilled an entire pitcher of beer. Atlanta was impressed. She would have never been good in the service industry.

"I heard you." Caroline was washing glasses, and as hard as she tried, Atlanta couldn't stop herself from looking straight down the light gray V-neck she was wearing. Was Caroline wearing a black bra? *Atlanta, pull yourself together.* Caroline finally glanced up into her eyes. "What do you want to talk about?" Restraint was a luxury she thankfully could afford, but damn, Atlanta wanted so badly to reach forward and gently brush Caroline's bangs away from her eyes. The vodka sodas Todd had kept ordering her were not helping matters at all.

"Why you really skipped the mentoring session."

"Sick dog. Remember?"

Atlanta watched her finish with the last few glasses, then turn the washers off and wipe her hands. "Caroline." Atlanta took a deep breath when their eyes locked again. "Will it help at all if I apologize?"

"No. Not really." Caroline's answer was so matter-of-fact it caused Atlanta's breath to snag in her throat. She watched Caroline's facial expression, watched as she finally moved her bangs from her eyes with the back of her hand, watched the way she steadied herself with the sturdiness of the bar top. All Atlanta wanted to do was crash through the brick wall she'd made Caroline build, but so far, there wasn't even a crack in the mortar. Caroline shrugged. "Four more weeks and you never have to deal with my horrible sentence construction again."

The thought those words provoked made Atlanta's hands ache. "Is that really what you think I think?"

Caroline let out a puff of air. "I'm cutting you off." Caroline reached for the almost empty glass. Atlanta took a huge risk by gently laying her hand on Caroline's forearm. Caroline's eyes moved up to Atlanta. She looked shocked, maybe a little scared, and right below the surface was something else entirely.

"Come to a session tomorrow." She studied Caroline. Was she considering a response? Or was she going to bat away the olive branch? Caroline blinked, swallowed once. She didn't break eye contact, which calmed Atlanta's nerves somewhat. "I have an opening at ten." She loosened her grip, but Caroline still stood frozen. "I would really like it if you gave me another chance." Her entire body filled with heat, leaving her cheeks on fire. *Oh God, please don't let my nervous splotches appear.*

"Thanks, but…" Caroline paused. She looked as if she was coming up with a lie. "I'd love to say I have to work, but I don't want to lie."

The sense of relief flooding Atlanta's being was as intense as anything she'd ever experienced. "Great. I'll see you then."

"I didn't say I'd be there."

"You just said—"

"I said I wasn't going to lie."

"So?"

"I'm not going to come in. Thank you, but I think I've had enough mentoring." Caroline's eye contact didn't falter.

Atlanta didn't know what to say. She'd really messed up. Not only was she never going to have a chance, but if Caroline went to the dean…

A wave of nausea washed over Atlanta. She hoped it was the alcohol, but she knew better. "Can I get…my, uh…my check?"

"You don't have one."

"You didn't have to—"

"Believe me, I didn't. Todd got it."

Wow. How the roles had reversed. "Oh." Now Caroline held the power? What the hell was Atlanta going to do to remedy the situation? She fished around her wallet and pulled out a twenty. She placed it faceup on the bar top and stood. "Have a good night." And she left, hoping like hell she wasn't stumbling.

CHAPTER TEN

"Tell me why you're making me go to this again?"

Sheri groaned as Molly pulled into a parking spot off the main thoroughfare in the touristy area of Sedona. "Because you've been unbearable lately, and we all want to have some fun." They were dragging Atlanta to the Fourth of July Music and Arts Festival.

"Me? I've been unbearable?"

"Yes, you." Molly slammed the door of her Kia and whipped around to face Atlanta, who stood flabbergasted. "Stop being such a fucking stick in the mud. You're allowed to have fun." Atlanta looked exasperatedly from Molly to Sheri, who had nothing to offer but a shrug as she turned toward the festival.

Live music was coming from a block or so away, and the smell of fried food filled the warm afternoon air. As the three of them walked, Atlanta took in the blue sky. There wasn't a cloud to be found, and the contrast between the sky and the red rock of the mountains was striking. The afternoon was gorgeous, and thankfully, it would cool down a bit as the sun continued to set. She hated to admit it—because she absolutely did not want to leave her happy, cozy condo in Phoenix—but Sedona calmed her in a way no other place had. There was something to be said about its spiritual energy…whether she believed in it or not. She'd always felt on edge and ready to explode, but here in the beautiful mountains, she felt as if maybe she could take a breath. Breathing easily was not normal. At all. She was forever on the verge of a breakdown. Trying to contain herself and color within the lines that had been drawn for her was hard, and it made everything about her life much more stressful.

Her friends were right: She was allowed to have fun, to see the sights, to experience this amazing place. The festival was the perfect opportunity. The streets were lined with kiosks filled to the brim with produce, baked goods, bouquets of flowers, and fresh honey. There were also quite a few vendors selling homemade jewelry, clothing, and home goods.

"This is exactly what I needed," Atlanta said when Sheri steered them in the direction of a frozen lemonade stand.

"See? I told you it would be fine. You're always so high-strung. Chill out. Take in this place. I swear it's done wonders for me." Molly handed over a twenty and paid for their lemonades. "And I think Rick Springfield is going to perform tonight."

"Shut up."

"I swear."

Atlanta laughed. "I love Rick." She felt herself getting lighter as they made their way from kiosk to kiosk. She purchased peaches and tomatoes from an older couple who'd retired to Sedona fifteen years ago from Indiana. They were so nice and generous. She looked through jewelry stand after jewelry stand until she found a beautiful pair of earrings, which she purchased from a tiny Yavapai woman who was wrinkled and worn but sweet as could be.

The three of them found a shady area on the side of the road where they sat on the curb. Sheri munched away on a plate full of fried vegetables, Molly drank her third frozen lemonade, and Atlanta kept stealing a bite and a drink of both.

"You know, I almost slept with a student once." Molly was still holding the straw between her teeth as she spoke. "Third year of teaching. Listen, I'm not proud of this." Molly let go of the straw, sighed, waved her hand through the air as if swatting a bug. "Whatever, though. Stupidity happens. His name was Tony Scarpelli and damn, he was cute."

"Molly, are you kidding?" Sheri's question was full of disbelief.

Molly nodded. "That year was crazy. But I got through it. You want to know how?"

"Is this where I answer yes?" Atlanta sighed.

"I lived my life. I didn't bottle everything up and act like a hard-ass all the time. I get it's how you think you need to be in order to survive, but it's not doing anything for you." Molly popped a piece of fried cauliflower into her mouth. "I didn't sleep with him, but…" Molly started with her mouth full. She swallowed and shrugged. "I probably should have."

"Stop," Atlanta said before letting out a deep sigh. "This isn't only about sleeping with a student. I can't…" She closed her eyes, took another deep breath, and let it out slowly. "I'm a mess, I guess. I don't even know where to begin."

"Do you want my opinion?"

"Not really." Atlanta glanced at Sheri as she rolled her eyes.

"Well, you're gonna get it anyway." She finished off the remaining fried mushrooms. "I think part of your problem is you really like Caroline Stevens, and you know you shouldn't."

Atlanta sighed again.

"And I think you know you can't do anything with her. Those conflicting emotions are causing you to feel super heavy here," Sheri placed her hand over her own heart and then her forehead, "and here. You need to figure it out because you cannot keep doing this back and forth."

"I'm trying to keep her at arm's length. Risking everything for someone I know nothing about is so dumb."

"Well, yeah, you're right. But maybe eventually you could?"

"What do you mean?"

"She's done after eight weeks. She's out. She's free. I mean, as long as she passes her classes." Molly nudged her. "She's a really cool lady, and she's insanely good at math."

Atlanta laughed. "You're such a geek."

"I know, I know." Molly took her sunglasses from her head and folded the arm over the neck of her shirt. "I think Sheri is right. And I never agree with her."

"This is so true." Sheri nudged Atlanta on the other side. "Just figure it out, okay?"

"You act like it's so fucking easy."

"Well, shouldn't it be? Find someplace where breathing is easier and pull some of this pure mountain air into those lungs." Sheri wrapped her arm around Atlanta's shoulders and squeezed. "Okay?"

Atlanta nodded, tried to smile, and looked toward the horizon. Clouds had started to form, which would lead to a spectacular sunset. As she started to open her mouth to suggest going to watch it down the street by the Pink Jeep Tours building, she heard Sheri gasp. "What?" She followed Sheri's line of sight to none other than Caroline Stevens. "Welp, there goes my plan to breathe."

"Stop. This is a perfect opportunity to bury the hatchet." Molly stood quickly. "Well, bury it *again*."

"Are you serious?"

"Yes." Sheri stood as well and held her hand out to Atlanta. "In through the nose, out through the mouth. Smell the roses, blow out the candles."

"Funny."

"Let's go."

Atlanta reluctantly stood and followed Sheri and Molly the ten feet or so over to Caroline. She was standing with people and looked relaxed, as if nothing in the world was bothering her. She was pushing a stroller, making Atlanta's heart swell, which was so crazy because she wasn't a huge fan of kids. As they approached, Caroline turned and smiled at Sheri and Molly. She looked shocked, and it was more obvious when she pushed her glasses to the top of her head. She had minimal makeup on, and her hair was pulled back, even her bangs.

"Oh goodness, Dr. Wright, Professor Higgins. What a surprise." Her smile was forced but gorgeous, and when she finally looked at Atlanta, she nodded. "Dr. Morris."

The feelings passing through Atlanta's mind as Caroline engaged in conversation with Sheri and Molly were hard to describe. A mixture of happiness, regret, fear, lust, swirled as if caught in a tornado. As Caroline stood there in short khaki shorts and a loose white tank top, Atlanta knew she was going to have far more to regret and fear than she ever thought possible. Because she felt herself making a decision. She was going to mend fences. She was going to stop the sadness she caused with her bitchy attitude. And she was going to turn on the charm.

"And this little guy here is my grandson, Oden." Caroline pushed the stroller forward a bit and looked down at her smiling boy. "This is my daughter, Samantha, and son-in-law, Andrew. These are my professors."

"Oh, it's so nice to meet you all. My mom has nothing but great things to say." Samantha smiled broadly. Caroline watched Samantha's eyes as they landed on each professor and how they changed entirely when she looked at Dr. Morris. Samantha had heard all the stories about Dr. Morris, so it came as no surprise to Caroline when her daughter couldn't control her glare. "Mom, we'll take Oden. You can have some adult time."

"Honey, thank you, but it's totally not necessary." Caroline felt her heartbeat start to race. She in no way wanted to be trapped with these women, especially Dr. Morris.

"Come on, Caroline." Sheri smiled. "You can join us for the Rick Springfield concert."

"Oh, fun." Samantha's sarcasm was hard to miss. She winked and pulled the stroller toward her. "Don't be too late, Mom." Samantha chuckled as she whisked the stroller down the street with Andrew following her.

"She thinks she's a real comedienne." Caroline shook her head as they all laughed. "Professors, Dr. Morris, it's so crazy running into you all here. How was the market?"

"Okay, whoa, whoa, whoa. I refuse to hang out with you today and also be referred to as Professor the entire time, so stop right this instant. I'm Molly, this is Sheri, and obviously, this is Atlanta." Molly shuddered as she ran her hand through her hair. "I hate the professor title sometimes—like, what exactly do I profess? Fucking math? It's so boring."

Caroline laughed while nodding. "Okay, okay. I will definitely drop the titles."

"Good. Yeah, so anyway, the market…"

Sheri shook her head while chuckling. "Molly is a trip."

"Oh, stop." Molly waved her hand, the bracelets she wore clanging together. "Everything's been awesome, Caroline. I bought way too many knickknacks. Atlanta bought a very cool pair of earrings and is gonna breathe more."

Caroline locked her eyes on Dr. Morris. *Atlanta…* No. She refused to call her Atlanta. Not until these awkward feelings dissipated. *If they ever did…* Dr. Morris also seemed awkward, uncomfortable, as if everything inside her was struggling. "Sounds like really good advice," she said as she let her eyes wander over Dr. Morris's facial features, her eyelashes behind her glasses, her nose ring, her hair, the beads of perspiration along her hairline, the way her clothes clung to her body. How could entirely too short ripped jean shorts and a linen shirt with colorful birds embroidered on the chest be *sexy*? Hell, everything about her was sexy, including the way Caroline could see through the fucking linen shirt. She groaned internally. She could not understand what her brain was doing, where it was going, and why it was going there. But she also didn't want to stop…Because stopping would mean everything she was feeling was wrong, everything she was questioning was wrong, everything she was thinking was wrong. Wasn't it wrong, though? She knew she shouldn't be in this spot with these thoughts with this woman, but dammit, everything about Dr. Atlanta Morris was causing Caroline to question every thought, every feeling, every quiver.

And to make matters worse, she was still wearing those damn Birkenstocks. Caroline hated those sandals.

She knew it was a little insane to find someone such as Dr. Morris attractive for two reasons.

One, and most important, she was a woman. While Caroline had definitely found other women attractive throughout her life, she'd only acted on those feelings in college after copious amounts of alcohol and weed. She was coupled with a man by her junior year, though, married right after graduation, and together with her husband for so long she never really watered the seed college planted. Now, though, the seed not only was being watered, but it must have been fed some fertilizer because it was growing as if it were a dandelion. And the meaner Dr. Morris was, the more she wanted to explore the world of lesbianism with her, which was scary and exciting and so very forbidden, especially because she was her professor.

As they all walked along the street, Molly and Sheri started asking hundreds of questions. How long had Caroline been divorced? Why did she move to Sedona? How old was her daughter? How long had they lived in Sedona? Where did she live before this? Didn't she love Chicago? Why would she want to leave such an amazing city? Why didn't she want to be a nurse any longer? Didn't she love it?

"Holy shit, you were *shot*?" Sheri gasped as they came to a stop near the stage for the concert. The live music was in full swing now, a local band by the name of the Mountain Jacksons. They were playing bluegrass, and it made Caroline relax a little. As she explained the circumstances behind the gunman, the wound, and why she wanted to get as far away as possible from the nursing field, she felt Dr. Morris's eyes on her. The sensation was freeing, a feeling she didn't anticipate.

Molly and Sheri launched into stories about their lives: why they wanted to escape the big city of Phoenix and exchange it for the red mountains of Sedona. They talked about spearheading the expansion, and how it was such a fun experience. They were both talking nonstop, and Caroline noticed Dr. Morris wasn't saying much. After their encounter last week, after the hours and hours and hours of obsessing, after the endless nights of little to no sleep and the intense dreams Caroline found herself having almost every night, she decided to not give up so easily. She'd made her point by not letting her guard down with Dr. Morris at the pub, but now it was time to be the adult. Time to see if those fine lines appearing were really a crack in her cold-as-ice exterior or if this was an elaborate ploy to crush Caroline's spirit once more. "What about you, Dr. Morris? Are you enjoying Sedona?"

Dr. Morris cleared her throat, and Caroline noticed how her eyes flitted to Sheri and Molly before they locked on to hers. "I really am. Sedona seems to have its own personality. I really love the idea of a town having soul. This one really seems to. Also, fortunately, I have a very awesome rental the college is footing the bill for."

"Yeah, the college really went all out." Sheri smiled. "Especially for this one. You should see the view."

"I bet it's amazing."

"I can see the sunrise every morning from my bed. It's incredible. Also, please, it's Atlanta." She smiled, and the sight really did take Caroline's breath away. "Call me Atlanta. I mean, since we aren't in class." She leaned into Caroline's space and winked. Caroline wasn't sure if she should laugh, smile, wink back, or run away screaming. She was completely bowled over. Dr. Morris said to call her Atlanta, and *did she really fucking wink at me?*

Before Caroline could obsess, the moment was over. The announcer came running onto the stage and started to pump up the crowd for Rick Springfield. The four of them started to hoot and holler for Rick, and when the first chords of "Jessie's Girl" rang through the streets, they all started to scream like teenagers. Caroline was having so much fun. She wasn't sure if it was too good to be true or not but decided to not worry about it. To live in the moment for once instead of thinking about the worst that could happen. Getting back to the easy-breezy attitude she used to have was difficult, but she knew she could do it. Stress caused by a traumatic event was not fun to deal with. The new environment, talking to people about what happened, hearing their words of encouragement, and seeing she wasn't damaged goods anymore was helping.

About halfway through the third song, a stirring cover of Katy Perry's "Firework," Caroline felt a hand wrap around her arm.

"Will you come with me? I want to get a drink," Atlanta said as she leaned into Caroline's space. Her face and mouth were entirely too close for comfort.

She did as she was asked and followed Atlanta through the crowd. The evening was beautiful: warm air, stars littering the night sky, and the sound of Rick serenading them.

"Do you want something?"

"Just a water." Caroline eyed Atlanta from the side as she raised to tiptoe to order out of the food and drink truck. Her calf muscles flexed, and the outline of her hamstring was visible. Caroline allowed her eyes to roam up Atlanta's backside, which looked so good in those shorts. Caroline closed her eyes, turned her head, and stifled a chuckle. How had she lived her entire life and never had these feelings about a woman before? Did this really happen? This late-in-life bullshit was for the birds. Figuring it all out now was confusing as hell.

She looked back at Atlanta as she paid. Her braid was hanging down her back, her nose and full lips in profile as she smiled and reached for the change, her drink, and Caroline's water. Everything about this woman was turning Caroline on, almost to the point of needing release, and if it continued, she was going to do something really stupid.

Or really smart, depending on how one looked at it.

Because there was no doubt in her mind it would be incredible. The sheer number of different ways she imagined it unfolding was laughable. Jesus, how many times had she thought about Dr. Atlanta Morris? At least a hundred, and every single time it left her breathless. Hands all over and mouths roaming, teeth biting, hair pulling, and clothes being flung in all different directions.

Caroline shook her head and bit the inside of her cheek so hard she almost drew blood. She needed to get her shit together. She was horny and lonely. She didn't really have feelings for this unbearable woman. No way. No how.

"Here you go," Atlanta said, as she turned and held out a water.

In a moment of pure boldness, Caroline reached for Atlanta's beer. She took a long drink from the plastic cup. She kept her eyes glued to Atlanta's the entire time; she didn't seem fazed at all.

She either had a great poker face or...the alternative...she wasn't fazed. At all. *Please God, don't let it be the case.* Caroline handed the beer back and took her water. "Thank you."

When Atlanta arched her eyebrow over the rim of her tortoiseshell glasses, Caroline thought maybe, just maybe, she really was affected. She brought the cup to her lips and drank. Caroline wished she was that cup, that beer...

"Fuck," she whispered, realizing not only had the word come out of her mouth, but Atlanta heard her.

"You okay?" Atlanta still had her beer raised when she asked, and the way her eyes were shining made something inside Caroline know she was not alone with these feelings. Not in the slightest.

She nodded and, then again without thinking said, "Would you get out of here with me?"

Caroline watched as Atlanta's key slid into the lock of the door to her rental. From the outside, the house was small, but it absolutely fit Atlanta's style. Especially when she opened the door to an open living area with wooden beams on the ceiling, slate floors, and an immaculate kitchen with a light turquoise backsplash, stainless steel farmhouse sink, and cement countertops. "This place is incredible," Caroline said as she ran a hand over the kitchen island. She crossed the living area with its brown leather couch, floor-to-ceiling bookshelves, and a large flat-screen TV mounted above the fireplace to the huge sliding glass door. She unlocked and slid it open, then walked outside to the wooden deck, which looked west to the red mountains. She breathed deep as she braced against the railing and closed her eyes. She took the couple seconds of alone time to center herself and settle down. She was so far outside her comfort zone, and trying to keep up the facade was stressful, but she was not about to chicken out now. She could do this. She could be put together, fun, spontaneous, and interested in a woman. Couldn't she?

She heard Atlanta approach, and when she appeared in Caroline's peripheral, she was holding a glass of white wine in each hand. After Caroline accepted, they clinked them together. She watched Atlanta sip the drink. Her lips weren't ridiculously full, but damn, they looked luscious against the clear glass. She finally pulled her eyes away before she sipped from her own glass. She wanted to smack herself. What was she doing? A week ago, she hated this woman.

Hell, who was she kidding? She'd never hated Atlanta. *Never.* She was intrigued by her from the moment she laid eyes on her in class: Atlanta's dark hair, brown eyes, light pink lips, glasses, tattoos, everything. The feeling was so intense it had become hard to ignore.

"I need to tell you something." Atlanta's voice broke through Caroline's thoughts, and she looked over as she leaned against the railing of the deck. Her shirt had shifted over her shoulder, exposing her bra and bare skin and *sweet Jesus, she looks sexy...* "I am so sorry for how I've treated you."

A silence fell around them, and it made a chill shoot through Caroline from her toes to the top of her head. She didn't know what to say. Should she respond? Should she say it was no big deal? Because she'd be lying. Everything Atlanta had done was a big deal to Caroline. A huge deal causing her to feel awful, insignificant, and worst of all, stupid.

"You do not deserve it at all." A small smile started on Atlanta's lips. "You are a brilliant writer. I need you to know that."

Caroline felt the emotion rise into her throat and lodge there. The compliment was all she ever wanted to hear: her words were worthy of something other than disdain and horrible marks. "Why, then?" She finally found her voice.

"Do you want me to be honest?"

"Why would I want you to lie?"

Atlanta laughed a small, soft chuckle, and it sounded amazing against the quiet backdrop of the night. "Good point." She turned and leaned against the railing. Atlanta locked her eyes on hers, which caused another chill to zip through her. "I am very, very attracted to you. And truthfully, I cannot be."

Her heart was beating so hard, she was sure Atlanta had to be able to hear it. Was this really happening? Her classmates were right.

"I don't expect you to do anything with this information." Atlanta held a shaky hand out, clenched it into a fist as if to hide the nerves, and half sighed, half laughed. Caroline hated and loved how adorable Atlanta looked: her eyes and the way she pushed her glasses back up the bridge of her nose with a gentle nudge of her fingers. "I'm really sorry. I didn't mean to make you uncomfortable."

"No," Caroline said, then realized it made no sense, so she waved her hand. "No, no. I mean, you didn't make me uncomfortable at all." She didn't sound convincing, so she took a step closer. "I promise."

"Okay." Atlanta focused on her glass.

"Look, I mean, of course it's a little shocking. I'm straight. Or at least…I think I am. I don't know." She was fumbling this entire conversation. She wanted to cut the scene, rewind, and start over. She glanced down at her own glass and swirled it gently. "I don't know what I want anymore."

"Caroline?"

"Hmm?" She kept her eyes on her drink, not because she was embarrassed, but because looking back up into Atlanta's eyes was going to make it harder not to fall into this affair, which simply could not happen. Not now, not with a woman, and not with her professor. The entire situation was against every rule, everything she'd ever believed in, and everything she thought she was made up of.

"Can you look at me?"

Caroline heard the question and knew if she answered out loud, emotion was going to show, proving she was a hot mess, so she shook her head.

"Please."

Against her better judgment, she made herself look at Atlanta, who'd closed the distance between them.

Atlanta placed her glass on the railing; the sound of it clunking against the wood was almost deafening. "I won't do anything. I promise."

The simple promise should have made Caroline feel better. She should have heaved a huge sigh of relief because it meant no forbidden affair, no need to tread carefully, no need to fear getting into trouble or getting Atlanta into trouble.

But the relief didn't come.

Instead, it made her heart sink so hard and so fast her stomach bottomed out, and her legs felt so weak, she wondered if she should lunge forward and make the first move. She could be the brave one. She could be the one who crossed the line that couldn't be uncrossed. She knew now Atlanta would follow her over the line, so why not? Why not throw caution to the wind and say fuck it and live life? She knew better than anyone how quickly life could be taken away.

But instead... "I should probably go," she heard herself say.

"Yeah." Atlanta's voice was barely a whisper. "I'll walk you to the door."

Caroline panicked as she walked through the living area toward the front door.

Turn around!

Stop and turn around and kiss her.

Be the person you've always been.

Fearless and assertive and fun and spontaneous.

When they got to the door, Atlanta opened it. "I'll see you in class on Monday."

Caroline nodded as she walked outside, then heard the door latch. She was frozen in place. She knew she needed to keep moving. This couldn't happen. None of what they were doing was right, but why did it feel so fucking good? As she took a step toward the driveway, toward her car, toward home while plagued with the reality she'd chickened out, she heard the door open, felt Atlanta grab her hand, and allowed herself to turn.

Everything happened so quickly, there was no time to protest. When Atlanta's lips landed on hers, her entire world seemed to click into place. A life that went from wonderful to horrible with the speed of a bullet was somehow back to wonderful again. Every breath... every boyfriend and her marriage and divorce...every patient, dead or alive...every thought and bout with depression...every single thing led her here to this moment, to this night, to this woman.

Atlanta's tongue slid into her mouth, and the feeling was exhilarating. Caroline backed into the outside wall next to the front door. The stucco was rough against the bare skin of her shoulders, and the pressure on her left scapula caused it to ache, but she didn't care. She placed her hands on Atlanta's hips and pulled her closer. The feeling of Atlanta's hands on her face, on her neck, on the back of her head, fingers pressing into the base of her skull, up her cranium to her ponytail, was *such* a turn-on. She wondered if any kiss ever had done this to her. She was ready to die and be reborn, as if life would never be the same, and for that, she was thankful.

She heard Atlanta moan into her mouth and felt the vibrations reverberate against her lips, teeth, tongue. She knew this entire situation was going to go from zero to sixty very fast, and if Atlanta wanted her, then she was all in.

Wait.

What the fuck?

She was not all in. There was no way she could be all in. Atlanta was her professor and a woman, and the last time Caroline had sex, she had to fake an orgasm to get it over with. The reality of the situation slammed into her like a freight train. She pushed Atlanta away.

"Fuck," Atlanta whispered. "Fuck. I'm sorry."

"Don't. It's okay."

"No, I'm sorry. I shouldn't have—"

"Stop." Caroline straightened her shirt and wiped her lips with the back of her hand. "I participated, so it's as much my fault."

Atlanta took one step back, then another. She folded her arms across her chest. Her lips looked used, possibly even bruised, and Caroline felt the same feeling of desire spring to life inside her again.

"You should go." Atlanta's voice was so soft.

"Atlanta?" Caroline had fucked up. Regret replaced desire instantly. She could taste it like she could taste the wine on Atlanta's tongue.

Atlanta turned and walked back into the house, closing the door on Caroline again. Except this time, she didn't reopen it.

CHAPTER ELEVEN

S o, you're telling me I need to dig a little deeper?"
Atlanta leaned back in her chair. The second student she was
mentoring was asking a million and one questions, all pertaining to the
journal assignment.

That was due last week.

That the student still hadn't turned in.

That she was begging for extra time for.

That she didn't really deserve.

"I'm telling you I needed you to turn it in on time. It has nothing to
do with digging deeper." She knew she was being condescending. She
didn't care. "I don't think you understand the concept of a deadline."
She shrugged. "I'm not trying to be mean, but I'm not giving you an
extension. If I give you an extension, then I have to give every student
one."

"I think that's fair."

"Laura, seriously?" She laughed when Laura nodded. "Listen, you
can turn in the journals tomorrow, okay?" Laura's face lit up as she
leaned forward, clearly excited by her answer. "I will read them and
comment and give you half credit. Sorry, but it's good as I can do."

"You are awesome. Oh my God. This will help me so much."

Atlanta glanced at the clock on her wall. "Time's up. I'll see you
next week." She watched as Laura hurried out of her office, closing the
door behind her. Up next was Caroline, and it was making Atlanta's
stomach roll. They'd successfully avoided each other since the night of
the festival. Since the night of the kiss...the kiss that rocked Atlanta's
world in ways she'd never experienced before. At least a week had

passed with no contact whatsoever, and it was driving her a little crazy. She wanted so badly to see Caroline, to talk to her, to tell her how sorry she was for kissing her, for jumping the gun, for everything. She knew Caroline didn't want to see her, though. Considering she'd skipped class on Monday and was nowhere to be found during the weekly study session in the community center lobby, her feelings were being made fairly obvious.

The fact she knew Caroline's schedule was ridiculous. She took a deep breath, holding it while she counted to seven. She was so stupid to let herself get to this point with this woman. *Shit.* Forget it was with this woman. She was a goddamn student.

What the fuck was Atlanta thinking? She was out of her mind. She did not need the drama this was bound to cause. Caroline Stevens needed to go back to not mattering at all to Atlanta, which meant what? Treating her poorly again? Treating her as if she didn't matter? Even though she mattered so much it was frightening.

Caroline's latest piece of work, which she had emailed instead of handing in, wasn't anything exciting: a research paper about teaching nursing to high school students in a career center setting. The amazing part was it was so thought-out and wonderful that halfway through, she had to remind herself to actually grade it. Her hold on herself was slipping when it came to all facets surrounding Caroline, and losing her grip on reality simply could not happen. She had to work extra hard to stay on track with the curriculum of her class because she found herself wanting to assign writing assignments so she could read more of what was in Caroline's mind. She was kicking herself for caring and for wanting to know more. She needed to let this foolishness go. No good would come of this if they didn't keep themselves guarded.

When a gentle knock sounded on Atlanta's office door, she felt her heart start to beat faster. The door opened, and Caroline's head poked through the opening, her hair cascading over her shoulder. Atlanta knew then letting go was as likely as an *Armageddon*-style meteor strike.

Possible but highly unlikely.

"How was your math test?" Atlanta studied her as she sat and adjusted her reading glasses. She slid them to the top of her head, pushing her bangs away from her face. Caroline sighed and shrugged. Clearly, this was affecting her, as well. She'd not made eye contact since sitting down, and it was making Atlanta's throat ache. She wanted to look at her, tell her it was okay, she understood; it was the right thing to walk away from this. "Did it go well?"

"I think so?"

"Molly—I mean Dr. Wright—said you're doing very well." Atlanta waited for eye contact. When she still received none, she stood and walked to the small table across from her office, where she pulled a stack of papers from her bag. She handed them to Caroline. "These are your latest journals." Caroline grabbed the papers. Still no eye contact. The papers wrinkled in her hand from being held tightly, and Atlanta wished she could take back the kiss even though it was one of the best kisses she'd ever experienced. If she had known all it was going to do was make their already tumultuous relationship worse, she would have walked away, never looked back.

Caroline's eyes flitted up and finally landed on hers. "Thanks."

The tiny gesture made hope spring to life inside her chest. "Are you going to look at them?"

"Nope." She shrugged. "I know what they say. I wrote them."

She willed herself to calm down, to smile, to be a human being with a heart. Caroline was biting back fiercely. If this was her way of getting Atlanta to back down, it was working, but only slightly. "Maybe you should look at them."

Caroline sighed, rolled her eyes, and pulled her olive messenger bag over her head. She slammed it onto the chair next to her. The attitude Caroline was carrying around right now was backfiring hardcore. Her hard-ass façade was even more attractive to Atlanta, which made the whole exchange even harder. She watched as Caroline started to thumb through the last ten journals. As she completed reading each, her facial expression morphed from irritated to confused to surprised to... *Is that the hint of a smile?* She stopped reading halfway through and looked up. "What happened?"

"What do you mean?"

"This isn't how you grade me." Caroline turned the papers over and pointed at a remark on the page. "'This is incredible,'" she read. "'Please keep putting this emotion into your work.'" She flipped to another one. "'Reading your words is like being inside your brain.'" Another one. "'I hope you take this passion into the classroom.'" Caroline looked from the papers to Atlanta. "I don't understand."

Atlanta shrugged. "I told you. I wasn't lying, regardless of what happened."

"Dr. Morris—"

"Atlanta," she corrected, and their eyes locked again. She noticed Caroline's makeup, the sparkle in her eye shadow, the curl of her eyelashes, the blush on her cheeks. "Please."

Caroline took a deep breath, causing her chest to rise, then fall as she let it out. "What happened the other night was a mistake."

"Was it?"

Caroline pursed her lips. She glanced at the ceiling, then back to Atlanta. "Mistake or not, I don't think we should talk about this here."

"This may shock you, coming from me, but you're right."

Caroline laughed the same girlish laugh from the other night, and Atlanta felt it in the pit of her stomach. "I never thought I'd hear those words."

Seeing the smile on Caroline's face was causing emotion to simmer. Atlanta cleared her throat and brought them back to business. "Keep the passion coming. I enjoy reading your journals." She paused and smiled. "A lot."

"I'll be honest," Caroline started and then, as if she decided against saying whatever was on her mind, she shook her head. "I was going to drop your class today."

Atlanta's guilt and fear collided. If Caroline dropped the class, her reasoning would be she wasn't being treated like the other students, fueling the gang of faculty members in charge. "Please don't." Being less of a bitch had nothing to do with what those professors thought, but losing a student halfway through the program would have raised some serious questions. Atlanta didn't need the added negative attention.

"I won't." Caroline's lips started to turn upward into a smile. "Are we good?"

"Do you have plans tonight?" Atlanta heard the words come out before she could stop herself. She hoped the regret in her mind didn't appear on her face. This was not the road they were supposed to be traveling. Yet there she was, wanting to know and letting herself ask. She knew Caroline was wondering what the hell was going on. She saw the questioning look appear on her face.

After waiting a beat, Caroline seemed to relax. "Why?"

"I'd like to take you to dinner."

Caroline rolled her lips together. She closed her eyes, and Atlanta knew she'd overstepped. Again. But Caroline opened her eyes. "I'll meet you somewhere."

"You won't let me pick you up?"

She shook her head, slowly. "Absolutely not." She stood, reached across the desk, the scent of orange blossoms and honeysuckle crashing into Atlanta, and grabbed a pen and Post-it. Caroline was scribbling something, but all Atlanta could do was stare at her face, the tiny lines at the corners of her eyes, her jawline, her neck, her hair. She was so close, too close, and her proximity was causing Atlanta's breathing to speed up. When Caroline finished writing, she glanced at Atlanta and did a double take. A blush filled her cheeks. "Stop," she said quietly.

"Why?"

"You're making me sweat." Caroline's lips looked so soft as a small smile appeared on them. "Text me." She turned and reached for the doorknob. When she swung open the door, none other than Dr. Brady was standing there.

Atlanta stood as Dr. Brady barged into the small space. Atlanta's feelings of excitement, happiness, and desire were quickly replaced with dread.

And only dread.

"Dr. Morris. A word?"

"Dr. Brady, I didn't realize you'd be visiting this week."

"Yes, surprise visit means they'll be unexpected, Atlanta." He glanced at Caroline and motioned for her to leave. "Session over, sweetheart."

Atlanta clenched her fists at her side. "Ms. Stevens, forgive me. We'll have to cut our session short." She tried to relay her sincerest apologies through eye contact, and thankfully, Caroline seemed to understand. She gave Atlanta one more small smile, then left, disappearing as she turned the corner. Dr. Brady moved quickly and oozed his great bulk into the chair where Caroline had been seated moments earlier. She tried to pay attention as he launched into a lecture about enrollment for fall, retention rates, and graduation rates. Her mind was racing. She was clutching the Post-it, hoping she wouldn't get caught and praying Dr. Brady would shut the hell up.

❖

"So, I have a question for you."

Atlanta raised her eyebrows and peered at Caroline over the top of her dirty martini. "Okay."

"What happened with the student?"

Oh, how nice it would have been to be able to play dumb. To furrow her brow, ask stupidly, "What student?" and carry on with the conversation as if nothing happened. Unfortunately, and Atlanta wasn't exactly sure why, she felt compelled to tell the truth. So she sipped her martini, let the salty deliciousness of the olive juice wash over her tongue and take the edge off the Tito's vodka, and said, "Her name was Melanie." She paused as the memories from the semester filled her brain. Not like they were ever tucked too far in the archives. She liked to keep those regrets toward the front of her filing cabinet of memories, if only to remind herself why getting involved with a student was so insanely stupid. *Yet here I am.* "She was a freshman while I was in grad school. I was a teacher's assistant for one of my favorite professors." Atlanta ran her finger along the rim of her glass, picked up the toothpick full of blue-cheese-stuffed olives, and brought it to her mouth. She slid an olive off and chewed it carefully. "Thankfully, it didn't go horribly far, but it has haunted me ever since."

"You're joking."

Atlanta laughed. She was shocked. "What do you mean?"

"That's it? That's all you've got for me? 'It didn't go horribly far'?" Caroline's impression of Atlanta made her chuckle even harder. "You're crazy if you think those answers will get you off easily."

"Well." Atlanta picked at the popcorn in the bowl that sat between them at the pub. Dinner had been amazing, but neither of them was ready to call it a night. The night was yet an embryo, and the evening air was warm, and there was entirely too much sexual tension between them to go home yet. Alone or not... Atlanta leaned forward and winked. "I have a feeling you have no idea what it means to get off easily." Caroline's eyes went wide, and her cheeks turned a lovely shade of pink. "Oh my God, I'm so sorry. I was only teasing." Atlanta grabbed her hand.

"You are crazy." Caroline started to laugh as she shook her head. "Dirty and crazy."

Atlanta laughed along as she released Caroline's hand. "I couldn't help it."

"Yeah, sure."

"So, you want to know the details? About Melanie?"

Caroline nodded. "You owe me now."

"Fine." She watched as Caroline played with the stem of her martini glass. Her fingers were thin, and even though she was divorced, she still wore what seemed to be a wedding ring. "She was cute. Nineteen, full of life, very funny. I remember getting coffee with her once or twice, and she would always be able to make me laugh. She was eager and ready to learn. Always. She'd write poems and short stories, and I'd critique them." She pulled a deep breath into her lungs. Quite a bit of time had passed since she'd last spoken about Melanie. About the way Melanie found a way into her every single thought. "She kissed me one day, and I pulled away. For more than one reason."

"What were the reasons?"

"I had no idea I was gay, for one."

"No way."

"I swear." Atlanta nodded. "Shocking, I know."

Caroline smiled as she leaned forward and propped her elbow on the table, chin resting on the palm of her hand, and sighed. "How old were you?"

"Young. I started grad school at twenty."

"My God. You were Doogie Howser, weren't you?"

Atlanta laughed. "I'm not a doctor."

"But you are."

"Oh, yeah, I guess you're right." Atlanta and Caroline both laughed. "A medical doctor, then."

"So, what else happened?"

"This is so boring…but honestly?" She shrugged. "Nothing. I mean, we kissed a couple more times, but I started to get scared, so I stopped it. She was devastated and embarrassed. She never made another move, thank God, but she told someone. I wasn't shocked she couldn't keep her mouth shut, but the person told someone else, who told someone else, and then yadda, yadda, yadda, the dean found out, and it all went downhill from there."

"So, you have this brand on you all because of a kiss you didn't even initiate?"

Atlanta nodded. "Fucked up, isn't it?"

Caroline was staring dreamily at Atlanta as she softly said, "Mm-hmm," and if it wasn't for the table between them and the fact that they were in public, Atlanta probably would have lunged at her. She adjusted her glasses and pushed her fingers through her hair, moving it away from her face. Caroline arched her eyebrow and smiled. "Do you have someone back in Phoenix?"

For the first time in what seemed like forever, Atlanta felt as if she was being pursued, and it felt foreign, absolutely not something she was used to, but at the same time, it was really nice to know if she let someone else see the real her, the icy exterior she worked so hard to maintain could be melted. Even if she shouldn't have allowed it. At all. "I do not."

"Definitely good news."

"Oh?"

"Mm-hmm."

"Caroline?"

"Hmm?"

"Are you tipsy?"

Caroline smiled, let out a small laugh, and leaned back in her chair. She was wearing a black sundress with small red cherries on it and little ruffled sleeves. The neckline was low-cut, and the view of Caroline's cleavage from her vantage point was making it hard for Atlanta to focus, especially since Caroline took her jean jacket off and discarded it in the seat next to her. "I am not."

"We have two weeks left of class."

A few loose curls had fallen from her messy bun, and when Caroline slowly and deliberately moved them away from her neck, she raised her eyebrows. The way she lightly dragged the tips of her fingers down her neck and across her chest, coupled with the look she had on her face, made Atlanta's stomach bottom out. She swallowed as Caroline ran her fingers over the bare skin of her breasts to her cleavage. "Yes. We sure do…"

"We are going to wait two weeks." Atlanta waited for a response, an acknowledgment, something, anything, because she needed Caroline to know nothing else could happen. "This isn't a condition I am willing to negotiate. Okay?" Caroline shrugged, and the ache Atlanta felt in her hands, her throat, her chest, moved through her body until it took up residency between her thighs. She was fairly positive the heat radiating off her body would have started a brush fire. She tore her eyes away from Caroline and bit down on her bottom lip. How the hell had she allowed herself to want Caroline Stevens so badly and with such intensity she was ready to use the ethics book she structured her career around as kindling?

"I'm not going anywhere."

Atlanta glanced at Caroline, let a deep sigh escape, and said quietly, "Do you even realize what I would do to you if I could?"

"Is telling me against the rules?"

"Probably." Atlanta pushed out a breathy laugh. She was shaking. She knew if she started talking about sliding her hands up Caroline's bare thighs to her panties, slipping her fingers under the material, dipping into her wetness, she would, without a doubt, cross every line known. "I don't know if either of us could handle all the details."

"I have a feeling you're right."

"It'd involve you needing new panties because I'd probably rip them off."

"Who said I'm wearing any to begin with?"

"Jesus *fucking* Christ." Atlanta breathed out, her eyes wide, and her heart lodged so hard in her throat no amount of swallowing would help.

Caroline giggled. She honest to God giggled, and it was absolute perfection. "I'm just saying."

"Yeah, well, fuck."

"Two weeks."

"Two insanely long weeks."

Caroline smiled and shrugged. "I suppose if I can survive getting shot, I can survive two weeks of anticipation." And Atlanta couldn't help but laugh right along with her.

❖

"Hold up. I'll walk you to the door."

Caroline stepped out of the car and waited as Atlanta rushed around the trunk to her side. Atlanta offered an arm to Caroline, who, against her willpower, was definitely tipsy. The truth came out when she stood at the restaurant, and her knees were wobbly. They left her car at the pub after Atlanta assured her more than once they'd come back the next day and pick it up. "Thank you," Caroline whispered. She didn't mean for it to come out as low and breathy as it had, but Atlanta's smile was a perfect response. Everything about Atlanta was perfect. She looked so stunning with her hair down and lightly applied makeup. Especially wearing those glasses with the clear, plastic frames and *damn, her hoop nose ring...*

"This was a lot of fun."

She turned toward Atlanta as they stood at the top of the steps to the door of her basement apartment at Samantha's. She leaned against the railing and reached to place her hand on Atlanta's arm but instead slid her fingers down until they could intertwine them. "You aren't as horrible as you make yourself seem."

"You aren't as straight as you make yourself seem."

Caroline chuckled softly. "Touché."

"Can I call you later?"

"Tonight?"

"Yes."

"It's one in the morning."

"So?"

"Why don't you come in?" Caroline knew she was being far too bold considering Atlanta's earlier stance of not going down the teacher/student road. She also knew she was turned on and ready to get some relief. So, even though Atlanta's protest hung loosely in the air, Caroline imagined a gentle nudge would send her flying over the forbidden line.

The forbidden line she knew that if she crossed, she'd be completely out of her element. The realization that only a week ago she wasn't ready felt odd, because now? Now she was raring to go. She guessed the hours and hours of research on the internet and the sheer number of fantasies her research produced was practice enough to get rid of her hesitation and nerves.

"Two weeks. Remember?" Atlanta's laughter sounded as if it was mixed with intrigue and nerves, and again, Caroline's inner voice told her to ignore the yield sign. "And besides, not in your daughter's house."

Caroline let out a low groan. "What if I told you I was being serious?"

"About?" Atlanta's eyebrows were furrowed.

Caroline moved their intertwined hands to the hem of her dress, which fell right above her knee. She placed Atlanta's hand flat on her thigh and then moved it up, up, up, until a surprised look flashed across Atlanta's face. "I wasn't lying."

"Caroline." Atlanta's voice was deep, but Caroline couldn't tell if she was mad or turned on, so she pulled back.

"Two weeks. Right?"

"You are killing me."

"I know…" Caroline pushed out a breath. "Go. Before I die."

Atlanta laughed. "You're *so* dramatic."

"Yeah, well, you're a tease, so?"

"A tease, eh?"

Atlanta's eyes said it all. Caroline wasn't sure if she should be turned on or frightened by the fire in those dark irises. So much had happened in the past couple of weeks, from anger and confusion to joy and certainty. Knowing the spectrum of emotions she'd traveled, she could only imagine what was going through Atlanta's head and heart. She didn't want to push Atlanta, but at the same time, she found herself unable to stop the force. She knew every action had an equal and opposite reaction, so what would happen if this all blew up in their faces? How would she be able to live with herself for putting Atlanta in the same predicament she worked so hard to avoid? Was it worth it? "Am I worth this?" she heard herself ask, saw the glimmer from the outside light above the stairs flicker in Atlanta's eyes, heard the sharp intake of air Atlanta pulled into her lungs. Her breath smelled of vodka when she breathed out, probably meaning she shouldn't have driven them anywhere. Caroline kicked herself for letting her brain be so motherly, so reasonable, yet at the same time so irrational and ridiculous. "Seriously, Atlanta…" Caroline's eyes welled with tears, so when she blinked, the drops slid down her cheeks. Warm and wet. "Am I worth this?"

"Do you think I'd be here if I didn't think you were?"

"What if, though? What if this isn't—"

"It's impossible to know." Atlanta shrugged. "Do you think I haven't thought all about this?"

Caroline shrugged. She wanted to say she barely knew Atlanta. She legitimately had no idea what went on in her brain, in her heart, in her soul. The only thing she knew with absolute certainty was she had never felt more alive and at peace than she did when she was around Dr. Atlanta Morris.

Atlanta wrapped her hand around Caroline's wrist. "There is nothing we can predict. If I could have predicted you, I would be in this same spot anyway, regardless of any warning sign."

"You don't know for sure." Caroline's inability to trust after being shot, after being left, after being heartbroken, was alive and well. She wanted to curse herself for being able to be as strong as possible one minute, then a hot, crumbling mess the next.

"I do know." Atlanta squeezed Caroline's wrist. "You are filled with so much light, so much soul. Even in a place as bright and spiritual as Sedona, I find myself feeling more alive and illuminated around you than I ever have." She smiled a sheepish smile and shrugged. "I know it sounds kind of simple and stupid… But it's how I feel. So, yeah." Atlanta loosened her grip on Caroline's wrist as she pulled her arm up and placed a kiss on her hand. "You're worth it," she whispered against Caroline's skin. The gesture itself made Caroline melt into a puddle on the concrete.

"You're obviously a writer." Caroline was unable to hide her smile.

And just like that, Atlanta took a step and started to walk down the stairs. She pulled on Caroline's wrist. "You coming?"

"What? You mean now?"

"Yes. Come on."

"Wait!" Caroline tugged on her arm, and Atlanta released it.

Atlanta stopped, turned toward Caroline, and smiled knowingly. "See?"

"See what?"

"You." Atlanta smiled while shaking her head slowly. "You're freaking out. I sorta knew that was going to happen."

"Are you serious right now?"

"Yes."

Atlanta looked completely heartbroken, but Caroline let out a laugh. "Now who's being dramatic?"

"What do you mean?"

"I was going to say I think we should go to your place so I can wake up and see the sunrise you bragged about." Caroline reached back out and smiled. "I am not freaking out at all."

"Seriously?"

"Yes, seriously. Come on." Caroline motioned to Atlanta to grab her hand. "You inspired me."

"How?"

"To show you the light inside me you went on and on about."

"You being so sure of yourself is such a turn-on." Atlanta's smile was sexy as hell, and Caroline knew if she didn't pick up the pace, she was going to pounce.

"You being hard to get is, as well." Caroline chuckled and let out a low whine. "Are we doing this or not?" When Atlanta bit her bottom lip and nodded, Caroline felt as if she could fly. "Let's go. Time's a-wastin'." Atlanta laughed as she skipped up the steps and grabbed Caroline's hand.

Chapter Twelve

Caroline couldn't lie; she was nervous as fuck. She remembered the first time she'd witnessed an attending physician crack a man's chest in the emergency room. Pinching a clamp on an aortic valve while a doctor worked like hell to save the man's life wasn't nearly as nerve-racking as the moment she was presently living. Atlanta slowly sliding the zipper of her black sundress down, down, down… She swore she could feel and hear every single tooth unlatch. Caroline felt woozy, her knees wobbly, her chest heavy. She felt cool fingertips on both shoulders. *Trapezius muscles*, she recited. *Over my deltoids. My God. There go the sleeves of my dress. Down my biceps. What is happening to me?* She wasn't sure if she was going to pass out, have a panic attack, or die. She made herself take a deep breath and hold it for one count, two, before she pushed it out slowly. If she hyperventilated right now, she would never forgive herself.

"You're shaking."

She could feel Atlanta's breath on her skin, and the number of goose bumps it caused was ridiculous. "I'm nervous." Her voice came out as a whisper, and almost instantly, she wanted to take it back. "Not in a bad way," she corrected, hoping it didn't break Atlanta's already fragile state. Or her own. "Just…nervous."

"Would it make you feel any better if I told you I'm nervous, too?"

Caroline chuckled. "Not really. You're supposed to know what you're doing." She heard Atlanta's giggle and felt her hand as she laid it flat against the small of Caroline's back.

"We do not have to do this."

Panic started to rise up Caroline's esophagus. "I want to."

"Are you sure?"

"Yes."

"Positive?" Atlanta moved in front of Caroline. She was already in her bra and panties. As nervous as she was, Caroline had no problem whatsoever stripping Atlanta of her dark blue skinny jeans and red tank top as they fumbled their way through Atlanta's rental, kissing, bumping into furniture, knocking teeth, laughing.

When Caroline opened her mouth to say yes, she saw her past flash before her eyes. All of her faults and successes, all of her boyfriends, all of the times she hated herself, loved herself, wanted to be more, wanted to be less. She saw her friends, her daughter and son-in-law, her grandson, her mom and dad. Would they be happy this was the life she was living? Would they want this for her? A lifetime of being a minority? Fighting to be recognized? Wondering if she'd ever be discriminated against? Would they want to see her happy? Truly in love and smiling? And completely and fully loved? "Yes, I'm positive. Just…" She paused, held back the tears that were threatening to escape, and shrugged. "Be gentle. Don't grade me like you graded my papers."

Atlanta's laugh was a welcome sound in the too quiet bedroom. Her smile was gorgeous, lit by only the moonlight shining through the window. "I'm so sorry," she said quietly, her voice dropping low at the end of the "sorry."

The tone of Atlanta's voice, the way she said "sorry," the sincerity in her eyes, how she pulled her bottom lip into her mouth afterward, biting down with her straight teeth, and the popping of a knuckle as she fidgeted made Caroline's nerves dissipate. The calming feeling which washed over her was odd, as if she somehow remembered how to breathe after holding her breath for so long. She felt something deep inside her spring to life, reminding her she was beautiful, sexy, kind, and worth every stare, every lick of the lips, every uttered word of praise. She was worth it all, and Atlanta was worth it in return. She was risking everything by doing this, and there was no way Caroline was going to back out. How could she? The idea of walking away was crazy. Atlanta was fulfilling a need buried so deep she'd never realized it existed until the day in the community center classroom when she saw Atlanta sitting there in all her young, hipster glory, cross-legged on the wooden table. The wooden table making appearances in more fantasies than Caroline would ever admit to…Atlanta's glasses, her hair, her tattoos, her stupid fucking nose ring. Everything about Atlanta awoke a starving beast, and the beast was not about to take "I'm too nervous" as a reason to not be fed. Caroline reached over to her shoulder and continued to push her sleeve down. She did the same to the other shoulder, and before she shimmied the dress over her hips, she said a silent prayer her fifty-five-year-old body wasn't a complete turnoff.

"Fuck." The word came out under Atlanta's breath, and she licked her lips afterward, and Caroline felt slightly better about herself. The last time someone other than her ex-husband saw her naked was in college. She laughed to herself. *How ironic.* Talk about coming full circle.

"Take your bra off." Atlanta's voice was sultry, full of passion, and for the thousandth time, Caroline regretted not wearing panties. She was so wet already, and with nothing to absorb it...How was she going to last if only hearing Atlanta's voice at that octave made her insides quiver? She complied, though, and reached behind to unsnap her bra. When she dropped the garment on the floor, Atlanta lunged at her, capturing her lips, her hands gripping her bare hips, sliding up her back, around her front, to her breasts, as she walked them backward to the bed. When the backs of her legs hit the plush comforter, she sat, scooted back, and Atlanta stripped herself of her own panties and bra. Her body was, of course, much tighter than Caroline's. She clearly worked out, but she had this adorable little stomach, and her breasts were much larger than her clothing led Caroline to believe.

Atlanta started to climb onto the bed, but Caroline raised her hand. "Wait a second."

"What? Is everything okay?" Atlanta sounded genuinely concerned, and it made Caroline fall a little harder for her.

"Oh yes." She nodded, smiled, and propped herself up with her elbows. "I wanted to get a good look at you." And that was the first time she ever saw nervousness pop onto Atlanta's face. She was sure if the lights were on, Atlanta would be fifty-seven shades of red. "Not used to being admired?"

"Not used to letting someone admire me..." Atlanta paused as she stood there. "It feels weird."

"Weird how?"

"Can I please come up there?"

Caroline laughed as she sat up, stretched her legs out in front of her, and crossed the left over the right. "No. I want to know why it feels weird, Dr. Morris."

"Come on…"

"If I have to give a presentation in class, so should you." She watched as Atlanta's courage seemed to absorb back into her pores. She placed her hands on her hips, and Caroline let herself take in all the different marks on her body. The medium-sized birthmark on her stomach in the shape of a continent…*Africa? Or is it Australia?* The outline of a sun was inked onto her side with "you are my sunshine" scribbled above it.

Atlanta took a deep breath, making her breasts move in a way Caroline never before thought she'd find attractive. "I tend to keep people at arm's length." Atlanta shrugged, hands still on her hips. "I don't let people in very often. If ever. So, this? You staring at me?" She spread her arms out and turned in a circle. "This isn't normal for me."

"You're handling it very well."

"Because I hope I am rewarded with making you come very, very, very hard."

Caroline's mouth instantly went dry.

"To make up for treating you so poorly before."

"Come here." She eyed Atlanta as she continued to stand there with a smirk on her face. Her dark, wavy hair had somehow found its way over her shoulder, and it was completely covering her left breast. Everything about her was making Caroline want to tear into her like a starving beast finally being given a substantial meal. "Come here. *Now.*" Finally, Atlanta did as she was told. She moved quickly, topping Caroline, straddling her hips, kissing her deeply, their tongues mingling, her hands roaming until her fingers found Caroline's nipples. She tweaked each lightly at first, then harder until Caroline couldn't contain the moan that burst from her lungs. In every dream, every fantasy, every single one, Atlanta would always take charge. She would love it because in her past life, she was always the one to initiate, and she was sick of that life. She was done with that life. She wanted to be dominated. She wanted to be taken advantage of. She wanted to be desired, admired, loved. And sweet Jesus, did Atlanta know what she was doing. She seemed to be in tune with exactly what Caroline wanted because she was barely trying, and Caroline could feel the pressure building between her legs, and *oh God…Is it an orgasm? Already?* No, no, no. It was too quick! She'd never be able to go again if she had one now. She broke the kiss, and before she was able to protest, she felt the orgasm sneak through the gates she tried her damndest to close and padlock. She leaned her head back as a moan ripped from her throat. When Atlanta latched on to her neck, she could hear her soft laughter as she moved to Caroline's earlobe.

"You are entirely too easy," Atlanta whispered before she bit down on the soft flesh of the lobe.

Caroline loosened her grip on the comforter. "That has never happened before," she finally managed to say between breaths. "What the hell?"

"Imagine how good it'll be when I get my fingers inside you…and my mouth on you." Atlanta started to make her way down Caroline's body, across her breasts, her now sore nipples, her stomach with the stretch marks, to between her thighs. When Atlanta gently nudged her legs open wider and settled between them, Caroline clamped her eyes shut. The nerves were back and with a vengeance. In preparation for this event she had no real idea was going to happen, she'd shaved for this woman. She hadn't been shaved down there since the early nineties. But all the research said…

"Did you do this for me?" Atlanta's fingers glided over the smoothness between her legs. Caroline nodded, her eyes still clamped shut. "Open your eyes." Atlanta's voice was soft, so she pried her eyelids apart and lifted her head. "I won't hurt you."

"I know," Caroline whispered. "I know."

"Good." And Atlanta did what Caroline was unaware could ever happen. She made her come twice in a row, and she changed Caroline's life for good.

Atlanta knew she was good in bed. She'd never had a doubt. She didn't want to brag, but she absolutely knew her way around a woman's body. She hadn't had tons of partners in her life. No, she just paid attention. And she was a very attentive lover.

So it came as no surprise when she completely rocked Caroline's world.

Caroline cried. Legit tears streaming from her eyes. Atlanta didn't want to say she felt a sense of accomplishment because it would probably sound very conceited and rude.

But…she totally did.

And when Caroline composed herself, and Atlanta slipped two fingers inside her, quickly bringing her to climax again, Atlanta felt as if she could conquer the world. She watched Caroline's body as she finished, the shaking subsided, the muscles unclenched, and her jaw relaxed. Caroline smiled, finally, her eyes still closed, and a laugh bubbled from her throat. She looked absolutely breathtaking with messy hair, smudged lipstick, and smeared eyeliner and mascara. "Atlanta Morris," Caroline said, as she continued to laugh.

"Hmm?"

Eyes still closed, Caroline held her hand in the air. "High five, because that was fucking incredible."

Atlanta burst into laughter and high-fived Caroline. "You are a nut."

"I have never…" Her eyes were finally open, and in the moonlight, she was glowing, and it was one of the most intense scenes to ever play out in Atlanta's life.

The realization that she could fall in love with this woman slammed into her like a rockslide. *Shit*…those thoughts were not what was supposed to happen. Or were they? "Never what?"

"Never felt like that before."

"I'm glad I could help."

Caroline propped herself up on her elbow and began to run her fingers over Atlanta's breasts, her nipples, to her tattoo of the sun. Caroline smiled. "You have a lot of tattoos."

Atlanta nodded.

"Any special significance to them?"

"What do you think?"

"I think you're too deep for them not to." Caroline's words seemed to snag on something in her voice. "What does this one mean?"

"My mom used to sing the song to me when I was little." She moved a little and showed the tattoo better. "The tattoo is in her handwriting."

"What about this one?" Caroline took Atlanta's wrist and stretched her arm out, lightly touching the one on her forearm.

"Lyrics from a song I used to love," she whispered.

"You don't love it anymore?"

"Not really. Sort of a painful reminder of a past love." *Please don't ask...*

Caroline seemed to hear her silent plea as she moved on to the next. "And this one?" Her fingers danced over the hummingbird.

"Another for my mom." She watched as Caroline's eyes flitted to hers from the tattoo. "The other is the day she passed away." Caroline swallowed so loud Atlanta could hear it in the quiet of the dimly lit room. "It's okay. I'm okay."

"Are you sure?"

Atlanta nodded as she smiled. "I promise."

"Tell me about it one day?" Caroline returned the smile and cleared her throat. "Okay, enough sad shit. Let's do this." Atlanta couldn't hold back her laughter. Caroline sat up, and before Atlanta could think another thought, Caroline was on top of her. "It's my turn to make you feel good."

"If you think none of what happened made me feel good, then you really have no clue how amazing lesbian sex is."

Caroline's low chuckle made chills erupt all over Atlanta's skin. "Oh, believe me. I'm starting to get the idea." She positioned herself between Atlanta's legs. Caroline ran her hands so softly over each of her thighs, knees, calves, moving each so her feet were flat on the bed. "Forgive me if I take my time." Caroline's eyes were locked on Atlanta's as she said those words, and if there was ever a time when she almost emotionally lost it, it was right then and there.

"Believe me, I'll never be upset."

"Good, because I want to..." Caroline paused and moved so she was on her stomach. "Taste and explore..." She gently ran a finger through Atlanta's wetness, who felt it in the pit of her stomach. "Every." She dipped a finger inside Atlanta. "Single." Then slid two fingers in. "Inch." And when she didn't think it could get better, she saw Caroline bend her head and felt her mouth surround her.

"Holy shit," she whispered. "Are you sure you've never done this before? Because you absolutely know what you're doing." She felt Caroline stop and let out a snicker before she started again. She was taking her time, and it made Atlanta feel as if she really mattered. Equal give and take sex was few and far between for her. Normally, she didn't want to take. She only wanted to give and get it over with, but everything was different with Caroline. Atlanta didn't want it to begin with because she knew she shouldn't. And honestly, she still shouldn't want it, but there was something about Caroline she desired on another level altogether. She truly hoped Caroline felt the same way because if all this did was fuck her up in the end, she was going to be so disappointed in herself for trusting her heart to make the decisions.

Atlanta knew her orgasm was close. She was never fast when it came to climaxing, but whatever Caroline was doing was, without a doubt, working. The combination of the tongue and the fingers was exactly what she needed, and as her orgasm built, she once again felt the words "I could fall in love with this woman" flooding into her heart and mind. As the release came crashing into her, so did everything else. The past, the future, the present. Including the fact Atlanta did what she swore she never would, which was sleep with her student.

Oh God, what am I doing?

Her entire body seized as she clamped her legs together. She turned, jerking herself away from Caroline, who bolted upright. She put her hands on Atlanta's thighs, concern written all over her face. "Are you okay? Oh my God, did I do something wrong?"

"Stop," Atlanta pushed out. "Don't…please…I'm sorry. But we have to stop."

"Oh no." Caroline placed her hand over her mouth.

"You didn't do anything wrong." Atlanta clamped her eyes shut.

"Then what is going on?"

Atlanta needed to answer, to tell her she was wrong, they shouldn't have done this, she was the one who jumped head-first into this stupidity, and she never should have. She was so passionate sometimes, and this was not the time for it. Ever. And now look what her ridiculous heart got her into. "Caroline." She let out a shaky breath. "I don't think…I don't think we should have done this."

"Excuse me?" Caroline must have had her hand over her mouth still because her words were muffled.

"This." She bit down on the side of her tongue as hard as she could without drawing blood.

"Forgive me for being dense, but you need to be more fucking specific."

Atlanta opened her eyes and stared. "This. It wasn't…We shouldn't have. What if…" She wasn't positive, but the pain in her chest felt an awful lot like heartbreak. "It was a mistake."

"Are you fucking kidding me right now?"

Atlanta was frozen, paralyzed with regret, sadness, and worst of all, fear. Fear that her impulses hurt a woman she finally felt actual love for. And the look on Caroline's face was enough to cause a myriad of emotions to fill her, but the most prominent was legit fear.

"You asshole." Caroline hit the bed with her fist. "You are not doing this right now." She pointed. "Do it when you leave, when you run back to Phoenix, but not now. I am not allowing you to do this to me right now."

"Do you have any idea—"

"Do I have any idea? About what? About what we just did?" Caroline was one decibel away from shouting. "Do *you* have any idea?" Caroline shook her head. "You don't. Don't you dare say all of this was a mistake." She clenched her jaw together so tightly Atlanta could see the muscles flex in her cheeks. "I know you're risking everything, but so am I. At the end of the day, I gave myself over to you, and you're going to walk away. You'll leave and go back, and it's going to break my heart. I'm prepared for it to happen eventually, but don't fucking do it now. After everything happening between us…Don't you dare."

Atlanta finally moved so she could be on an equal playing field. She sat upright, cross-legged, and pulled a pillow in her lap while staring at Caroline. "If this ever got out, I'd be crucified."

"Why do you think I'm going to say something?"

"Because I barely know you."

"Then why did you do this? If you barely know me? Why? Tell me, please, because I'm dying to know why you slept with me if you barely fucking knowing me really bothers you."

This was not how Atlanta saw this night going. She looked out the bedroom window. "I think…" She took a deep breath and pushed it out through her lips. "I think I could fall in love with you." The emotion she'd been doing such a good job of squashing was rearing its ugly head with wrathful vengeance. She swallowed once before she looked again at Caroline. "I can't fall in love with a student."

"I'll only be a student for two more weeks."

"Did you even fucking hear me?"

Caroline pursed her lips and nodded. She didn't have a pillow in her lap, so she was completely exposed, and if the conversation wasn't as intense or as packed with hurt feelings as it was, she would have looked so sexy.

"I barely know you." Atlanta took a breath and waited a beat before she finished with, "And I'm almost all the way there."

"Atlanta…" Caroline's voice cracked, and it made Atlanta's eyes fill with tears.

"I can't."

"What if I told you…" Caroline paused. "What if I told you I'm right there with you?"

"I'd tell you you're crazy. And it's impossible. And stupid. And we barely know each other."

"But…"

Atlanta reached out her hand, and Caroline took it. She was crumbling all over again. She had no legs to stand on. She should have never crossed the line, but she did. Her heart was so far in she didn't know if it was possible to stop. "Don't leave."

"You are so confusing."

Atlanta shrugged. "Welcome to being a lesbian," she said with a small smile.

CHAPTER THIRTEEN

"Eight weeks really flew by."

Caroline shrugged. Had they? She didn't really feel as if they had flown by. From feeling like an idiot to being confused about Atlanta to not really knowing what the hell she was doing anymore... Eight weeks definitely didn't seem to fly by. They *crawled.* And she crawled right along with them and hoped to God every second the stupid program didn't kill her in the process.

"You don't think so?"

"Absolutely not." She laughed when Kate scrunched her face and shook her head, causing her small ponytail to bounce. "You are nuts. I never thought it was going to end."

"Yeah, well, you passed, didn't you?"

"Barely."

"Whatever. You got straight As." Kelli laughed. "I'm sure we'll never know the real truth behind how you pulled out an A in Dr. Morris's class."

Caroline's mouth dropped open. "What are you insinuating?"

"Oh nothing." Kelli and Kate both descended into giggles as Michael slid into the booth.

"What's so funny?"

"Caroline somehow got straight As." Kelli's voice was covered with sarcasm. She was still in her softball uniform from her part-time job as a summer coach for the high school. She had dirt all over her, including a huge smear across her face. They'd agreed to go to the game to offer support, but on one condition: beers afterward.

Michael let out a loud, dorky, one-syllable laugh and smoothed his hand over the scruff of his beard. "Well, I wonder how that happened?"

Caroline took a long drink of beer. "No comment."

All three of them snapped their heads up and stared. "Excuse me?" they said in unison.

"I earned the A, okay?"

"Whoa, whoa, whoa," Kelli said as she held her hands in the air and waved them wildly. "What the hell?"

Just as the question came out of Kelli's mouth, Caroline caught a glimpse of Atlanta walking into the pub. Atlanta waved and walked over to the booth, leaned down, and kissed her on the lips. "Hi," Caroline said softly, and Atlanta kissed her again before she pulled up a chair and sat.

"Oh," Kate whispered.

All Kelli said was, "Hmph," and pursed her lips in a semi-approving manner.

"Okay, then." Michael let out another laugh, this one much calmer than the one before.

"How's it goin'?" Atlanta smiled as she glanced at Michael, Kelli, then Kate. "How was the game?" She was looking at Caroline now, and it was one of the best feelings Caroline had ever experienced.

"They won," Kate finally answered, which, thankfully, broke the tension. Kelli, who seemed to understand they all needed a subject change, launched into a story about her favorite player's home run, and Michael regaled Atlanta with a tale about his dream to play in the major leagues. Atlanta paid attention and listened to every word, occasionally rubbing the top of Caroline's thigh.

None of their situation was perfect, but it was working. They'd made it through. And Caroline was so happy. Happier than she'd been in forever. Her new life in Sedona was the reason.

As well as Dr. Atlanta Morris, who took a minute or two to thaw, but offered a lifetime of love.

PRIVATE EQUITY

Elle Spencer

CHAPTER ONE

Let's get one thing out of the way right now. My feelings about my boss are complicated.

It's 3:15 on a Thursday afternoon, and in about two minutes, she'll come into view. She always looks so sexy after her weekly massage. Her hair's a little messy, and her cheeks are usually flushed, just like I picture her looking after sex. I realize that's a very inappropriate thought. I've been having a lot of those lately.

My boss is Julia P. Whitmore. She always signs her name with that goddamned *P*. My coworkers like to guess what it means based on her demeanor. Pompous. Pretentious. Particular. Patronizing. Funny how patient and personable haven't ever been proposed. Ninety seconds from now, *perfect* will probably cross my mind. When it comes to Julia P. Whitmore, I have issues.

You've probably figured out by now that I mean *that* Julia Whitmore. "Laser-like focus and unmatched intellect give this VC the Midas touch." That's what the *Times* said about her when she cracked their top ten list of the world's leading venture capitalists. Working at WhitCap, her private equity firm, is the opportunity of a lifetime. When it's not a complete pain in the ass.

Julia works long hours, which means I work long hours. We're friendly but not friends. She made it clear that anything less than total professionalism will not be tolerated. Still, she shows her appreciation in very generous ways, like the new company car I drive and a great benefits package. And then there are those quarterly bonuses. I really want to stay with her for as long as possible and learn as much as I can, so I do whatever it takes.

I dress the part daily, keeping my long hair pulled back and wearing only designer suits thanks to another perk I like to call my "dress like the boss" clothing allowance. My black hair and olive skin mean I can pull off the bright colors, but I keep it pretty simple. Most of my wardrobe consists of black, navy, and gray suits and dresses. Sometimes I'll throw in a red blouse, but most of them are a shade of white.

I don't dress exactly like Julia. She has more style than I do, and her clothing budget is probably ten times what mine is. But I try, and she appreciates that. I'm sure of it.

As she comes around the corner, I see she's changed out of her business attire. I had packed her a little bag with casual clothes to change into, but I didn't think she'd actually wear the jeans, tight T-shirt, and cashmere cardigan. This is a rarity indeed, and I'm going to appreciate the hell out of that T-shirt.

Julia is tall and slender. Her blond hair is usually low-maintenance short, but she hasn't been to her stylist recently, so she has short bangs that she slicks to one side. And I was right about how she'd look after a massage. God, she looks sexy as hell when her hair is on the messy side.

"She's here, Sean."

Sean was hired to be our driver while we're in Seattle. Really, he's part bodyguard and part driver. Julia likes to have security when she and her daughter are in different cities for any length of time. Julia's profile isn't insignificant, and even though it sounds like the plot of a TV movie, the risk of a ransom kidnapping actually does exist. As you might imagine, Julia is someone who likes to anticipate all possible risks. That's why she's so good at what she does.

Sean gets out of the car and opens her door. "Ms. Whitmore."

He always greets Julia with a smile, but it isn't always returned. Even after a massage, when her body is fully relaxed, her head is still in the game. She usually mumbles something back to him, gets in the black SUV, and starts barking orders at me. That's what I expect now too. I wait with pen and pad in hand, but she's silent.

I look over, and she's laid her head back against the seat. She has a smudge of mascara under one eye and a lazy smile that isn't usually there. I bet she's beautiful first thing in the morning, her head on a pillow and her face so relaxed that the worry lines on her forehead don't exist.

Shut up, Cassidy.

I try to force the thoughts from my head. It's ridiculous, really. Julia is beautiful and brilliant. I think I may have mentioned that. But she's also demanding and reserved. Aloof is how one journalist put it. And despite all that, I still manage to worry about what her head looks like on a pillow. Jesus. How long's it been since I've gotten laid anyway?

"How was your massage?"

"Heavenly," she replies. "My shoulders were a mess."

I try not to be distracted by her very relaxed, sexy voice. "As good as Hans?"

"No one is as good as Hans, but the headache is gone."

"Yeah, this project has been a headache from day one."

Julia opens her eyes. "You feel the project's going poorly?"

"Well, no, I didn't mean that."

"If you didn't mean it, why did you say it?"

"It's just, I mean—" Okay, I really need to stop stammering. "It's just been a bit hard to extract some of the data we need."

"Which data? Why is this the first I'm hearing about it?"

God. What the hell is wrong with me? I know better than to casually mention issues with an investment. When you bring a problem to Julia, you'd better damn well bring a solution along with it. "Because I just got the numbers. The updated figures are in your files." I motion toward the paperwork I'd left on the seat next to her. "It just meant a few late nights with the CFO, but everything's straightened out now."

"Good. I count on you to keep me apprised of any developments related to our projects, Cassidy."

My former boss made the mistake of bragging about me to Julia. Told her he had the best of the best. His loss was my good fortune. My title is Chief of Staff to Julia Whitmore. If anyone wants to get to her, they have to go through me.

I've gotten used to Julia's looks. I mean, I've sort of gotten used to her looks. Obviously, I've been sitting here hoping she'd emerge from the massage having neglected to fasten the third button of her blouse. Did I mention I have issues?

When we met, I was stunned by Julia's beauty. And it's not like I didn't do my homework. I read all the interviews I could get my hands on. I watched I don't know how many hours of CNBC. I'm telling you, none of it does justice to those piercing blue eyes. The memory of it still makes me cringe when I think about our first meeting.

"Hi, I'm Julia." She'd extended her hand.

It was at that moment that I apparently decided to break from long-held traditions that would require me to take her hand and, oh, I don't know, maybe return her greeting. Instead, I decided to stand there and do nothing. I didn't reach for her hand. I didn't introduce myself. I just stood there speechless for a good five seconds.

Five seconds may not sound like very long to you, but just imagine standing in front of a stunning woman whose reputation and genius precede her. She absolutely commands the room. She's just flashed a smile that makes your heart stop. She approaches you. She says her name. She goes to shake your hand and anticipates your reply.

One, one thousand. Two, one thousand. Three, one thousand. Four, one thousand. Five, one thousand.

How does five seconds feel now? God. I'm a complete idiot.

Fortunately, Julia seemed to take it in stride. At the time, I figured she wrote it off as me just being nervous. Of course, now I know Julia well enough to know she hates having her time wasted. Five seconds lost was six seconds too long.

"And you must be Cassidy," she'd said.

"Yes. You can call me Cassidy."

"I believe I just did."

Because yes, I actually did that. Even now, I want to ask Sean to open the trunk so I can crawl in it and never have to look Julia in the eye again.

By some miracle, I managed to recover after the "call me Cassidy" debacle. Would you believe I managed to come off as smart and competent? Of course, I always gloss over that part of the story in my head. It's so much more fun to obsess about how I spent five full seconds doing an impression of a wax figure at Madame Tussaud's. And not one of the really good, lifelike ones.

Anyway, I obviously got the job. I'm sure it helped that my last boss had one too many whiskey sours and inadvertently pitched me to Julia in the most glowing of terms, or so I've been told. Not by Julia but by others who were at the party. I suspect poaching me had some allure too. Julia is nothing if not competitive.

"I'm so happy to be out of the snow." Julia takes her phone out of her purse and opens the weather app. "It's seventeen degrees in Chicago right now."

"And snow is expected tonight," I tell her. "A couple of inches, I think."

Right now, we're working in Seattle, where I'm from. I grew up here. I went to college here. I came out here. Seattle is where I have friends I haven't seen in years. It's also where my parents told me that they don't have a gay daughter and promptly erased me from their perfect lives.

If I was worried about going home, Julia had eased my mind. Our time in Seattle would be about work and work alone. Our first morning here she'd said to me, "Cassidy, I trust you understand this isn't a vacation. I know you've spent time in the area, and I'm sure you have acquaintances here, but I expect the same level of commitment as always. You shouldn't anticipate having much in the way of free time."

Spent time in the area? Apparently, that's what Julia calls a childhood.

Chicago has been my home for going on five years. I'm happy there. Happier than I ever was in Seattle, but I don't tell Julia that. I'd rather she thought I had a perfect life here, with kind, loving parents. Not that she thinks about it. But if she does, she doesn't need to know the truth.

We're working on Julia's latest investment, and nothing is going right, hence the hastily scheduled massage. We're staying at the Four Seasons. Julia and her five-year-old daughter, Lily, are staying in the penthouse suite, which also serves as her office away from home. I have a premium suite on a lower floor. The mini fridge is stocked with bottled water, protein drinks, and fruit. My meals usually consist of a quick bite on the run and the occasional dinner with Julia and Lily. What I'd really love to do is go to the cheese and olive happy hour they have in the hotel bar, but I haven't had the time.

I focus on my phone, but I can feel Julia staring at me. It makes me nervous when she looks at me for too long. I worry she'll see something I really don't want her to see. Like that I'm human or something. I'd pull my hair to the side and cover my face a little bit, but it's slicked back in a tight ponytail. I look out the window to see if we're anywhere near Lily's school. Shit. We're not far from Seattle Center where the Space Needle is. Unfortunately, that means we're a good ten minutes away from the top of Queen Anne, where Lily can rescue me from Julia's gaze.

"Cassidy?"

"Yes?" At some point during our first meeting—you know, after I'd gotten my shit together—I'd actually told Julia to call me Cassie, but she never does. I swear she uses my full name just to remind me what an idiot I'd acted like during the interview.

I grab my notepad and wait. She doesn't say anything, so I turn and look at her. Her usual hard stare has melted into more of a soft gaze, which makes me wonder what the hell is going on. Was the massage so relaxing that it changed her into a nice person? That's not fair of me to say. Julia isn't mean. She's just demanding. That's what I tell myself anyway.

"What do you like to do for fun?" she asks.

Okay, something is definitely wrong with this picture. It feels like a trick. "Fun? What's that?" I ask, attempting a joke.

"You know, that thing you're supposed to do when I'm not working you to death?"

"Oh, that thing. Well, I like to go to the movies. I love to get popcorn and candy and escape for two hours. Not have to think about anything. Just sit there in the dark."

"With someone?"

"What?" I heard the question. It's just so strange to hear it coming from her mouth. She gets irritated when she has to repeat herself, so I quickly reply, "Not usually." And with that answer, she probably thinks I'm a psycho. I turn away and open my window a crack to get some air. This sudden interest in my life is disconcerting.

Julia doesn't know I'm gay. I don't think she does anyway. I don't know why she would. I've been working for her for six months, and my sexuality has never come up. I mean, not that it would. Or should. I don't hide it or anything. She just isn't one for small talk, and anything about my personal life would be considered small talk. Julia keeps it strictly professional, which I'm fine with. My personal life is pretty much nonexistent at this point and not worthy of conversation. Where's that damn school?

One of the drawbacks to living in Chicago is having to endure a long, cold winter. Even if the work here in Seattle doesn't take a full four months, that's how long we're staying. After a negotiation that involved a sizable donation and an agreement to stick around a full semester, Lily's been enrolled in kindergarten at one of the best private schools in Seattle.

"I can't remember the last time I went to a movie," Julia says.

"Honestly, neither can I."

"You enjoy it, but you don't do it?"

Yes, Julia. It's like sex that way. We can enjoy things we don't do. As usual, I have the perfect reply in my head but no idea how to respond in person. If I lived like Julia does, I'm sure I'd watch movies all the time. She has a small media room in her high-rise apartment in Chicago, but from what I've seen, it rarely gets any use. If Lily watches movies or cartoons, it's usually on her iPad.

"I should take Lily to a movie sometime," she says. "I don't think she's ever been. Are you dating anyone?"

For a split second, my mind focuses on the first half of her statement. *Your child has never been to a...* Wait. What? What the hell did she just ask me? As mentioned, Julia P. Whitmore does not make small talk. The best-case scenario is her body was somehow snatched during her massage. Maybe the therapist is like a zombie or a vampire or whoever it is that takes over your body. Clearly, I don't care much for scary movies, but you get the point. I see Sean quirk his head slightly. He obviously wants to know the answer as well. I smile at her even though I want to open my door and roll across the pavement. "No, I'm not currently dating anyone."

Julia doesn't respond. She seems to be taking this information in. Or maybe she's just moved on to another topic in her mind. "You certainly seem like the type of woman who would have no problem attracting attention. Have you tried one of those apps?"

Sean winks at me in the rearview mirror, and I smirk back at him. He tries to chat me up on a daily basis and refuses to believe me when I tell him he has a better chance of winning the lottery. I turn back to Julia. "It's not a priority right now. I'm really too busy to date," I lie. I mean, I sort of lie. I actually am too busy, but it's not like I haven't been on a date in the last year.

"I'm certain you could make the time if you wanted to."

I don't know what to say, so I try to turn it around. "If it's so easy, why aren't you dating?"

That makes her turn away. "Too busy. And I suck at relationships. It's not worth the trouble with the size of men's egos."

I nod but don't reply. I know all about men and their egos, even though I don't sleep with them. Julia is my first female boss, and it's been so refreshing to not have to worry if my blouse is sending the wrong message. I glance over and have to laugh at myself because Julia's T-shirt is sending the perfect message. The roles have been reversed, and I'm the one doing the ogling. I quickly look away because I really need this job.

I'm saving up to buy my first apartment. And then there's the MBA that has always been a goal, but that'll have to be put on hold for a little longer. There's no way I can go to school while working for Julia. She requires too much of my time. But I'm not complaining. I like my job, even if I don't understand the weird conversation I'm currently having.

I look out the window again. Why is this taking so long? Did they put the school farther away? I swear it's farther away. I look at my watch because we can't be late for Lily's school play.

"What are you doing this weekend?" Julia asks.

"David has Lily, so you should have plenty of time to review the proposals."

David is Lily's dad. He and Julia have been divorced for three years. He's a nice enough guy, but I fail to see what Julia ever saw in him. There's just something about him that's a little bit douchey, if you know what I mean. She deserves so much better.

"I didn't ask what *I'm* doing; I asked what *you're* doing."

Damn. Obviously, I can't dodge every question she lobs my way. I guess it wouldn't hurt to tell the truth since it's my first weekend off. The impersonal memo from HR informing the staff of the full weekend off per month rule is the stuff of legend in our office. It laid out the statistical analysis that had found productivity increases when people have two days off in a row. "No big plans," I tell her. "Just a party with some old college friends."

She's feeling very relaxed. I know this because she just turned her entire body toward me. She's resting her head on the back of the seat with her hands tucked between her thighs. If I look her in the eye, I just might melt.

"A party? What kind of party?" Her voice is expectant. Excited almost. That doesn't make any sense since she hates going to parties. She finds them tedious but necessary in her line of work.

"I'm meeting some friends tomorrow night. I haven't seen them in ages, and they're having a big birthday party at a club. That reminds me, I need to get a gift." I'm looking out the window, alternating thoughts between how weird this is and what to get my friend, when I get a text. Oh good. Things just got weirder. It's from Julia:

Take me with you.

I look over at her in shock. My body snatching theory suddenly seems more plausible. Julia is looking down at her phone when she whispers, "Please." I keep staring at her, not knowing what to say because what the actual fuck? I feel my phone vibrate again.

I'm sick of falling asleep to Disney movies in Lily's bed. I could use some adult fun.

Good God. I could certainly show her a night of adult fun. I tell my inner voice to shut the hell up. I make a mental note to research whether or not sexual harassment can be perpetrated by the employee even though I know perfectly well that it can. But I'm pretty sure things that occur in my head don't qualify. Thank God. I shake my head, partly at Julia and partly at my own ridiculous thoughts. "You wouldn't—"

She puts her finger up to stop me. "If you're about to say I wouldn't enjoy myself…" She glances at Sean, then back at me and whispers, "Unless you'd rather take someone else?"

I shake my head while trying to avoid breaking out in hives. Also, is she implying that I have a thing for Sean? So not happening.

CHAPTER TWO

The car stops—finally—and I open my door to find Lily standing on the curb with her teacher. I've never been so happy to see this little cherub. I take a couple of deep breaths as she crawls across me to hug her mother. Then she jumps into my lap like she always does and intertwines our fingers. She likes to have my full attention when she talks to me, and holding my hands is her five-year-old way of keeping me on task. It works too because who could resist the mini Julia?

"Did you remember my bunny rabbit costume?" Lily asks.

"Yes, honey. It's in the back. Did you practice your lines?"

"I know them by heart."

"Okay, good." I smooth her blond hair and hold her face in my hands. "Now, remember when you're on that stage to just look for me or Mommy, and we'll blow you kisses so you're not scared, okay?"

"Okay, I will." Lily wraps her arms around my neck. "Thanks for getting my costume."

I kiss her cheek and rub our noses together before she jumps off my lap and gets out of the car. I start to get out of the car too, but Julia grabs my shoulder and says, "Thank you for being so good to Lily."

The truth is, I love that kid. She's sweet natured and precocious as hell, which makes me laugh. The other day, Lily's teacher told us about a lesson they were doing on money. Apparently, they set up this town, and the kids all got different assignments. Before accepting the role of store owner, Lily asked about the store's market position and capitalization. It's possible we've involved her in a few too many work discussions. And you'd think dragging her around to our projects would take its toll, but Lily seems to acclimate well. I'm sure things will change as she gets older, but for now, she's a miniature WhitCap executive. I want to tell Julia that I adore her daughter because I do, but I shrug it off instead. "It's my job."

"No, it's not, actually. Taking care of Lily isn't in your job description at all, but you do it anyway, and I really appreciate it."

Who is this woman? Julia is not one to dole out compliments or concern herself with job descriptions. Like, not at all. Regardless, she's right. Lily has a full-time nanny, but the kid and I seem to have a connection that goes beyond job descriptions. "She's a wonderful kid, and you're an amazing mom."

"I'm a better mom now that I have you running my schedule. I'd be lost without you, Cassidy."

I know I said before that I told her to call me Cassie, but I sometimes love it when she uses my full name. She makes it sound so classy. I try not to blush as we get out of the car and walk into the school. For a brief moment, I manage to forget I'm just an employee. I feel like a proud mom waiting for her child to walk onto the stage.

We've rehearsed Lily's lines so many times, I know them by heart, but I tell myself not to mouth them for her. She has them down. She'll remember every word. Plus, I can only imagine how the other moms would react. *Julia Whitmore is so important she has her assistant do her stage momming for her.* Omg. I just said "other moms."

We work our way through the crowded auditorium. "Here." Julia stops at the third row where two aisle seats are marked *Reserved. Whitmore.* Whenever we're at an event, Julia has us sit on the aisle in case we need to make a quick exit. I can't imagine that will happen here, but apparently, the habit has stuck.

From what I can see, they're the only reserved seats in the house. Julia must've arranged it because I didn't. We sit, and Julia is the picture of poise. If I hadn't spent fourteen hours a day with her for the past six months, I'd never know how nervous she is. But I see her sitting just a little too straight, gripping her program just a little too tightly. The small auditorium is filled with nervous parents. I just never expected Julia would be one of them.

I can't let myself get lost in the fantasy where Lily's my daughter and Julia is my wife who I need to comfort because she doesn't know how much Lily and I rehearsed those lines. In my fantasy, I wrap my arm around her and kiss her cheek and whisper, "She'll be fine, honey."

In reality, I lean in and whisper, "She's Julia Whitmore's daughter. She's got this."

She pats my hand and seems to reassure herself by saying, "Of course she does, Cassidy."

In my head, she said, "Good answer, honey." Wait. Did she just pat my hand? That part wasn't in my head, was it?

I take a breath and remind myself over and over exactly who I am, or more accurately, who I'm not. A man kneels on the floor next to my chair. "I hope you don't mind," he says. "I was late getting here, and I promised Jack's grandma I'd get some video for her, but my seat is way in the back."

"No problem." I'm grateful for the distraction. Julia and I rarely have reason to sit this close to each other. Lily is usually sitting between us. "Jack has been very sweet to Lily," I tell him. "She told me he always shares his baby carrots with her."

"Ah. Well, I wish I could say it's because Jack is a true gentleman, but the truth is, he's not a big fan of vegetables." He offers his hand. "I'm Tim."

"Cassidy. And I know all about the battle with vegetables. I'd love to know how Jack gets Lily to eat those carrots because we sure can't."

"It must be true love." He grins and looks toward Julia. "Are you Lily's other mom?"

I stop breathing. Julia leans forward and shakes his hand. "Julia Whitmore. And please keep packing those carrots. They just might be the only vegetables Lily eats that day."

She didn't correct him, and I'm not sure what the hell to do except cover my chest with my hand so they don't notice it turning bright red. Luckily, the lights go down. Tim gets his phone ready. "Here we go," he whispers. "I'll make sure I get Lily in the shot too. She's the bunny rabbit, right?"

I don't dare look at Julia, so I nod. "Thanks, Tim."

I want to hug Julia for not being offended by Tim's mistake. I also want to rejoice in the fact that someone would mistake me for Lily's mom and, by default, Julia's partner. I'm not getting an angry vibe from her. She hasn't stiffened in her chair or put any distance between us. My shoulder is still grazing hers.

The crowd starts to applaud so I join in. Julia is clapping with a fervor I've never seen before as Lily hops her way onto the stage. I glance at her proud mama and have to stare for a moment as she claps for her little girl. I imagine she's been very underappreciated by the men in her life, her intellect and business acumen always being overshadowed by her beauty. Men rarely appreciate both in one package.

A wave of bravery washes over me, and I put my hand on Julia's just because I can in this instance without it seeming awkward. "She's gorgeous," I whisper. And then I try not to let myself drown in the scent of her.

"And a pretty good dancer," she whispers back.

"Does she take after her mother on both counts?" I can't believe I just asked that. Luckily, she doesn't seem to think anything of it.

"Hey, I can bust a pretty good move."

I try not to laugh. "Oh yeah? Did we just go back in time?"

Julia laughs with me. "Just a decade or two."

See? This is why I'm so confused. Just this side of ninety-nine percent of the time, Julia is pretty frosty. We don't share moments or play "get to know you." Her office nickname is actually "IQ." I mean, no one would ever say it to her face, and it's not a name I ever use at all. Here's a hint: it rhymes with ice queen. Oh wait, sorry. That's literally what it means.

When all the little forest animals take a bow, we give them a standing ovation. Julia whistles loudly with two fingers in her mouth. I stare at her in awe. She looks at me and shrugs. "Another one of my many talents."

Of course, my mind goes straight to the gutter, wondering what else she can do with that tongue. And also wondering what she tastes like. God, I'm so gay. I need an escape, so I offer to go find Lily backstage. When I spot the bunny ears, I open my arms to her. "You did so good, Lily."

She grins and runs into my arms. I pick her up and kiss her cheek even though it's got a perfect circle of pink makeup on it. "I remembered my lines," she exclaims.

"You were a great bunny rabbit. That hop? You rocked that hop, Lily." I make a fist and she bumps it, then hugs me.

I carry Lily out to the audience and whisper, "We have to be quiet while the other kids perform." I stop short when I see my seat has been taken by Lily's dad. He's in Seattle ostensibly to visit Lily. He's staying at the same hotel as us; for Lily, he says. But my money says he wants to get Julia back, and if he appears to be a doting father, he thinks he'll win her heart again. At least, that's my take on the situation.

I may have seen three different Julias today, but I don't think there's a Julia in any universe who'd fall for his routine. It might be wishful thinking, but you've probably figured out by now that wishful thinking is kind of my thing. In my spare time, I pray he gets bored in Seattle and cuts his trip short. Not that Julia has given any indication that she'd be interested. But I'll take a work trip with Julia and Lily all to myself over a work trip invaded by the arrogant ex-husband who didn't know what he had in Julia when he had it. He had his chance, and he blew it. As assholes do.

I set Lily down and kneel next to her. "Your mom and dad are right there. See them?" She nods, and her furry ears flop up and down. She's so cute, I could die right now. "Okay, honey. Walk slowly down the aisle to them. Don't run, okay?" I watch until she reaches her dad. Julia doesn't look back to see where I am. Of course she doesn't. Why would she?

I see Sean standing against the back wall, so I join him. He leans in and whispers, "Lily did good."

"She did great."

"Sorry, David took your seat," he says.

"Oh, it's fine. He didn't know it was mine."

"He did, actually. He saw you get up."

I don't know what Sean's reason is for telling me this. I shrug it off.

"Sorry, Cassidy. I know how hard you worked with Lily to get those lines memorized."

I don't want Sean to see my disappointment. Yes, I'd rather be sitting next to Julia right now with Lily on my lap, telling her how well she did and seeing Julia's proud smile. But that spot was never really mine. I lean in and whisper, "I saw Lily's part up close. That's all that matters."

CHAPTER THREE

Julia looks at her watch for the second time. "They're late. We're sitting in their conference room, and they're the ones who are late?"

I've been dreading this day. We're waiting for the executive team of Ionius Punk. Their combined age is one hundred and twelve. That might sound like a lot until you realize there are five of them. You do the math. Anyway, IP is the software company we're investing in. They try to act cool, but the truth is, they're a bunch of sentimental softies who've been at this since they were seventeen. Julia's about to tell them that ten percent of their workforce is deadweight and needs to be let go immediately. I hate the days that start this way.

I refill our coffee cups and sit back down next to Julia. "Lily did great last night, didn't she?"

"Don't change the subject, Cassidy. Focus on what's happening right now."

I look around the empty room. "Nothing's happening right now."

"Precisely."

The door opens, and five people walk in. The "executive team." They all sit across the table from us with the CEO in the middle. "Sorry, we're running late."

Just then, a sixth attendee joins us, an older woman in a pink suit. She goes to the serving area and starts pouring beverages. She looks at me, holds up the coffee pot, grins, and mouths, "Coffee?"

I smile back and point at my cup. "We're good," I mime back, shaking my head.

Julia leans forward and rests her arms on the desk. "Gentlemen, you'll find my instructions for paring down payroll in the folders sitting in front of you."

The CEO opens his folder. "Don't you mean your recommendations?"

"No, Paxton, that's not what I mean," Julia says in that tone that lets everyone know she doesn't like to be contradicted. "You're overstaffed with underqualified people, and if you want me to invest in your company, you'll take care of it immediately."

The other employees open their folders, and all eyes go to the woman in the pink suit who's still pouring coffee. She sets the pot down. The room is silent as she walks over to the table and opens one of the folders. She looks at the list and then at Julia. "Mrs. Whitmore, you can't fire me. I've been here from the beginning."

"And you've been a bookkeeper from the beginning, Mary. That was fine for a company in a garage, but IP needs a real CFO now. One day we'll take this company public, and I'll be damned if a bookkeeper is at the helm. I'm confident the SEC would agree with me on that front."

"But, but..." Mary stammers. "I can't afford—"

"Can I afford to have you looking after my ten million dollars, Mary? Or would a qualified CFO be a better choice?"

"Mary is my aunt," Paxton says. "She's done a fantastic job with the books."

"Oh, she's your aunt." Julia's tone goes to full-on sarcasm. This won't be good. "Paxton, you have thirty seconds to convince me that my money is more important to you than your aunt and any other family members who might work here. Are there more?"

Ouch. Mary closes the folder and sits. She puts her hands in her lap and keeps her head down. Paxton swallows hard and looks at the list again. "There are three more family members on this list."

Julia looks at her watch. "Twenty seconds from now, I will walk out that door and never look back."

Paxton wipes his brow and takes a deep breath. "My wife is going to kill me, but I'll take care of it."

Mary puts her hand over her face and starts to cry. I kind of want to go over there and comfort her. I mean, who knows what her situation is at home. Maybe she has an ailing husband or two grandkids in college.

"Good," Julia says. "And I assume you've given them all some sort of equity deal. If you haven't, that's on you."

Mary cries a bit harder. Paxton looks beaten down. Everyone else just looks stunned.

Julia stands up. "Excellent. And for future reference, I don't tolerate people being late for meetings."

I follow Julia out of the conference room, feeling a little stunned myself by her callousness. I wonder if I'll ever get used to it. We get in the SUV and sit in silence while Sean drives us back to the hotel.

"Good meeting, ma'am?" Sean asks.

"Apart from the late start, it was perfect. Wouldn't you agree, Cassidy?"

Her chipper tone is a bit too much for me right now. I look out the window and don't respond.

"If Paxton listens to me," Julia says. "If he follows my counsel and implements my instructions, in two years, he'll be wealthy enough to support Mary and any other family members he wants." She turns to me. "You'll see, Cassidy. I did him a favor today. He just doesn't know it yet."

No, he doesn't. And Julia seems just fine with that. That's the difference between the two of us.

❖

It's terrible to think this way, but I'm really hoping Julia will be too tired to go out with me tonight. I hope she'll want to stay in with a glass of wine in one hand and her *New York Times* crossword puzzle in the other. That way, I can relax too and maybe get her off my mind for a little while. Plus, I'm still reeling from her "take no prisoners" demolition of Mary this afternoon.

The idea of Julia seeing me in a social setting and, God forbid, meeting my friends feels overwhelming. Yeah, I know this flies in the face of all my fantasies about Julia Whitmore, but I've said it before, and I'll say it again. My feelings for Julia are...say it with me now... comp-li-cated.

Besides, it was silly of me to get caught up in Julia last night at Lily's play. Pretending, even just for a moment, that we're anything other than employer/employee isn't a good way to keep my job. No, job security relies on me being my professional self and getting my head out of the gutter. Like, right now, I shouldn't be staring at Julia's ass while she stands at the dining room table and snacks on the fruit plate that room service just delivered.

She has one hand tucked in her pocket, and it's pulling the gray trousers tighter across her backside. Her blouse has come untucked on one side. I imagine myself standing behind her, telling her that it's untucked, but instead of fixing it for her, I untuck it all the way and slide my hands under the blouse while I whisper in her ear, telling her how fucking hot she is. Then I'd pull the blouse up over her head and—

"You have to taste this pineapple. It's outstanding."

She walks to my desk and holds the fork out. Her fork. The one that was just in her mouth. I should take it and slide it into my mouth and drag my lips across the fork, but I'd be sorry if I did. Why couldn't she have offered me watermelon? Or a grape? "I can't eat pineapple. It gives me canker sores."

She blinks a few times. "How did I not know that?"

"Why would you?"

"You're right." She looks at her watch. "I guess I'll know a lot more in a few hours."

It's my turn to blink.

"We're still going to that birthday party, right?"

"Um."

Julia straightens her shoulders and intensifies her stare. That's never a good sign. "Don't disappoint me, Cassidy."

I think the disappointing part will be when she sees where we're going. "No. I mean, yes. I mean, of course." I seriously need to stop fumbling over my words. "We're going. As planned."

"Excellent." Julia goes back to her desk. "What should I wear?"

How about the tightest jeans you own and a low-cut shirt? Stop it, Cassidy. "It's casual. Like, totally casual."

She focuses on the paperwork on her desk and says, "Choose something for me, will you? And don't make me look like a one-percenter. I want to blend in."

Blend in? In this club? Like that's even possible. My God, what will I have her wear? "Sure. I can do that." I try to sound chipper, but inside, I'm dying a slow death. It's not that I don't see the opportunity here. It's just that it's a lot of pressure to pick out an outfit that's slutty enough for me to thoroughly enjoy without it being obvious that I've selected an outfit that's slutty enough for me to thoroughly enjoy. Now do you see the kind of pressure I'm under?

CHAPTER FOUR

Oh God. What if she hates what I chose for her to wear, and that's why she's late? I look at my watch again, and then I see her. She's rushing toward me, and all I can do is stare. She looks ten years younger and sexy as hell. But she doesn't look happy. She walks right up to me and looks me in the eye. "I have no idea if I look good or not."

"You look great."

"So, this isn't a joke?" She points at the rainbow heart on her white T-shirt. Well, my white T-shirt that happens to be a tad too small for me, but it's hugging Julia just right.

"You said you wanted to blend in." I look her up and down. The jeans I ran out and bought for her are faded and worn, unlike the jeans she sends to the dry cleaners that are still as dark as the day she bought them. The shirt is as low-cut as I hoped it would be. I can just see the lace of the bra her breasts are filling perfectly. "You look hot." God, I shouldn't have said that. "I mean, casual. Do you like the shoes?" All she brought with her were fancy dress shoes, leather boots, and running shoes. It wouldn't hurt for her to own a pair of low-heeled suede ankle boots. It's purely a coincidence that I'm wearing boots with a heel that makes us just about the same height.

"Very comfortable." She hands me the short jean jacket I also picked up for her and runs her fingers through her hair. "I didn't have time to shower."

"You smell great." Oh my God, I need to keep my mouth shut tonight. "I mean, you always smell great." Because that made it better.

She takes the jacket and puts it on. "Do you have a gift for your friend?"

"Yes."

"What are we waiting for, then?"

I want to tell her that she was the one who was fifteen minutes late, but I look at my phone and then scan the hotel entrance. "He's here. There he is." I wave at the silver Camry, and the driver pulls forward. "Okay, let's go."

Julia scowls at the car. "Who is that?"

"That's Michael, our Uber driver."

"Where's Sean?"

"He has the night off."

Julia doesn't move.

"Have you never taken an Uber before?"

"Of course I have," Julia snaps. She gets in the back seat, and I follow, feeling pretty sure this is her first Uber ride.

I need to tell her where we're going so it isn't a complete shock. If she hates the idea, we'll go have dinner somewhere, and I'll get my friend's gift to her another time. I look over, and she's staring out the window, probably deep in thought about work or something. "Julia?" She turns to me. "It's a gay club we're going to."

"Why are you saying it like I should be afraid?"

"Am I? No, I just wanted to give you an out if you need one."

"An out?" She rolls her eyes. "I see you're not wearing any rainbows. Should I be questioning the decision to let you choose my outfit tonight?"

I shake my head. "No. Everyone wears rainbows." Okay, fine. Maybe not to a club. But still. People wear them. "I have like, five gay T-shirts." She raises an eyebrow, so I say it out loud. "Yeah, I'm gay."

She stares at me for what feels like forever. "Do you hide that from everyone or just me?"

"No, I'm not in the closet. It just hasn't come up."

"I see." She looks out the window again.

"Just say no," I blurt out. She looks at me again. "At the club tonight, you know, if someone, a woman, asks you to dance, you can politely decline."

"I think you know I'm perfectly capable of handling unwanted advances, Cassidy."

"It's just that a woman like you will stand out in a crowd like that."

"A woman like me? What is that supposed to mean?"

"Refined. Put together." I can't hold her stare. "Beautiful," I whisper.

"Well, thank you for the advice. And the compliment. I will definitely politely decline. Unless, of course, I would rather dance. Then I'll politely accept."

There's a playfulness in her tone that I usually only hear when she's talking to Lily. I'm the only one at WhitCap who spends any quality time with Julia and Lily together. Maybe that's why I'm able to see past her IQ reputation and appreciate this other side of Julia. Or maybe it's just that she has a great ass.

I smile at her, then focus on my phone. This was a bad idea. I don't say it out loud, but I yell it in my head. Bad idea, Cass.

Okay, it wasn't my idea, but like a fool, I agreed to it. One of the reasons Julia and I work so well together is that I never seem to be able to say no to her. I should work on that. The driver stops at a light, and I feel the need to warn her about something else. "You'll have to ignore my friends. They love to harass me about dating."

"Because you don't?"

"When I lived here, they were always trying to set me up. The problem is, they didn't have a clue about what I liked. They thought they knew, and then I'd go on a blind date and walk away wondering what they could have possibly been thinking. Which is why I don't do blind dates anymore." But why the hell am I telling her this?

"So, you don't let your friends see the real you?"

I look at her sideways and debate jumping out of the car. Why is she asking me these questions? Why am I answering them? "That's not what I said."

"That's what I heard."

Julia has an uncanny ability to get at the heart of an otherwise meaningless statement. I've seen her do it a thousand times in pitches. These poor start-up founders come in with all the confidence in the world and leave convinced they have no idea who their audience is or what they have to offer. Well, her tricks won't work on me. "Come on, Julia. Does it take me baring my soul for my friends to know I'm probably not right for a girl who made her skirt out of fabrics she found in people's trash and thinks daily showers are a waste of precious resources? Who thinks money is the source of all evil and therefore refuses to take part in the system, so I'll need to pick up the check?" I take a quick breath. "Oh, and who introduced herself by shaking my hand and announcing how high she was?"

Crap. I just raised my voice and got all emotional. Julia is my boss, not my friend. I need to remember that tonight. "Sorry," I say under my breath. I sneak a glance at her, and I can tell she's trying to suppress a smile.

"No need. I think I knew her in college."

"We all did," the driver says.

I can't help but giggle along with the two of them. It's not often that I see Julia laugh. Sometimes, I think she saves the best of herself for Lily. I love that about her.

As I get out of the car, I take a deep breath of the fresh air and try to clear Julia's amazing scent from my head. It's different from her usual perfume. Softer. Sweeter. She thanks our driver, closes the door, and turns to me. "Okay. Be serious. Did that blind date really happen?"

"Oh, yeah. One in a long line of Sarah's epically bad fix-ups."

"Sarah's your friend?"

Julia's going to know way too much about me after this, but I'm in it now. No escape. "It's her birthday party we're going to tonight. And since I forgot to tell her I have a plus one, she'll probably have two or three girls already lined up for me to dance with. That's just how Sarah is. Also, I can't speak for their wine selection. You might be better off sticking with martinis."

She scoffs at that. "Don't make me sound like such a snob."

I grin. "Hey, have the wine. But don't say I didn't warn you." She *is* a wine snob. And a clothes snob. And a food snob. The truth is, I've learned to enjoy the finer things in life, thanks to her. Especially good wine.

We walk down a short alleyway to the club's nondescript entrance. It's only nine, so the line isn't long. A hot dog vendor is setting up just outside the door, apparently getting ready for the rush of drunk customers who will think a hot dog is a terrific idea a few hours from now. I catch Julia giving him a quick glance and imagine she's wondering what the hell she's gotten herself into. Or maybe she's thinking *so this is what it feels like to stand in line.*

We get to the front of the line where an absolute behemoth of a man asks for our IDs. Julia reaches into her back pocket to produce hers. I suddenly wish she'd asked me to get it for her. Because I have issues.

We stop at a table to pay the cover charge. When I go to pay, Julia puts her hand on mine and says, "No, let me."

She pulls a hundred dollar bill out of her pocket and hands it to the cashier. I'm not sure I've ever seen Julia use cash before. The bill must be fresh from the Four Seasons ATM. I wonder if she planned it. Did she know there'd be a cover? Did she get cash in case the club didn't take cards? Who am I kidding? She's Julia Whitmore. Of course she planned it.

After Julia pays, we walk down a short dark hallway and see the entrance to the club. I haven't been here since college, but I know exactly what's on the other side of that door. Fucking pandemonium. This club is mixed, so we'll see plenty of women getting to know each other better—aka grinding on the dance floor—alongside shirtless, sweaty men who are clearly just there for the exercise.

I open the door to the club and immediately feel like I should close it and take Julia out for a nice dinner instead. This is most definitely not her scene. The music is so loud. And have strobe lights always bothered me, or is this a new thing? And also, what is that smell?

It was never my scene either. I only came here back in the day because Sarah loved it. In fact, it reminds me of when I was so insecure I could barely look at another girl let alone ask her to dance. I shut the door and turn to Julia. "We can just skip this and go somewhere else."

"Cassidy." Why do I feel like she's admonishing me? "Didn't you RSVP?" Oh. Because she is.

"This isn't really that kind of—"

"Did you tell your friend that you'd be here tonight or not?"

I give her a reluctant nod. "I did."

"Then it's settled."

She motions for me to open the door that I've now been standing in front of for entirely too long. I turn back around and feel Julia's hand on my back. My heart stops for a second. It starts again when I feel the pressure increase and realize Julia is pushing me through the door. Sarah's already texted to let me know they've taken over the small raised area in the corner with pool tables and a few barstools. I look in that direction. She spots me and hurries over, dragging a girl behind her. I give her a kiss and hug, and I'm about to introduce Julia when Sarah whispers in my ear. "Just work with me, okay?" She pulls the girl from behind her, and I immediately lose the use of my voice. The girl looks barely old enough to even be in this bar. Her head is shaved, she has a cigarette tucked behind each ear, black lipstick, eye shadow the shade of dried blood, and several facial piercings, one of which looks rather infected. My eyes fall to her chest where a torn-up wifebeater is proudly announcing in big block letters how much she LOVES PUSSY. I mean, I love pussy too, but Jesus. I'm sure Julia is wondering what she got herself into.

Sarah's yelling the girl's name in my ear, but it's not registering. Rudy or Trudy, maybe? "Trudy?" I ask Sarah. It takes me a second to realize Julia is saying something behind me. Is she calling me *honey*? I look down when I feel her arms wrap around my waist and freeze all motion when her chin rests on my shoulder. I can't move. I can't speak. What is happening?

"Honey, aren't you going to introduce me?" She offers her hand to Sarah. "Hi, I'm Julia."

I clear my throat, trying to find my voice. "Um, Sarah, this is—" *My fucking boss*? I decide to leave that part out for now. "This is Julia."

Sarah stands there looking just as stunned as I am. Infected Nose Ring Girl rolls her eyes, pulls the cigarette from one ear, and lets it hang from her lips unlit. Sarah starts jumping up and down and shouts, "Oh my God! Cassie has a girlfriend." And I just want to disappear.

"Hey, Sarah, just give us one sec. We'll be right over," I tell her.

Sarah shrugs. "Cool, but no disappearing all night to make out in the bathroom like that one time." She spins around and trots off with Nose Ring Girl in tow.

I look at Julia. "First of all—"

"What?" she shouts, pointing to her ears. "I can't hear you! The music!"

I put my hand on her shoulder and pull her closer. My mouth is about an inch from her earlobe. So, you know. God. Focus, Cassidy. "First of all, that thing Sarah said is not true, and I should tell you now that I've never liked Sarah. Second of all, what the hell was that back there?"

"What the hell was what?"

I raise an eyebrow, letting her know I'm not buying her innocent tone. "The *honey* thing?"

"I just made sure I wouldn't have to watch you and that teenager make googly eyes at each other all night."

"She's not my type."

She puts up her hands in defense. "I'm not judging. If that's what you go for—"

"It isn't. I told you, Sarah is a terrible matchmaker." My God, this is getting worse by the second. "Julia, I can't introduce you to everyone as my girlfriend. I can't lie to them like that."

She folds her arms and lifts her chin as she scans the crowd. "Don't be so melodramatic, Cassidy. I'm certain we can rectify things if necessary."

Shit. Is IQ back? If so, this could be a long night for all of us.

"I would hate to stand in the way of you and a young lady who," she glances over at Nose Ring Girl, "loves pussy so much." She flashes a wide smile and gives me a wink.

Did you hear that? She winked at me. God. What is my problem? And Julia Whitmore just said *pussy*. It's official. I'm in an alternate universe. I have to say, much as I hate lying to my friends, her idea has some merit. I imagine myself fighting off Rudy/Trudy all night. I put my hands up in defeat. "Okay, okay. I see your point. I'll keep up the charade."

She looks down her nose at me. "Well, you're going to have to do better than that if you want me to be your girlfriend. It's no wonder you're single."

I look at her, utterly confused.

"Ask nicely."

Oh. My. God. She is so messing with me. Fine. I can do this for the next three hours and forty-five minutes. Thank God last call in Seattle is early. So, why is my mouth so dry? Why is my stomach in knots? She's looking at me, waiting. "Um, okay. Yeah," I stammer. "So, um, Julia, would you, you know, um, would you…"

"God, Cassidy. This is worse than I thought." She grabs my arm and pulls me toward the area where my friends are. "We'll work on this another time."

I know what you're thinking. I'm thinking it too.

Am I in hell?

Sarah is in the back where the pool tables are. She's pointing at us and making big hand gestures. Everyone stands and claps. Shitballs.

CHAPTER FIVE

After introducing Julia to everyone as my girlfriend, I fight my way to the bar for drinks. I'm going to need them. I order a shot of Patrón and a Mosaic Pale Ale for myself and a Belvedere martini for my girlfriend of eight minutes. I slide my card to the toned, tank-topped bartender. I imagine he does well for himself.

"You wanna keep it open?" he yells.

"Nah, just run it," I yell back. The way things are going, I can't imagine we'll be staying long. When he turns around to run my card, I throw back the shot of tequila. Maybe it'll help me relax and actually enjoy this night, though I know it's not likely.

I take the two remaining drinks and work my way back to my friends. And my boss. As I approach the table, I see her laughing with Sarah and Jane, our old college roommate. I can only imagine what story Sarah "No Filter" Frye is telling now. I know I've asked you to kill me multiple times up to this point, but this time, I really mean it. Please kill me now.

"Hi." I hand Julia her martini. The glass is wet because I've spilled half the drink on the way over. And before you judge, you walk through a crowded nightclub with a full martini glass.

"Thanks, babe," she says with a smile. She doesn't acknowledge that the drink is dripping on her. "Your friends are great. They've been filling me in on your misspent youth."

"Omg, hoochie mama." Sarah cackles. "How could you not tell us about your little jujubee?"

I raise my eyebrows and look from Sarah to Julia.

Jane chimes in. "She told us what you call her. It's adorbs."

I look at Julia for an explanation, but she just shrugs. Jujubee? For context, you should know that the woman who just announced how "adorbs" we are is in her third year of a surgical residency at the University of Washington. Sarah leads hiking expeditions on Mt. Rainier. These women—neither of whom I trusted to drive my car— have other people's lives in their hands on a daily basis. To be fair, my car was a stick shift. Meanwhile, my boss, Julia Permafrost Whitmore, has apparently created a backstory for a relationship we aren't in.

Seriously, though. Why me? This is a far cry from the world I live in by day. You know, the world where my boss is not only *not* my girlfriend, but who is actually a model of professionalism and self-control. What was I thinking, bringing her to a place where self-control is frowned upon? A perfect example being the dude who just ran past us in his tight briefs and combat boots with the words *dance, suck, repeat* written on his chest in black Sharpie.

Julia casually sips on her martini, acting as if that didn't just happen. Meanwhile, I can feel the heat working its way up my chest and neck. I feel so embarrassed right now, I could die. Also, I'm a terrible liar. Surely, Sarah's going to realize this whole thing is a farce and hate me for it. Not to mention what it could do to my working relationship with Julia. Honestly, I'd rather be sucking on that girl's infected nose ring than sitting here pretending that my boss is my girlfriend. I need my job, damnit. Also, I just grossed myself out.

Before anyone can start hammering me with questions about how I met Julia, I stand and offer my hand. "Let's dance."

Julia's eyes widen. "What?"

I motion with my head and mouth the words, *We need to talk, Jujubee.*

She takes my hand, and I lead her to the dance floor. I kind of love how her hand feels in mine, but I can't focus on that. We need to get our story straight. I get to the middle of the crowded dance floor where no one can hear us and turn to her. "How did we meet?"

"What?"

I throw a hand in the air. "This charade, Julia. We're lying to one of my best friends, so tell me how we met."

"She's one of your best friends, yet she doesn't know you at all."

"Oh, like you're an open book." I shake my head in frustration. "Sorry. I'm just a little confused right now."

"We should dance." She puts her hand on my hip. "You don't want them to think we're fighting, do you?"

With her hand on my body, I lose the ability to think anything at all. I also lose my resolve to get our story straight. I'm melting like butter in a hot pan.

She puts her other hand on my hip, and I really have no choice but to touch her back. I put my hands on her arms and try to breathe so I don't faint right here on this dance floor in Julia Whitmore's arms.

"I like those big hoop earrings. I could never pull those off, but they look great on you," she says.

I didn't want to look like I'd tried too hard after telling Julia to dress super casual, so I kept my hair pulled back and put on some hoops, a pair of jeans, a loose blouse, and wedge sandals. "Thanks. You look great too."

"You're nervous, Cassidy. I can feel your hands shaking. Are you uncomfortable with this?"

I rest my forehead on her shoulder. I have so many conflicting emotions right now. I'm scared and turned on and happy and confused. I feel her breath on my ear. "It's okay. We can go if you want."

It's a tone I've never heard her use before. Soft, comforting. If I raise my head and look at her, will she still be my cold, calculating boss? Or will she be someone I can trust? I raise my head and look her in the eye. "Are you having fun, Julia? Because I want you to have fun tonight. Just ignore my anxiety."

She gives me that smile that I love so much but rarely see. "I am having fun. Thank you for letting me tag along."

"Oh, you're not just tagging along. You're my girlfriend for the night. In a few weeks, I'll email Sarah and let her know that unfortunately, it didn't work out with the hot chick I brought to the bar. Problem solved."

"Hot chick?"

"Seriously? That's the part you focus on?"

"It's a good plan, Cassidy. This is why I hired you. Along with all of your other fantastic attributes, you're also a problem solver."

"Ha! I wish I could solve the problem I have with Sarah. I mean, really, Julia. What kind of vibe am I putting out into the universe to make Sarah think that girl she had waiting for me is my type?"

"Hmm. I think Sarah's trying to tell you that you work too hard."

"Really?" I can't tell if she's bullshitting me or not.

"Hence the young, high-on-my-own-bad-attitude type."

That comment gets me laughing. "Oh, you nailed her."

"And how could I, as your girlfriend, compete with that? I should just quit while I'm ahead. I mean, she's so young and vibrant and full of life with that black lipstick. She looked happy; didn't she look happy?"

"I think her nose ring is infected. So, my guess—not completely happy."

We stare at each other for a few seconds and then burst out laughing. Also, Julia just called me her girlfriend, and I'm not even worried this time. I think I'm falling in love as I listen to her. Or maybe it's just the tequila. Something is making me giddy.

Now she's telling me about a blind date she once had. The guy had an old motorbike and no helmets, or something like that. It's hard to hear over the music, and honestly, I'm just getting lost in those eyes. We're the same height since I'm wearing three-inch wedges. Her lips are right there. Everything is right there.

I decide to forget about how stupid this is and wrap my arm around her shoulders, then lean in so our cheeks are touching. She stops talking. And I close my eyes.

It takes me a minute to realize that Julia is actually dancing with me. She's not talking or trying to lighten an awkward moment because it's no longer awkward. It's hot as fucking hell. Like an idiot, I run my hand up her arm and into her hair and let my breath hit her neck. She doesn't pull away like I expect her to. Because the truth is, we don't have to dance this close to pull off her little ruse. But she doesn't pull away; she grips my hips tighter.

I'm not even sure if the music is still playing. All I can hear is our heavy breathing. I don't know what this means, and the tequila's making me not care anymore. I thought I was better than this, but I don't want to stop. I'm not going to stop. My desire to make sure this doesn't happen has turned into an even greater desire to make sure it does. I can't even begin to describe how good she feels in my arms, moving against me. She's perfect. In every way.

Her hands move from my hips to my lower back. Her grip on my body tells me she doesn't want this dance to end just yet.

I pull back enough to rest our foreheads together. I can't look her in the eye, or I'll lose the courage to do what I so desperately want to do. I'll blame it on the tequila if she hates it, but I'm going to kiss her. I lean in, and her lips meet mine. She wants this too? I guess we'll both blame it on the booze.

I kiss her lightly, letting our lips brush together. When I deepen the kiss, she welcomes me in, her tongue there to greet mine.

I just found heaven in Julia's mouth. Soft, warm, inviting, tantalizing. I know, it sounds like I'm describing her pussy. I don't think there's enough tequila for that, so I pull back a little. I can't read her eyes. It's too dark in here to know what they're telling me. She hasn't pulled away, but she hasn't smiled or pulled me in for more. God, now what do I do? I hesitate for a second, and then I take my hands off of her. "Sorry. I got carried away."

"The tequila?"

I smeared her lipstick, so I gently rub it off of the corner of her mouth with my thumb. "Yeah, the tequila."

"I could taste it."

Her tone is so neutral, I have absolutely no idea what she's thinking. Maybe she wants to keep me guessing. Maybe she's trying to spare my feelings by acting as if it's no big deal. This was her idea, after all. Okay, maybe not the dancing. I'm the one who dragged her out onto the dance floor. But pretending to be something we're not? That's all on her. "We should go back to the table." I take her hand and lead her through the crowd.

As I bump shoulders with other dancers, I feel Julia's grip on my hand tighten as if she doesn't want to lose me. And when I feel her other hand touch my back, and her fingers slide into the waistband of my jeans, I realize that my world will never be the same.

Julia will go on with her life, and I'll be stuck here in this moment. The moment when I lead my girlfriend back to our table as if it's the most natural thing in the world. The moment when I let go of her hand and wrap my arm around her as I kiss her cheek as if it's something I've done a thousand times before. The moment when I let myself believe for five seconds that she's mine, and I'm hers. The moment when she wraps her arm around my waist, and we both look up as Sarah *takes a photo*? She motions to me that she'll send the pic to my phone and gives me a big thumbs-up. Fuck.

This whole thing needs to stop. And I have to get Sarah to delete that damned photo from her phone. The last thing I need is for Julia to end up all over Sarah's social media accounts with us wrapped around each other. In the meantime, I need to get my shit together because Julia has a look of concern on her face, which means I'm probably turning bright red. "We should sit," she says.

I lead her back to the table and put my face in my hands. What the hell was I thinking, kissing her like that? I feel as if I should apologize a million times and get her out of here, but when I sit back in my chair, she smiles and rests her hand on my leg. She's talking to Sarah, who's sitting on the other side of her. All I can do is stare at her hand.

Her fingers are long and slender. Short manicured nails polished a blush color. It's moments like these when I know for sure just how gay I am. A woman's hand on my body, even just resting in my lap, makes me feel things. I have a thing about hands, and Julia's are perfect. I take a calming breath and decide to allow myself to have this moment. It'll be over soon enough. I might as well enjoy it for what it is—temporary bliss.

Julia leans over to ask me about someone sitting across from us, and without thinking, I whisper the answer in her ear and let my lips brush against her temple. Her eyes bore into mine when she pulls back. Then she smiles and gives me a nod, letting me know she heard me. And I hope, *felt* me.

I can feel her hand burning its way through my jeans. Part of me wants to remove it so I can breathe normally again. The other part wants to hold it in mine. She's still talking to Sarah when I slide my hand under hers. She doesn't look at me, but she intertwines our fingers. And I watch closely as her thumb caresses my hand. She giggles at something Sarah says and then turns to look at me. Her smile turns into a look of concern. "Are you okay?"

I want to tell her no, I'm nowhere near okay. I'm much closer to totally screwed because she's so gorgeous, and her hand is so soft, and I'm probably falling in love with my boss who is so straight she's been married and divorced twice. Instead, I give her a half-hearted smile. "Fine," I whisper.

"You're flushed. Do you need some water?" She lets go of my hand and gives me her bottle. I chug half of it down and pray her hand doesn't work its way back to my body because I just might cry if it does. My eyes flutter closed when I feel her fingers squeeze my leg.

I am so fucked.

CHAPTER SIX

Singing happy birthday to Sarah is a distraction I can get behind. After we've all sung out of tune on purpose, I stand and hold up my shot of tequila. "Here's to the worst matchmaker in the history of the world."

Sarah laughs and flips me off. I throw back my third shot of tequila and slam the glass on the table, then flop back onto my chair. Julia has a mischievous grin on her face. "What?" I ask.

She leans in and whispers in my ear. "Have fun. I'll get us home."

I want to kiss her so bad. My eyes fall to her lips. "Do you have *any* idea how sexy you are?" Am I starting to slur? God. I think I am.

"Cassidy, where's the restroom?"

She ignored the sexy comment. That's good. I point behind us. "I'll join you." Drunk me has apparently lost all common sense.

This time, she's leading me through the crowd. I could get used to this hand-holding thing. We see Nose Ring Girl again, and I act as if I'm checking her out as we pass by. Julia shakes her head. "Whatever, drunk girl."

"Hey, I can tell she wants me," I practically shout.

"Uh-huh. I'm sure you'd be very happy together. Make sure you get her name tattooed on your ass because that's *always* a good idea."

"Are you speaking from experience?" Oh God. Now I'm dying to know whose name is tattooed on Julia's ass.

She lifts an eyebrow. "The only name I'd put on my ass is my own."

"Oh. Well, that'd be weird. I mean, who puts their own name on their body? Maybe someone with an ego the size of Texas would do that, but talk about an eye-roll move."

She pulls me close and says, "You're rambling. Are we going in the right direction? I can't see over all of these extremely handsome, muscular men."

"There are men in this bar?"

"Smart-ass."

"I'm kidding. Straight ahead."

I'm amazed at how comfortable Julia is in this bar. She hasn't once seemed as if she was out of her element. She's more comfortable being here than I am. "Hey, Julia?"

She stops and turns around before we get to the bathroom. I practically run into her, so I grab her shoulders, trying to balance. Definitely too much tequila. "Thank you for not being offended by all of this gayness."

"Gayness? I don't think that's a word, but you're welcome."

"You know what I mean."

"Yeah, I do. And you don't ever have to be shy about your life, okay?"

I smile, grateful that I can blame the fact that my hand is caressing her side and getting dangerously close to her breast on the alcohol, and before I can stop myself, I'm laying another kiss on her lips. My right hand finds her breast, and the second I touch it, I back away so fast, I almost lose my balance. She grabs my hand, and I grab my forehead. "Oh God. I'm so sorry. I…fuck." I practically run back to the table to try to get away from her.

I see Sarah corner Julia as she comes out of the bathroom. I have no idea what they're talking about, but I'm fine with it since I need to sober up before I say another word to her. And really, the only words that need to come out of my mouth for the rest of the night are *I'm sorry.*

I jump when Nose Ring Girl sits in Julia's chair and puts her feet up on the table. Yep, that piercing is definitely infected. She flashes me a smile and says, "I noticed you and your girlfriend are in a fight. What do you say we sneak out of here and go back to your place?"

The nerve of this girl. "I'm going to go with a hard no on that one."

"Are you sure? Sarah knows how fond I am of older women. That's why she introduced us." She puts her feet down and leans in, giving me an even closer look at her nose. "I never leave a woman unsatisfied."

How can I explain to her that I'm so preoccupied with how red and puffy her nose is, I couldn't possibly be enticed by her offer? Also, she just called me *old*.

"Pardon me. You're in my chair."

We both look behind us and see Julia standing there. Miss Infection gets up. I want her to leave without speaking another word, but it's clear she has other plans since she's looking down on me now. Her pussy loving shirt is right in my face, and all I can smell is stale smoke.

"If you change your mind, you know where to find me," she says.

I look her in the eye because *really*? "Actually, I have no idea where to find you. I don't even know your name." I point at my own nose. "But you should get that checked."

She rolls those heavily made up eyes. "I meant Sarah." She takes a cigarette from her ear and puts it in her mouth. "Sarah knows where to find me, okay?"

The cigarette bobs up and down with every word, and I want to laugh so hard, but I force a smile. "Good to know."

Julia watches her walk away and then sits next to me. "Wow, that was close."

"What do you mean?"

"If I hadn't shown up when I did, who knows where you'd be right now? Maybe in the park across the street, scoring some weed?"

"Very funny."

"Maybe making out behind the building? Or riding on her bicycle back to her parents' place? The possibilities are endless."

"She wanted to go to my place, if you must know."

"At least you'd know the sheets were clean," she says with a smirk.

"She told me that she likes older women, and she never leaves them unsatisfied. It was tempting."

"You're kidding, right?"

"Do you think I would let that nose ring anywhere near my—" My God, I almost just said the word *vagina* out loud. "Never mind."

She stares at me for a few seconds, then says, "Okay, then."

"Okay, then." I tilt my head. "What are we saying okay to?"

"Ending this conversation."

"Thank God."

I say my good-byes with Julia by my side. We get to Sarah, and she pulls us both in for a hug. "I expect an invitation to the wedding."

Oh. My. God. "Sarah, we're not, I mean it's not—" God, if you're out there, could you please turn back time for me? I don't ask for much, but this one thing would really help me out. I just need to go back to the moment when Jane invites me to this party and I tell a big fat lie about where I'll be instead. Maybe the local library? Volunteering in a nursing home? Anywhere but here.

"I'll call you." I probably won't call Sarah, but I need to wake up from this nightmare, and the only way to do that is to get back to the hotel, hide under my covers, and hope that when I wake up tomorrow morning, Julia will have forgotten that our lips ever touched.

I follow Julia outside. "It was stuffy in there," she says. "Mind if we walk for a bit? I could use some air."

I nod and fold my arms tight across my body. The cool air is refreshing, but the energy between us feels more awkward with every step we take back into reality. I'm kind of sad that my life will never be the same. I love my job. I love working so closely with the smartest, savviest businesswoman I've ever encountered. Every day, I learn something new from her. She's a great teacher, and she seems to love sharing her knowledge and experience with me, even if we haven't shared much else until tonight. I let out a big sigh and try to cover it up with a cough.

Next thing I know, she has my arm and is tugging me into a little corner store. I stand at the door and watch her go to the cooler and pull out a bottle of water. She's paying the cashier and glancing at me with a look of concern. God, she's so fucking beautiful. Even under these harsh fluorescent lights, she's simply stunning. I close my eyes for a second and imagine my hands unbuttoning one of her crisp white dress shirts, her lightly freckled chest coming into full view, the curve of her breast where it meets her bra—

"Drink this."

I open my eyes and take the bottle from her. "Thank you."

We're back outside, breathing in the cool air. I'm slowly getting my mixed-up emotions under control. Julia is making light conversation about my hilarious friends and how the real estate that the club sits on must be worth a fortune. And how she might be a bit too old to appreciate the strobe lights. She prattles on as if prattling on is normal for her. Nothing serious. Nothing about what just happened between us. Maybe she can blow it off and act as if it was no big deal. Maybe I can too, if I try hard enough. Maybe we really can get back to life as we knew it before this train wreck of a night happened.

"Can I see the photo Sarah took?" she asks.

I'm surprised by the request, but I pull out my phone and hand it to her. I haven't even looked at it yet. I don't want to. The last thing I need is a visual reminder of the best moment of my life. Oh Lord. I just called it the best moment of my life. Julia's right. I *am* melodramatic. I'm guessing you already figured that out.

I manage to get out of my head long enough to see Julia smiling at my phone. Now I desperately want to see us right after our first kiss. Correction, our only kiss. I take the phone back and stop dead in my tracks. We look so happy it makes me want to cry.

"I had fun tonight," Julia says. "I needed that."

"A night of gayness?" I reply, trying to make light of the situation.

"A night out. Just you, me, and Nose Ring Girl."

"Oh, I got her number before we left." I open my purse and pretend to look for it.

Her mouth gapes open. "You did not."

"No, really. She wrote it on a cigarette butt. I know it's in here somewhere." I dig around some more and try not to laugh.

"Did she write it in her own blood? Is the number 1-800-I-LOVE-PUSSY?"

I shake my finger at her. "I knew there was a sense of humor hiding in there somewhere."

"Your gayness brings it out in me."

I grab her arm and stop when I see we're standing in front of a donut shop. "What's your favorite kind of donut?"

"I don't eat donuts."

"Not on a regular basis, but if you were going to splurge?"

She considers it for a moment. "When I was a kid, I liked the ones with cream filling and chocolate glaze on top."

"Tonight, you're a kid." I take her hand and pull her into the shop. "Have a seat. I'll get them."

I get two donuts and sit across from her in the booth. "Okay, cover your eyes for a second."

She scowls at me. "Why?"

"Just do it." I wait for her to close her eyes before I get the candles and lighter from my purse. I poke as many candles as will fit in the donut and light them. "Okay, open your eyes." I start singing "Happy Birthday," even though I have a terrible singing voice. Lucky for me, a few people sitting near us join in.

"Okay, make a wish and blow out your candles."

I can tell Julia's embarrassed by the attention, but she blows the candles out. We all clap for her, and I pull the smoking candles out of the donut. It's a holy mess now, but Julia still takes a bite, probably for my benefit.

I'm hesitant to say what I'm about to say to her, but I don't want to leave it unsaid. "Happy birthday, Julia. And thank you for spending it with me. I had fun."

"Do you always carry birthday candles in your purse?"

I shake my head. "No. I just thought that if the opportunity arose tonight, I'd throw one in a hamburger or something."

"Thank you for not telling Sarah," she says. "I didn't want to take away from her big celebration."

"Can I ask why you spent it with me? I mean, you could've done anything tonight. Gone anywhere. It's your fortieth birthday, right? That's kind of a big deal."

"Only if I make it a big deal. Truthfully, David wanted to make it a thing, which I really wasn't interested in."

I gasp. "Julia, I'm shocked at you. Not wanting to spend your fortieth at a pretentious party full of business associates invited by your ex-husband."

"So you see my point. I had to come up with plans, and they turned out to be a refreshing change of pace." She wraps up the rest of her donut in a napkin. "You mentioned a hamburger, and since I'm blowing my healthy diet today, I might as well go all in."

"Yes, you should definitely go all in tonight. Be decadent. Spend money you don't have. Watch porn. Get drunk on cheap wine. Too bad there's not a zipline nearby. A zipline would be good."

"Kiss a girl?"

I freeze because I can't read her expression. Does she regret it? Does she wish she could turn back time? Push me away instead of going all in? "Consider it a birthday kiss between friends. Totally no big deal. Sarah and I kiss like that all the time."

"Do you?"

"No. I'm just trying to make sure I don't lose my job over this."

"You won't, Cassidy. And you're right, it was a sweet birthday kiss, and I'm glad I went with you tonight. And tomorrow, everything will be as it was. Deal?"

Sweet isn't the word I would use. Breathtaking, amazing, hot, sexy, fuck let's do it again. That's what kind of kiss it was. But this is fine. This works. I'll take it. I'll take anything I can get with Julia Whitmore. And then, I tell the single biggest lie of my life. "Deal."

CHAPTER SEVEN

Everything's going to be fine. I repeat the mantra in my head on my way to Julia's suite. Just another normal day. No big deal. As I turn the corner, I see David standing by Julia's door, looking at his phone. His room is several doors away on the same floor, but Lily is at school, so I have no idea what he's doing here. "Hi, David."

"Cassidy." The tone in his voice isn't exactly friendly. "Can I have a minute of your time?"

Damnit. I'm already a few minutes late. "What can I do for you?"

"Take me to a gay bar and show me how the other half lives."

"You need a date?" I hold his stare because I refuse to be intimidated by a man who would cheat on a woman like Julia. At least, that's the rumor. Julia has never confirmed it. She doesn't ever say anything about him one way or the other, but I've seen the frustration written all over her face when he doesn't show up for Lily.

He steps closer, getting well into my personal space. "I always knew there was something off about you. I just couldn't quite put my finger on it."

"Off? How charming."

"You know what I mean."

"No, David, I don't. Why don't you spell it out for me?"

"I don't like being stuck babysitting Lily while you take my wife out for a night of—"

"Fun. That's the word you're looking for. We went to my friend's birthday party, and it just happened to be at a bar."

"A gay bar."

"You've obviously discussed this with Julia already, so I was just wondering if she informed you that she's not actually your wife anymore."

"We're working things out. Why else would I visit her in Seattle?"

"Oh? I thought you were here to spend time with your daughter."

What an asshole.

"You know, you're just someone's personal assistant, so get off your high horse—"

"I'm chief of staff, which you'd know if you worked at WhitCap, except last I checked, you don't," I say, interrupting him. "More to the point, I'm not just *someone's* chief of staff. I'm Julia's chief of staff, and any direction I take will be from her." I pull the keycard out of my jacket pocket. I start to insert it but turn back to David. "And P.S., it's not called babysitting when you're spending time with your own child." I open the door to Julia's suite and walk in, shutting it behind me. She's sitting at her desk, looking as beautiful as ever. It looks as if maybe she got her hair trimmed over the weekend. "Good morning."

She doesn't look up from her paperwork. "I heard talking in the hall. Was that you?"

"Yes. I ran into David out there." Her head shoots up, and she stares at me for a few seconds, then goes back to her work. I could vent to Julia about what an ass I think David is, tell her how threatened he obviously is by my presence here, but we have work to do, and I don't want to give David the pleasure of taking up any of Julia's time. Any of Julia's time with *me*.

"There's another company here in Seattle I've been watching, and I'm meeting with the founders for lunch."

My head shoots up this time. "You didn't tell me about another company. Are you sure we could manage it right now with everything else? I mean, Chicago is already going crazy leading the round for Ionius Punk."

She sets her pen down and looks at me. "Are you questioning my judgment, Cassidy?"

I'd never question her judgment. But her sanity is a different story entirely. I shake my head. "Of course not. What's the name of the company? I'll do some research."

"No need. It's a last-minute lunch. I've already done some recon on my own. If I like what they say, then we'll put our analysts on it."

"Got it." I open my laptop and bring up her schedule. "You have three conference calls with IP today."

"Cancel them."

"What? That doesn't seem like a good idea, considering how busy you are."

She drops her pen on the desk. "Do we have a problem, Cassidy?"

"No, I just know what your schedule looks like and—"

"When and if the time comes that I desire your opinion, I assure you, you'll know it."

"Okay, it's just that—"

"Cassidy, stop." She stands. "Our relationship hasn't changed. I'm still your employer, and I expect to be treated with the same amount of respect and deference as before."

"Of course. I apologize." I go to the wet bar and get my coffee cup out of the cupboard. It feels as if she had that little speech ready to go. She just needed an opening to use it, and apparently, I gave it to her. And just like that, IQ is back. I may need to see a chiropractor soon about my whiplash.

I draw out the coffee-making process to ridiculous lengths so I don't have to look at her yet. My hands are shaking, and I don't want to appear too affected by her words, even though I'm hurt she would think so little of me. As if I'd suddenly walk around as if I owned the place now? I take my cup back to my desk and try to avoid eye contact.

"You're right about the office," she says. "I should've left you back in Chicago to run things."

I don't dare respond. I'm not entirely sure what she means, but I know enough to know she might think I'm questioning her judgment if I remind her how qualified the team in Chicago actually is. Also, she probably wishes she left me back there for other reasons involving a steamy kiss.

I resist the urge to go over there and straddle her legs and hold her face in my hands and tell her everything will be fine. In my fantasies, she would run her hands up my thighs and grip my ass. She'd keep her hands there and look at me with those amazing blue eyes and say, "I know, honey. As long as I have you, everything will always be fine."

Oh good God, could I be any lamer? I could be on the verge of losing my job because yeah, being in the same room feels awkward as hell, and I know Julia feels it too. I blame tequila and that tight T-shirt.

She's trying to hide her feelings with the tough boss act, but I think I see some pain in her expression. And yet, I can't get her out of my head. Her scent, her touch, her kiss: it's all so close it feels as if it happened only seconds ago.

Before I can look away and pretend to be working, her eyes meet mine. If we could speak the truth out loud, what would we say to each other? Would she apologize for scolding me just now? Would she admit that the attraction is mutual? Would I tell her—

"Have you ever used Ryder?"

She interrupted my thought process, damnit. Would I tell her how much I love it when she takes off her suit jacket and her shoes and paces in her office barefooted? Or when she—

"Cass?"

She called me Cass. Why did she call me Cass? "Yes? Sorry."

"Have you ever used Ryder?"

"The moving company?"

"No. It's a dating app."

Where is this coming from? She wants to know where I find all of my nonexistent dates? "I don't really need to. Sarah considers herself my dating app."

"That's here in Seattle. What about in Chicago?"

Do I really want to admit I haven't had a single date since I moved to Chicago? No, I don't. "I've never used a dating app for my, my, you know, connections in Chicago." Oh God. I sound like a prostitute. Or a drug dealer. Pathetic, seeing as I live more like a nun.

"Will you take a look at it for me? I'd like your opinion."

I pick up my phone. "Why me?"

"Because this app is for your demographic."

"Millennials?"

"Lesbians."

My heart skips a beat. My eyes shoot up from my phone. One kiss and she's on a lesbian dating app? "And you care about a lesbian dating app because…"

"That's who I'm meeting with at lunch today. I might invest in the company."

Okay, this is so out of the realm of where Julia invests her money. There's no way a lesbian dating app is going to offer the profit margins she looks for. "Why?"

"Because there's a lot of money in the promise of love, Cassidy. Grindr sold for two hundred and fifty million, and they aren't even fully monetizing their user data from what I can see. Maybe Ryder should lose the E."

She writes herself a note while I stare at her, slack-jawed. When she sets her pen down, I close my mouth and bring up the app. "I would have to sign up to see anything."

"Please do that, then report to me before my meeting."

Julia's in the other room on a call when I start setting up my Ryder profile. The splash screen is pretty much written for Sarah. Two women with perfect bodies, their faces slightly obscured by ridiculous amounts of highlighted hair. And then the tagline.

Ryder
The most single lesbians on planet Earth

Planet Earth? Ryder isn't lacking in confidence. I scan the main page and wonder why Julia is interested in this now. The nightclub debacle was just over two days ago. Even if she was interested personally, she wouldn't involve her company. For Julia, the lines between business and pleasure are clear. One of her credos is "Personal lives are for personal time. Business is business."

I keep thinking back to what she said. *I've already done some recon on my own.* Recon? What recon? Looking at Grindr? I can't say I know much about it, but I'm pretty sure Grindr and Ryder have different value propositions. Julia's not stupid. She'd never think of the LGBTQ demo as homogenous. In my heart, I know what the recon was; I just don't want to admit it to myself.

"Well? What were your findings?"

I'm walking with Julia down to the hotel restaurant for her meeting. I haven't been invited to stay and take notes, so I'll probably get something to go. "It's a solid app. The reviews are good. When users report problems, they seem to be on top of it."

"Would you feel comfortable using it?"

"If I was into that sort of thing, sure." I pull up the app and show her the main screen on my phone. "They allow the users to make it clear what they're looking for, be it a quickie or long-term relationship or even just friendship." She looks away from my phone and picks up her pace. "Also, they seem to have a solid search engine. I put in the words 'Chicago' and..." Oh God. Did I seriously almost say that out loud?

"And what?" Julia stops and turns to look at me. She has that look of arrogant impatience she gets when anyone on Earth hasn't provided a satisfactory response. "I don't have all day. Just show me." She grabs my phone from my hand. The app's already up. She taps a few times and pauses. She doesn't react other than to say, "Oh. Okay, thanks." She hands my phone back and walks into the restaurant.

I look at my phone. The filters are right there, plain as day, mocking me.

What are you looking for?
Location: Chicago Area
Age: 40–45
Education: Graduate School
Employment: Professional
Height: 5'8" or above
Keywords: Short hair, blue eyes, finance

I should probably think about getting a new job. I could just run out the door right now. I've got my phone and my wallet. Do I really need anything else? I decide to consider it more carefully on a full stomach.

I grab a menu from the hostess so I can place a to-go order. I'll try to drown my sorrows in truffle fries. With a chaser of the triple chocolate chip cookies. A high-pitched squeal from across the restaurant grabs my attention. I watch a very excited woman rush into Julia's arms. After a long hug, she introduces Julia to another woman, and they all sit at the table.

"Cassidy."

Shit. It's David behind me. I turn and force a smile. "Yes?"

"Where's Julia? I thought I'd ask her to lunch."

"Someone beat you to it." I focus on the menu again. Damn, it felt good to say that to him.

"Who?"

"I don't know their names."

"I thought you knew everything. Every move she makes."

"And every breath? No, David. Just the work-related stuff."

"So, it isn't a work meeting?"

I shrug. "Hard to say."

"Why are you being so coy? Who is she with?" His jaw flexes when he spots Julia and her lunch guests.

"It's not my job to keep you up to speed on your *ex*-wife's whereabouts, David." I make sure to draw out the "ex" and raise my voice just a wee bit to make my point.

As David stomps out of the restaurant, I turn back to Julia. She's laughing with the woman who just hugged her as if they're long-lost friends. No, this isn't just a work meeting, and I feel as if I'm watching something I shouldn't be watching, but I can't take my eyes off her. That is, until she looks my way. I expect her lips to tighten up because I'm still here when I should be back upstairs working, but she waves me over to the table. I look around, point at myself and whisper, "Me?" She waves me over again and stands when I arrive at the table. I feel her hand on my back, so I put mine on hers.

"Ladies, I'd like you to meet my chief of staff, Cassidy Bennett. Cass, this is Rory and Piper."

Rory and Piper? Seriously? Isn't anyone named Jennifer or Michelle anymore?

There's an upbeat excitement in Julia's voice that wasn't there a few minutes ago. I shake Piper's hand first, the one who had squealed at the sight of Julia. "Pleasure to meet you."

"And you as well, Cassidy." Piper's eyes fall to my chest for a split second. She's an elegant woman, much like Julia, while being a tad less subtle about it. Her jewelry is a bit larger, with more shimmer. Her lips are full in the way that costs money, and her freckled chest tells me she's spent plenty of time on a beach somewhere.

Rory appears to be closer to my age. I'm guessing early thirties.

She has a silver ring on every finger and a firm grip. She's wearing a tie clip, which turns out to be a good thing since her preppy plaid skinny tie would've otherwise ended up in her drink when she stood and leaned across the table to shake my hand. "It's certainly my pleasure, Cassidy."

Julia moves her hand from my back to my waist and pulls me closer. "Piper, I would brag about how great Cassidy is at her job, but I'm afraid you'd steal her away from me, just like I did with her previous employer."

"Damn right I would. And I'd pay her better too. What do you think of Seattle, Cassidy? Would you like to move here?"

"Actually, I grew up here."

Piper throws her hands in the air. "See? It's meant to be."

Julia doesn't loosen her grip on me, and honestly, I don't want her to. I want a few more seconds of my fantasyland where we're a couple chatting with another couple. Which makes me wonder if Piper and Rory are solely business partners or if there's something more to their relationship.

"Hey, Pipe," Julia says. "Do you want me to invest in your company or not?"

"I want all kinds of things from you, Whit, but we can start with your money."

Okay, so Piper would like to devour my boss right here in this restaurant if her flirty expression is any indication. Rory looks as uncomfortable as I feel right now, and Julia just took her hand off me. I don't think an invitation to sit is in my near future, so I take a step back. "Nice to meet you both. Enjoy your lunch."

CHAPTER EIGHT

An hour later, I'm busily cleaning out my inbox when Julia bursts into the penthouse suite and heads straight for her bedroom. I follow behind her and stand at the door. "Everything okay?"

"The sun is out. Finally." She throws a pair of jeans on the bed. "I'm going to pick Lily up from school and take her on the ferry." She stops and looks at me. "Would you like to join us?"

"Are you sure you don't want to take Piper?" Why the hell would I say that? Lily is more mature than I am sometimes.

"What do you mean by that, Cassidy?"

"I don't know why I said that."

"Stop. You're out of line again." She walks over to me and folds her arms. "Because Ryder is a dating app for lesbians, you're choosing to assume Piper is gay?"

"What? No. That never crossed my mind. It was the way she looked at you. Straight women don't do that."

"Stop." She goes to her drawer, pulls my rainbow T-shirt out, and hands it to me. "I meant to give this to you earlier."

"Okay, but you and Piper are friends, right, Whit?" I just threw in the newly discovered nickname for good measure. It's actually cute and has grown on me over the past hour, but Whit doesn't need to know that. Whit, Whit, Whit. See? It works.

"What we are is none of your business. Now, would you like to go with Lily and me or not?"

I search her eyes for some kind of clue that she actually wants me to go, not just to help her with Lily but because she'd enjoy my company. Her hard stare tells me nothing. "I have a busy day."

I turn to walk away, but she grabs my arm. Her touch is gentle, and her eyes have softened. "I'd like you to go. Lily loves your company."

"What about you?"

She gives me a smirk. "Just don't get drunk, and we'll be fine."

"But I'm so fun when I'm drunk." I can't believe I just said that. Luckily, she laughs and goes over to the bed. She unbuttons her dress pants, then looks at me. "Could you close the door, please?"

"Oh. Right. Okay." I close the door and head back to my desk, chastising myself for standing there like a big ol' gay dufus, ready to enjoy the Julia-gets-undressed show. God, what a show that would be. The pants fall, revealing those long, firm legs. I know they're firm because back in Chicago, Julia swims laps every morning. I haven't had a reason to visit the pool so I could see for myself, but I don't have to. I know they're sexy as hell.

The panties would be black. No, maybe red. Either works just fine. They'd hug her ass and be lacy in the front. She'd turn away from me, unbutton her shirt, and let it fall away. Then she'd—

"Are you going to wear those heels on the ferry?"

"What?" I was so lost in my fantasy, I didn't hear her door open. "I mean...what?" Is my face red? It's red. I know it is.

"Your shoes, Cassidy. Go change and meet me at the car."

Did I ever say I was going on the ferry? I don't remember saying that. Apparently, it doesn't matter because IQ has decided I'll be accompanying them. Look, you and I both know I was going no matter what, but that is not the point. The point is, I would like Julia to at least pretend I have a say in the matter. That's how relationships work, or so I'm told.

She's wearing the jeans I bought for her with a white T-shirt and white Stan Smiths. My God, she's adorable and sexy, and I probably shouldn't go with them. I'll just stare at her the whole time. Also, I wouldn't miss this for the world, so I jump up and head for the door. "Give me five."

I haven't been on a ferry in years. As public transportation goes, it really doesn't get any better than the ferry on a sunny day. Julia's decided we'll go to Bainbridge Island. I suspect mainly because it was leaving within a few minutes of our arrival. We're walk-ons, so we don't need to wait. I'm actually glad she picked Bainbridge. It's not too long a ride, and if we feel like a little walk, there's a cute town on the other side. If we're lucky, we'll see a pod of orcas on the way. Three dozen orcas once circled the ferry as it approached the Bainbridge terminal. I'll settle for a small pod to delight Lily.

Julia breaks some crackers into her clam chowder. "You were right, Cassidy. This chowder is delicious."

"It's a ferry thing. Or maybe it's a Seattle thing. People love the ferry food."

"That's because it's yummy," Lily chimes in between bites of chili.

"It sure is." I take a spoon and steal an extra-large bite of hers.

"Hey!" Lily acts put out, but she's laughing. "It's okay, Cassie. I'll share with you." She nudges her bowl toward me.

"It's okay, squirt. I just wanted one bite. I'm not too hungry. I mean, if they had corn dogs, I'd make an exception."

Julia looks up from her phone. "But they do have corn dogs."

"They only have chicken corn dogs," I explain. Then I turn to Lily with a serious look on my face. "Lily, what I'm about to tell you is extremely important. The very concept of chicken corn dogs is an affront to everything that is good and true in this world. The only thing worse is a veggie corn dog, which should be disqualified from even competing in the corn dog category."

Lily giggles. "What's an affront?"

"It means it's something that offends people," Julia says. "Particularly people who are really, really picky about their corn dogs." Lily seems to take this in before pivoting in the way that only five-year-olds can. "Mom, can we go up front?" She points to the bow of the boat where people are leaning against the railing, taking in the view.

"Of course, sweetie."

"Yay!" Lily jumps up and grabs my hand. "Come on, Cassafrass, we're going up front."

"Okay, silly Lily, but jackets on first. It looks windier than Chicago out there."

❖

Julia and I sit on a bench at the back of the small platform. Lily spots a little boy near her age and tries to make friends. Apparently, Beckham lives on Bainbridge, and from the way he's pointing out the sights to Lily, it seems he's on this route regularly. "That's Blake Island." He points excitedly at the small island off in the distance. "They have lots of deers there because back a really long time ago, people would hunt them, and the deers swam to Blake Island to escape."

Julia smiles at the kids, then gives me what seems like a playful nudge. "So, corn dogs, huh?"

"Well, I didn't put this on my résumé, but I'm basically a corn dog connoisseur. Not surprisingly, the best one I've ever had was *not* on a ferry. It was at one of those little shopping mall carnivals, where people you'll never see again set up for a few days before they're on to the next town. State fair corn dogs run a close second, but the shopping mall carnival dog has yet to be beat."

"I was never allowed to go to those. My parents said they didn't trust the carnies to set up the rides correctly."

"Did you seriously just say carnies?"

"I did indeed. I know a lot about carnivals. I considered investing in one."

Did Julia just try to make a joke? "You did not. I know every one of your deals: closed, unrealized, and apparently, imaginary."

"Fine," she says with a sigh. "My parents didn't trust the temporary employees hired by the traveling carnival organizations to properly set up or manage the rides."

"Huh. I guess my parents didn't love me enough to stop me. In fact, they let me go alone with my friends when I was ten. I ate so much cotton candy, I had a stomachache for two days."

"I'm not sure at what age I'll let Lily go anywhere alone, but I know ten is not the answer. Probably twenty-five."

I gasp. "You'll ruin her. She won't know how to function in the real world. She won't know how to order a freakin' corn dog. Or how to talk to strangers. She'll be a psychopath, Julia."

She giggles at me. "Is that your medical opinion, Doctor?"

"It's not just my opinion. You have to give kids the freedom to make choices and fail. You have to let them skin their knees and eat dirt and get in trouble at school and do their time in the principal's office. And then, you have to love them through it. You have to be there when they shed tears, but you can't protect them from the thing that caused the tears."

"And this information is coming from?"

"Oh, for God's sake, IQ. Don't you know I've read every one of the eight thousand child-rearing books you have on your office bookshelf?"

She pulls back a bit and looks at me. "Did you just call me IQ?"

Shit. Did I say that out loud? "It means you're super smart. You know, like, she has an IQ of one-eighty-five."

"Ha! Nice try."

"But you are. You're the smartest person I know." Also, the hottest, but that's better left unsaid. Unless I just said that out loud without realizing it too.

"Again, nice try. I know it stands for Ice Queen. According to some, I have a heart made of ice, and I live in the depths of an enormous iceberg off the coast of Iceberglandia."

I shake my head. "Not a place. You actually live in Norway. Rumor has it, you and Elsa from *Frozen* are neighbors."

"Ha! Don't mention *Frozen* unless you want an impromptu and very loud singalong of 'Let It Go' with a five-year-old in front of everyone on this ferry." She gives me a side-eye. "And surely by now, you know I know everything that goes on in my office."

"Mmm-hmm." I agree, though I've suddenly taken a keen interest in the view. Any minute now, she's going to tell me how out of line I am.

"She's a college friend." Julia wraps her jacket around her a bit more tightly. I look at her, and she says, "Piper. She's a college friend."

"Oh." We sit in silence for a moment after that quick change of subject. Lily has moved on from Beckham to a little girl with what looks like a beagle puppy. That should keep her busy for a while.

"We were more than friends for a bit," Julia says. Again, I look at her. "Piper," she adds.

"Oh." Well, this is fucking news. I'm sure I sound as stunned as I feel.

"So, no, Cassidy, you weren't my first lady kiss."

I let that sink in and then blurt out, "You know what was special about that corn dog at the carnival?"

"What?"

"It was my first. You never forget your first corn dog."

She smiles at me. "Or your first kiss?"

"Or your first *lady* kiss. Piper is a stunning woman. You have good taste, IQ." Now that the cat is out of the bag, so to speak, I feel free to use the nickname.

"She is. That hasn't changed."

Her tone is wistful, but I don't see this as a bad thing. I turn to her and say, "That's a relief, actually."

"How so?"

"Ever since that night at the club, I've had this feeling that I showed you something you didn't want to see."

"About you?" she asks.

"Well, yes. I mean, no. I mean, I meant going to a gay club, and obviously, my friends aren't like your friends." I'm babbling. Why am I babbling?

"You did show me something new, but I like that. I've never been in a gay club before. It was an eye opener. The whole evening was an eye opener." She turns on the bench toward me. "But did you really think I didn't know you're gay?"

She knew? The whole time, she knew? "Wait. So, you came with me to a gay club, knowing you were going to a gay club?"

"I didn't know for sure, but I hoped that's where we'd end up. Great research for the app."

Oh my God. No wonder she seemed as if she was having a grand ole time at the opry. She was collecting data the whole night. Doing recon, as she put it. Sizing up her future clientele. God, I'm such an idiot. Again. "Well, I can't imagine you gleaned any vital information from that place."

"Are you kidding? Information started pouring in before we even walked through the door. I mean, the entrance is past a row of dumpsters, and really, a hot dog vendor?"

"Hey, I'm sure he does well. He'd probably do even better if he sold corn dogs."

"And I applaud his entrepreneurial spirit," she says. "But that doesn't change the fact that there's clearly a gap in the market."

I hate this. I hate that my stomach had flip-flopped when she asked if she could join me that night. I hate that I swooned a little when I thought she wanted to spend her birthday with me. Okay, fine. Not a little but a lot. I hate that it was all just her stupid recon. "All right, fine, Julia. Educate me. What's the gap?"

"You're a sophisticated, successful woman, Cassidy. Is going to a place like that really how you want to meet women, or would you rather pick both the woman and the place where you meet instead of relying on Sarah?"

"I don't rely on Sarah or anyone else. I'm quite capable of finding my own dates."

"Where?" Julia asks. "If ten percent of the population is gay, and half of those are men, and most of the women don't meet your high standards, or at least the high standards I think you should have, you're looking at a very small percentage of the public. And how in the world would you single out those women and approach them?"

"I don't approach any woman who I don't first know is gay."

"Which is my point. If you were to use Ryder—which, by the way, Sarah and Jane have used, and Jane is dating someone she met on there now—you could immediately rule out Infected Nose Ring Girl with age parameters. Not to mention interests, employment, etcetera. Eventually, the app ought to have a pretty good idea of who's right for you based on who you interact with and who they've interacted with in the past."

I've been around Julia long enough to know she's talking about an algorithm for my love life. And sadly, she's right. In all the times I've gone to that bar with Sarah, I've never met anyone I'd want to date long-term. "I get what you're saying, but people have tried building lesbian dating apps and failed or at least haven't reached the kind of success you would be looking for."

"Maybe they're not doing it right. Or maybe they were built on a shoestring budget and don't have the funding required to update or expand or just keep up with and implement new technologies in general."

She's probably right about that too. Companies that have tried to cater to lesbians are depressingly underfunded. Or at least it sure seems like it judging from the crap product out there. I mean, have you ever seen a lesbian movie on Netflix?

"I looked up your college friend Piper. She has plenty of money, so why is she coming to you for funding?"

"It's true, Piper could throw money at Ryder for years and not feel the loss, but she doesn't have my experience. I think coming to me was a very smart move on her part."

"Okay. I have a question. Just how much of that night was research?"

"I told you, Cassidy, that wasn't my first encounter with another woman. I didn't need to kiss you to know how it would feel. That's what you're asking, right?"

"How *did* it feel?"

"It felt like an HR nightmare. Something we should probably discuss at some point. The sooner, the better. In fact, I like your suggestion. Let's call it research that got out of hand. Nothing more, nothing less. And we can both sign something to that effect if you're in agreement."

It feels as if the temperature just dropped a million degrees. Ice Queen indeed. Are we really reducing our night together to research that got out of hand? And documenting that in a signed document? Apparently so. "Whatever you need."

I close my eyes for a second when what I really want to do is disappear. She didn't feel a thing when we kissed. Not a damn thing. And here I am, slowly falling in love with her. Because, you see, I know that's what's happening. And if I have even a single brain cell inside my head, I'll stop those feelings before they take hold and consume me.

CHAPTER NINE

We're not being ourselves with each other, but I don't know how else to act, other than strictly professional. After our conversation on the ferry yesterday, I managed to maintain a level of friendliness I didn't feel in my heart. In other words, I faked it until we got back to the hotel. Today, I'm not doing such a good job of hiding my hurt feelings.

"Hungry?" Julia doesn't wait for me to reply. She picks up the hotel phone.

"I thought I'd go down to the lobby and—"

"Yes, I'd like to order two cobb salads and a fruit plate, no pineapple."

"Get a muffin," I say under my breath, finishing my reply. Then I look at her. "You didn't have to do that."

"Get lunch?" She looks at her watch. "It's almost two. Do you really want to see me get hangry?"

Would I know the difference? Probably not. "No, the pineapple thing. You like it. Lily likes it. Don't leave it off just for me."

"I'm sure Lily and I will survive without pineapple."

"That's not the point."

"No?" She glares at me. "Then what exactly is the point of this inane conversation?"

"The point is, I want a muffin, not a cobb salad." I grab my purse and storm out of the suite. God, she makes me so mad sometimes. Who does she think she is leaving the pineapple off the fruit plate just because they give me canker sores? And then ordering a salad for me without asking? Granted, they make a great cobb salad, but she stepped over a big line this time. Huge line. Specifically, the Cobb Salad Line, which everyone knows exists.

Speaking of lines, there's a long one at the coffee bar. I throw my hands in the air because now I have to go back up there with my damn tail between my legs and eat that damn salad. I turn around to do just that. That's when I realize who's standing right in front of me in line. I wish I could tell you it's Beyoncé or someone equally interesting. I'd build up to the reveal and have you guessing about the mystery woman in my story. No such luck. It's not Beyoncé. I turn back around just to make sure I saw who I thought I saw. And then I say it. "Mom?"

She turns around and sounds surprised. "Cassie. I was just on my way to your room."

Was she? Because she looks as if she's in line for a latte. I look at the baristas and then back at my mother. I think I've achieved a suitably skeptical look.

"I thought I'd bring you a muffin. You always did like muffins. Do you still?"

I stifle a laugh. My mother has always had a knack for being completely unaware of the innuendo she unleashes upon the world around her. "I do indeed." I haven't seen my mother in years. Her dark hair has started to gray, and the wrinkles around her green eyes have deepened. She was always so beautiful to me, but she looks tired now. Sad almost. "How did you know I was here?"

"Sarah told me."

Note to self: Kill Sarah. "Yeah, I'm here for work. I was planning to call; we've just been too busy." I wasn't planning to call, and she knows it. Why would I when they treated me so badly after I came out?

"We hoped you'd make that effort one day."

I tilt my head. "You did? Because as I recall—"

"Let's not talk about our past mistakes, Cassie. We all made them. Don't you think it's time to put all of that to rest?"

Is someone fucking kidding me? Let's not talk about our past mistakes? That's the kind of thing only the mistake maker says. Sure, just kick me out of your lives and then show up at the Four Seasons acting as if I should have called. Ugh. These people. "I don't know, Mom, is it really time to put all that to rest? I'm still gay, you know. When you say we all made mistakes, is that what you think mine was? Do you still think it's a choice I'm making to hurt you?"

"Hello," my mom says to someone behind me. I turn and find Julia standing there, looking concerned.

"Mom, this is Julia. Julia, my mom, Jasmine."

"Sarah told me you had someone special, Cassie. I take it you're the same Julia? Sarah had the most wonderful things to say about you."

Oh, great. Just great. The nightmare never ends. "Mom—"

"Pleasure to meet you, Jasmine," Julia says as she shakes her hand.

I feel Julia's other hand on my back, and I want to scream. This is not happening again. I am not going to pretend Julia is anything but—

"Julia is my boss, Mom. She owns WhitCap. That's the company I work for, but you wouldn't really know that."

"Sarah keeps us apprised of things."

"How accommodating of her." I fail to keep the sarcasm out of my voice. And by the way, Sarah is going to get the biggest piece of my mind before I kill her as previously promised. Julia's hand drops away from my back, and I instantly miss the contact. God, I'm so confused. "What I meant to say is, that's nice of Sarah, but you could always call me yourself and find out how I'm doing."

"Well, I'm here now," she says. "Maybe you could join us for dinner tonight." She looks at Julia. "Both of you, if you'd like to come as well."

"I have a daughter. Lily." Julia rests her hand on my back again. "Would you mind having a five-year-old tag along?"

"Of course not. We'd love to have a little one around the house again." My mom takes a tentative step toward me and leans in, giving me a light kiss on my cheek. "See you at seven."

"If I remember the address," I mumble as I watch her walk away. That woman's ability to turn me into a petulant teenager is unmatched. And did she really just invite the woman she believes is my girlfriend to dinner tonight? Has the world turned upside down? "I don't know what just happened," I say to Julia.

She takes my arm. "Let's talk on the way upstairs."

The elevator doors close, and we lean on opposite walls. "How long has it been since you've seen your parents?" she asks.

"Years."

"How many?"

"Not enough."

She looks at me with raised eyebrows, apparently expecting a less sarcastic answer.

"It doesn't matter. This isn't your problem, and you don't have to go with me tonight."

"Would it help if we were there? Maybe make it less awkward?"

"Or more awkward. She didn't invite you because you're my boss. She invited you because she thinks—"

"I know what she thinks," Julia says, interrupting me. "It seems like a pretty big deal *why* she invited me. That must be a huge step for them."

The doors open, and I walk out first. "I'm tempted to stand them up."

"And where would that get you?"

I open the door to the suite. "No worse off than before, that's for sure. I've lived without them for more than a decade. No reason I can't keep on doing it."

"Cassidy."

I feel a hand on my shoulder. I set my purse on my desk and keep my back to her. I can't turn around when I feel as if I'm about to cry. How dare my mother show up as if it's nothing? Oh sure, let's just call it water under the bridge. Leave the mistakes in the past, as she says. Bygones and bullshit, that's what it is. As if ignoring what happened will somehow keep all the horrible memories of their anger and disappointment at bay too.

I feel Julia's arms surround me from behind, and it does me in. I start heaving for air. I feel a kiss on my shoulder and her breath on my neck. Soon, the sobs start, and I turn and fall into her arms because really, there's no one else in the world who could possibly ease this pain. I know she can't take it away, but I wonder if she can calm the storm that always lingers inside me. That's how it felt when we kissed. She made me feel worthy of love, if only for a moment. Only Julia can do that. Always Julia.

CHAPTER TEN

I t's the fourth house on the right."

We're on my parents' street now. The house looks the same. Still stuck in the '70s when it was built. It's a split level with vertical cedar siding. The old long-needle pine tree in the front yard still towers over it. Every spring, my dad would threaten to cut it down because he was sick of having to clear the dead needles from the gutters. I would cry and convince him not to, and he would call me a tree hugger. And then I'd wrap my little arms as far around the trunk as I could to keep him from cutting it down, which I realize is basically the point of tree hugging. It was years before I clued in that pine trees don't lose their needles, and he was really just bitching about the mess from another long, rainy winter.

My eyes are still a little red from the crying earlier, but I freshened up my makeup and curled my hair. It's silly, but I want my parents to see the woman I've become without their influence in my life. That also explains the rather expensive leather boots I have my jeans tucked into. And the diamond tennis bracelet on my wrist. Yes, I'm being shallow, but I don't give a damn.

Too bad I can't really claim the gorgeous woman sitting in this car with me as mine. Or the little girl sitting between us, for that matter. Julia insisted on coming with me tonight. I felt so embarrassed to be crying on her shoulder earlier, but truth be told, I've been craving her touch ever since that night in the bar. Pain and pleasure warred with one another while she held me. They're still warring because I can't really claim her. But she's here, and that gives me some comfort.

"I hope your mom is a good cook," Julia casually states.

"I hope you like fish sticks and overcooked broccoli."

"Ew," Lily says. "I hate broccoli."

I smile at Julia. "Don't worry. She's a great cook. I've missed having that in my life."

"Don't you mean *her?* You've missed having *her* in your life?"

"That's TBD. Let's see how tonight goes."

We all get out of the car, and Lily grabs my hand as we go up the brick steps to the front door. "Do your daddy and mommy have a backyard?"

"They sure do," I answer. Lily leads a pretty cosmopolitan life. She's seen a lot for a five-year-old, but she's missed out on some of the everyday experiences I had as a kid. Her dream of having access to the mythological place known as a backyard is something her mother and I are both well aware of.

Her eyes widen. "Is there a swing set?"

Crap. Childhood dreams shattered. "Ah, sorry, kiddo. They used to have one when I was little, but not anymore."

"Oh, that's too bad. I love swings."

She looks so cute in her little red sundress and matching sweater, I could just eat her up. When we get to the door, I lean over and kiss her chubby cheek. "I'm so glad you came with us, Lily. You can call my parents Mr. and Mrs. Bennett, okay?"

"Yep. Mommy already told me."

I straighten back up and look at Julia. She's wearing a tan linen jacket over a white blouse with her dark jeans. She looks amazing. "Thank you for this."

She gives me a wink and says, "You should probably ring the doorbell."

"Right." I turn back around, and the door opens. It's my dad. His hair is more salt than pepper now, kind of like my mom's. "Hi, Dad."

He opens the screen door and smiles. "Hey, pumpkin."

Lily giggles. "Your daddy called you a pumpkin."

"And who do we have here?" My dad leans over and offers his hand. "You must be Princess Lily of the Chicago clan. I hear your people are very brave and very good dog trainers. Is that true?"

"I want a puppy dog so bad," Lily says. "A girl on the ferry has one, and his name is Scooter."

"Well, it just so happens that I am in need of a dog trainer, Princess Lily."

Lily gasps. "You have a dog?"

"Would you like to meet her?"

Lily gasps again. "It's a girl dog? What's her name?"

"She doesn't have one yet. That's one of the things I'd hoped you'd help me with, Princess Lily."

Lily turns to Julia and in a very serious tone says, "Mommy, I need to help Mr. Bennett give his doggie a name."

My dad steps out of the house and kisses my cheek. "You've never looked more beautiful. Let's get off of the porch, shall we?" He reaches for Julia's hand. "Good to meet you, Julia. I'm Lyle."

"Good to meet you, sir."

We follow my dad inside and climb the six stairs to the main level. Lily spots the dog kennel in the living room and runs to it. She kneels down and starts cooing at the little one inside. I look at my dad. "You got a puppy?"

He shoves his hands in his pockets and bounces on his heels. He always did that when he had a surprise for me.

"Dad, what did you do?"

"Our neighbor two doors down had a litter, and when I heard about your little one, well, I just couldn't resist."

I look at Julia. "Dad, we're at the Four Seasons." I widen my eyes at her and whisper, "Sorry."

"We'll keep her until you go back to Chicago. And if in the end it doesn't work out, we'll keep her forever."

"No, you guys, it's okay." Lily grabs both of our hands. "Remember my friend Ryan, Mom? She lives at the hotel too, and she has a dog, a great big one. And they have a place to take him out, and the housekeepers even leave treats and everything."

Lily drags us over to the little puppy, who I believe we're going to call I'm Going to Kill My Dad. I look over at Julia and mouth the words *I'm sorry.*

Lily turns around with tears in her eyes. "Mommy, I love her so much. Can we get her out of the cage so I can hug her?"

I turn to my dad and shake my head. My mom steps up behind him. "I tried to talk him out of it." She points at the dog crate. "I'll just help Lily get her out."

Lily gets the little puppy in her arms and giggles as she tries to lick her face. "Mommy, she likes me!"

Julia takes her phone out of her pocket. She's been so quiet about the whole thing, I have no idea what she's thinking. She takes a few pics of Lily, and the smile on her face makes me think she's not super angry about it. Obviously, my dad has no idea who he's dealing with.

He claps his hands together. "Okay, ladies. We have red, white, and a fine, six-week-old light beer."

"I'll have a glass of red," Julia says.

I feel as if I should keep my wits about me. These are not the angry, tearful parents I left behind. These are people who buy children's love with puppies. And just to be clear, I've never been opposed to that sort of thing. It certainly worked in my favor when I was a child. "Just a diet soda for me, Dad."

I watch in awe as my mom sits on the floor and discusses puppy issues with Lily. I still can't believe this is happening. Why now?

She gets up off the floor and puts up her hands. "Let me wash these, and then we'll have dinner."

We get the little chocolate brown puppy back in the crate. I'm not sure what breed she is. Maybe a mix of some sort. I take Lily to the guest bathroom and help her wash her hands. She looks up at me and says, "She's the prettiest puppy I've ever seen."

"She is a pretty little girl. Have you thought of a name for her yet?"

She shakes her head. "I'm going to think about it while I eat. I'm hungry."

"Me too." I rinse off her hands and wipe them dry with a towel.

"Me too." I look up and see Julia leaning against the door frame, her thumbs tucked into her front pockets. She's grinning from ear to ear.

"What?" I ask.

"I like your parents."

"Me too," Lily shouts.

"Yeah, they're nice people." I want to make some sarcastic remark about how it's easy to like them when you're not their daughter, but Lily doesn't need to hear that. "Or so I've been told."

In Seattle, you have to take advantage of sunny days when you can, so I'm not surprised when my mom leads us outside to the redwood deck on the back of the house. Dad gives us our drinks and offers Lily a juice box. "It's strawberry apple. Mrs. Bennett thought you might like that flavor."

"Thank you, Mr. Bennett." Lily takes the box and holds it carefully while she sips. That would be due to the little lesson about having good manners in other people's homes she got from Julia before we left.

"This is beautiful." Julia steps up to the edge of the deck. "Do you back up to a forest?"

"Sort of." I stand next to her. "We're on the edge of the subdivision. Beyond the trees is a golf course."

My dad stands next to me. "Cassie loved it when she was a little girl. She called it her enchanted forest." There's an unexpected softness in my dad's voice. I turn to him, and he smiles at me. "Does Lily dress up like a princess the way you used to, honey?"

The way my dad's voice just cracked has me worried. I hope he doesn't cry in front of everyone. "She does. A pink dress, just like mine."

He nods and turns back to the trees. "She'd probably love the enchanted forest, then. Think of all the adventures she could have." He points to a spot on the left. "Remember when we camped out just beyond the trees?"

I look at the spot. "Yeah, I remember. We were rained out."

"That was part of the adventure," he says. "Don't you remember how we huddled under a tarp until the castle guards gave up on trying to find us? We waited until we couldn't hear the hoofbeats of their horses anymore, and then we ran as fast as we could toward the sound of the wind chimes."

"And Buddy's bark." I can't believe I remember this part. "Buddy went home when it started to rain."

"Smart horse," my dad says with a wink.

I turn to Julia. "Buddy was our dog. A big golden Lab that I used to try to ride like a horse. He'd run back home that night, but he kept barking for us to come home too."

Lily tugs on my hand. "Cassie, I want a doggie I can ride like a horse through the enchanted forest."

"Sounds like you had some great adventures with your dad and Buddy," Julia says.

"Buddy is buried in those woods." My dad's expression changes from excitement to sadness. "His grave is probably grown over by now. I'm not even sure if I could find it."

"I could. I know exactly where he's buried." I turn to him. "Maybe we could go look for him after dinner."

He puts his head down and nods. "I would like that."

I'm leading the group single file through the trees. Lily has her puppy wrapped in a blanket and is whispering something about birthday cake to her. I inhale deeply, taking in the musty pine scent of the forest. It brings back only happy memories and makes me realize what a great childhood I had. My dad made sure it was full of adventure, and my mom made sure I always felt safe and looked after.

What happened to them? Why was my coming out such a blow to them that they wanted nothing to do with me anymore? How could they just abandon me like that? And why am I letting them off the hook for it?

I stop dead in my tracks when a memory shoots to the front of my brain. I turn around and find my dad, mom, and Julia staring at me. I should turn around and keep going. We're almost to Buddy's grave. Twenty more steps and we're there. But I can't. I can't do another thing until I know.

"My sophomore year, you two started going on dates every Sunday afternoon. I thought you were going to R-rated movies without me, but that's not what you were doing, was it?"

My parents lower their heads. Julia raises her eyebrows and silently asks me what's going on. I focus on my mom. "Did you join that church your friends were trying to get you into?"

My mom raises her head and looks at me. "We didn't want to force it on you, honey. We knew it would be a lot for a girl your age to understand. We wanted to wait until you were a little older before we introduced you to it."

I turn back around and keep walking. This isn't a confrontation I should have in front of Julia and Lily. But my parents were going to some evangelical church behind my back? No doubt they'd been indoctrinated with homophobic bullshit. Probably counseled to shun me lest they go to hell with their daughter.

We get to the tree Buddy is buried under. The rope I'd tied around a branch about ten feet off the ground is still there, though you'd never know it had once been a bright shade of red. I kneel down and clean the needles off the rock we'd used as a marker.

I didn't expect the tears that fill my eyes. I place my palm on the rock and whisper, "Good boy, Buddy."

My mom crouches and places a little bouquet of wildflowers she and Lily had picked along the way on the rock. She moves out of the way, and Dad crouches down next to me. He hands me a photograph of Buddy. "We had an extra copy. I'd like you to have it."

"Thanks." I give him a quick smile and wipe the tears from my eyes.

Lily wraps her little arms around my neck. "I'm sorry Buddy died."

I give her a squeeze and kiss her cheek. "Me too, baby."

Chapter Eleven

Julia closes the door to Lily's room. "She was out like a light."

I stand there with my arms folded. I should've left the suite once we got Lily in bed, but I've been pacing from the window to the door. "You don't have to accept that puppy. It was wrong of my dad to make such a huge assumption."

She takes off her jacket and pushes up her sleeves. "You're wound up like a tight rubber band. How about a glass of wine?"

I watch her get a bottle from the bar. "Did you hear me?"

"I heard you. I also felt you shaking your leg the entire ride back. You do that when you're stressed."

"I know. Sorry."

"Don't be. You were ridiculously brave tonight."

"I wasn't. I was...weak. I should've stood up for myself. I should've yelled and pounded my fist on something."

"You could have. But instead, you showed them what an amazing, strong woman you are. And I think they showed you something too."

"Ha! The only thing they showed me was how to bribe a five-year-old."

"Oh, you already knew how to do that. All of those stuffed animals in her room didn't come from the concierge."

"I can't help it. That's different. She owns my heart."

"And you own your parents' heart. I could feel their regret. They know how much they've missed out on. But they also know you don't owe them a single second of your time."

"How do you know that?"

"Because they let you leave without a commitment to return."

"No, they just made sure I'd have to by giving Lily a puppy."

"It's your decision what you do now. I can get the puppy when it's time."

The puppy didn't make it home with us tonight. When Julia broke the news that their suite wasn't pet-friendly like Ryan's, Lily took it fairly well. In other words, Lily extracted a promise from her mother that we would look into moving them to a pet-friendly suite tomorrow. If one isn't available, Lily helpfully suggested that we would simply negotiate with the hotel to make the current room a "dog room." I have no doubt Lily will be able to arrange that with the hotel manager without help from her mother or me. Hard-nosed negotiation runs in the family.

"Look, it's cool," I say while trying to shake it off. "It's nice that they reached out, and yes, it's a big deal that they included you." I fall back onto the couch. "I just need to take it for what it was and let the rest go."

Julia sets two glasses of wine on the coffee table and sits down next to me. "Bullshit." She takes my hands and holds them between us. "These are your parents. They're the only ones you get. Being rejected by them isn't something you just let go of."

I don't respond. I can't. Her hands are warm. I focus on her slender fingers.

"I'm a pretty good judge of people," she says. "That's why I do what I do. And from what I can see, your parents are looking for forgiveness. They're looking to be in your life again. And yes, they suck at articulating it, but they're ready. You might not be able to accept that yet, or ever, and that's okay, because it's finally up to you. But don't reject it just because you believe it's not possible. And for God's sake, don't beat yourself up for not being able to just let it go. You're not a bot."

I don't know what to do with this. She sees me. I love that she sees me. I also hate that she sees me. "You were so great tonight. So patient. I didn't see you check your phone at all." Yes, I'm turning the conversation around to focus on her. I know it's lame; you don't have to tell me that. But still. Julia Whitmore didn't check her phone once. That's almost as big a deal as my parents inviting my supposed girlfriend and her child over for dinner. And then, you know, giving the kid a puppy.

"I was there to support you," she says. "And if your parents had said or done anything hurtful, I would've gotten you out of there as fast as humanly possible."

Just between you and me, I love this woman. Since I can't say that, I go with, "I don't know what to do with all of this support. I don't know what I should be feeling right now."

"I imagine you're feeling all kinds of things after seeing your parents again." She looks down at our joined hands and back up at me. "Don't confuse your feelings right now with whatever you feel for me. This isn't about us."

Us? There's an us?

"You're firing on all cylinders, Cassidy. Emotions are high. The attraction is intense. I get that. But…"

Is she trying to kill me right now with that soft, sexy voice? I pull my hands away and stand. I take a step away from the couch. "But it's one-sided. You've made that clear."

"What?" She looks confused.

I volley back. "What?"

She stands up. "What you just said, Cass."

"Oh. It's fine. We don't have to talk about that. Let's just drink wine." I try to go around her to get my glass, but she blocks my way. And there's that intense stare again. I can't tell if she's angry or—

"I think you should leave."

Okay, so it is anger. I pick up my purse. I don't even bother to put it on my shoulder. I carry it like a clutch with the straps hanging off. How I could possibly think of this as a quality storm-out-of-the-room moment, I'll never know. "Thanks again for tonight." I turn to leave.

"It's never been one-sided. Not since the day we met," she says. I turn back to see her slowly shaking her head. "Not for one second has it been one-sided."

"You could've fooled me."

"And you're smart enough to know that was my goal." She takes a step closer. "But after seeing what you've been through with your parents, I can't let you leave here thinking you aren't good enough. I won't stand for it. Your parents seem like lovely people, Cass. But if you think I didn't want to give them a piece of my mind for rejecting you, you're sorely mistaken."

"You… you did?"

"Yeah, I did. It took everything I had, for Lily's sake and yours.

There's potential with your parents, but that doesn't mean it doesn't break my heart that they made you think you weren't good enough because you so are, Cassie. You're brilliant and beautiful and kind and a lot of things I'm not. You make my life easier and brighter, and God knows you do the same for Lily."

We stand in silence for a moment. And by "moment," I mean one, one thousand. Two, one thousand. Three, one thousand. You know the drill. I finally break the silence. "But?"

Julia has a pained expression on her face now. "You know what the *but* is. You know I can't afford to lose you as my chief of staff."

"You know what it sounds like to me?" I drop my purse and remove the distance between us. She said it's up to me now. Sure, she was talking about my parents, but maybe she meant more than that. "It sounds to me like you can't afford to kiss me right now."

She's weighing the pros and cons, but when her eyes fall to my lips, I know I've got her. She's remembering what I taste like. She knows what it feels like to kiss me, and she wants more. She wants my tongue in her mouth. She wants my hands on her body. She wants to hear me panting in her ear, begging for more. She needs that more than she needs me as her chief of staff. She needs—

Our lips collide.

Me. She needs me. And God knows I need her.

When should I tell Julia that I'm in love with her? Should it be right now, when I'm on top of her, and we're naked and sweaty and grinding on each other? Probably not. That's inappropriate, right? Too early or too hot or too something, right? Her body is everything I thought it would be. Having her legs wrapped around my hips like they are right now has happened so many times in my mind.

Now it's real. And I can barely breathe, I'm so turned on. So wet. So on fire. So ready to come. But I want Julia to come first. I want to hear her say my name and cry out in pleasure, so I drop onto my elbows and kiss her with a passion I've never felt for anyone else before. I can't get enough of her lips. Her tongue. The taste of her.

But I need more. I need to sink my teeth into her shoulder and suck until I leave a mark.

"Oh God," she whispers. "Cass," she says between quick breaths. "Take me. Take me now."

I can't help but grin as I suck a little harder. Ms. Control Freak likes to be taken in bed. This is excellent news. I get up on my knees and move down to her breasts. I've already been there, but I want her very wet by the time I reach my ultimate goal. I worship one with my tongue and then the other. I slide my hand down her smooth stomach and let my middle finger slip into the wetness. She groans, and then I groan because, God, this is everything.

I circle her clit for a few seconds while I watch her reaction. Her eyes are closed, and her hands are gripping my shoulders. "Take me," she says again.

She's wet enough that I don't have to be gentle. I'm so glad I don't have to be gentle. I slide two fingers in as far as they can go, and her hips buck. Her eyes open, and she says, "Fuck me, Cass."

Those words practically make me come and yes, I will fuck her all night long if she wants me to. Her nails dig into my shoulders, and her hips buck, and her groans of pleasure get louder as I push into her. She grabs my face and shoves her tongue into my mouth, and again, I'm so close, and she hasn't even touched me yet.

I need to taste her. I need to run my tongue through her folds and suck her swollen clit into my mouth. So I stay inside her and kiss my way down her stomach. I mark her again when I reach her hip. Just a little something to remind her where I've been.

As my tongue touches her clit, I push in hard again. "Oh God," she says.

I alternate between licking her with a flat tongue and the pointed tip. I don't want her to come too fast. I go slower than I know she wants me to. I want to stay here a while and revel in the fact that I'm here at all. Because fuck, I'm really doing this.

When I feel her body tighten, I take my fingers out and grab onto her hips so I can focus on her clit. The joy I feel when she grabs my hands and squeezes them with all her might as her climax hits her hard is indescribable.

I let her catch her breath for a few seconds before I lie on top of her again. She's limp under me. Her brow is sweaty, and her blue eyes are void of any stress or concern. She looks beautiful. And perfectly relaxed.

"I don't know what to say," she whispers.

I kiss her lips softly. "Don't say anything." But now that the deed is done, she ignores my command.

"Primrose."

"What?"

"Primrose. My middle name. That's what the P stands for."

I giggle. In this moment, what do I do? I fucking giggle. "I'll worry about that later." I slide my hand down her body and back between her luscious thighs. "For right now, I'll assume it stands for something else."

CHAPTER TWELVE

I doubt a double espresso will compensate for the lack of sleep, but it's worth a try. We'll both be functioning on adrenaline and caffeine today, but God, it was worth it. I hope it was for her too.

I snuck out of Julia's suite before sunrise. I didn't want Lily to find me naked in her mother's bed. Though I did amuse myself with the thought of it while standing in line for coffee. "Oh, this," I'd say innocently. "Mommy and I were just exercising. Other favorites include 'can you believe we fell asleep after bath time' and 'Mommy had a tummyache, so I rushed right over.'" For now, sneaking out seems like the safest way to handle things, considering I have no idea how Julia will treat me after last night. Will she be aloof or warm? Stern or flirty? Your guess is as good as mine.

The elevator doors open on Julia's floor. David doesn't wait for me to step out before he gets in. In fact, he blocks my way.

"Good morning, David."

"You ever heard of Little League baseball?"

"Of course. Why—"

"Yeah, that's not you. You're below that. You're in the T-ball league where the ball isn't even pitched to you. They just put it on a tee right in front of you, and you still can't hit it. You know why?"

Really with this shitty analogy? "Because what you're actually describing is golf?"

"Nice try. It's because you're T-ball, and Julia is the best team in the world. She's the Red Sox, and you're T-ball."

As false equivalencies go, I'm pretty sure this one's unmatched. He's basically saying, "Julia is Chanel, and you're a sewing class."

Remember the first thing I said about him? Douche. Bag. But he wants to play baseball, so I'll play baseball. "Are you saying it'll take Julia eighty-six years to win, and then she'll have to overpay to do it?"

"What? No, I'm saying you're T-ball, and Julia—"

"Is the Red Sox. I heard you."

I've caught him off guard. He has no idea my grandpa was only the biggest baseball fan I've ever known. I grew up watching the game with him. He always said it was a game for smart people and challenged me to learn all I could about it. I memorized stats and got treats for my knowledge. The truth is, I loved it. And I still do. And the Red Sox? If you want a shitty analogy, talk about throwing me a softball.

"So, what you're saying, David, is that Julia's gonna come this close to winning," I hold my thumb and forefinger together, "and then the first baseman's going to have the ball go through his legs, and the Mets will win the series?"

You may have figured out by now that there is no way I'm going to let Douchey David get away with trying to insult me by using the single dumbest analogy I have ever heard.

He waves his hand. "Okay, just forget about the baseball."

What a moron. "David, did you actually plan this speech?" I pause to laugh at him a little more. "Is this your way of telling me I'm out of my league? Because you could've just said that in the first place, and then I wouldn't have made you look so far out of yours." I walk away because mic drop.

He catches up to me. "Where did you two go last night?"

"Oh, Julia didn't tell you? We went to a softball game. The ball was moving and everything. Not like that lowly T-ball. It was the super lesbian kind where nachos and beer and toaster ovens are sold. I got the super high-end model."

"I have no idea what you're talking about," he says. A moment passes, and I don't say more. We just stare each other down. Finally, he adds, "I guess I don't speak lesbian."

"Or baseball." Again, what did Julia ever see in this asshole?

"So, you were watching sports?" he stupidly asks.

"No, David. We were actually at a play. It was a revival of the classic musical *It's None of Your Fucking Business, David.* You should try to get tickets. The reviews are fab." I swipe the keycard and go into

Julia's suite. I shut the door without another word to him. Hopefully, the door whacked him in the nose. God knows nothing else is big enough.

Lily is standing in her doorway, still in her pajamas. "Hi, Cassie."

"Hi, sweetie."

"I have a tummyache." She grabs my hand and leads me into her bedroom. "Mommy's busy."

I can hear Julia talking in the other room. She must have an early call with clients in Europe.

"Will you play with me till she's done?" She climbs back into bed and pats the spot next to her. "Please, Princess Cass-A-Lot?"

She hasn't called me that in ages, but it gets me every time. I drop my bag, set my coffee down, and kick off my heels to cuddle with my favorite little girl. I lie down and lift my arm so she can snuggle in close. "How's this?"

"Good."

I kiss her head. "I think so too."

I hear my name and bolt up. "What happened?" I blink several times and try to focus. Okay, I'm in Lily's room. My skirt is hiked up to mid-thigh, and my mouth tastes like crap.

"You fell asleep." Julia is standing there with a smirk on her face.

I push my skirt down and plant my feet on the floor. I feel a little woozy. "Sorry. Lily asked me to sit with her while you were on a call, and I must've dozed off."

"Or snored like a bear in hibernation."

I slap my forehead. "Oh God."

"I'm kidding." She sits next to me and pushes the hair off my shoulder. "Big night."

"Yeah." I let out a giggle. "Huge, actually."

Her hand goes to my lower back, and she leans in and kisses my shoulder. "Hi," she whispers.

"Hey," I whisper back.

"You left early."

"I did."

She kisses my shoulder again and caresses my back. "Thank you."

For what, I wonder. Making her come so hard? Twice? I pause to think about that one. Because twice. Then I realize she's talking about Lily. She's being normal. I can do that too. And yes, I breathe a sigh of relief that we seem to be okay. I let my eyes run down her body. She's wearing gray pants with gray boots and a semi-sheer button-up blouse. She looks amazing. I wave my finger up and down her body. "This is hot."

She smiles. "Your dad and a certain little puppy and an ominous-looking envelope are here."

"What? Why?" I try to smooth my ponytail down.

"He said he needs to talk to you. I'm guessing it's regarding whatever is in that envelope. And of course, Lily is feeling so much better now that little what's-her-name is here."

"Okay." I stand and slide into my heels.

Julia stands in front of me with her hands tucked in her pockets. "We'll have to talk about what last night means."

I try for a casual tone. "Yeah. Sure. Whenever you want."

"I'm having a late breakfast with Piper."

"Piper?" Wait. Hold up. Plot twist. How did *she* come back into play? I tell myself that now is not the time to get all jealous and possessive. "Right. Piper. The Ryder app."

"That'll give you some time with your dad. We'll talk after that."

"Okay." I resist the urge to lean in and kiss her good-bye. Instead, I ogle her fine ass as she leaves the room. I had my hands on that ass last night. Despite all of my insecurities in this moment, if I could give myself a fist bump, I would. If I had time to rush into the bathroom and relive it with my hand in my panties, I'd do that too.

My dad is sitting on the floor with Lily and the puppy. I sit in a chair near them. "Does she have a name yet?"

"Hey, Cassie," Lily shouts. "You were snoring in my bed."

"Great." I sigh and shake my head because now I know Julia wasn't just kidding.

My dad starts in on his version of my snore. It sounds more like a pig snorting. Lily joins in, of course.

"Okay, you don't have to reenact the whole thing." I see the envelope Julia was talking about sitting on the table. "What's up, Dad?"

He gets up off the floor and sits in the chair next to me. "I thought I'd bring Mr. Chickles down for a visit."

"That's not her name," Lily says.

"That was the name of my stuffed monkey when I was little." I turn to my dad. "Good memory."

"I came for another reason too." He grabs the envelope off the table and stares at it. "Do you have any dreams, Cassie? Things you'd like to do? Places you'd like to go?"

"Dad, you don't have to give me money. I don't want it anyway."

"It's not mine to give. It's always been yours, from the day you were born."

"Huh?"

"Yeah! Huh?" Lily echoes my sentiment. She's used to knowing what's going on and evidently doesn't like being kept in the dark. In this moment, I love her more than I ever have.

"We set up a trust for you right after you were born," he says. "We planned to use it for your education and maybe give you a down payment on a house when you graduated from college. Life stuff. You know?" He sucks back a breath. "But we weren't there for any of those things. You did it on your own." He takes a tissue out of his pocket and wipes his eyes. "I bought shares in a few companies over the years and did the same for you. Small amounts. Nothing big." He holds the envelope toward me.

I stare at him. Speechless. I don't move. I can't move. This whole thing has been a lot to take in, and I don't know what to do with most of it. I'm sure my expression says as much. He pushes the envelope closer to me. I finally take it.

"This doesn't in any way obligate you to let us back into your life. But if you can find it in your heart to forgive us—"

"Just say sorry, Mr. B." Lily's holding the puppy like a baby and patting its back. Also, she calls him Mr. B.? "That's what Cassie taught me. When you say sorry and you mean it, people will forgive you."

My dad gives Lily a sad smile. "If only it were that easy, honey."

"It is that easy," she says with all the naïve conviction of a five-year-old. "But you have to mean it. It only works if you really mean it."

My dad's eyes fill with tears. So do mine.

"Cassie will forgive you, Mr. B. Won't you, Cass?"

My dad covers his face with his hands and breaks down in sobs. "I'm so sorry, Cassie. So very sorry."

I grab his hand and squeeze it while Lily pats his knee. She's looking at me as if I should say something. "It's okay, Dad. I—" Lily's eyes widen, telling me I should say it. "I forgive you." She smiles at me, and I do the only thing I can do. Through tears, I give her a wink.

❖

"Why don't you stop staring at that envelope and just open it?" Julia puts one leg up and sits on the edge of my desk. That's something she's never done before. She usually just kind of sidles up to my desk, which is hot. But this sitting on my desk thing is way better.

"Sorry, I was lost in thought. How's Piper?"

"We're getting closer to making a deal."

I try to busy myself with paperwork, but she grabs my wrist. "Don't change the subject. Why won't you open it?"

"I don't know. I just...can't."

"Is it money? Are they trying to buy your love back?"

"It's not like that. At least, I don't think it is. My dad said he started a trust for me on the day I was born." I pick up the envelope. "I guess this is it."

"It sounds like it's time to stop guessing. Would you like some privacy while you open it?"

I let out a big sigh and pick up the letter opener. "Stay here." I go straight to the bottom line. Then I stop. "Holy shit," I say.

"What is it?"

I look at her and then back at the document. "It would seem I have a three-million-dollar trust."

We're both silent for a moment. Memories come flooding back of my dad sitting at his computer. On the screen were squiggly lines that I now understand were stock charts. He spent hours in there while I played on the floor with my dolls. I had no idea all of his research would amount to such incredible gains.

"Cassidy?"

I set the papers down and focus on Julia again. "Yes?"

"What's the first thing you would do with that money if you didn't have this job?"

"I'd get my MBA." Holy shit, I just blurted that out without thinking. She's staring me down, but I have no idea what she's thinking.

"I expect to have your resignation on my desk by end of day."

She walks away, and I bolt out of my chair. "Julia."

"End of day, Cassidy."

CHAPTER THIRTEEN

Third row up on the right side, two chairs in. If I get to class early enough, that's where I always sit. A girl named Heidi likes to sit to my left. It doesn't bother me as long as the aisle seat stays free. Heidi sort of reminds me of Infected Nose Ring Girl, minus the infection. I imagine she was named after an aunt. I suspect she hates it, and that gives me a tiny bit of satisfaction.

I find her bloodred lipstick and slow way of speaking endearing now. Plus, she's smart as a whip and makes a good study partner.

"Hey, babe." She sits and gives me a wink. I forgot to mention she's also a big flirt. Bless her heart. "We have a guest speaker today," she tells me as if it's big news.

"Yeah, that's what I heard."

"She's hot too, so don't sit too close. She might think I'm taken."

I give her a side-eye. "Yeah, I'd really hate to ruin your chances with—" Julia walks in, and I freeze.

"Julia P. Whitmore," Heidi whispers. "You know what the 'P' means, don't you?"

I don't say it out loud, but yes, Heidi. I know exactly what it means.

"Please, Please Me," she says, nudging me. "I'm going to go down there and introduce myself. Wanna come?"

"Nah, you go." I keep my eyes on the back of Julia's head. She stands up to greet our professor, and my eyes naturally fall to her ass. She's wearing tight black pants with suede ankle boots and a crisp dress shirt. Her hair is barely brushing her collar. Standing in front of her, I'd be just about an inch and a half, maybe two inches shorter. I love that thought.

I was angry at Julia for insisting I resign. I'd come to believe I was irreplaceable. Turns out, no one is. She did it for my own good. I know that now.

She turns slightly to shake Heidi's hand, giving me a view of her profile. God, she's so fucking gorgeous. They talk for a minute. Julia ends the conversation and goes back to her seat. Heidi plops back down next to me and whispers, "She smells awesome. I think I'll slip her my number later."

I lean in and whisper, "Isn't she a little out of your league?"

Heidi puts her hand over her heart. "No, girl. I'm a player. Head to toe."

I giggle and shake my head. Our professor introduces Julia, and even though I'm probably not supposed to, I pull out my phone and take a photo of her standing behind that lectern.

"Oh, good idea," Heidi whispers.

Heidi forgot to turn off her flash, causing Julia to look our way. She pauses when our eyes meet, and my tummy does a thousand flip-flops.

I lean forward on the little desk attached to my seat and rest my chin in my hand. Over one hundred thousand per year in tuition, and all we get is a little desk attached to an auditorium seat. I want to hear every single word she has to say.

After Julia's speech, Heidi grabs my hand and drags me to the back of the line where Julia is shaking hands and signing copies of her new book, *Deal with It.*

Heidi rips a piece of paper out of her notebook and scribbles down what I imagine is her cell number. She folds it up and puts it in her hand, then offers that same hand to me. "This is how you do it, Cass. It's like giving the maître d' a tip so you get the table by the window."

I shake her hand, and she slides the paper into my palm. "Very smooth, Heids, very smooth."

"Right? Give it back now."

I give the note back to her, and she starts nervously bouncing from foot to foot. I have to admire her audacity. In fact, maybe I should do the same thing, so I grab a pen out of my bag and quickly jot my number down, then fold the paper into a small square.

I try to make Heidi go first, but she pushes me forward. "No." I fight back. "You can't even."

But she does. By now, you have to know my taste in friends is downright unforgivable. I have no choice at this point. I put out my hand while holding the note against my palm with my thumb. "Hi, Julia." She shakes my hand and looks at the folded piece of paper that somehow ended up in hers. I silently thank Heidi for teaching me how to palm a bill. Or a note. Whatever.

"Hi," she says with a big grin. "It's nice to see you. You don't even know how much."

I reach into my bag. "Will you sign my book?" I hand it to her along with a pen.

"Of course I will," she says. "Anything for you."

She seems a bit flustered, but she tucks the note in her pocket and takes the pen in her left hand. She opens the book and pauses to look at me again.

"It's Cassidy. Cassie, Cass. Any of those work," I tell her. I look behind me to see if Heidi's watching. She's holding her phone up to take another photo.

"Here you go, Cassidy." Julia hands the book back to me. "I hope you enjoy reading it."

I want to look inside and see what she wrote, but I control myself. "Thanks. I have no doubt I will."

The nudge on my back tells me our eyes have lingered on each other for longer than Heidi's comfortable with. I give Julia a smile. "Thanks again."

"You're welcome again."

"Are you kidding me with this?" Heidi whispers behind me.

I put my hand on her back and push her forward. "Heidi, this is my girlfriend, Julia Whitmore."

"Yes, we've met," Julia says. She takes the book from Heidi's frozen fingers and signs it while I put my finger under Heidi's chin and push her mouth closed.

❖

I open the door to our apartment, and the smell of Italian cooking hits my nose. I drop my book bag and kick off my shoes by the door. Milka—oh yeah, I should tell you that Lily named her puppy after a German candy bar. The little world traveler says her puppy and a Milka bar are the exact same color of chocolate brown. Anyway, Milka almost knocks herself over, her tail wags so hard when one of us comes through the door. I lean over and let her lick my hand. "Hey, sweet girl. Where's Lilybug?" She barks and runs to the kitchen, which is exactly where I want to go. A certain cookie jar is calling my name. I get a running start and slide into the kitchen on the smooth tile. "Hi, I'm starving."

Lily stands up on the barstool and wraps her arms around my neck. "How was school, Cassie?" She loves asking me now that we're both in school.

I pick her up and walk over to the stove. "Well, this really pretty lady came to our class and told us very important things about business. How was your day?" I lift the lid on the pot and moan. "Hmm, spaghetti and meatballs."

"There's bread in the oven too," Lily says.

Julia steps up behind us. I turn and get a kiss from her. "Hey, babe. Good class today."

I feel her hand slide down to my ass. "Yeah? Did you like what I wrote in your book?"

I put my free hand over Lily's ear and motion for Julia to cover the other ear. "You're so naughty," I whisper. Her eyes fall to my chest, and she shrugs.

I will definitely have to hide that book somewhere so no one will ever see that she wrote, *Cassidy, your tits look great in that sweater*, then signed her name three times as big as she usually does. Tonight, I'll probably straddle her and slowly pull this sweater over my head so she can have a real good look. And then I might open negotiations with Julia P. Whitmore. I wouldn't bet against me.

ABOUT THE AUTHORS

AURORA REY is a college dean by day and lesbian romance author the rest of the time, except when she's cooking, baking, riding the tractor, or pining for goats. She grew up in a small town in south Louisiana, daydreaming about New England. She keeps a special place in her heart for the South, especially the food and the ways women are raised to be strong, even if they're taught not to show it. After a brief dalliance with biochemistry, she completed both a BA and an MA in English.

She is the author of the Cape End Romance series and has been a finalist for the Lambda Literary and Golden Crown Literary Society awards. She lives in Ithaca, New York, with her dogs and whatever wildlife has taken up residence in the pond.

ELLE SPENCER is the author of several best-selling lesbian romances. She is a hopeless romantic and firm believer in true love, although she knows the path to happily ever after is rarely an easy one—not for Elle and not for her characters.

Before jumping off a cliff to write full-time, Elle ran an online store and worked as a massage therapist. Her wife is especially grateful for the second one. When she's not writing, Elle loves a good home improvement project and reading lots (and lots) of lesfic.

Elle and her wife split their time between Utah and California, ensuring that at any given time they are either too hot or too cold.

ERIN ZAK is the author of several best-selling lesbian romances including *Casting Lacey*, a Goldie finalist. She is a hopeless romantic and firm believer in true love, although she knows the path to happily ever after is rarely an easy one—not for Elle and not for her characters.

When she's not writing, Elle loves working on home improvement projects, hiking up tall mountains (not really, but it sounds cool), floating in the pool with a good book, and spending quality time with her pillow in a never-ending quest to prove that napping is the new working.

Elle grew up in Denver, and she and her wife now live in Southern California.

Books Available From Bold Strokes Books

Face Off by PJ Trebelhorn. Hockey player Savannah Wells rarely spends more than a night with any one woman, but when photographer Madison Scott buys the house next door, she's forced to rethink what she expects out of life. (978-1-63555-480-9)

Hot Ice by Aurora Rey, Elle Spencer, and Erin Zak. Can falling in love melt the hearts of the iciest ice queens? Join Aurora Rey, Elle Spencer, and Erin Zak to find out! A contemporary romance novella collection. (978-1-63555-513-4)

Line of Duty by VK Powell. Dr. Dylan Carlyle's professional and personal life is turned upside down when a tragic event at Fairview Station pits her against ambitious, handsome police officer Finley Masters. ((978-1-63555-486-1)

London Undone by Nan Higgins. London Craft reinvents her life after reading a childhood letter to her future self and, in doing so, finds the love she truly wants. (978-1-63555-562-2)

Lunar Eclipse by Gun Brooke. Moon De Cruz lives alone on an uninhabited planet after being shipwrecked in space. Her life changes forever when Captain Beaux Lestarion's arrival threatens the planet and Moon's freedom. (978-1-63555-460-1)

One Small Step by MA Binfield. In this contemporary romance, Iris and Cam discover the meaning of taking chances and following your heart, even if it means getting hurt. (978-1-63555-596-7)

Shadows of a Dream by Nicole Disney. Rainn has the talent to take her rock band all the way, but falling in love is a powerful distraction, and her new girlfriend's meth addiction might just take them both down. 978-1-63555-598-1)

Someone to Love by Jenny Frame. When Davina Trent is given an unexpected family, can she let nanny Wendy Darling teach her to open her heart to the children and to Wendy? (978-1-63555-468-7)

Uncharted by Robyn Nyx. As Rayne Marcellus and Chase Stinsen track the legendary Golden Trinity, they must learn to put their differences aside and depend on one another to survive. (978-1-63555-325-3)

Where We Are by Annie McDonald. A sensual account of two women who discover a way to walk on the same path together with the help of an Indigenous tale, a Canadian art movement, and the mysterious appearance of dimes. (978-1-63555-581-3)

A Moment in Time by Lisa Moreau. A longstanding family feud separates two women who unexpectedly fall in love at an antique clock shop in a small Louisiana town. (978-1-63555-419-9)

Aspen in Moonlight by Kelly Wacker. When art historian Melissa Warren meets Sula Johansen, director of a local bear conservancy, she discovers that love can come in unexpected and unusual forms. (978-1-63555-470-0)

Back to September by Melissa Brayden. Small bookshop owner Hannah Shepard and famous romance novelist Parker Bristow maneuver the landscape of their two very different worlds to find out if love can win out in the end. (978-1-63555-576-9)

Changing Course by Brey Willows. When the woman of her dreams falls from the sky, intergalactic space captain Jessa Arbelle had better be ready to catch her. (978-1-63555-335-2)

Cost of Honor by Radclyffe. First Daughter Blair Powell and Homeland Security Director Cameron Roberts face adversity when their enemies stop at nothing to prevent President Andrew Powell's reelection. Book 11 in the Honor series. (978-1-63555-582-0)

Fearless by Tina Michele. Determined to overcome her debilitating fear through exposure therapy, Laura Carter all but fails before she's even begun until dolphin trainer Jillian Marshall dedicates herself to helping Laura defeat the nightmares of her past. (978-1-63555-495-3)

Not Your Average Love Spell by Barbara Ann Wright. In this romantic fantasy, four women struggle with who to love and who to hate while fighting to rid a kingdom of an evil invading force. (978-1-63555-327-7)

Not Dead Enough by J.M. Redmann. In the tenth book of the Micky Knight mystery series, a woman who may or may not be dead drags Micky into a messy con game. (978-1-63555-543-1)

Not Since You by Fiona Riley. When Charlotte boards her honeymoon cruise single and comes face-to-face with Lexi, the high school love she left behind, she questions every decision she has ever made. (978-1-63555-474-8)

Tennessee Whiskey by Donna K. Ford. After losing her job, Dane Foster starts spiraling out of control. She wants to put her life on pause and ask for a redo, a chance for something that matters. Emma Reynolds is that chance. (978-1-63555-556-1)

30 Dates in 30 Days by Elle Spencer. In this sophisticated contemporary romance, Veronica Welch is a busy lawyer who tries to find love the fast way—thirty dates in thirty days. (978-1-63555-498-4)

Finding Sky by Cass Sellars. Skylar Addison's search for a career intersects with her new boss's search for butterflies, but Skylar can't forgive Jess's intrusion into her life. Romance is the last thing they expect. (978-1-63555-521-9)

Hammers, Strings, and Beautiful Things by Morgan Lee Miller. While on tour with the biggest pop star in the world, rising musician Blair Bennett falls in love for the first time while coping with loss and depression. (978-1-63555-538-7)

Heart of a Killer by Yolanda Wallace. Contract killer Santana Masters's only interest is her next assignment—until a chance meeting with a beautiful stranger tempts her to change her ways. (978-1-63555-547-9)

Leading the Witness by Carsen Taite. When defense attorney Catherine Landauer reluctantly becomes the key witness in prosecutor Starr Rio's latest criminal trial, their hearts, careers, and lives may be at risk. (978-1-63555-512-7)

No Experience Required by Kimberly Cooper Griffin. Izzy Treadway has resigned herself to a life without romance because of her bipolar illness but wonders what she's gotten herself into when she agrees to write a book about love. (978-1-63555-561-5)

One Walk in Winter by Georgia Beers. Olivia Santini and Hayley Boyd Markham might be rivals at work, but they discover that lonely hearts often find company in the most unexpected of places. (978-1-63555-541-7)

The Inn at Netherfield Green by Aurora Rey. Advertising executive Lauren Montgomery and gin distiller Camden Crawley don't agree on anything except saving the Rose & Crown, the old English pub that's brought them together. (978-1-63555-445-8)

Top of Her Game by M. Ullrich. When it comes to life on the field and matters of the heart, losing isn't an option for pro athletes Kenzie Shaw and Sutton Flores. (978-1-63555-500-4)

Vanished by Eden Darry. First came the storm, and then the blinding white light that made everyone in town disappear. Another storm is coming, and Ellery and Loveday must find the chosen one or they won't survive. (978-1-63555-437-3)